I0614848

FOX DEN

B O O K S

Oregon

The Red Witch of Tirdonne

Fox Den Books may be ordered through booksellers or by contacting

Fox Den Books
PO Box 39
Brightwood, OR 97011

Fox Den Books rev. date 5/1/2017

A fantasy by

Miranda Mayer

The Red Witch of Tirdonne

Miranda Mayer
www.mirandamayer.com

Photography:
Payton Hibberd
Photographer/Graphic Designer

Model:
Marissa Long
Instagram
@marissaangeline

Costume and Cover Art"
Feffie's Cottage

Dedications

To all the witchly ladies out there. Persist.

MIRANDA MAYER

Chapter 1

It was not the kind of day one would associate with bloodshed. It was the lazy, quiet, rainy day that one ought to spend by a fire making lace. That was exactly what Evvie was doing. She hung over her lace pillow, hands working the bobbins thoughtfully, until she felt a chill. She rose, and placed a slab of apple wood onto the fire. She wiped the dirt and moss from her hands and then shook out the crinkled petticoats that were sticking to the back of her knees. She stretched, pushing forward her hips and lower back and listening to them pop. The fire was hungry and lapped around the wood, singeing the dried moss that clung to the bark, burning through it in attractive orange patterns. Evvie added a sizable piece of oak on top—which would take much longer to burn—and walked to the window.

The private drawing room was dark and cozy. The heat of the fire pressed back the cool damp that was the day outside: a bleak grey, darkened by heavy clouds that hung low, rumbling together crossly as the rain spit down against the leaded panes of the window. She couldn't see very far out into the garden because of the fog. Outside, a young golden squirrel was playing on the sparkling lawn, leaping and twisting, rolling and running. Evvie sighed wistfully at the sight of the playful creature that seemed so joyous in spite of the miserable weather.

Her smile was a brief, fleeting thing. The brooding, weighty sadness that had been hanging over Evvie for the past few weeks lingered. She sighed wearily, her breath trembling. One of the logs popped loudly. She looked to the hearth, observing the flare of sparks, and the momentary brightness shed out onto the hand-woven rug. The wingback where she worked was worn and old; her lace-making pillow stood in front of it on a turned-wood stand, the beaded bobbins still swinging from her quiet work. The deeply stained paneled walls made the room seem darker than it was.

The austere visage of her father stared down at her from the mantel. She gazed at it for a second. She'd never liked that painting, she mused. It was nothing like the man who'd doted on her and adored her as a child. She sighed and turned to face the window again.

Her scream slashed through the cozy peace like a jagged blade. A wild-eyed, livid face glared back at her, inches from her own, only the leaded panes between them. The stranger bashed his shoulder into the center frame where the glass window-doors came together, and the latch snapped. The doors flew open before her, hitting her in the shoulder. She stumbled back, falling against a credenza that backed her father's favorite worn napping sofa. An old, beautifully made spice urn fell onto its side and rolled off the edge of the table, shattering on the floor.

Evvie pressed her hand under her breast, her breath quick and frightened. Faintness washed over her. Her stays felt like they were constricting around her ribcage. The crazed, furious stranger hesitated at the threshold for a moment, darkening the window. A delighted little grimace curled his lip as he took her in, appraising her loveliness with a greedy eye. Evvie scrambled to her feet, pressing herself against the table. Wondering how quickly she could throw herself over it and the back of the sofa to the door.

The intruder's rain-soaked garments were stained in dirt and what looked like blood, Drops of watery blood fell from his hands and his nose. He clutched a pistol. He laughed at her, making as if he was about to step over the threshold into the room. Before he did, he shuddered violently, and a spot of blood blossomed on the front of his belly, spreading out quickly as the waterlogged fabric wicked it from his wound. It spread like rose petals unfurling across his filthy shirt and frock. His gaze dropped shakily to peer down at his front in astonishment. His eyes then traveled back up to Evvie with a gape of incredulity. He collapsed to his knees, revealing another silhouette behind him. The second man yanked a bayonet from the back of the attacker and the body tipped, folding back onto his calves. A convulsive jolt from the body, and he died, gargling blood.

Evvie cried out through her terrified tears, dropping back to the floor in front of the table. Her fingers clutched the edge. Her head swam as the killer stepped forward and looked through the open doorway. He gave her a quick sweep as if to determine that she was not injured.

He was a towering triangle of a creature, his shoulders so broad they spanned almost the whole doorway. He was so tall he had to duck to look in. He stood there for a spell, gazing in at her.

He was monstrously large, she thought, and frightening. A tree of a man in a feathered helm, he wore a uniform of the infantry: brown wool breeches, hardy boots, gaiters in the same muddy brown as his leggings, and a forest-green wool jacket with a short frock, decorated with gold braid and bullion. The edges of his collar were piped in scarlet. There was a large pack strapped to his back, and he carried a tall rifle, tipped with a bloody bayonet. The odd thing was he bore the tattoos of a northern man: a man born of a different kingdom entirely. It was not usual.

He looked too savage for his uniform. Foreign to it even, but he wore familiar colors of the Attash army. His dark eyes were partly sympathetic, partly voracious. Behind him, a sudden rush of bodies darted by, silhouettes of varying shades of grey, one after the other. Countless feet splashed noisily on the damp earth. Armed figures in the same muted colors as her savior loped across the immaculate lawn. She spotted the occasional diffused glow of a torch among them, and then heard the thunder of hoofs, followed by a flickering horde of mounted soldiers galloping by. Some were only mere suggestions of shape and shadow because of the heavy rain and mist. This was all accompanied by muffled, staccato sounds.

Musket fire followed, the crack of each shot suffocated by the fog—which sounded much like the popping of the fire log. These were accompanied by eerie flashes in the fog. All the while, the soldier simply stood there, staring as rivulets of rainwater ran down the side of his nose and poured off the grizzle on his chin. His right foot was planted between the dead man's knees. Suddenly he snapped to, and gave her a purposeful look.

"Lock your doors," he said to her in a strong northern accent. "The Adrin have crossed the border." He reached into the room and grasped the window doors, pulling them closed as best he could. He then moved off in the direction of the troupes. The room brightened immediately from his absence. Outside, the army raced by. Horses, runner dragons, infantry thundered past in the rain, reducing the grass to muck. Above, two large dragons soared past, blotting out even more light for two brief lapses, their bulk carried on silver-grey skin wings, the membranes riddled with ball shot holes. She wondered how they kept to the sky. One of the dragons roared, the incredible power of the cry causing the items in her room shiver in their places.

Behind her, the drawing room door opened and Farrick entered, his ragged breathing and heavy step a comfort to Evvie. He was soaked, his brow creased with worry. His apprehension seemed to abate a bit when he spotted her safe on the floor behind the sofa.

"I'm sorry you were left alone, Ma'am. Are you hurt?" She shook her head. "They're heading back eastward," he continued. He helped her to her feet and then turned to inspect the broken window-latch, briefly taking in the hulk of dead man lying on the stone patio outside her window. His jaw rippled. "They should be thinning out soon, I hope. The Attash are charging for the border. They are flowing all around the manor to the orchards."

They both froze as a deafening boom shuddered the windows in their panes. Farrick frowned. "The Adrin have come as far as the bridge at Mellim… and evidently, a few made it as far as the park. I've sent for the Damantros brothers to assemble a guard for the house. A Colonel of the Attash has come to the door… wishes to speak with you." He pushed the doors closed and then kicked a cast-iron plant-pot in front of it.

Evvie was glad to hear that Farrick thought to call for the estate's guard. It was the first time she could recall ever having to call them into action. They might as well put their continued training to use. She reached up and mopped the tears from her face with the back of her hand, which was trembling. "And the dead man?" Her body shook as if the earth were moving beneath her.

4

"I willtake care of that. You needn't worry… do not look at him." He tugged the curtains from the tiebacks, and let them drop over the window. "I'm so sorry I wasn't here. Come, Sit down."

Farrick, the Butler, had served her family from childhood. His father still served the house, and his father before him had been the manager of the household, as well. She and Farrick were as much family as they were anything else. He was a good man, well-spoken—so much so he could be mistaken for a high born—simply because he was raised alongside Evvie and her siblings.

He took a kerchief from his pocket and gave it to her. She accepted it gratefully, using it to dry her face. She trusted this man with her life. She clutched his hand for a moment, which he held, looking at her with concern. He reached out and gently took her arm, supporting her as he guided her back to the hearth. "Shall I invite the Colonel in?"

She pulled away from his grasp, sniffing in her tears, dabbing her eyes with the little square of muslin. "Of course…" she made her way to her chair on her own, knocking her lace pillow and its stand over. She cursed under her breath. Farrick bent to pick it up. He gestured for her to sit, and she plopped down into her chair, trying to compose herself. "Where's Faye?" she asked, her eyes glassy with concern.

He looked at her anxiously. His wife, who also happened to be Evvie's personal companion and closest friend, had gone out to town that morning to buy some sundries for the mistress and had yet to return.

He shook his head. "Likely still in town. I haven't heard of any attacks there. I can only hope she is unharmed. She's sensible enough not to go wandering about in circumstances such as this. I willwager she's with her family for now."

Evvie swallowed hard. She glanced stiffly at him, the concern plain in her eyes. She loved Faye like a sister.

"Would you like to go to the formal parlor perhaps? Get out of here? With that cadaver out there…" his words tapered off into nothing.

She shook her head. "It is fine. It is warm here and that'll be cleaned up soon." She waved dismissively towards the window. "I feel safer here." She remembered the figure that had filled her doorway and saved her life.

5

Farrick's brows shot up dubiously, but he knew better than to argue with his mistress.

"Please be so kind as to open the curtains again, and then you may send the Colonel in," she muttered, patting down the front of her skirts. She regained some poise and focused on the fire, which snapped and popped as cheerfully as usual. The guns had faded into the distance, past the orchards now, she imagined. The fire was the dominant sound.

"Yes, ma'am. I willsee that the Adrin savage is removed from the window," Farrick assured her with no lack of bitterness in his voice as he threw the curtains back. He then ducked out of the low doorway, mumbling something to the waiting visitor as he exited.

The door had barely swung closed when a hand stopped it. The arm was encased in a sharp, crisp edge of a shirtsleeve—underneath the dark blue cuff trimmed in gold, over a forest green sleeve... A soggy-plumed, velvety black Bicorn with a green and white cockade ducked through the doorway. The gentlemanly, kind face beneath beamed at Evvie.

The man was short next to Farrick—boyish next to the soldier that had stabbed the intruder. He was lean, and had the look of good breeding about him. His cheeks were flushed from the cool air. He wore an elegant greatcoat hooked on one shoulder, a chain looped around the high-collar of his uniform held it on. There were some fancy gold aiguillettes draping from his other shoulder. The greatcoat swung gracefully as he strode into the small room. He had mud on his boots, and rain was falling off the edges of the thick wool capelets of his garrick—yet none of these imperfections made him any less well-looking—and he seemed to be keenly aware of it.

He took off his hat, and bowed elegantly before reaching up to untie the chain from his greatcoat. He shrugged it off with a smooth gesture and draped it over arm of the napping sofa, placing his hat atop it. Then, without invitation, he moved to the wingback across from hers, which mirrored the other in position and sank down, a smirk on his fair face.

Evvie had not gotten to her feet when he entered, as was customary, for she still felt weak at the knees and was unsure that she could stand steadily enough to greet him appropriately. Secondly, Evvie was in no way motivated to greet him appropriately to begin with. His raffish air and engaging expression only served to make her dislike him.

Her feelings in regards to men in general were not very high at the moment, and the last thing she wanted to endure was flirtation from a dapper, almost arrogantly confident fellow like this one. She did not want to make him feel welcome, but rather to make him uncomfortable so that he would be brief and go away. He introduced himself as Colonel Rath, and Evvie returned the favor and gave him a shallow curtsey.

The Colonel had jaunty, sandy-golden hair cropped in a shaggy, raffish manner. He had thick, well-trimmed sideburns running down to his jaw. His cheeks were red, eyes a bright, dancing, cheerful blue, and a fine set of teeth. He glanced briefly to the window. From where he sat he would have a bit of a view of Farrick and two of his men dragging away the corpse of an enemy that had somehow fallen right in front of the tall window doors to the garden.

"My apologies Madame. It seems the Adrin chose your family's land to stage a little incursion. But never fear, we have had word of their army's movements for several weeks now, and have been moving a full brigade into the region. We were surprised by the early incursion today, but they will be easily subdued and pushed back. I must apologize for the sorry state of your park as well. The cavalry, cannon and the dragons have done some measure of damage…"

"It'll grow back," Evvie interrupted, her hands clutched together tightly. "I'm surprised we borderlands received no warning of these movements from your end. It would have been nice to know something was going on. Perhaps to prepare or prevent some of the events that occurred today," she said with a touch of acidity. "We have our own men here that could have stopped this, if the numbers are as insignificant as you describe."

The Colonel nodded and did not argue. He had no excuses. He paused to take her in, finding himself quite taken by how lovely this lady was. She was remarkably beautiful. Her hair was an unusual deep, dark red almost like wine in this low-lit room. A mass of beautiful natural curls were piled up on her head and enhanced by a sky-blue silk ribbon that wrapped around her coif. She wore a simple thin gold chain with a pearl pennant, and two tiny dangling pearls on her ears. She had a delicate appearance: a pale face—heart-shaped with a small widow's peak— and huge butterfly eyes of vivid and astonishing bluish-white; enhanced by thick lashes and delicate arched brows.

On her right wrist a fine, subtle gold bangle hugged close to her skin. A marriage bracelet with a sorrow symbol added onto the seal— the mark of a widow. Colonel Rath had to admit she was without a doubt one of the prettiest women he'd ever laid eyes upon. He wondered about her husband, who he was, and how he died. He sat up straight and leaned his elbows on his knees.

"I understand you recently lost your father, and your husband," he asked. She nodded once, her expression numb. "My condolences, ma'am."

He had assumed when reading about this estate, that she'd be a spinsterish sort of creature. He was quite surprised to find the opposite. It was unusual for so young a lady to manage an estate alone. He knew she was a widow returned to her ancestral home, but she looked too young to be such a thing.

Her family's estate was an old one, once a part of Adrin before the wars that changed the borders some hundred years past. Colonel Rath had studied the history of the region as he led his men towards the Eastern borders. He was now looking at the member of a dwindling, ancient family line.

Sweet and petite, she sat before him with trembling hands, which she tried to hide in the folds of fine voile of her gown. She wore a simple white day-gown of sheer muslin expertly white-worked and embroidered around the hem and the elbow-length sleeves. It was a gown of the most recent fashion, with a small, high-waist bodice that was fitted snugly to her shapely back and shoulders, with a wide, flattering neckline, which was filled with a sheer lace tucker. Yards of skirting cascaded from underneath her bosom, and draped down over her curves in the most appealing manner.

The gown folded and pleated around her lovely form and pooled at her tiny, garnet-red slippered feet. She sat on a smart-looking shawl that she had shrugged off at some point. The yards of the stylized-leaf pattern fabric draped elegantly and artfully over the arms of her chair, as if she were sitting for a portrait. The only things that seemed to affect the perfection of her pose were her reddened eyelids and stiff, frightened demeanor. Her eyelashes were still wet with tears and clumped together, which only made her exquisiteness more dramatic.

"The reason I am here is to secure your permission for my men to garrison on your land. The Adrin border is so close, and the only way we can protect your estate from further incursion is to set up a stronghold near the border."

"Of course," she whispered, her voice trembling. "Do what you must. Speak to Farrick about supplies from our farms. He is my manager. Just try to avoid felling trees."

He looked reassuringly towards her. "I hope it should certainly increase your sense of security knowing an entire brigade of men will be guarding your estate, should it not?"

She didn't look impressed. "Indeed," she muttered flatly. "Please pardon my manner, Colonel, I am a bit shaken by the man in the window…"

"Yes, I saw. Dare I ask what happened?"

"He came through the door. He was going to attack me. One of your soldiers stopped him, ran him through before he could do me any harm. I was reassured once I saw your soldier's colors, but it didn't make the whole thing any less shocking… one moment it was peaceful, the next all those people and beasts were charging past… It was almost impossible to believe to be true. I'd like to find that man and thank him."

He admired her delicate nature, drawn to her fragile vulnerability. He reached out and boldly took her hand, patting it gently. "Never you fear, Madame. You are secure now. Our armies outnumber the Adrin invaders a hundred to one—and they are all as brave as the one that killed your assailant. The incursion is squashed, and any new intrusions will have infantry, cavalry, dragonry, and five elder dragons awaiting them. I also hope you will send for me if you have any concerns or questions. I will always be nearby. Any of my men can relay a message to me."

"Of course, thank you Colonel." She tugged her hand out of his grasp and gathered up the ends of her shawl, piling it over her lap and legs.

"I understand you are also the owner of the Redstone House in town." He leaned back in his chair as Evvie gave him a nod. "It is not let?"

"The gentleman that occupied it passed away last year," she answered.

"I would like to secure it if I could. The Throne has assigned us to this border county and it looks like we might be here for some time, and I am encouraging my officers to take residence here and bring their families. Word is that we might take advantage of this incursion, to take back the Valley perhaps…"

Evvie's eyes narrowed and she furrowed her brow. "Carath is staging its own offensive?" She found it odd that he would disclose such ideas to her. Perhaps he trusted her as a land owner to receive this knowledge. But she found it out of turn, and almost as if he wanted to impress her with it.

"Perhaps. They've been discussing broadening the no-man's-land a bit. For now we are securing the border, and we maintaining security until we receive further orders."

"When you speak to my land-manager, I'm sure he can help you with the process of finding residences for you and your officers. There are plenty of available homes and lodging around these parts. It is the consequence of being along the border with Adrin. Nobody stays for long."

"I will speak to him the moment I find him," he declared. He crossed his legs and wagged his foot, gazing at her intently.

"I'm afraid my staff is preoccupied, Colonel. I cannot offer you tea or refreshments. I apologize."

He took a moment to take her hint, and then, appearing slightly bewildered, said: "I best be on my way then." He did not move, however. He found her coolness off-putting. He was not accustomed to having his charms roll off of a lady like water off of a swan. She seemed wholly indifferent to his wiles; in fact, she seemed almost disgusted by them.

"Good day, Colonel" Evvie turned her face back to the fire, ending her discourse with him.

He finally rose from the chair, bidding her farewell with a playful tip of his hat before putting it on his head. Still puzzled by her disinterest, he ducked out of the small room. She never looked back at him, her eyes fast on the fire.

Evvie did not look away from the flames until she heard the latch close behind him. With an intolerant sigh she got to her feet and adjusted her shawl over her arms. She walked back to the window. Outside it was peaceful again. The squirrel had not returned, but the only evidence of what happened was the torn, mucky earth that had once been a fine lawn.

She reached down and shoved the pot aside and pulled the glass doors open to the rain and mud drenched garden. She stepped out only as far as the stone threshold and looked around. There was no more blood to be seen staining the doorsill or the grass by her window. The army was long gone, threaded through the orchards towards what they called the back-land, which was mostly hay fields and, beyond that, forest. The border was two miles beyond.

She saw a lingering soul here or there among the fruit trees, assisting Farrick's men in collecting the remains of other unfortunate Adrin soldiers who'd been stampeded by the charge of soldiers, mounts and dragons. She did not see the soldier who'd saved her. She stood there in the misty rain for a while until she saw the cautious little squirrel warily creeping down the trunk of the oak once again. For some reason, the sight of the little creature overwhelmed her.

She watched it scurry about, her eyes blindly trained upon the creature, but her focus elsewhere. She took in the prospect of the gnarled, osteal silhouettes of the apple trees in the distance, almost completely obscured by the fog. It was a familiar sight. One she had only briefly been separated from once in her life. Somehow, with all that had happened in this short morning, something felt different about the familiar view. It felt tainted.

She went back inside, closed her windows, added another piece of apple wood to the fire, and pulled her lace pillow back in front of her knees. She stared at the work in progress for a moment, and then suspired. With a small shake of the head, she set to work, her hands moving with liquid, purposeful grace as she wound and crossed the bobbins under the forest of pins on the pillow. Her movements became feverish and almost manic as time wore on, a look of deep concentration darkening her brow.

Her hands froze suddenly and her work faded out of sight. She was overcome with an odd feeling. It was a bizarre sense that something needed to change. She ascribed that thought to the morning's close-call, and was about to force herself back to her lace-making when Faye finally appeared carrying a tray of tea.

MIRANDA MAYER

Chapter 2

"Oh Faye, you're back!" Evvie called out to her friend, leaping to her feet.

Faye was Evvie's favorite person. A rotund, sweet, merry creature, Faye's dark curly hair and shining hazel eyes warmed Evvie's soul. To see her friend safe nearly made her cry in relief. Faye only shook her head in amusement at Evvie's overt joy and gave her one of her radiant smiles.

"I'm fine, ma'am. Please sit down, you needn't have worried so," she declared, setting the tray on the sideboard before serving her lady a cup of tea.

Faye was pregnant. Her belly swelled beneath the flowing skirts of her printed cotton day gown, a lump under the high-waist of her bodice. Her plump arms were covered in soft muslin false sleeves and she had a little fichu of the same lace-adorned fabric draped over her shoulders, the ends pinned to the front of her bodice. She wore a frilly voile cap over her hair. Evvie thought she looked too matronly dressed as such, but Faye was to be a mother, and this was the customary attire for a mother-to-be. Evvie looked forward to the arrival of the child. A child was most rare and welcome creature in this large old house.

"Truly, I am fine," Faye assured Evvie, who was still gaping at her with misty eyes. She handed Evvie her cup and saucer. "Nobody we know was hurt. Farrick was relieved to see me, too."

"I shall never send you away again," Evvie blurted.

Faye laughed and sat down in the chair where the Colonel had sat earlier. She balanced the saucer on her belly for a moment as she sipped from the cup. She then put them both down on the small round table by the right arm of the chair. "Nonsense. If you do not send me anywhere again, then how are you to be assured you get *exactly* what you want? Nobody else knows your tastes like I do. I acquired all sorts of lovely things for you today. You should see some of the Ambrian floss I found. It shines like spun pearl. Drink your tea, have a little cake and we'll sort through all the little things I found. That ought to cheer you up and get this ghastly day out of your thoughts."

Evvie nodded compliantly, only willing to accept such orders from Faye.

The plump girl sighed. "I understand you had an officer visit you…"

"Yes. He thought quite a lot of himself as well. He was roosterish and ridiculous in his attempts to be charming." There was no filter to the spite in Evvie's voice.

"I can hardly blame him. You are an astonishingly handsome woman. And nothing draws the eye of such a man more than a delicate lady requiring his assurance and strength."

"Ugh…" Evvie rolled her eyes and sipped her tea. "I'm sick of men."

"Farrick said you were quite shaken."

"Who wouldn't be? But the savage did not get in. A soldier killed him before he had a chance to. It was a fright. All that blood…"

"Thank the gods the man was there when he was. What if he hadn't been? I do not want to even imagine it," Faye cried. She reached over the left arm of her chair, retrieving knitting from her basket by the fire. She shook out the little blanket she was making for the child growing in her belly and began to work her needles furiously. "You were most fortunate today, ma'am. Most fortunate." Faye yanked some slack in the yarn from her basket.

Evvie listened absently and continued her lace making, hands working, mind elsewhere.

It was the morning of the following day. The men were garrisoned and now ambling about the town en masse. Dareth was among them, his pillar of a figure making him most noticeable amongst the averaged sized men milling about outside the public house. He tried not to stand out, which was hard considering he was taller than everyone else in town by at least a head. He stepped back in the thick of a crowd of militia, and bent his knees a bit, his eyes fast on the open coach as it drew into the market square and pulled to a stop

In it was a fresh-looking mother-to-be with some generous curves and a mighty bosom nearly spilling from her gown, held back only by a strained cotton chemisette. She wore relatively plain clothing. Sitting across from her was the woman he had saved from the hands of an Adrin savage—the woman whose face he could not shake from his mind. He was thrilled to see her again. He found himself exhilarated just being so close.

The Lady was so strikingly attractive. He actually felt a thrumming discomfort in his stomach when he looked at her. She was in a long redingote and a cream bonnet adorned with expensive, exotic feathers and silk ribbons that flounced in the wind. She was so refined and delicate looking. But he knew what she was. She was that, and so much more.

In his present state, a southern lady such as she would scarce look at him. He also imagined that even if she understood who he was, she would still perceive him as naught but a northern savage. In his mind, Providence had led him to her.

He could see her pale profile, the dark rim of lashes around her icy eyes. She was focused on her companion's face while the plump girl chatted amiably. He stared brazenly, using his fellow soldiers as camouflage to do so. He heard some brash comments about her from the militia around him, praising her in the coarsest of ways.

"Shut your mouths. Have some respect for a lady," he snarled. The soldiers around him glanced up at their fearsome comrade and quieted down.

The lady's companion was helped down into the street by a footman. She lifted her hand to the Lady to indicate that she would be right back, raised them hem of her skirts, and tiptoed gingerly through the muck towards a shop.

The lady waited, staring straight ahead, ignoring the scores of militia crowding the normally quiet marketplace. Suddenly she turned her head, and looked directly at him. Her gaze was like the blow of a hammer it was so direct and powerful. He was irrevocably locked into it, and any effort to disguise himself was lost. He straightened and stared back, unable to tear his eyes from her wolf gaze. His heart raced at the power of it. His mind was a fuddle.

She gestured for him to approach. Her fingers, slender and graceful, were wrapped in near-white kid leather gloves. As if he was not in control of his own actions, he answered her bidding. He forged through his fellow soldiers and reached the open coach and peered at her expectantly, stunned by her beauty.

"Your name?" Evvie's voice was commanding but also kind.

"I am Dareth of Ilmeer," he muttered, almost reluctantly.

Evvie was not sure why the man appeared so abashed. His display when they first met at her window bespoke of a great strength and courage. Now he was tentative. His accent was exceedingly strong—the northern guttural dialect was often thought of as dissonant and unpleasant. Evvie found it manly and beautiful coming from the lips of this monster of a fellow that stood before her transfixed. He was taller than everyone in the square, which was amusing to Evvie. She hadn't realized how large he really was until she saw him compared to the Carathian soldiers around him. Most northerners were large people. The men and women of the north were built strapping and brawny, perhaps to survive a life of hard work and hard weather. He shaved his whole head which bore the special markings common to northerners. The tattooed whorls crept up his neck and onto the back of his head. His exposed wrists also showed evidence of markings sleeving his arms and likely, his whole chest, according to the reading she'd done on the subject. His jaw and lip were covered in the dark, smoky growth of a few days, which only served to feature his full, masculine mouth. His nose was strong, and his brow a hard line. A pair of brooding, hematite eyes gazed up at her from under heavy lids rimmed in thick raven lashes. He was a mass of muscle underneath his uniform. Evvie noticed that his right hand was covered in little scars and nicks.

He, and a hundred others dressed like him, had gathered outside the public house. It was probably full inside, so they were passing drinks out the door to the men that stood outside.

"It is reasonable to assume that I am right when I say that you are the man who slew the Adrin at my window yesterday morning?"

16

"Yes My Lady, you are correct," he replied. His gaze was powerful and bold. He did not shy away as most subordinates would when addressing a Lady. He looked straight on, and she returned it with unflinching steadiness. "You nearly ended up a hostage or perhaps even a victim," he added.

"Nearly," she said. "Thanks to you nothing happened. As gruesome as the sight was, I have to say I was never more grateful." She paused, and then glanced at the public house. "You are here for ale, Mr. Dareth?"

He turned to look at his milling friends, and then faced her again. "Yes, My Lady."

She stood up in the coach. She held out her hand to him, which she evidently expected him to take to assist her down from the coach. He complied, wrapping his massive, calloused, scarred hands around her delicate fingers. She lifted the hem of her skirts, and stepped off the coach, hopping down next to him. She reached only his shoulder in height.

She kept hold of his hand, and walked towards the Public House. Surpassing the common entrance, she made her way to the door at the side which only gentlemen were permitted to enter. Dareth stopped, and she was abruptly halted by his action.

"Come along," she said firmly. She led him to the door, and opened it. It was already bad enough that she was a Lady entering this part of the Public House, but she entered with a common foot soldier. But Evvie had no patience for convention, not at this time. Not when she had Dareth on her arm. She would shock them all. Because he deserved the distinction.

Inside, a few of the officers were scattered about, many seated in the ample chairs scattered around the private room. Among them was Colonel Rath, who seemed wholly shocked by her appearance. Many of the patrons were idling about in their shirtsleeves, and the sight of a lady sent them all a fuss, trying frantically to tug on their frock coats again. The owner of the public house, Farrick's brother Trudo, merely bowed at the sight of his Lady, and greeted her warmly.

"My Lady, what a pleasure to have you here." He appeared quite unaffected by her presence. The patrons, at least the non-local ones, were aghast. The Colonel buttoned his frock coat, and approached Evvie and her guest, bowing curtly.

"My Lady," Rath tried to capture her gaze with a bold, flirtatious flicker of his eyes, but she simply gave him a shallow curtsy, and extended her hand. This time he greeted her properly, brushing the top of her knuckles with his lips before straightening. "To what do we owe the pleasure?" He smirked tightly, and gave the soldier beside her a quick once-over. The downturn of his mouth made his disapproval obvious.

Evvie, still clutching Dareth's hand, pulled him forward. She laid his hand over her arm, patting it affectionately. Daring the Colonel to object. "Colonel, this is the man who slew the Adrin warrior that threatened to harm me yesterday. I would like to recognize him for his efforts and bravery. I'd also like to buy him an Arretta ale. I would also like to purchase enough ale for those of the men outside."

Trudo nodded and went into the back room. The Colonel appeared perplexed, but didn't argue. Trudo reappeared a moment later with a tall glass mug of mahogany- colored ale and, giving the Dareth a knowing look, he handed it over the bar to the Lady. Evvie passed it to her companion who accepted the drink. He appeared comfortable in the posh room, almost aloof. Evvie had a sense that he was no stranger to the posh side of the public house. She tilted her face up so she could see him clear of the brim of her bonnet, and smiled at him.

Dareth looked down at her, and felt his soul melt into her sparkling eyes. The lacy circle of her cap and the shadow from the brim of her bonnet made them seem even more vivid and lively.

"Thank you My Lady," he said in a low voice, sipping the thick ale. It was a treat of the likes he had not enjoyed since leaving home. It was beer from his country, best served river-chilled. But despite the fact that it was too warm, it was still delicious with a wonderful, buttery aftertaste lent to it by the buttergreen that was added in addition to the lush hops. How thoughtful of her to buy him Aretta Ale, he mused.

"Thank you, My Lady," Dareth repeated loudly, purposefully thickening his accent a bit simply for the sake of ruffling more feathers in the room.

The officers stilled. Some sat at the tables, others in plush chairs; some at the bar, but all were silent and frozen, as if waiting for normality to resume, and for the intruders to disappear from their retreat. Dareth drained his beer, savoring its familiar flavor, and emitting a coarse grunt of appreciation when he was done. He passed the glass to Trudo and bowed his head in thanks.

"I will certainly give serious consideration to your recommendation to distinguish this soldier for his valor Madame," the Colonel finally said.

"Well, I choose to distinguish him in my own way as well. I think he deserves it." She took Dareth's hand again and led him out of the public house. Outside, Trudo's sons were hammering a bung into a brand new keg, preparing to serve some locally brewed ale to the crowd of soldiers outside.

Dareth helped the Lady back up into her waiting coach. Her companion was already inside with packets on her lap, looking puzzled.

"Mr. Dareth, please come by the house this evening to dine. Be there by half-past six. If your superiors give you trouble for your absence, they can speak to me." Evvie gave the coachman leave to go. The assemblage lurched forward. Darth remained where he stood, a little smile on his lips.

"There will be no trouble," he muttered. "I will be there."

As they drew away, she acknowledged him with a nod and then peered forward. Dareth waited for her to look back. Just before the barouche took the curve and disappeared from sight, she did. Her pale eyes met his one last time. For Dareth, that was all that was required for him to make a decision.

"What *are* you thinking?" Faye exclaimed once they cleared the village gates. The coach slowed down to pass a line of Attash soldiers marching towards town.

"What do you mean?"

"I mean no offence my Lady, however… a common foot soldier? I am as common as they come and even *I* can see that what you did was rash and highly improper."

"You are wrong, Faye. And, if I might add, presumptuous, to castigate me so." Evvie laughed. "He is not as common as you believe, nor are *you* by any means. Do you know anything about the Bask?"

"Not really, except they're tall and they like their beer cold," Faye mumbled.

"The markings on his head, arms and neck… those are called drest, and they indicate a person's rank among Bask society. The more tattoos a person has, the higher the rank. That man is covered. It is likely that you will share a dining table with someone that outranks me. I will show you. I have a book at home that illustrates what I mean. You will see. Moreover, he saved my life, Faye. He saved my life and he deserves recognition for it."

Faye shook her head in astonishment. "This is most unlike you, ma'am. Most unlike you."

"It is not unlike me!" Evvie insisted. "I give gratitude where it is due. It is always been who I am."

"No, Ma'am. That is not what I meant. To been seen with so low a man. And to flirt so openly with him to boot!"

Evvie's eyes widened and a line of red appeared across her nose and cheeks. "I beg your pardon? Faye, you are overstepping in a way I've never seen before!"

"He's a savage, My Lady. And you smiled at him, and took his arm, and went inside the gentleman's entrance of the public house," Faye snapped quickly and impulsively. "You do not even trust me, and here you are sailing about with a barbarian!"

Evvie's eyes widened and for a moment she was rendered speechless by her friend's assertions. Her brow darkened and she frowned in disapproval at Faye. "How dare you speak to me in such a way?"

Faye's eyes moistened and she realized what she had done. "I am sorry, Ma'am." She reached into her sleeve cuff and withdrew a handkerchief, dabbing her eyes.

Evvie relented a bit, and slumped back against her seat. "He's not a barbarian," she insisted. "He's more than that. That I do know. And it is the first man I can look at since—well, you know—who doesn't make me want to retch."

Faye snorted out in laughter. "Well, besides Farrick. He doesn't want to make you retch."

"No. But Farrick is like my brother. He doesn't count in that way."

Faye studied the kerchief in her lap, fiddling with the lace. Evvie exhaled and chose to no longer argue with her friend. Instead, she watched the country roll by as the large horses drew them back to the manor house.

"Look at that," Faye muttered a few moments later.

Evvie followed Faye's gaze and saw what she was ogling at. In the north field of her farmland, amid the stubble of the recent harvest, were dragons. Colossal dragons, all quietly at rest, taking in the warmth from the earth as they slept. They were lying like enormous scaled tubes, their necks curled back like swans, noses tucked underneath the pits of their winged legs. She could actually hear one of them snoring in the distance. One flicked the tip of its tail like a cat.

"I've never seen one this close before," Faye whispered.

"They are magnificent, aren't they?" Evvie replied distractedly. The coach rolled past without drawing even one of the dragons' large, pearlescent eyes. One of the riders was trying to wake the nearest dragon, his strange saddle contraption over his arm. The dragon wasn't having it and continued napping in spite of the puny man patting his neck.

Chapter 3

Evvie had not always been so jaded or distrusting of men. It was her recent past that made her so—a fleeting, doomed marriage that had rendered her bitter.

It was a marriage made for the sake of her home— Ravensroost. It was an old house. Almost four hundred years it had watched a succession of generations of the same family pass through its doors. Once a vibrant, large family, Evvie of Ravensroost and her brother Effery and his children were all that was left of the direct line. There were some cousins and other branches of the family that were neither consequential nor stood to inherit.

Evvie had inherited the whole estate, mostly because her father adored her, but mainly because Effery had been disinherited of most of his legacy and stripped of this title because of his lewd and scandalous behavior. Effery now lived in Darumet, where he had been given a knighthood, and lived mostly off of the generosity of an extremely rich step-uncle. He'd tamed his wildness since, married and had just welcomed a son into the world, but it was too late to regain his father's respect or his goodwill.

Had Evvie *had* children, they would have inherited the estate after her as her father had arranged. She'd been married to a middle-aged Duke and had lived in the Duchy of Ivran for almost exactly four months.

Her father had arranged the match. The Duchy of Ivran was a close ally and relative to the Throne of Adrin. Lord Ravensroost wanted to ensure that, despite the family's once direct links to the Adrin noble lines, Adrin would have no further reason to target his estate should the Adrin decide to confront the throne of Carath which the family of Ravensroost now served. It was an act of insurance to protect an estate that had existed for nearly half a millennium.

Evvie's father had been conflicted about marrying her off for political reasons, but she'd encouraged it, understanding his desire to protect the line. She foresaw having children and keeping the family going. Love had never been a consideration, and rarely was for young women of status like her. She was resigned to being married to someone who she might not care for, and accepted this as her duty to the family. She decided she could throw herself into motherhood, and find happiness in doting on her children.

So her father made the match. Not long after, the Duke collected his bride-to-be and took her south to his Duchy. He was delighted at the beauty of his new acquisition. He was a pleasant enough fellow as far as the ambitious and prideful could be. He was not mean, or rude or cruel while he courted her. He was detached and entitled—as to be expected of a highly ranked member of the nobility. He spent most of the long coach-ride gazing at his fiancé with an avarice he had long-since thought himself no longer capable of, considering himself mostly jaded and bored with women in general. This fresh young thing was as attractive and exotic as he could have ever hoped for. She would please him, and her beauty and status would make him the envy of all of his peers.

The wedding was quickly arranged, and she was bound to him in a ceremony where they both donned the wrist-rings that would never be removed. The metal grew hot and singed Evvie's wrist—in spite of the protective leather pad slid between—as the jeweler sealed the gap with molten gold. She was terrified by the leering, hungry look in her husband's eye as the ceremony progressed. When it was done, she was whisked away to her own apartments. The servants freed her of her ruby-red wedding gown and all the underpinnings and she was prepared by ceremony for her wedding night. They washed her body, doused her in fragrant waters, adorned her with jewels, and draped her in a wrap of sheer white muslin, which represented her purity. They guided her to sit on a chair in the center of her room and told her to wait. She was left to sit there for half an hour.

The Duke walked into the room without ceremony or address. He simply took her arm and guided the trembling girl to the bed, tore off the draping fabric, climbed atop her, and without gentleness or affection, took her innocence. Thenceforth, whenever he had a free moment, he continued to take her as he pleased.

In the beginning, Evvie kept to her apartments on the most part, not bothering to explore the vast old fortification that was his home. She learned, however, that by doing so, she was easy prey for his frequent demands. He would simply walk in, shoo away any attendants, and open the flap of his breeches. He would grasp Evvie's arm and push her into position, most of the time not even bothering to undress her, but instead, hiking up her skirts and having his way. If she resisted, he would beat her without the slightest hesitation, his hard, bony hand would slash across her face and stun her into submission. He would then do as he wished, and simply withdraw when he was done, buttoning up his fall fronts, and stalking out.

It irked Evvie how seemingly charming he was with other people—and even to herself, but only when he was in company. A man of society, he laughed, flirted and entertained with his peers in a way that made him likeable and affable. But then after they were all gone, and Evvie was alone with him, she became little more than an object to him. Something upon which to sate his desires. And he made no effort to engage or please her. He did not brook refusal, and Evvie earned the bruises to show it. She grew to hate him.

Evvie discovered, after a time, that absence was of immense advantage. First she took to riding out for hours on end, but when the Duke could not find her at his convenience, he soon put a stop to that freedom. So, Evvie instead developed a sudden and keen interest in various parts of the ancient castle keep, primarily, the conservatory and the old library. Not the new, clean, recently stocked library, but the ancient one in the bowels of the castle. It was a vault of a chamber with a high ceiling and towering wall-to-wall shelves crammed with old tomes. There were walkway mezzanines that were stacked up four levels, all connected by a spiral staircase of carved oak that wound up and up. There wasn't much for comfortable places to sit and read except three flattened cushions on the wide window-ledges of the windows that overlooked the cliff side. They were one over the other on each of the three upper levels of the library. She brought a little blanket, some pillows, and made herself a nest on the third level window. She would sometimes bring a carafe of water with a cup, and other times something to eat.

In the morning after breakfast, she'd stroll to the towering hot-house conservatory to watch the wasp-birds buzz about the hothouse flowers looking for nectar, and then she would venture down the many winding halls and flights of stairs to the archive library where she would crawl onto the wide sill on the musty cushion, encase herself in pillows and a blanket, and open up an old forgotten book to read. Sometimes, she'd sit there and just cry.

When the Duke had trouble finding her again, he assigned a servant to remain with her at all times. Evvie was able, however, to escape their scrutiny quite easily, which often caused the termination of that person's employment, and the assignment of another. But Evvie was still able to slip away. When hiding in her library, nobody ever bothered her. The people who did use the library—a low clerk or advisor—would come in to look for a book here or there, but they ignored her, or gave her understanding glances as they browsed the spines of the books. Nobody ever once revealed that she frequented the library.

This routine helped her avoid all manner of daytime assaults by her uncaring spouse. And at night, he would castigate her for running off, satisfy himself with her, and then roll over to sleep. It was usually quick enough for it to not be too much of an imposition, and he wouldn't bother her too often come morning, if he stayed through the night.

The Duke never got bored of her—as she often wished. Sometimes, when she was in her hiding places, she could hear someone calling for her during the day. Likely because he was desirous and sending the staff to find his prize. During her full tenure there, nobody ever thought to look in those two places, or if they did, they looked at the wrong time.

By the time the fourth month of this routine was about to conclude, Evvie was beyond miserable. She'd shed so much weight, she looked gaunt. She was listless and disinterested, and occasionally didn't even come to her room at night, finding instead other places to catch some sleep. There were countless bedrooms and apartments to choose from. Someone would inevitably find her, take her to her apartments and try to feed her. She would then await the expected, the brief and insincere concern of her husband passing through her as if she were made of gossamer, followed by the inevitable abuse of her body.

Four months nearly to the day that Evvie first arrived at the Castle Ivran, she was in her room, lying listlessly in bed, refusing to get up. She'd been there for two days, claiming she was ill. It didn't stop her husband from crawling in with her at night. The servants were beside themselves with worry. A messenger arrived at the door of her rooms in a frenzy. The servant began to disclose the most horrific news. The Duke had been killed. He'd been attacked and stabbed multiple times, the noble's ring cut from his hand, finger and all. For the first time in days, Evvie sat up. Two days later, she and all of her personal belongings were on their way north again, back to Ravensroost where her father happily welcomed her back with kind and loving care.

From the moment of her return she wanted nothing to do with men. Until Dareth arrived. For the first time since her ill-fated marriage, she could look upon a man without disgust or anger. There was something deeply significant to Evvie about this. In her mind, this meant something greater. And she was not going to let it pass. She wanted to trust again, and Dareth looked like her only option to do so.

Her feelings for this stranger, who she'd only met twice, were particularly sharp. Almost unnervingly so. She began to ponder where he was from, and how far it was from Ravensroost and all that was familiar—everything that reminded her of her father, and the life she had before her terrible marriage.

She dwelled on the soldier's earnest, brooding eyes, and his sweet, barbarian's face. There was attraction in that gaze, she could not deny it. And she could not help but admit that it was there in her heart as well. She knew that there was the possibility it was based entirely on his being a rescuer—when she most needed to feel rescued. Her suspicions of his being highborn were perhaps a vain hope, because in all truth, Evvie wished to pursue something with this man. What, she was unsure of. But he represented so much. Attraction; safety, and most of all, change.

Whatever happened from this day forward, Evvie resolved two things, as she sat and worked. She would give the estate back to Effery, and she would leave Ravensroost. One way or another.

Chapter 9

Ravensroost Manor had its fine, elegant rooms for receiving visitors, and also its private, cozy rooms that few others would see. The family drawing room was the most personal of spaces. Like many of such quarters, it was filled with old, beloved furniture pieces. It was where Evvie and her father used to spend their free time. She would make lace, draw, or paint at the work table or by the fire. He would sit at the heavy desk in the corner and write, nap on the sofa that faced the entrance, or sit by the fire with her and read.

Lord Bareet had been a learned man. He spent many hours at the capitol, or at the House of Lords. However he loved his home and his estate and contrived to spend most of his time there. He read extensively, and was captivated with Northern cultures. He claimed their family descended from the Bask, and was endlessly fascinated with the society. It was from his obsession with this subject that Evvie gleaned her own knowledge.

She also remembered exactly where her father kept his books on that subject. When she and Faye arrived at the house, she scurried right through the large entry hall, shedding her bonnet, redingote and gloves on haphazard pieces of furniture here and there. The grand hall opened directly to the right of the entrance. From there, she entered the family library to which the small drawing room was connected. She found a large book on the shelf in the library and toted it to her father's desk in the private drawing room. She sat down and snapped a tinder-grass stem into flame, touching it to the wick of the candle on his desk. She adjusted the light-reflector and opened the book.

Faye had followed her at the pace of a pregnant, plump woman, and arrived at length, looking a bit beady with sweat and mostly annoyed. She sighed loudly when she came through the door. "Ah look. Farrick saw to the latch being fixed. They added some stronger locks too." She went to the window doors to inspect the new hardware attached to the frames, giving it a vigorous shake to make sure it was secure.

Evvie nodded absently, and then pointed to the book. "Here he is. Here's his family. I *told* you. Ilmeer… See?"

Faye groaned and made her way around the credenza towards the desk, circling the round work-table where Evvie had once worked on many a project in her father's line of sight as he sat as his desk.

Evvie turned the book so she could see. "His father is a Viryet. I'm not sure what that is yet… hold on." Evvie got up to refer to another book, going back out to the library. While Faye studied the map of the family's estate in the Northlands and read the extensive lineage, she heard Evvie shout from the library: "Count. It is like an Earl. His family is very high up, Faye. I cannot find the book on the tattoos and what they mean, where could it be?" She then appeared in the doorway of the drawing room again. "How odd… that he is here fighting a war for another monarch, and at the bottom of the pecking order. A common foot-soldier. Oh, never mind that. He's a hero. If he hadn't been here, I'd likely be dead." She bustled to the desk and sat down, poring over the pages of the book. "He deserves exceptional treatment for that. You will not mention this to him or anyone else, understood? It is up to him to reveal who he is if he decides to." She then looked up at Faye. "Tell the kitchen to prepare for an extra person at dinner tonight, please."

Faye complied and waited for Evvie to go back into the library before she exited the room. Faye was concerned by Evvie's interest in this foreigner. Evvie had been most unenthusiastic about men since her return from the ill-fated marriage to the Duke. Now she was all a fuss about this soldier. She'd never, in all her years knowing Evvie, seen her so excited about a man, even before her marriage to the duke. She hoped the Duchess was right and that this man was high-bred. But it still didn't explain why he was swilling ale with the chaff of the Attash infantry. Faye shook her head in resignation and walked towards the kitchens, cursing the fact that everything in this house had to be so far from everything else.

It was well known that the people known as the Bask were different from the other people of the southern nations. They were larger than the rest of their race—taller, stronger—products of a life that required greater size and strength. The Bask also lived by a different set of rules as the rest of the civilized nations. They did not sway much to the norms and fashions of the rest of the mainland. They were known to eschew the formalities of southern societies, were rumored to be rather raucous and loud, to treat women with a more equal standing, and to engage in violence to settle disputes and gain rank. Violence was part of life for the Bask. While their society remained relatively close to that of the southern nations, they still possessed distinctions that made them purely Bask. Their land was harsh, often unforgiving, and they were not inclined to worry about the larks of the south when they had a short growing season and winters that buried their stone buildings under several feet of snow.

They had a basic ruling system and various royal bloodlines; however rule was not entirely based on inheritance from father to son. It was based on strength, and contenders among the royal lines of Bask rulers battled for power. These were called Titular Bouts, and a person's rank in society could be determined by who they defeated in the bouts. Although there were few people who could transcend class and enter the peerage this way, it wasn't unheard of. But from the King all the way down to the village chief, positions could be usurped and claimed by anyone in their class capable of winning the fight for it.

The Bask was mostly a culture of fighters. Strength was lauded. The warrior caste was called the Baskreth, and it included almost all governing families including the royal lines. Intelligence and knowledge, however, were also tremendously valued. Scholars were treated almost like a separate people. Intellectuals among the Bask, known as Brii, lived in individual communities, innovating and thinking mostly without the boisterous disruption of their war-like brothers.

They partook in leadership only in the advisory role, and although they had their own structure of peerage and nobility, it was not fought for, it was inherited. The Brii royals did not govern all of Bask, only their own communities. These settlements were called Emmebrii, and these were sacred among all the Bask people.

The central Bask throne was located in Tirdonne—a city which contained one of the largest Emmebrii communities. The mighty Royal castle was a spired, buttressed monstrosity cut and formed from the summit of a cone-shaped mountain. The city itself wound around the lower slopes like a coiled, spined serpent. The largest Brii conservatory in the land sprouted high up next to the palace, dominating half the mountaintop. The city was one of the few places where the Brii and the Baskreth coexisted.

Tirdonne was also known across the world as one of the most desirable places to obtain an education. Many foreign scholars sought to study there, and longed to visit the legendary libraries which were rumored to contain more books of literature, philosophy and knowledge than all the rest of the libraries of the world combined.

However Tirdonne accepted very few foreign scholars and even fewer were permitted to enter the sacred libraries.

As Tirdonne was a city of leadership and education, the city's society was significantly more sophisticated than the rest of the Bask nation. It resembled much of the southern cultures, save for the unmistakable Bask identity that could not be rubbed away by southern fashions. The harsh weather and somewhat stolid nature of the Bask acted as deterrent to most others making their nation and its largest city largely isolated and unwelcoming to foreigners. Even with Tirdonne being so appealing in its progressiveness and culture, it remained almost purely Bask.

According to the tattoos on Dareth's neck and arms, and the artful scrolls climbing up the back of his neck and onto his skull, he was a highborn, but he had yet to secure his father's title. Which would likely mean he would have to fight others—and possibly his own father—to secure it, were his father unwilling to give it up and retire.

Evvie's eyes were wide with shock as she turned the page of the book. There, she saw a linotype of two well-formed male figures—one depicting the front, the other the back. The almost nude figures were covered in a filigree of scrolled pictograms showing the typical markings of a Bask Count. She turned the page back one to the linotype of the markings of an untitled heir to insure that these were indeed the same markings as her rescuer. She shook her head, incredulous.

Evvie slapped the book shut, and put it back on the shelf where her father had stacked his rather impressive collection of Bask-related books and papers.

Her eyes fell upon the portrait of her mother which hung in the library over the dark fireplace. The image stared back at her from its frame. Like Evvie, her mother was a striking red haired beauty with pale, ghostly blue eyes. Evvie scarcely remembered her. A glimpse of a memory, the haunting sound of her laughter, and the gentle, smooth touch of her hands. Little more. She wasn't sure how she could miss someone she hardly remembered, but she did. She gave the portrait a final glance before emitting a cleansing sigh.

She rubbed the back of her neck and walked into the small room where she spent the majority of her time. She sank down into her worn chair where her lacework waited, and leaned back, staring off into the ether for a moment. *Why on earth would he be here? It is impossible,* she thought. *An heir to a Bask Count in the Carath Royal Attash. Perhaps he was an imposter. Perhaps the markings were put there under pretence.* She found herself doubting that in the deep, visceral core of her being. She knew that Dareth was, indeed, the son of a Bask count. She knew not, however, the why of the whole thing.

What she did know was that this was the first man she felt attracted to. In her entire life. To discover that he was equal to her made seemed like serendipity. She could not for the life of her explain why she felt this way, and she was wholly unfamiliar with the strong physical reaction she experienced when he was nearby. She suddenly understood in earnest, what she thought was romantic drivel that she had read in books. She could not stop thinking about this man. She had the idea that it was the same for Dareth. She hoped.

Something deep inside her mind told her this was the man she was meant to marry. To have children with. To find the change she'd felt the desire for so strongly just before the incident at the window. It was perhaps a foreshadowing of his arrival, and the possibility that he could take her away from everything familiar and depressing. To bring her to a new life. She thought perhaps she was presuming too much.

Speculating herself towards a self-inflicted disappointment. With a frown, she focused on her lace.

She rearranged some pins on her lace pillow, pulled out some slack in each thread, and worked quietly, the bobbins clicking pleasantly together. She lost herself in the task as she often did. Lace-making brought a peace to her busy mind like nothing else. She forgot herself, her time and her confusion.

Dareth was brought to a room that was familiar to him. It was the same room where he first set eyes on Evvie, terrified, crouched in a pool of snowy-white embroidered skirts in front of a narrow table, tears streaking her pale face. He could close his eyes and see her face as it was: the stark recognition that he had just saved her, the silent terror melting away into shock, the unspoken reassurance that he would never hurt her—then into something else, something profound and powerful. He'd had a hard time walking away that day, shutting her windows and rejoining the wave of fighting. He almost hadn't. He'd almost stepped inside, scooped her up into his arms, and carried her home to Ilmeer. Almost. But that wasn't honorable. He needed to be honorable because this woman was special.

The gangly boy who let Dareth in had led him through a decently stocked library to the room where he now stood and gestured for him to go through the open door. The boy made no formal introductions, and didn't even alert the lady that she had a visitor. Instead, he stumbled away. Dareth peered through the doorway.

To his right were a cluttered desk and a work table with a paper-quilling project left unfinished on the smooth oiled surface. All so genteel in southerner fashion. It made him think of his aunts, and a smile crossed his lips. They would adore Evvie.

An ancient, threadbare sofa faced him. Behind it, the window that he knew all too well, and to his left, the soft clicking of lace bobbins, a fireplace burning fruit wood, two ugly wingback chairs, and her. She hadn't even heard him approaching. She was absorbed in her task. A skein of lace the length of his arm hung over the back of the stand she was working on, making it longer.

He stood there for a moment to drink in the image of her in the peace of her task, content to be cozied up in a shabby room tucked inside a palace. The room showed much use, much love. She was of this world—of society and of fashion—but somehow not. Somehow, simple things suited her. She was a strange thing, this creature. Strange in a way that suited Dareth. He straightened his shoulders and held onto his resolve.

He cleared his throat. The bobbins stopped, swinging and knocking together in diminishing clicks. Her face was almost ghostly when she turned to him, those bewitching pale wolf-eyes wide and questioning. She dropped her hands, and smiled with her soft pink lips. She wore another white gown, this one simpler—no embroidery—with long, clinging sleeves. The square neckline was filled by wispy, sheer fabric ruched around her neck and tucked in the front of her bodice. Lace frilled at the ends of her sleeves—covering her knuckles—and all around the neckline. Her wine colored hair was tied up in a band of green silk.

"Mr. Dareth, when did you arrive? Have you been standing there long?" Evvie was startled to find her guest suddenly looming over her.

He shook his head. She gestured for him to sit across from her. He sank down awkwardly in the chair that was tragically undersized for his bulky frame. He looked uncomfortable. She could see why—poor thing. The furniture was not made to accommodate a Bask man. She studied him with an open gaze, and he simply watched her as she did. It was a bold appraisal. "I am glad you came. You are welcome here, Mr. Dareth."

He grinned. "I thank you, Lady. For the distinction. For everything."

She scoffed at him and laughed. "I am the one who owes you gratitude. Your bravery is the reason why I am able to sit here today, performing my most mundane task. Silly as it seems, I am happy to still be here to do these little things... they make me happy." She paused. "May I ask... what brings you here? To Carath? To our Attash Legion specifically. I can say I have lived a life of four and twenty years, and I have never met a Bask before. I've only ever seen one from afar once. I have only read about your people. My father was *most* engrossed in your culture—a lifelong obsession, and so I have learnt a bit in part. His dream was to visit Tirdonne and to see the mountain castle and the Brii academy. He would have loved to have met you. It would have been his greatest delight to meet a Bask in person."

"Yes, we tend to keep to our own on the most part," he replied, his voice strong and words clipped.

She looked at him expectantly, awaiting an answer. He shifted in the small chair, and scratched the back of his head. He seemed to be formulating an answer. She wondered if perhaps he wished to formulate an answer that would satisfy her curiosity without giving away too much of himself.

"I needed to explore," he finally muttered. "To see the greater world."

"That is not surprising. From what I understand, few races visit your lands."

"Some do. Especially at Tirdonne. But there's more to my removal than that. A restlessness, I suppose. A mission, the purpose of which I am unable to describe."

"Finding yourself perhaps?" Evvie suggested.

He seemed a bit surprised by her exclamation for a second, and then he half-smiled, "Yes. Finding *something*." His gaze was intense.

"Do you have any idea when you will go back north?"

"I didn't until recently. But now I'm fairly sure I will leave soon."

"I'm surprised that you ended up here. Serving our throne," she said.

"We Bask find a sort of peace in the art of battle. It balances us, and tempers our aggressive natures. With our more… civilized society these days, we need an outlet for that facet of our nature. I followed and served with the Attash to find that equilibrium, perhaps so my mind can be free to reflect on my questions, and why I am here. I think it has helped me sort some of that out."

"So you are ready to go home then?"

"Almost."

"That is too bad," Evvie declared with a regretful sigh. "I was hoping for the chance to get to know you better. If not for my own personal selfish needs, than to honor my father's desire to know more about your people. To learn first-hand what he sought in books…"

A head poked into the doorway. It was the servant girl Nanneet, who meekly interrupted them. "Dinner, Ma'am."

"We'll be right there, Nan. Thank you." Evvie stood and patted down her skirts.

Dareth did not move. He seemed hesitant. Finally, after a moment or two, he got to his feet, towering over her. He was dressed in his regulars. They were a bit shabby and worn; the forest green of his frock coat was darkened to almost black near the seams. There were various repairs on the legs of his black breeches, and the leather of his boots was scuffed and worn.

"I believe, Lady that I should disclose everything," he exclaimed unexpectedly.

Evvie, who was just stepping out of the room, paused and turned to face him. There was puzzlement on her brow along with something else—anticipation, maybe. A twinkle of it in her icy blue-white wolf-eyes.

"I am not who you think I am," he confessed. She folded her hands together, saying nothing, just waiting for him to go on. "I am a Bask noble. I am from the grant of Ilmeer—my family is the line of Ilmeer, an old line. Close to the throne. And I am doing what we call a Completion."

"A Completion?" she asked.

Nan appeared in the door again. "My Lady, dinner is served…"

"Yes, Yes, Nan. I told you we were coming!" Evvie snapped. The girl withdrew and scurried away.

Dareth sighed. His brow furrowed as if thinking about how to elucidate the concept. "It is hard to explain. A Bask may not claim high leadership without doing a Completion. It is like what you said… finding yourself. Learning to be alone, because in a place of leadership—when one must decide on difficult matters—one is always alone. Learning to understand one's own being, one's essence, one's motivations, one's strengths. Learning to accept one's weaknesses… these are supposed to make you a better leader… to learn self-sufficiency."

"I understand," Evvie said softly. "And you've found your answers then—come to terms with who you are?"

"I believe I've discovered who I am as a person, and what I want. I think I have known for a while now. I confess I should have gone home sooner."

"But you were seeking something else?" she said, guessing at his thoughts and prying out the inevitable.

"Yes," he replied, his stiff posture softening. He turned towards her. They stood in stark silence for a long, strange moment, his eyes burning down into hers.

Evvie simply waited. She knew what it was. She'd known since she had locked her terrified eyes onto his as the body of her assailant had fallen away like a curtain and her fearful gaze melted into intrigue, into trust, into gratitude... perhaps even a strange surrender to the power of Dareth's hungry gaze. He'd staked his claim that very morning. He'd taken possession of her.

"I am not a man of gentility, of taste or manners. I didn't come here to dine," Dareth finally said in his guttural tone. "I am going to return north in four days. I will be removing myself from service to the Attash and selling my commission. How I go home is dependent upon certain things. I would like you to come with me."

Chapter 5

Evvie was neither shocked nor surprised by the request. She stood there, hands daintily folded against her stomach, her fine shawl draped over her arms and across her back in an elegant swag. The calm reflected on her exterior was not at all what was going on inside her head. Her thoughts were filled with jubilation, fear, anticipation, and incredulity all at once. She chewed her tongue, questioning what seemed like madness, while simultaneously embracing the situation.

He looked around at the simple yet cozy room. "I am sure you will be most suitable for life in my ancestral home. Your preference for this room proves to me that you would not find it beneath you in style and comfort."

"I have an appreciation for simpler things," she replied. Somehow, his offer did not surprise her in the least.

"The city house would offer you a finer option when I am at Tirdonne," he said. She could feel the flush cross her cheeks as he talked about these domestic things—causing her to imagine them both together. Alone, in intimacy. The rage of feelings inside her made her blush deeply, and she cleared her throat, trying to bring her thoughts to the present. He looked around again. "This is your home, your own ancestral home, and you might miss it. I cannot demand that you leave it behind, so I understand if you feel obliged to decline my offer. However if you do wish to accompany me, I must know now, so I can provide adequate means for you to travel comfortably. Otherwise I will buy a horse and set off alone."

"I am an accomplished horsewoman, however it is far to travel in the saddle. If I were more accustomed to that, perhaps so… but a coach might be necessary. Maybe I can manage both," she mused.

"And leaving here?" he asked.

She peered sentimentally around the familiar room. "The things I value most are mostly portable. The rest, the house, the possessions, those were valued most by my father and my brother. My father has only been gone for three months now, and I respect his wishes as best I can, for he was the most important person in my life. But I had already resolved to give my brother back his rights to Ravensroost, even if it meant my living in one of our smaller houses nearby so he can raise his son here. I think Effery deserves to have his birthright back. I think father would understand. Another month in respect to my father, and I was going to take Redstone house and call my brother home. There's no sense in waiting now."

The clock ticked loudly as they shared a moment in silence. Evvie wondered what he was thinking. Was his heart pounding as hard as hers was?

"The things you do wish to take can be sent by carriage. Is four days enough time for you to prepare?" he asked.

"Of course." She was curious, however. It would be wholly improper for them to travel alone together as unattached adults. Even if they were engaged to be wed.

Apparently he had already thought of that. To her astonishment, his hand shot out and grasped her right arm with the wedding band on her wrist. He slid his free hand into the large back pocket in the tail of his coat and withdrew a pair of blacksmith's clippers. He opened up the black, flattened, iron pincers, slid them over the delicate band, and cut through the soft metal as easily as they bit into hoof.

She gasped in surprise. This was never done. In her country, one wore the bracelet until death.

The clippers cut through the band like butter. Dareth bent the band away from her wrist, sneering at the burn-scar left from it, and hurled it into the fire. He did this with almost an angry air about him, as if spiteful of the ring that had bound her to another man.

With his huge hand still wrapped around her tiny wrist, he pulled her towards him and bent down low, cupping her face with his other hand. He kissed her, surprisingly gently. She felt the core of her being light up the touch of his lips and her own still tingled when he withdrew. She tried to follow his lips as he pulled away, but he was too tall. Her eyes opened in a flushed flutter, and she sighed. He reached into a breast pocket of his apparently well-supplied frock-coat, taking out a heavy pendant with typical Bask-style art enameled onto it. The items crammed into the pockets of his frock showed preparation and anticipation of this moment. She imagined him plundering the smith's tent before stalking towards the house. The image made her smirk.

Dareth gave the pennant to her, placing it in her hand. It was a solid, circular piece about three-fingers wide.

"This is my family insignia. My personal marking is here." He pointed to a tiny image of a raven. It was sitting underneath the enameled images of a black bear and a white horse rearing away from one another. "I knew when I saw the depictions of ravens on your house, and on your family crest, that this was meant to be."

Evvie's eyes shone, and her face glowed. All she could focus on was the fact that she really wanted another kiss. Her heart was still madly thumping from the last one.

He touched the pennant in the flat of her hand. "To become engaged to a woman in our tradition, I give you my pendant. I am supposed to put it on your neck. That is, in essence, claiming you as mine." He frowned. "But I do not have a chain."

Evvie reached behind her neck, unfastening the gold chain that held a single luminous pearl. She slid the pearl off, and he took it, putting it into his pocket. She took the pendant and slid it on the chain, and he picked it up by the ends, lacing it around her neck, and fastening it closed.

"There. We are engaged then." Evvie patted the pendant resting on her breastbone. "What do I do? To return my claim on you?"

"You accepted my kiss. And you have given me a token." He patted the pocket where the little pearl was nestled.

"That is not an acceptable token…" she admonished. "That has no meaning to me." She moved purposefully to her father's desk, and sat down in his chair. She tugged open one of the drawers, reaching in and rummaging around. She found her desired item. She also took something else, and closed the drawer, returning to Dareth with a pretty smile.

He was so tall, she mused, gazing up at the beautiful, manly face she hadn't been able to get out of her mind. How lovely the Goddess of Fate had worked things out so well for her. After her disastrous marriage to the Duke, she had wondered if she were ever destined to be matched with someone who displayed such kindness and gentleness—someone who she would not mind touching her. Someone whose simple presence made her feel protected and safe. She was even more pleased to discover that his kiss sent her into a flutter. Her cheeks and her neck flushed as she thought about that kiss.

She opened her hand and two items sat on her palm. One was a small crest much like his pendant with her family insignia on it: a southern raven smaller than the kind he knew standing with wings spread, beak agape. It was embossed over an oak tree.

"This was the medal my father wore when he was formally attired for public or official events," she explained.

The other item was a little miniature painting on a ceramic cabochon set on a filigree gold frame. It was the size of a locket. Her father had her sit for the portrait just before she left for the Duchy. The little ceramic painting depicted her fresh, pale face, large eyes and striking hair, the expression a little sad. Her father had kept it in his desk so he could see her face whenever the house seemed empty without her.

Dareth took the painting, admired it, and placed it with the pearl. He then examined the insignia.

"There. Now we both have each others' crest. I believe we have formally exchanged tokens," Evvie declared.

He smirked, and tucked the medal in his pocket, too. He ducked down and stole another kiss, much to Evvie's delight. She realized that in all her days with the Duke, he'd never kissed her. He'd been given access to the most intimate aspects of her being, and yet he'd never bothered to kiss her—except once, when they were bound and wed. It had been a cool, wet kiss with no warmth, no passion, and no reaction like this one that made her long for more.

"We are free to travel together as betrothed now. We will marry at Tirdonne with my peers and family present."

She was content with the arrangement. She could not even begin to imagine what her life would be like once they arrived at Tirdonne. A strange land, foreign culture, no family, no friends. These things caused her to wonder, but in truth, she was not afraid. It was the change she wanted, and that change came accompanied by the most devilishly handsome companion who sent her blood boiling whenever he was nearby. She'd never felt this kind of attraction before. She knew to trust her instincts now. To listen to them instead of talk herself out of them as she had with the Duke. Yes, she thought, the idea of what was to come was almost too much to fix upon. As her father once told her when she expressed trepidation for her marriage:

"Do not fear great change, dearest daughter. Most people only recognize change after they've walked through it. You must merely move forward moment by moment, and you will come through it before you even realize it." She resolved to move forward, moment by moment, and embrace whatever might come of it.

"I will arrange for a large box carriage to collect the things you wish to take with you. If I could take this whole room for you, I would."

She looked at the things that endeared the space to her: the old sofa, some odds and ends on her father's desk. Mostly, she wanted books, some artwork, trinkets and some other small furniture pieces peppered around the house and in her private rooms.

"I will see to it that it is done in time," she agreed.

"Good. I sent word via wyvern today that I would be returning home with my betrothed. They will be expecting us. I will return for you when we are ready to depart. I have other preparations to make. I want to move before the winter comes in earnest, or we will miss our window to cross the mountains. That means I may not see much of you in the next few days." Evvie was not too keen on his disappearing for so long after this proposal. But she understood.

Evvie was amused that he'd presumed so much as to send the good news before he even asked her. She watched him turn away, and he exited the room just as Nan was about to come back in.

"What of dinner, Ma'am?"

"I will eat in here. Can you please see to it that Faye attends me here at her earliest convenience?" Evvie said. She then sat down at her father's desk and took out one of his embossed parchments. She picked up a plume, dipped it in the inkpot, and began to scratch out a nice, long letter.

Chapter 6

Faye was incensed. She never calmed, all the way up to the day of Evvie's departure which was exactly when Mr. Dareth had said: four days after his unusual proposal. It had been a strange time. Dareth had not returned to see his intended, however things began to arrive: messages with information and instructions that Evvie would need, the large carriage that would make its way north—first by horse, then by river, and then by horse again until it reached Tirdonne—and the best seamstress in the village. She'd apparently been paid a significant sum to quickly make Evvie some warm traveling gowns to tide her over until she reached Avradelle, a large city about fifteen days north of Ravensroost.

The seamstress had been commissioned to take Evvie's measurements to forward via the wyvern to a colleague there. Wyverns had become the quickest method of long-distance communication since the little dragons began to migrate up from the Wyver Isles after the great conflagration of ninety years past; where their native islands were swallowed by volcanoes.

Before that, the people relied on the rider relay, a service still heavily in use, and more markedly, on homing pigeons. Wyverns, being as intelligent as they are, and having discovered particular taste for plump, healthy squab, quickly deduced with their clever little brains, that the stream of homing birds came from and returned to the same places; which were invariable crammed with more birds. The little serpent dragons nearly destroyed the practice of carrier birding by following pigeons back to their cotes, raiding the pigeonries and eating the entire fleet and the eggs. However, it wasn't a vast leap for a famous dragon-master known as Halen Hux, to conceive of the idea to train the wyverns as carriers instead, and to reward them with meals of squab in turn. It was an arrangement that worked out quite well for two of the three parties.

The wyverns were still a costly way to send messages, as the pigeons had been, but the little dragons could carry more, as they were larger. Most general correspondence still travelled in the large bags on the sides of rider-relay saddles. Wyverns were used for high-priority messages and even the occasional small package.

Dareth had dropped a pretty penny to make sure that the modiste had a timely message, and Evvie's measurements quickly and early enough to have a suitable wardrobe made up by the time Evvie reached Avradelle. Dareth was glad to pay the high fees simply so that his wife-to-be would arrive at Tirdonne with a suitable wardrobe.

After leaving the city of Avradelle, they would cross the Avradelle River, and climb the foothills of Mount Rothro, where the temperature would drop quite significantly. Evvie considered it thoughtful of Dareth to ensure she was well-prepared for the journey.

Other, less important things arrived that were no less welcomed by Evvie. He sent her a freshly hunted pheasant, two men to help load the carriage with her belongings, some lovely, delicate jewelry, new traveling trunks, and a number of other items here and there. Obviously, despite being busy, he was thinking of her.

Evvie's cheeks warmed at the idea that this large, brawny, barbaric looking man took the time to see to such details for her comfort and consideration. She felt a deep, instinctive rightness about him with each new gesture. She wanted to see him again, but she knew she had more time to get to know her future husband better as they traveled. She knew the essentials already. He was protective, deeply thoughtful, and even doting, even in his absence. She tried to show Faye this, but Faye would have nothing of it

She wondered where he'd stored his funds while he was on his somewhat violent pilgrimage to nowhere, finding himself, discovering that the answer to his needs was a small, southern woman who would probably stick out like a sore thumb against his strapping family. She and Faye packed her trunks while Faye wept almost continually.

"You're mad! You do not know he's a real Count's son, Evvie. You do not know! You spoke to him in earnest only once or twice, and yet you agree to marry him! He could be taking you anywhere! I do not mean to sound insulting, Evvie, but the man looks so savage... how could you promise yourself so quickly? How?" Faye dabbed her eyes and sobbed while still helping her dearest friend and companion carefully lay her many delicate muslin, silk and heavier wool and linen gowns into the trunks.

Evvie could not explain it. There were no words that existed that could adequately describe the sense that this is what she was meant to do—the feeling that this was meant to be. That it was what Evvie had survived her horrible marriage for. It was more than the fact that Dareth made her feel safe and cherished for the first time since she returned from her short, violent marriage. It was deeper than even she understood. But she knew if she did not follow this path, she would only regret it, and her life would be a sad, empty sort of existence. Perhaps a life of lonely widowhood, being aunt to her brother's children. Perhaps a second marriage to someone she felt less for, but perhaps knew better. The idea of another unwanted match made her shudder. These were what awaited her if she stayed.

The carriage with the big items was already on its way. It was slow moving and heavy, and would need lots of time to get where it was supposed to go. Now they packed the trunks that would travel with Evvie. She was becoming weary of Faye's blubbering. She remained firm and determined.

"Faye, after enduring a marriage like my first, I think you should credit me with the experience and the instinct to choose what is best for *me*. Unlike the Duke, I *like* Dareth. I have from the moment I met him. Even in that moment of violence, I felt secure in the quality of his character. I *know* how I feel about him, and I'm confident he feels the same way about me. His determination and his decisiveness are qualities that I admire in him. He has been attentive even in his absence, and considerate of me from the moment we spoke. He never forced me to make any choice, Faye. He offered me every chance to gracefully decline if I wanted. I cannot explain why I want this, or why I'm doing it. It is something I do not fully understand, but it is also something I cannot ignore.

"Dareth is not the type to dance around words or feign something he does not feel. He knows what he wants, and I can relate to that. From the moment I met him, I knew I wanted him. The truth is, even if he wasn't covered in tattoos that show that he is a Bask noble, and he were indeed just a foot-soldier, I probably would have felt the same way. I would have married him in spite of it, and I would have elevated *him* with my own fortune so that this stupid, fussy society would think him worthy of me. I am *not* mad to want to be happy. Especially after this past year. I welcome change, and I welcome a life with Dareth in it."

No matter what Evvie said, Faye's tears did not wane. Even Farrick was irritated by Evvie's decision, but he admitted he could not set aside Dareth's actions, or deny that he was brave and strong. Evvie was guaranteed at least those good qualities to protect her.

None of these things diminished the power of the farewell. Effery had written back to indicate he would be returning home to live within a month, and he bade her goodbye and promised to visit her at Tirdonne within the year. Faye and Farrick were significantly more difficult to leave behind, but she knew they belonged with Ravensroost. She embraced her weeping friend, and then Faye's husband who was oftentimes more of a brother to her than Effery had ever been.

The misty morning brought the arrival of a very fine coach. Riding behind it was the man that Evvie had entrusted with her future on little more than instinct. He dismounted.

Dareth was a different man from the one who had left her four days earlier. His shabby clothes had been replaced by the garb of a gentleman. Even his demeanor had changed to some degree, but he could not hide the rough-edge of his fighting nature. He supervised the placement of her trunks on the coach while she shared some last-minute words with her friends.

"Here." Faye handed Evvie her lace stand and her supply basket.

Evvie took them. She handed them off to the footman who was putting a number of items in the coach cabin with her so that she could occupy herself during the long, dreary voyage.

"If it is a girl, I'm naming her Evvie," Faye said through her tears. "I do wish you wouldn't go… I was so lost when you went away before, what am I to do this time?"

"Effery has a wife and children. Just promise me you'll take good care of them and make them feel at home. I would never dream of taking you and Farrick from this house. It is your home as much as it was mine. But I confess I will miss you both the most. It will be strange to be in a foreign place, with nobody familiar at my side."

Faye sniffed.

"I will miss this old place, but without father… it just is not the same. Nothing has been the same." Evvie let her words taper off.

She gave Faye and Farrick one final affectionate embrace, told them they should come and visit her, and then Dareth handed her into the coach. Evvie settled onto the wide, comfortable bench. Dareth closed the door, and mounted his horse again. He gave the servants a polite nod, and the coach rolled forward. Evvie waved goodbye to them out the window until the coach disappeared 'round the bend of the long lane to the road. She heard Faye succumb to bawling as the coach drew out of view.

Evvie then sat back, and sighed. No more Ravensroost, no more border skirmishes, Adrin infiltrators, frightened tenants, political matches, stupid officers smirking at her or simpering fortune hunters finding excuses to visit. Everything would be new. And she wouldn't feel too isolated as long as Dareth was there. Even if things did turn sour, there was the promise of that massive Brii archive, she thought with an amused smirk. She glanced at the window where Dareth paced the coach, watching him ride the heavy northern horse with an easy grace.

He glanced down at her and actually smiled. Not just his stiff, uncomfortable smile that he'd given her in previous encounters. No, this was an uncomplicated, happy smile, and she couldn't keep herself from delightedly returning it.

MIRANDA MAYER

Chapter 7

The northbound roads passed through a populous region, mainly because the road followed a large river that flowed from the north, cutting through the land, and opening up into the southern seas. The river Corridan carried many a ship along its sinuous length—some having sailed against the gentle current from the ocean to carry wares from exotic places. Nothing connected people like waterways, and nothing brought a larger variety of races and nationalities together more than a large port. They were never wanting for places to stay as the coach traveled along, Dareth riding alongside. Sometimes he rode on the seat next to the driver, and several times—during particularly heavy downpours—he rode inside with Evvie. He spent most of his time gazing at her while she worked.

They spoke quietly. He was tentative, it seemed, in engaging her. Allowing her to open up to him. She talked of her childhood at Ravensroost, and of her father mostly. He listened quietly, thoughtfully, his dark eyes on her. She could not help but flush under the weight of his gaze. Twice, he fell asleep for long spells during which, Evvie found herself studying his manly face, learning the curve of his lips, the soft cleft of his chin, the ringless holes in his ears, and the tendrils of ink that peeped up from beneath his high collars. She wanted to reach out and grasp his calloused, scarred hand, and press it against her cheek. Why did she feel so much for this stranger? She asked herself. She did not know. Some powerful, inner voice inside her was telling her that this man was the one she needed. That was all she could determine.

Evvie made lace. Lots and lots of lace. She read books, and watched the landscape and the towns and farms roll by. She watched the ships on the water with their clouds of sails and wondered what they carried. She noticed that things began to change as they traveled along. The style of buildings, the crops being grown, the appearance of the people all began to vary from what she was accustomed to. The colonnades and austere architecture gave way to darker stone, and simpler, less decorative styles. Boxy, flat-faced buildings, with yawning windows like dark eyes peering out at passing traffic. The towns were denser; there were fewer isolated country villages, and more populous settlements, older ones, with scruffier looking residents.

On the eight day of travel they left the Empire of Carath and entered the Duchy of Darumet where the river veered sharply north and cut through the Moridden Peaks, the waters carving a broad gorge. The road, for the depth of the mountain range, cut right through the rock of the ravine. The tunnel was ancient. How old, Evvie did not know. It had been modified over the years, made beautiful by the addition of paintings, colonnades, arches and friezes by artisans and sculptors.

It was forty three miles in length, and climbed a bit towards the end to accommodate the higher altitude of the high countries. It was there they would enter the country of Adderat where they would climb the foothills to Rothro. Evvie would pick up her wintery garments after they climbed into the mountainous country, to cross at the mountain pass city of Avradelle. From there, the road would lead into Bask.

They entered the tunnel on a day where the rain spit down and made a wash of the windows and the occupant quite dreary. Dareth had chosen to ride in the downpour this time. He was a dark figure—sometimes riding alongside the coach, other times behind it—swathed in an oiled leather garrick with several capes off his wide shoulders, and a broad brimmed hat which dripped rain like a little waterfall.

The coach entered the expansive tunnel and the thunderous downpour on the roof was instantly halted. One side of the coach was lit by the weak yellow light of the occasional lantern sconce hanging from the carved wall on her left. On the right, grey, rain-washed daylight poured in, interrupted by the occasional passing shadow of a column. Mammoth arched windows looking out of the gorge had been chipped out of the mountain wall, leaving swaths of native stone to support the bulk of the mountain above. The deep windows were placed regularly along the eastern wall, and they brought in much-needed natural light.

Evvie folded down the window and peered out. The arches looked out over the gorge and the great river. The water below churned from the copious runoff from the rain storm, and the opposite cliff side was garlanded in waterfalls. A boat negotiated the river, riding the swollen current downstream.

The road had been so worn by centuries of iron wheels, that the divots that had been worn into it had been paved with cobbles, making the coach rattle loudly. The echo within the corridor was not a pleasant noise.

Evvie wiped the window down with a kerchief before she closed it again. It shut out most of the din. She continued to watch, riveted, at the prospect of towering, rocky walls of the gorge across the way as they shed rain in what looked like fountains. She took in the trees that stubbornly grew at impossible angles, the frothy river of teal, and the odd mountain goat clung to tiny ledges, their bodies hunched against the downpour.

Along the way, there were six massive, cantilevered viewpoints each near a tunnel village. These were spots where coaches and riders could pull out over the river to rest and water the horses. There was ample room for the conveyances and horses to park and for the passengers and riders to disembark. There was a broad stairway led either up or down, giving access to a cavernous settlement. A variety of shops and homes were carved right out of the cliff. There were raised walkways that edged the gorge tunnel where myriad stairwells disappeared up into the rock leading to all manner of passageways. Some people called the tunnel the rabbit's warren.

Evvie spotted walkers strolling the walkway all through the corridor as the coach entered the partially darkened space. She never imagined a tunnel could be a little city of its own.

The coachman chose one of the villages to rest. He pulled the coach off the road through an archway marked with chiseled letters which read: Diamond Rock. The archway led to a cantilevered patio. A marvelous and astounding contraption of an awning had been fanned out over the patio like an accordion, creating a temporary roof from the rain. The water battered the treated canvas, dropping like a curtain all around them, but did not permeate it. Gusts of air forced some in, along with wood-scented smoke from the cliff side chimney flues, but the majority of the space was dry.

The coachmen put the horses to drink. Stone troughs were built into the railing of the broad half-circular area. There were a few horses and one other coach tied along the edge. Some coachmen idled about on the benches near the wall, eating cheese and drinking ale.

Dareth dismounted. He removed his horse's bridle, leaving on the halter that was beneath, and tied the animal to a ring. He loosened the girth on his saddle, and flipped his stirrups over the pommel. He patted the animal's neck thoughtfully, then strode over to the carriage, and yanked the door open. Evvie stood, her legs tingling for freedom, and he lifted her down to the ground.

He looked rather tired. "I suspected you might like to enjoy a meal outside of the coach today. We can also stay the night, if you wish to have a longer rest than our usual pace allows."

"What about the animals?"

He pointed to a pair of rough wooden doors embedded in the side of the tunnel near the stairway. "There's a livery. The coach will have to stay where it is, but there's a stable there for the horses."

Evvie offered him a smile. "If you aren't in a great hurry, I wouldn't mind a longer respite. Given the location, I cannot deny a desire to stay the night. It is so unusual here."

"Then so we shall," he said. He took her arm and led her across the tunnel to the broad alcove where a set of stairs beaconed. They climbed to the landing, and then turned left to climb parallel the tunnel, turning once more to the left at another landing. The corridor was brightly lit with sconces, and the residents had painted the smoothened walls in cheerful colors and tasteful designs. The stairs opened up to a broad dome shaped cavern with a big bow window on the gorge side that allowed light to shower the beautiful space. The inclement weather was shut firmly out.

The floor was tiled in a bright checker of ruby red and gold. A colossal candelabrum occupied the center apex of the ceiling, but it had not yet been lit. The sides of the walls featured doors, more stairways rising and falling from the great hall, small corridors leading away from the main thoroughfare, and shops just like any street. Windows displayed wares, and signs advertised services. There were two and three stories of windows above this ground level overlooking the cavern. In the center was a circular raised bed containing plants and a small evergreen tree.

People were scattered about the square. A lady was selling fresh blossoms from a basket. A performer was playing a theorbo and singing in a dulcet voice by the window, the music echoing all around them and enrobing them in its beauty.

"This is the nicest of the prospect villages, I think," Dareth explained. "And it has the best public house in the tunnel. When winter sets in, and the galleries are shuttered, these villages are like oases from the gloom and darkness."

Evvie looked up at this tower of a man, gripping his arm tighter. He led her to a little inn near the great window. He ushered her through the door into the foyer, shucking his sodden coat and hat, and hanging them on the wooden hooks to drip dry.

They entered a room that looked nothing like a cave. The stone walls had been wrapped in warm wooden paneling and painted eggshell white. Bright paintings adorned the walls. One wall had windows that looked out onto the river and the rain. There was a broad common space with a mix of sitting and dining spaces. A blend of heavy, leather-covered sofas interspersed with more delicate, southern style furniture with finely carved saber-style legs, and jewel toned jacquards wrapping the plush seats. There were several shelves containing books, stacks of cards, and a variety of board games, some familiar to Evvie some not. A fire roared in a fireplace by the stairway. Two men sat in different areas. One, an older fellow, sat by the fire reading. The other, younger, read his book near the window. Both men were southerners by the looks of them.

A willowy woman with pure white hair and a long, oval, sweet face greeted Evvie and Dareth as she emerged from a set of swinging doors disguised to look like the paneling. Her hands twisted into the bottom of her apron which was pinned over a sky blue gown. Her hands dried, she shook out the apron over her skirts, smiling bashfully and dropping into a polite curtsy.

"Welcome, Madame, Sir. I am Mrs. Zsall. I am the proprietress here."

"We require two rooms, Mrs. Zsall, but if we could have something to eat first," Dareth said.

"Of course, of course. I will have Gillie prepare the rooms. Please make yourselves comfortable. I will inform the kitchen that a meal for two is in order. Would you care for anything to drink? My husband has only just brewed up a grog. And there is always spiced wine."

"Oh, spiced wine sounds lovely!" Evvie exclaimed, her fingers working the frogs on her redingote.

Dareth dotingly stood behind Evvie, and helped her pull the long coat from her shoulders. Mrs. Zsall moved sinuously towards them, and relieved Dareth of Evvie's coat. She swished back out of the room through the doors carrying the garment.

Evvie wore a simple flannel gown of a deep midnight blue. She was dressed for comfort. She hoped to change into something presentable for dinner, but for now, she just wanted to be free of the outer layer that was her norm since travel began.

The steady heat of the fire felt so wonderful after never being quite warm enough in the chill of the coach. She sailed towards the fire, offering the gentleman who was reading near it a nod of greeting. She held out her hands and let her palms soak up the warmth. The man gave her a sweeping glance, then his gaze caught Dareth, who slid up behind her like a looming shadow, and he averted his eyes immediately.

Dareth scooted a chair closer to the fire, placing it just behind her knees, and she sank down into it gratefully. Dareth then flopped down near her. She looked at him with gratitude and affection, and his answering smile warmed her soul. She felt his gaze on her even as she returned her attention to the lively fire.

After a plain but tasty dinner of mutton pie with an assortment of autumn vegetables, Evvie retired to the sitting room again, sipping a dry port and listening to the soft music from the plaza filter in through the windows. Outside the rain and river roared. Most everyone had gone to their rooms for the night. Even Dareth had abandoned her temporarily to exchange his boots for slippers.

Mrs. Zsall brought Evvie a glass of cold water. The proprietress paused as she deposited the tall, frosted flute on the table by Evvie's chair, and she threaded her fingers together. "If I might ask, Madame, is this your first time traveling north?"

Evvie nodded.

Mrs. Zsall sank down in the chair across from her. "Are you familiar with the people of the north?"

"To a degree."

"They will think you are something special," Mrs. Zsall said with a conspiring little smirk.

"Oh?"

"Yes. The red hair, and that widow's peak. You also have the magic mark. They are superstitious that bunch. You will be treated as sacred there. With all the northern-borns."

Evvie's russet brow rose up in puzzlement. "I have a magic mark?"

The woman nodded. "Yes. Your wolf-eyes."

Evvie gazed at her, confused. "I do not understand."

"They are the mark of a magic-bearer. At least so it was in the days of the old gods."

Evvie's was amused. "So Dareth chose me perhaps because he thinks I'm some sort of wizard?"

"Oh, I imagine he chose you because you are lovely. But the mark was surely received as a sign of fate for a man of his upbringing. He likely believes you are destined to be his wife, because he found such a rare gem in the southlands. My husband chose me for similar reasons, as those of snowy traits," she touched her hair, "are thought to be also of magical origin. I'm not sure if he has been disappointed that I am not a witch, and instead weave magic in the baking of my cakes and flummeries." She laughed merrily, and Evvie responded with a broad smile. "I felt it necessary to let you in on this little eccentricity that is common to northerners. They cling fast to the old religions and myth. And if they bring a southern woman home, it is likely because there is something particularly unusual about her. Be prepared to be admired and fussed over, dearest lady."

Evvie laughed cheerfully. How she loved all these new experiences. Such a stark contrast to the journey she'd taken a little over a half year before.

MIRANDA MAYER

Chapter 8

Morning dawned and with it a touch of regret, for Evvie had so enjoyed her evening in the cliff side room she had been allocated. She had scarce been able to sleep until the darkness became so thick that the sight of the gorge was no longer visible. But she had lingered in her wispy nightgown and soft hand-quilted dressing gown by the tall window, watching the water cascade from the fissures to spray the river below. She had observed the mountain goats as they hopped with astonishing agility towards a cavern almost out of her line of sight, and gathered at its rim in a row, like soldiers, lowering their heads as they dozed off to sleep. The rain pelted the stone and the water rushed below. It was a soporific song that lulled her to sleep.

She awoke before dawn, stretching luxuriously beneath the heavy covers, emitting an unfeminine groan. Then she exhaled as if expelling a year's worth of worries. The room was warmer than any of the ones she'd stayed in prior to this one. The fire had been stoked before she'd woken, and the light was just starting to fill the window. She'd left the curtains slightly parted that evening just so she could lie on her side and gaze out first thing, to watch the morning sun wash the cliffs of the gorge in its golden-blue light.

She was startled by the sound of the door opening. Mrs. Zsall entered, looking surprised to see her awake. "Good gracious, I am so sorry! I thought you would be fast asleep still."

"I'm an early riser by nature," Evvie replied, twisting onto her back and scooting upright.

Mrs. Zsall carried a tray with a stout little teapot, a rattly cup and saucer, and a plate with a small assortment of fruit and biscuits. "These will keep you sorted until breakfast is served," she said, moving with purpose to the small table by the window. She pulled the curtains apart just a shade more, and fluffed the pillow on the wingback for Evvie's comfort.

Evvie stood, and drew on her dressing gown, tucking back a tendril of her fiery hair as she moved towards the table. The pale lady watched her with interest.

"You are from Carath going by your accent," Mrs. Zsall said, quite boldly.

Evvie, undeterred by the question, sank down into the chair and poured a little cream into her cup, before adding some steaming tea to it. "Yes. Just north of the border of Adrin."

"Your family hails from there, I venture?"

"Oh, yes. For generations," Evvie replied. She dropped two little pearls of sugar into her tea and stirred it thoughtfully.

After giving her a questioning look, which Evvie responded to with a gregarious nod, Mrs. Zsall sat down in the small spindly chair opposite. "I've always wanted to go to Carath. I've heard such stories about the cities. How elegantly designed they are, how grand and lofty the buildings. I've seen lithographs of sights from Maraneet, including the grand assembly rooms at Tynick's. Have you ever been?"

"Yes. They are grand rooms indeed, but I do not much fancy balls and large parties, migrating from one amusement to the next. I am country-born and country-raised. I prefer a quiet evening by the fire more than dancing underneath the hundred-candle chandeliers of Tynick's."

"Then you will be suited for the north, I wager. Those long winters can be trying."

"Are you from the Basklands?" Evvie asked.

"No, no. My family is from Kessin."

"My goodness. A lady from the eastern seas! How fascinating. I've never seen the ocean in all my days. I am fated to be landlocked, it appears." Evvie feigned lamentation. "Was it there your husband found you?"

"Yes. A fair number of the ladies in my family are wintry as I am. He was fascinated with them, but mostly with me." Mrs. Zsall flushed. "I have the same color eyes as you."

"Yes, I think you do," Evvie agreed.

"He thought I was a white witch because of them," Mrs. Zsall laughed. "He's Bask, naturally. And the Bask value witch-kind." Her expression was one of immense amusement.

"And my magic mark makes me a witch too?"

"Oh yes. A red witch. My husband, who only glimpsed you briefly while you dined, has been nattering on about you all morning. You're a rarity, and he's all in a titter about it." She giggled and pressed a lock of her snowy hair aside. "Nothing prepared me for the kind of respect and deference ladies like us receive when in Bask company. The moment I saw you I thought I simply *must* let you know. It will likely begin in earnest once you near Avradelle, as that is a city that is heavily Bask, in spite of it being still part of Rothro."

"That is where I will be collecting my trousseau for my new home." Evvie sipped her tea, and put the cup back in its saucer.

"This idea that Dareth would value me more because he believes me to be a witch seems like nonsense, no unkindness intended," Evvie laughed. "He's never even mentioned it."

"I imagine not, as you are a pragmatic southerner. They know we do not ascribe to those superstitions. But the Bask are very closely tied to their old religions, and the witchery comes with it. There are several of my husband's relatives who claim they are witches. Black witches, in particular. I have not spent much time with his family; I prefer to stay here in the tunnel. I am only a white witch in their eyes, only slightly more esteemed than the common witches. But you, you're a red. I hear my husband talk of those with reverence. You are the prize of prizes."

"Goodness, what a laugh," Evvie chuckled.

"Indeed. I very much doubt your husband will have expectations of your magical skills, as mine does not. I think it is more about the idea of status than anything else, at least in the case of my marriage. Old habits, old standards, influencing what they seek in women."

"I would hope Dareth chose me for me, and not for my eyes and hair," Evvie lamented.

"Oh, I am sure he chose you because he found you lovely. But he will have seen the eyes as a sign of the right choice." Evvie could not help but feel that she too, felt a sign of the right choice too when she looked up on her Bask fiancé, but she did not say this to Mrs. Zsall. Perhaps it was a little bit of that witch—she mused with a soft smile—that made her so certain of her choice.

"You will be cherished. As I am. More so now, that I am with child," Mrs. Zsall declared. "That is what you will experience for having red hair and such lovely eyes."

"Well, that is nothing to complain about," Evvie laughed softly.

Mrs. Zsall stood. "Thank you for your graciousness. I rarely am able to sit and have a discourse with ladies my age," she said wistfully.

Evvie nodded, swallowing her tea. "If you come to Tirdonne, do seek me out. I will have my betrothed give me a card to give to you."

"Oh, that would please me exceedingly!" Mrs. Zsall exclaimed. She curtsied. "It was very nice to meet a fellow witch." She laughed easily.

Evvie giggled quietly too, and rose, reaching for a piece of apple, and popping it into her mouth. "Thank you, Mrs. Zsall."

"Call me Tarren," the young woman replied. "As I am with child, my husband is insisting I take my confinement in Tirdonne. So I will be leaving here in a few weeks, and will be traveling to stay with his family at the clan village. He believes it is better to have me with the family with access to better doctors and services in the city.

"Then you *must* come and visit, for I have no acquaintances or friends there," Evvie pled. "I have even left my abigail behind, and she was as dear to me as a sister. She, too, is with child, and married to the family's estate manager, so there was no question she should stay behind."

Tarren sighed. "I know that feeling well." She reached out and placed her hands on Evvie's. "I will be there in no more than a month. My husband quails unceasingly about my minding my health and that of the child. I shall be grumpy and my ankles will be bloated like sausages, but I will do my best to be of good company to you, Miss."

"Evvie, call me Evvie."

"You will be a married woman by then, I wager, so it will be proper for you to have a matronly companion to visit with," Mrs. Zsall declared decisively. "My sister in law comes to take my place in the kitchens and as hostess until it is deemed by my husband and his family that it is safe for me and the child to return to Diamond Rock. But do not despair, for we visit Tirdonne often because of my husband's family. So we can be fast friends."

"This gives me such comfort to know there will be a friendly, familiar face in this new home. I am so glad to have met you, Tarren," Evvie said.

"Good. I must away. My husband awaits me in the kitchens to serve breakfast. I will see you off later." She curtsied and exited in a rustle of skirts.

Evvie took a deep, hearty sigh, and felt a weight lift from her shoulders. She dressed on her own, choosing a light woolen dress and heavy petticoat. She also had some knitted wool stockings lined in cotton she had gotten for Adrin's icy winters. She pulled on these garments, anticipating a lower temperature in the carriage, as the road would begin to climb even before the end of the tunnel. She wound her hair up onto her head in a loose arrangement, and put a cap over it, arranging the lappets carefully on her shoulders. She selected a book from the little compartment in her trunk. She had resolved to read instead of craft, sure the light from the gallery would suffice.

Like every morning since she departed Ravensroost, she looked forward to seeing Dareth. The thought of his quiet, attentive company filled her with warmth. She put her garments in her trunk, and gathered up the little incidentals that she had removed during the evening. She gave the room one last look before bustling out, book in hand.

Dareth awaited her as he had done each morning, sitting at their assigned table. A coffee steamed in a cup, the tall silver pot with its high, short spout, beside it. Her pot of chocolate sat beside it, also tall, but with a long spout that originated at the bottom, and rose up like a swan's neck. How thoughtful of him to have ordered it, she thought.

Dareth would sit and read the periodical each morning, as he was this morning. His large frame and barbaric-looking tattoos were at odds with the sophisticated cut of his frock coat, and the crisp fold of his cravat. He lowered the paper at the sight of his wife to be, and a soft smile crossed over his full, attractive lips.

"Good morning, lovely Evvie," he said in a soft, deep bass voice, his accent sending chills up her spine. She could not help but think that they were only days away from arriving at Tirdonne, and would soon be married. "I hope to get to Avradelle to the pass at the end of the day tomorrow, if all goes well, and you are outfitted properly against the cold. If there is a delay, there is a delay. We are not leaving Avradelle until you are fully outfitted. In the meantime, I ordered the coachmen to put heated bricks into the seat bins to keep the coach warmer for you."

"What about you? Will you sit in the coach?" She tried to control the rise of her voice, as she desired nothing more to be in his company in quietude again. Sadly, he shook his head, unaware of her hopes. Evvie was not bold enough to simply ask.

"I am accustomed to the cold, my dear," he answered, flipping the periodical a bit to straighten a slumped page. She sat down. He looked at her over the paper. "I am however, tempted to sit in the coach simply to that I can gaze upon your loveliness. But that would be awkward for you, I imagine," he laughed.

She smirked and shook her head clumsily, wanting so to tell him that this was not the case, but feeling oddly bashful about her feelings on the matter. It was the first time she felt this way. She wasn't sure how to manage these emotions.

Mrs. Zsall brought a tray of pastry, ham, boiled eggs, bread, butter and fruit and put between them.

Dareth served a generous portion of each item onto his plate, and ate heartily. Evvie had a large appetite as well, foreseeing a lunch of cold foods from the hamper and a long wait for dinner. So she filled up, her husband-to-be watching with a bit of shock and amusement at how much she put away.

Nourished and rested, they rose and put on their outer garments. Dareth graciously helped Evvie put on her redingote, and drape her shawl around her shoulders. She took a moment to bid her new friend farewell.

"I hope to see you at Tirdonne soon. I shall dote upon you and your expected one until he or she comes into the world," Evvie promised. She slipped Tarren a card with her affianced's name and directions upon it. Tarren flushed, and nodded eagerly, clearly touched by the notion of finding a friend.

Dareth gently ushered Evvie away, and they followed their trunks down the stairs to the waiting coach. Evvie took off her bonnet the moment she was inside the coach, and was delighted by how warm it was. It was warm enough for her to take off her redingote. She wrapped herself in her shawl, put her book on the seat, and settled in while the trunks were loaded.

The coach was drawn back and then it jerked forward. By the time it was en route again; she was nestled in, her book open, the diffused daylight flashing between columns to illuminate the pages.

MIRANDA MAYER

Chapter 9

After spending an uncomfortable night at a shabby little inn just outside the tunnel, the coach carried Evvie out of a dense forest. The landscape abruptly opened up to a featureless hilled plain that rose steadily towards the peaks. They crossed this space encountering nothing except a herd of squat little ponies the color of cinnamon, with bushy manes and tails.

They arrived at length at Avradelle in the early afternoon. It was a densely populated city built in a narrow gorge, stretching across both banks of the Corridan River. The buildings were tall and close, all with the prickly angles of northern style architecture, mostly made from sharply cut stone with shale roof shingles. The city was gloomy and grey, with garlands of grayish-green hag's hair dripping from eaves and corbels, with lichens and mosses of rust, gold, olive and red flocking as many rocky surfaces they could. Ravens peppered the ridges of the sharp rooflines, cawing out dissonantly. The streets were flat-cobbled, which made for a smoother ride through town, but they were narrow and the progress was slow. There were constant issues with traffic coming from the opposite direction that required careful maneuvering to pass. To complicate things, there was a steady flow of foot traffic on streets with no walks. Heads bobbed past, some boldly gaped at Evvie.

She had never been much for cities, and this one seemed to have all the features she despised distilled into a smaller area. There were few trees and little greenery because of the elevation, for Avradelle was above the timberline. It was here that the Corridan River originated. Fed by two greater rivers down in Rothro—one of which they crossed using a broad bridge the day before—the river was sourced from the peaks on the west of Avradelle. What remained of the Corridan now was a tumbling, roaring whitewater about three coaches wide. As they approached the city, Evvie could see the falls and streams at the city's edge, which fed the river, cascading from the mountain peaks that towered over Rothro's smooth, barren hills. There was snow at the very peaks, but not yet where the city stood.

She was relieved when they reached the inn. It was still fairly early, which was nice. The coach drew under an archway into a round courtyard, and stopped. She descended onto the cobbles. The cold struck her like a wall, and she gasped, her breath rolling out in a whorl of steam. The heated bricks had efficiently warmed the cabin of the coach to protect her from the cold, and ward off the depth of it until this moment. Dareth swept off of his horse, and withdrew his garrick, drawing it, still warm from his large body, around her shoulders. She clutched it close, shivering so hard her teeth chattered.

"Do not worry. Avradelle is at a higher elevation, so it is colder here in autumn than it is in Tirdonne. We are fortunate it hasn't snowed yet. Believe it or not, sometimes it is actually too cold to snow," he said. "The vapor disappears in this air. The roads can be frightening. They are already icy. Luckily the horses we will have tomorrow will be shod for it, and the coach we will hire is from Tirdonne, so it is designed to navigate the mountains."

He bustled her towards the stairs that led up to the entrance. The door opened directly into a cramped, heavily timbered common room with low ceilings. It was crammed with people.

"Sorry," Dareth muttered. "It is the best inn in Avradelle. Any others would be much worse. The people are mostly here to dine and to drink. They will be gone once night falls."

Evvie was not quite as irritated by the noise and people as he assumed. The inconvenience of it was overshadowed by the embracing warmth from the massive stone fireplace, the lively fire crackling and popping within its yawning opening.

The innkeeper stood at a counter. The moment his eyes fell on Dareth, he wended his way out from the counter and through the crowd. He, too, was a strapping man of the Bask warrior caste, but his tattoos were far less prominent and dense. He was also padded and thickened from a life of leisure, with a round belly and a generous double chin. He bowed deeply to Dareth.

"We are to stay, if there is room."

"Of course!" The innkeeper's eyes then fell upon Evvie and her preternaturally pale eyes, the twin coils of fire red hair peeping from the sides of her cap. His eyes widened. He bowed to her even more deeply. "You will have my best rooms. I will see to it."

Tarren was right, thought Evvie, smiling furtively to herself.

A servant led them up the steep, narrow stairs into the portion of the inn that was dedicated to overnight guests. The stairs led to a sky bridge that passed over the next street. A coach rumbled beneath as they walked through it. Evvie peered out the windows to the fjord of buildings that pressed against the slender street. This side of the building was quiet. The skywalk led right into a single corridor capped with a stairway down to the lower floor. The corridor was lined with four doors on each side. The servant put them across the hall from one another.

Evvie swept into her room only after handing Dareth his coat. She was warm again, and so happy to enter the low-ceilinged room. It was wrapped in deeply stained paneling and box beams, furnished with stout, strong furniture made of heavy hardwoods, and swathed in warm fabrics in dark earthy colors. There was a fine piled rug with rich tones on the floor, two bay windows with built-in seats overlooking a street where people wove in and out of the steady stream of coaches, drays and riders. A stripe of daylight shone down the narrow chasm between the buildings. The sky was a cold blue with a few cloud streaks.

She took off her redingote and hung it in the old armoire. There was a knock, and her trunk appeared in the arms of a young fellow of Bask descent. He did not make eye contact. He merely deposited the trunk at the foot of her bed, and bowed out of the room. There was another knock and a young girl of about fourteen years entered. She was also Bask, by the look of her dark features, and the small tattooed florette inked on the top of her left hand. She had deep brown hair and wide dark brown eyes.

"I have been assigned to be your abigail ma'am." Her accent was the same as Dareth's, but her tone was coarser and more common. "My name is Eyna."

Evvie allowed Eyna to help her out of her traveling clothes, and to outfit her in something suitable for the warmth of the indoors. Evvie put on one of her sheer white, embroidered gowns with long sleeves over a deep blue linen under gown. A tiny, sleeveless spencer of navy blue— decorated with intricate needlework on the front — covered her bodice. She also wore a ruffed, lacy chemisette to fill the broad neckline.

The young girl removed Evvie's cap and bound her hair up into a delightful arrangement of braids around a twisted bun. Eyna produced from a pocket of her apron a string of pale white marbled beads, and without asking, wound them beautifully into Evvie's hair.

"What's this?" Evvie asked.

"They're called mountain pearls. I thought they would be most handsome against your lovely red hair, and I was right."

Evvie leaned towards the burnished silver mirror and tilted her head so she could see them. "They're beautiful!"

"Every Bask woman should have a set of them. They come from Dekarat, which is the highest mountain in the Bask nation," the girl explained.

"May I purchase them from you?" Evvie asked.

Eyna shook her head. "No. I wish to gift them to you. I read once that it is good fortune to bestow a gift onto a red witch."

Evvie sighed and laughed. "I am no witch." Her pale eyes twinkled with humor.

Eyna only laughed shyly and stepped back. "Take them anyway. We Bask hold true to our traditions, and I have already bestowed them upon you."

"Well, let me give you something in return," Evvie suggested. She stood and walked to her trunk. "Do you read much?"

"Whenever I can," the girl replied. She looked dubious.

Evvie knew that books were a costly endeavor for most people, often a luxury only accessible to the rich. Even lending libraries—the largest buyers of books—required a subscription fee, which was often too much for those of lower income. It was also uncommon for people of the lower castes to know how to read at all. But this girl had a learned, bookish air about her.

Evvie fished through the little assortment of books she had brought in her trunk. The bulk of her collection was in the box cart heading north. She pulled out a small volume bound in thick, red leather with gilded letters and attractive embossing of oak branches, leaves and acorns all along the edges. She straightened and moved to the girl.

"Here," she said with a delighted grin. "It was my favorite when I was your age. It is a story of a Mettin princess warrior named Reela. She's wonderful, and I dreamt of being just like her when I was a girl!"

The lass's eyes lit up. She accepted the book, and turned the striking little volume in her hands.

"I read it so much, I frayed the cover and flaked off the spine. My father had it rebound in this cover for my fifteenth birthday. Is it not beautiful?" Evvie asked.

The girl agreed shyly, looking almost cowed by the value of the gift. "I cannot accept this."

"Of course you can! It is time it was passed down to a new owner," Evvie insisted decisively.

The girl flushed and her eyes misted over. "This is of such greater value than the beads, ma'am," she whispered.

Evvie scoffed and waved her hand dismissively. "Do not be silly. Value is relative. I think these beads are of tremendous value because you gave them to me. This book I have enjoyed for many years, and I am older now. It no longer appeals to me the way it used to. But it will suit you. You take it, and do not say another word about it. I am delighted to know that it will bring you as much joy as it brought me."

The girl curtsied deeply and smiled shyly. She scurried out clutching the tome to her breast as if it was made of gold. Evvie did a few final primps to her appearance, found the book she was reading, and then sailed out of the room, closing the door fast behind her. She padded down the steps in her sapphire slippers, and crossed the sky bridge again.

Dareth had not yet arrived in the common room. She found a little spot in a corner by the tall, divided light windows, and when the boy came to see to her needs, she ordered a grog for Dareth and a pot of tea for herself. She had only just settled in and was watching the traffic pass outside, when the proprietor pushed his way through the customers to speak to her.

"My girl seems to have made off with something of yours, Madame, and I am most apologetic for the transgression. She has told me a lie and said you gave it to her." He held out the copy of the Princess of Swords. The girl stood by the counter, her eyes red with tears.

Evvie's brow furrowed in irritation. "I beg your pardon, sir, but I gifted the book to the girl. She was very sweet to give me a string of pearls for my hair, and attended to me so well, I decided she deserved it. She was not being untruthful to you."

"A string of mountain pearls is of no true value, and this is too fine for the likes of my girl. A book of this quality is lost on her," he retorted, giving the book another jab towards Evvie.

Her brow darkened and her eyes narrowed. "No, sir. I have bestowed the gift upon her. It is hers," Evvie said with a little more force.

The innkeeper looked befuddled.

"Jakin, you are insulting the lady by returning her gift," a deep, resonant voice interrupted. Evvie glanced up to find a tall, lanky fellow of Bask descent looming over them. The tattoos on his arms and the side of his face marked him as Brii caste. The tattoos were text, not stylized scrolls or creatures. The scripts were in dense patches where they were visible. Two came up his neck under his ears, and a few snuck out from under his long cuffs onto the top of his hands. He had been sitting by the fire, chewing on the thin stem of a long pipe. He had gotten to his feet as he eavesdropped on the interchange, and approached to intervene.

"It is too much for a child. Too fine a gift," Jakin muttered.

"That is not for you to decide," Evvie exclaimed. "That was a transaction made between her and me."

"Yes, It is not for you to interfere," the Brii man concurred. "And you truly choose to reject a gift from a redcaste?"

Jakin looked at the Brii man, and started as the man snatched the book from his hand. He wove around the tables full of people towards the girl, and knelt before her, presenting her with the book and a sympathetic smile. She took it, hiccupping through her tears. He said something to her and the girl came to Evvie, and curtsied again.

"Thank you for such a beautiful gift, ma'am."

"You already thanked me, my dear. No need to do it again. It is yours."

Her father seemed confused and slightly ashamed of his reaction. He bowed curtly and shuffled away.

"Thank you sir," Evvie said to the gentleman.

He bowed elegantly and took her hand, touching her fingers to his forehead. "Madame." His black eyes took her in with an unmistakable appraisal. "I am always pleased to see someone who encourages literacy. If I might be so bold as to introduce myself, I am Ando Ryse-Mevvick."

Evvie reclaimed her hand and politely curtsied in return. "Evvie of Ravensroost."

He smiled at her openly. She had to admit he was a handsome fellow. Handsome in a different way than her betrothed. Unlike Dareth, he had a full head of hair, thick and raven black in tousled curls that were swept forward onto his temples. He had a strong, prominent nose and his eyes were black like Dareth's. He sported a set of sideburns that were artfully shaped into dandyish points on his lower jaw. He wore a black frock coat and waistcoat, and a crisp white shirt with a black cravat. He tugged on the shirt cuffs protruding from beneath the velvet cuffs of his frock coat. His air was formal, which was the opposite of Dareth, whose air was one of easy confidence and indifference to formality. Dareth was high born and had nothing to prove. This man was, perhaps, also high-born, but was impressed with the manners and appearances of such, by a family of intellectuals, most likely.

"If I might ask, what brings you north, my lady?" His eyes took her in with a fascinated avarice, lingering on her deep red hair and her long-lashed wolf-eyes.

"Marriage," she replied bluntly. She found something off-putting about the manner in which he appraised her. Dareth, in spite of his possible beliefs about witches, never once looked at her like she was a fine piece of livestock like this man did. Her betrothed might have seen her red hair and wolf eyes, but it was not those things he was focused on when he first met her. It is why she never found the idea upsetting when Tarren told her about it. Evvie was fully confident that Dareth was not bringing her home because he had found himself a witch. She knew he was bringing her home because he wanted to be with *her*. The fact that she was or wasn't a witch was not relevant to him.

This man, the Brii, was in no doubt, from the moment of their introduction, keenly focused on Evvie's traits, and there was an expression he could not keep hidden that reminded her of her brother in his days of gambling and drunkenness—when he was sure he'd found the horse that would win him his fortune back. There was an immediate sense of delight and desire that made Evvie feel like little more than a pretty object. His eyes devoured her greedily, and his mouth twitched with what looked like a little victorious grin.

At her mention of the word marriage, his brows arched. His gaze immediately sought and finally discovered the bonding token hanging on her breast over her chemisette.

"I see," he muttered. The disappointment was thinly veiled in his answer.

It was at that moment that Dareth appeared. Stopping beside Ando Ryse-Mevvick, Dareth gave him a curious sweep of the eye before sitting almost gloatingly at the table with Evvie, and crossing his legs. He'd changed out of his frock coat into a fashionable banyan, and was wearing long trousers with tapestry slippers on his large feet. He had done this a few times during their travels—obviously feeling comfortable to loaf about the common spaces at inns in his state of undress. It did not bother Evvie. It might be perfectly acceptable to do so in Bask country. She paid no heed to it. Mr. Ryse-Mevvick on the other hand, managed a rather turgid expression of disapproval as Dareth took his place.

"Who do we have here, my dearest?" he asked.

"A Mister Ando… I'm sorry…" She looked to Ando for the family name that had slipped her mind.

"Ryse-Mevvick," he replied.

"Ah, I know that name. You hail from Tirdonne. A prominent family."

"And you are…?"

"Dareth of Ilmeer," Dareth replied with a bit of a hard look in his eyes.

Ando's expression was unreadable. "Also a prominent family."

Ando looked a bit bristly and arch.

"The Brii do not often mix with the Baskreth caste, even at Tirdonne," Dareth explained to Evvie. She merely sipped her tea thoughtfully. "It was a pleasure to meet you, Mr. Ryse-Mevvick," Dareth added. He waited for the man to bow curtly, and turn away before looking at Evvie. "This is going to be a bit a problem, I'm afraid."

"What's that?" Evvie asked over her cup of tea, her gaze locked on Dareth's handsome face.

"Men of the Bask will find you irresistible. It is the red hair," he said.

"Yes, my witch mark," she said tauntingly.

He looked taken aback, and even reddened a little on the ears.

"I was warned about this by the lovely proprietress of the Diamond Rock inn, Mrs. Zsall. She said that my features were desirable to Bask men," Evvie said.

He straightened in his seat uncomfortably and frowned. "That is not why I…"

"I know, Dareth," she assured him, stopping him from making further excuses. "A lady knows when she's viewed as little more than an object, and when she's not. Especially me, as I've been treated like one before," she said with a soft, sad lilt to her voice. She sipped her tea again.

He shifted uncomfortably and bent over the table towards her. "You are the most precious thing in my life, dearest Evvie. It is not your red hair or your ghostly eyes that makes you so. I knew the moment I saw you that you were for me. Not because of those things, but because my heart spoke to me first."

Evvie lowered her cup and placed it daintily on its saucer, returning his gaze. "Beloved Dareth, I am assured of this even without these lovely words. I, too, knew you were for me the moment I saw *you*. I thought of nothing but you until I found you again at the public house. I never would have abandoned my home for anyone else. I left my home once for a terrible man, and I vowed I would never do that again."

His brow arched in surprise. Evvie had yet to use one of the moments they'd spent together in intimacy, to confide in him the details of her previous marriage. She had never spoken to him about the man who had fastened the binding bracelet to her narrow wrist and scarred her forever. She'd lived with such shame and humiliation over it, she could scarce think of it herself, let alone vocalize it to someone else. But she knew that if she wanted a happy marriage with this man, she would have to tell him who she was, and hope to be accepted for it—and more importantly, she hoped she could accept herself for it too.

With a sigh, she addressed his look of curious concern, and—speaking in a low voice and shameful whisper—told him everything. Sometime during her missive, he reached across the table and enclosed her hand with his. His gaze, although sympathetic, also grew increasingly angry as she told him openly and quite plainly, what she had endured. She finally finished. "I returned to my father in shame, only to lose him to the Temmet's Palsy almost immediately after I arrived…"

Evvie shook her head, her eyes shadowed with sadness and shame. Dareth squeezed her hand tightly and reached across the table boldly, caressing her pale face, his eyes stormy with emotion.

"You will suffer no such indignity with me, my beloved. Never. You will never know anything from me that you do not desire. I will never touch you without your assent. I will cherish you regardless, for you are meant for me, and I am meant for you. I will endeavor to make you happy as best I can, and I will never, ever harm you."

The words he spoke caused feelings to well up in her breast and the burn of tears filled her eyes. She looked away, out the window. He withdrew a kerchief and gave it to her. She dabbed her eyes. As she turned to look into the room again, she saw Ando's gaze on her, and he looked angry. He must have believed that Dareth had made her weep. She looked away and turned her attention to her betrothed. She accepted his assurances with an affectionate gaze.

"How can I not love you for those words?" she asked.

He returned her smile, his gaze imbued with devotion and affection. Her towering warrior. A gentleman through and through.

He drank his grog and she her tea. They watched the majority of the clientele leave one by one as the afternoon wore into evening, until only a few people remained. Ando stayed, sitting in his chair by the fire, coils of smoke rising from his pipe, his eyes as often as possible on Evvie.

Chapter 10

That evening a large trunk arrived for Evvie along with the modiste who was responsible for filling it. Dareth had sent notice to her soon after they'd arrived that they were in town and awaiting the delivery on commission.

The modiste—Mrs. Anlin— was a stout, kind-faced Carathian woman who declared herself keen to see what Evvie had brought before they even began to delve into the new garments. Mrs. Anlin was fascinated with southern fashions, and even offered to buy a few pieces off of Evvie. Evvie was able to part with two of her nicer gowns and a spencer that she didn't wear very much. She also gave the woman an open robe with a wine-stained train. The modiste loved it, and was determined to shorten the train and salvage the beautiful striped taffeta garment.

Evvie's new wardrobe was made for a northern woman. These were items of taste and refinement, but made of thicker, better insulated materials for the cooler climate. They consisted mostly of finely woven wools, linens and heavier woven cottons, as well as items from highly polished cottons and some rusty deep jewel toned gowns made of scrumptious thick crepe silk.

What caught Evvie's eye at once was a striking redingote made of a rich, tawny, raw silk with a hood. Mrs. Anlin had lined it in a jet silk and edged the cuffs and hood with an impossibly soft black fur. The back had yards of the heavy, textured, lovely silk pleated into a train. Evvie fell in love with the garment and put it on at once so she could look at it in the mirror.

"Crag-rabbits," Mrs. Anlin said. "Softest fur you will ever touch. They can only be found north of Avradelle. I had the pelts on hand and when your commission came in, I knew at once they would be for you. Lovely, is it not?"

Evvie turned slowly to admire the cut and silhouette of the garment, and then pulled the heavy, floppy hood over her head. The fur tickled her cheeks. "It is astonishing! It is my favorite piece."

Mrs. Anlin grinned proudly. "Well then, let us see what else there is, dear." The woman showed Evvie that her current items would suit for the short Bask summer, and that she had plenty of time to commission more summer items in the northern styles when she was settled in. "I can recommend a modiste or two from Tirdonne that I know will serve you well."

"Can I not have them commissioned from here? Everything you've made me is so beautiful and you did so in such a short time!"

"Oh, I appreciate your kindness, Ma'am," Mrs. Anlin declared. "But I will not deprive the modistes local to you of your patronage, for the life of me. They are as good as I am, if not better. And given they will have more time to work, the quality of their work will be better. I am fortunate to have a small battalion of girls stitching away by lamplight, my dear lady. With my location, it is often we receive similar commissions for northbound travelers. It is with these that we devote most of our time.

"We stuff a form to provided measurements, and make a few basic patterns to work from. It is easy after that. This piece was sewn by my best apprentice." Mrs. Anlin slid the fur trimmed redingote from Evvie's arms and shook it out. "This will be too warm for the coach, but it will be wonderful for when you are out and about in town or walking around your husband's family-village or the city itself."

The word family-village surprised Evvie, but the woman did not give her a chance to ask her further about it. Mrs. Anlin busied herself with showing Evvie her new wardrobe, and putting all of the items she'd taken off Evvie's hands into a carpet bag she had carried in with her. She watched Mrs. Anlin fold her favorite new coat, and put it on the top of her new trunk.

The next day's departure was an early one. They breakfasted on warm porridge with diced crisp apple and a dollop of fresh cream mixed in. They were fussed over by the cowed innkeeper whose apologetic air still hung over the whole meal like a gloom.

The bricks had been freshly heated and stored again in the lined seat bin when Evvie was helped into the coach by her husband to be.

"The horses have studded shoes, and the roads are liberally salted. But to be sure, I have ordered the men to keep the pace slow and careful. I'm sorry, this will lengthen today's ride, but the switchbacks are dangerous even in summer," Dareth said as he closed the door.

She settled in. Once their trunks were loaded, they were underway.

Dareth was not exaggerating. The road was precipitous indeed. Although the switchbacks had sensible stone railings on the cliff side edges, the pitch of the coach and the sound of the metal studded horse shoes scraping on the cobble road were hair-raising. The coachman applied the special wooden wheel-brake most of the way down, and by the time they reached level ground, it smelled like it was smoldering. But flat ground they did reach, to a degree. It was no longer inclined so steeply that Evvie's book would keep sliding from the tufting of the seat whenever she put it down.

There were a few villages scattered along the road as they made their way north towards Tirdonne. But what was more intriguing was the forest that appeared almost immediately after they began to descend from Avradelle and its sparse greenery. The switchbacks began as barren, with the occasional stunted evergreen bush here and again. But as the road began to descend in earnest, they were soon moving between the tops of towering conifers which became a wall of heavy-boughed, needled trees dominating the roadsides. They did not thin out either. In fact, the further the party got from the mountain pass at Avradelle, and the deeper they drove into Bask, the thicker the woods became and the more varieties of trees grew.

The conifers became interspersed with beech, rowan, yew and birch, oak and elm and aspen. Chestnut trees and maples began to appear as the coach rose up again with the land. The villages here were more isolated from one another than they were south of the Morriden mountains. The forests had not been felled for sprawling open farmland as they were at home. There was no need for the poplar wind-blocks that criss-crossed the Carath flatlands like a leafy swaying gingham weave.

Bask architecture, which this far south was still strongly influenced by Carathian and other southern styles, still had a distinctness to it that was uniquely northern. Here, the buildings were designed to belong to the land. Made of stone, like those in Avradelle, even the small houses were imposing. They had roofs tiled in dark slate or shale, with tall smokestacks and narrow windows. There was lushness and greenery everywhere. Mosses on the rooftops, vining on the faces of the buildings, lichens in warm oranges and yellows, reds and ochres making a calico of stone walls and buildings.

There were intriguing details in the stone and woodwork. An archaic yet profoundly grave humor to the curve of the windows, the dip of a roofline, the scrollwork on the weighty corbels, or the many, many carved faces of the Geshinn—the nymphs and satyrs that peopled ancient Bask mythologies and adorned the framework of the buildings they passed by. Everything was built to withstand hard, long winters, to keep heat in, and the cold out, and to keep the moisture from wicking away the strength of the building.

The trees changed the quality of light in the coach. It made reading less pleasant. With the difficult descent and now the darkened coach, Evvie's book remained unread for the whole day.

They stayed in a large guesthouse that was apparently the only one between Tirdonne and Avradelle. It was an enormous building built around a courtyard livery. There were many rooms of middling quality. Even for a man of Dareth's rank their best room was shabby, but comfortable. After the day she had, Evvie hardly remembered eating supper or sleeping.

Come morning, they were breakfasting when they saw Ando again. He, too, had arrived sometime in the evening, and was preparing to embark at the same time they were. He rode with Dareth behind the coach, although from what Evvie could discern from her occasional glances through the window, there was little conversation to be had between them.

Just before supper time, Tirdonne appeared on the horizon. Evvie was so relieved to hear the coachman announce it, she folded down the window in spite of the rain. Shocked again by the cold air, but undeterred, she peered out at the city.

They had entered a partly open area where there were some cultivated fields and pastures interspersed with copses of oak and maple, with picturesque farmhouses settled beneath them. As the coach drew on, more houses began to appear. Then the great spires of the Brii conservatory and the royal palace towered on their mountainous foot, with the city climbing up towards it in a web of spiraling streets. The sun was setting and myriad windows glowed gold with candlelight.

Ando tipped his hat to Dareth, and then passed the coach at a canter. He gave Evvie a respectful, yet meaningful bow from his grey horse, before cantering up the main throughway and into the city. The coach rumbled on, Dareth as ever, in its wake. And only half an hour later, Evvie finally caught sight of her new home.

The family village was, in essence, a compound. It was a collection of buildings and gardens that fully enclosed a square with a large central stable and livery. It was accessible by two archways with iron gates. Above the archways, carved in the stone, was the family's name written in old Baskreth text, which thanks to her father's obsession, she was also able to read. The figures spelled out: ILMEERI. The letters looked sharp and precise as the lamp sconces on the side of the arch cut the shadows like paper.

Dareth had drawn his horse forward to lead the coach. He stopped and rang the bell, and a young man unlocked the gate and let him in. The coach followed, and the gate was closed behind them. The coach came to a stop by the livery, the silence of it was almost deafening. The city's noise was closed out by the enclosure of buildings. Windows shone bright into the square, and the silhouettes of people could be seen peering out as if to ascertain that their relative was indeed home with his new betrothed.

It was a large compound, a village in its own right. Houses hugged together, but a few sported little skirts of gardens. Others were tall and imposing, and a few were but cottages. They all faced the square

Dareth assisted her as she descended from the coach to the cobbles. "You will be residing with my aunts, if that is acceptable. Until we are wed, it will not be acceptable for you to sleep under my roof. But you will spend as much time there during the day as you please. I do, however, think you will like my aunts, and I am most certain they will like you."

Evvie, utterly exhausted and relieved that the travel was over, exhaled gratefully. He led her across the pavement to a two-story, narrow townhouse wedged between two much larger homes. There was bustling at the door, and as Evvie drew near, she saw two ladies squeezed together at the entrance, wringing their hands in anticipation. When she entered the weak circle of light cast by the sconce by the door, the two ladies threw themselves into raptures.

"Oh, Arah, is she not perfection?"

"Yes, yes, perfection, Nerah. She must come inside at once. Stop fussing about and step aside!"

Dareth glanced down at Evvie as they climbed the four short steps leading to these ladies. Arah, the older lady—who had hair the color of steel—literally shoved her sister aside with her elbow. Nerah—whose hair still had a luster of black remaining to it—was so enthralled by Evvie, she stumbled aside a few steps but seemed not to notice it at all. She grabbed Evvie's elbow, Nerah did the same. They tittered and made such a commotion as they ushered her through the door. They were both tall women, and Evvie felt diminutive beside them. Dareth had not uttered a single word. He took off his water-stained hat and ducked under the doorway behind them.

"Here girl, let me take that bonnet," Arah muttered, reaching up and unlacing the veil that Evvie had used to bind the hat to her chin. Arah pulled the delicate little thing off the bonnet and Nerah plucked the hat from Evvie's head. As they did this, they slowly guided her towards the small, formal sitting room where a cheerful little fire crackled in an elegant stone hearth.

"Aunts," Dareth boomed.

The ladies turned at once—noticing him at last—and both of them scuttled towards him and showered him in kisses and embraces. He bent down and succumbed to this demonstrative behavior quite happily. This was not the sort of thing Evvie had ever seen family do in front of strangers. Her father had been a loving man, but he was affectionate without the hugs and kisses she witnessed here. His words were kind, and his gaze warm. But he rarely kissed Evvie or hugged her. Except when she left to be married. He had clung to her very tightly and kissed both of her cheeks. The aunts were so elated for

Dareth's return, and their round, red-cheeked faces beamed love at him. Evvie was a little envious of this, but also a little uncomfortable.

"Your father was worried you'd turn out like Farnid and never return from your completion. Find that outside world too tempting, perhaps. You did find something tempting out there, but you had the good sense to bring her back here!" Arah exclaimed.

And lo, they threw themselves back towards Evvie, who shrank from all the attention.

"Miss Evvie of Ravensroost," Nerah intoned with pride. She wore a tall frilly cap over her hair, and—like her sister— had exactly three perfect curls hanging against each temple like little sausages of silver. They had no shortage of lace, either of them. Their throats were festooned with ruffling and pleating, chemisettes simply layered with it, and tuckers around their necklines to boot. Their gowns—Nerah's in navy blue, Arah's in an autumny red—were meticulously trimmed and embroidered. Nerah had false sleeves with more lace, and Arah wore mid sleeves with old fashioned elbow ruffles of lace. They were astonishingly adorable in all their bother and flushed excitement.

"Welcome to the family, Miss Evvie. As you are family, I will dare to call you Evvie, and you will call me Arah. Or aunt. You may call me either."

"Or both. You may call me either or both. Aunt Nerah, if you please. Welcome home indeed! We've prepared your room to be as cozy and comfortable as possible, and we have a delightful supper awaiting you. When Dareth's message arrived yesterday at lunch, we were so excited we could scarce eat our pork pie!"

"Thank you," Evvie managed to utter.

"You must be simply wasting away to a shadow with hunger, dear girl. Dareth, surely was too much in a hurry to let you stop earlier for supper. Thoughtless boy. You're a thoughtless boy, Dareth," Arah declared.

"Indeed I am." His deep voice was a rumble. His dark eyes glinted with laughter.

"We are happy to see you, Dareth, but we must bid you away. Your father wishes to see you at once, and we must be permitted to dote upon our guest," Arah said firmly.

"She requires doting," Nerah declared.

Dareth bowed, giving Evvie a wry smile. "I willhave your trunks brought in haste, my dear. I will see you in the morning. I will breakfast here with you, if that is acceptable to my aunts."

"Yes, yes, now go." Arah dispatched herself to herd her nephew out onto the square. When she returned, her sister had already seen to removing Evvie's redingote and was pouring Evvie a glass of port.

"My goodness, Evvie you are lovely to behold," Arah said.

Nerah handed the girl the port and bade her to sit.

Evvie clutched the port. "Thank you."

"We were concerned Dareth would not find *himself*, let alone find his match. And find these things he did. A true red witch!" Arah declared.

"Oh, not that again!" Evvie laughed. "I've heard little else since the tunnel."

"You do not believe in such things?" Nerah asked.

"As most southerners do not," Arah reminded her sister smugly.

"If I *am* a witch, I'm a useless one," Evvie replied in good humor. "I haven't an ounce of magic." Evvie had heard many a tale of magical things, but never once witnessed such a thing for herself. Most southerners were of the belief that magic and witchery were things of myth. She found it amusing how the aunts were so earnest in their belief of what she thought to be utter nonsense.

"No such thing. Southern witches are simply untested because the society of the south is primitive and closed-minded." Nerah waved her hand dismissively. "Witches of Bask are as real as they were when the ancient gods were worshipped. You will learn what you need in time. We knew you would need teaching since you hailed from below the spine of Morriden, so we have decided to teach you."

"Teach me? Are you witches too?" Evvie asked, her eyes twinkling.

"But of course we are, girl," Arah snorted. "We are not red witches. Not *powerful* like you. We are black witches. Black witches are most vulgarly referred to as common witches here."

"Common my arse," Nerah snorted under her breath. Her sister shot her a glare, and Evvie could scarce keep her countenance. She sipped her port to hide the smirk on her face.

84

"We must rely on spells and talismans to perform our powers, unlike your kind, but we are still sisters in magic nonetheless. It is our duty to see to your education on these matters. It has been many generations since a red witch has crossed the Ilmeeri gate, let alone the city of Tirdonne. The rumor of your existence alone has elevated our family's status amongst the various family clans of Tirdonne. Dareth's letter upon meeting you was met with acclaim by the whole family. And word has been spreading since," Arah said.

"That does not sound good," Evvie admitted. "I prefer *not* to be the center of attention."

"Too late for that!"

"Nerah!"

"Well it is true," Nerah said. "But the family can shield you from most of that. Our village is our village and you will be protected from the fuss as long as you are here."

Evvie groaned audibly and shook her head. The last thing she needed was to be ogled by strangers.

"Dareth never much cared for all these traditions, so we were surprised to hear that he'd found you, and was bringing you home. But even our skeptical nephew cannot argue with fate. He told me he would never marry if he did not know in the depth of his soul that the woman was the one for him. To feel that towards you, and to have you be what you are, well. That is fate indeed, Evvie. Fate indeed." Nerah nodded gravely as she spoke.

"Well, if it is fate that brought us together, I won't complain about it. But I am most certain you will all be quite disappointed, for I highly doubt I willever be the creature you think I am. I just hope that you will still hold me with some regard when that disillusionment occurs," Evvie said.

"Do not be a fool, child," Arah snapped, but with good humor. "There is no way you could possibly be a disappointment to us, or to Dareth. Even if your hair and eyes turned a mousy brown."

Evvie was amused by that declaration.

"Dareth has been a difficult creature from the moment he was born," Arah continued. "Willful and confused. Half-hearted at best in many things. We often thought he would never fall in love, for he found no pleasure in the flirtations of his lady peers. He's a handsome boy. You would think he would have had his lion's share of romance. But no. You are the very first creature he has ever expressed any interest in. And it wasn't just interest, it was decisive and knowing. That is enough for us. To know our nephew has found someone who can love him and ground him. Give him something to truly fight for when he battles for his place."

Evvie had forgotten that he still had that hurdle ahead of him. These were dangerous battles. She read that sometimes, the battles were to the death. It was a risky endeavor. She frowned thoughtfully.

"Never fear, dear girl." Arah patted her hand. "There is one thing Dareth has a talent for, and that is violence. It has been his constant companion from childhood, and he has scrapped his way into manhood and marched with an infantry. The matter of one bout is nothing to concern yourself with."

"Well, if he decides to stop at Count," Nerah added. "He might desire a higher set of drest to adorn his skin. Especially with the prestige of a redcaste wife."

"Oh, do shut up, Nerah!" Arah barked. "Do not be a simpleton. The boy cares as little about rank as you care for common sense. He will do his duty and take his father's title. Like his father, he will be content with what he was raised to be."

Evvie looked on in a sort of stupor. Her head was exploding and there was a deep knot of discomfort in her stomach. She realized that she was hungry. "Well then," she interrupted their glaring exchange. "Dearest sister-aunt-witches, might I be so bold as to ask when supper is? For I am utterly famished!"

Chapter 11

Evvie's little apartment in the Aunties' home was exactly as she would have imagined it would be: Cozy, welcoming and comforting. She had been given a pair of small rooms connected by a broad, hardwood archway. The larger room was the sleeping room, where a heavy, old-fashioned pedestal bed dominated the space with its pilasters and draperies made of yards and yards of tapestry. The second room was a small sitting room with a sofa, fan-back chair set by the fireplace, a petite, round work table—much like the one in her father's office—with a matching chair, and an embroidered fire screen standing tall before the hearth. A pocket door led to a wash chamber with a round bowl-shaped tub made of copper, a stand with a washbowl and decanter made of fine white porcelain, and a chamber pot chair.

The house was old. The rooms weighty and dark. The aunties had made a concerted effort over the years to bring brightness and cheer to the spaces by applying painted wainscot and plaster to the walls, and warming the dark, lustrous wooden floors with fine carpets.

The furniture was a blend of the old and the new. Some items were clearly imported from the southern countries, and seemed flimsy and fragile next to the solid, larger, heavy northern pieces. The effect of this blend was oddly pleasing. The aunties had furnished her with a goose down coverlet to replace what surely would have been layers of heavy quilted blankets. The sheets were clean, crisp cotton as white as snow. There was a modern vanity with handsome cabriole legs, which looked brand new and still emanated the aroma of newly worked wood and freshly dried lacquer.

She had not bothered to unpack the evening before. She'd eaten a good supper, and was ushered to bed, with the promise of her own abigail come morning. And when morning came, there was indeed a fresh-faced young girl of twenty or so entering her room carrying a tray with a rotund pot of steaming tea. The girl had extremely kind eyes, and a sweet disposition. She helped Evvie dress in a warm linen morning gown, and put her hair up into a simple twist on the back of her head. The ladies then set to unpacking the trunk into the large chest of drawers and the big armoire that dominated the back wall of the bedroom.

"These are so lovely," the girl, whose name was Imbrah, said, picking up the white gown Evvie had been wearing when Dareth had saved her that very first day.

"It won't be of much use right now," Evvie sighed, lifting the embroidered hem.

"Let us dedicate this trunk to all of your lovely summer clothes. I will arrange them between cedar to keep the moth worms from them. Then it can be put away for the season."

"An excellent plan," Evvie declared. Imbrah fetched a sack of cedar pieces and they laid out her wardrobe. "I have more garments coming with the box dray too; we shall have to add to the summer trunk when it gets here, providing you stay with me when I am moved to Dareth's home."

"Oh, I will if you will have me."

"Of course I will, dear," Evvie assured her.

The trunk emptied, they laid the gowns between sheets of paper, and placed the lovely, fresh cedar shapes in between the layers. It was quick work. Evvie stopped to take tea.

"Breakfast will be served in three quarters of an hour, Miss Evvie," Imbrah reminded her as she folded another gown and carefully let it pleat itself into the trunk.

Evvie acknowledged her reminder with a nod, and continued working while the girl hung the winter garments up on the pegs in the armoire, and tucked her underpinnings and other items into the drawers. Her collection of slippers—like silken gems—were arranged on the bottom of the armoire, along with several pairs of boots and half-boots.

"You will be here for at least two weeks, as there will be time needed to make all the wedding arrangements. You might as well make yourself at home," Imbrah postulated. She had arranged Evvie's books on the small, built-in corner shelf in the sitting room, along with the lace-making supplies and other accessories.

As Imbrah picked up the final stack of items that had been taken from the bottom of Evvie's trunk—things that could be sorted into the shelves in the sitting room and on her chest of drawers—something dropped from her grip, clattered onto the portion of the bare floor, and rolled to a stop near the skirt of the hearth. Evvie put down the gown she was folding and picked up the glinting object of the floor, turning it in her hand. The hairs on the back of her neck rose up and her stomach suddenly chilled in a blossom of icy fear.

"What is it, ma'am?" the girl asked.

Evvie stared at it in confusion. "It is a ring," she replied. She was awash with puzzlement and a little fear. In her hand was her former husband, the Duke of Ivran's, crested ring. The one that had been cut off his finger when he was killed. *How in the world did it end up in my trunk?* She had left a few items inside little cubbies on the bottom of the trunk when she returned from Ivran. Things she wanted to keep, but didn't require immediately. But she had not packed the ring. It did not belong in her trunk. It did not belong anywhere near her. She put it down on the dressing table by her box of jewelry and gazed at it, her stare painted with a touch of horror.

"And there!" Imbrah declared. "Finished."

Evvie's large trunk was fully emptied of its contents, and the smaller one was now dedicated solely to summer garments and accessories. Her various bonnets and hats were stowed on the top shelf of the armoire, and the doors closed. Evvie had been so absorbed in the mystery of the ring, she hadn't seen Imbrah finishing it all up. Just as the girl spoke, the bell downstairs tolled the half hour. Almost simultaneously, the front door bell jangled as well.

"Breakfast, ma'am," Imbrah declared. Evvie startled out of her reverie and bustled to the door. With a final glance at the bright, gleaming ring, she went downstairs.

Dareth noticed that Evvie seemed shaken when she came down the stairs to join the aunts and him for breakfast. He'd just been let in and was removing a rain-soaked hat and coat. He paused before handing them to the Aunties' ancient housekeeper. "Good morning, my dearest Evvie," he said, taking in her waxen face.

"Dareth, good morning," she replied, dropping her hem as she cleared the last step and grasping his hands in greeting.

"You look peaked. Are you unwell?"

"I've had a bit of a shock," she admitted.

"Come, let us go and sit down to breakfast. You can tell me about it."

She took his arm. He led her into the little dining room where both aunties were already seated and sipping coffee from delicate cups painted with tiny blue birds scattered in a loose pattern over the white background. Arah was reading some correspondence, and Nerah was sipping warmed milk from a double-handled bowl. Their dark brows arched in delight at the arrival of their guest and their nephew.

"Aunts," Dareth greeted them. They scarcely acknowledged him; instead they peered at Evvie in curiosity.

"My dear, you look like you've seen a ghost," Arah exclaimed.

"I might as well have," Evvie replied, sitting down at the table where Dareth held out her chair. He then positioned himself beside her and served her some tea and himself some coffee.

"As Imbrah and I were unpacking my things, we discovered an object that should in no way be in my possession. An object belonging to my late husband," Evvie explained.

"How odd. Could a servant have put it in there by accident?" Nerah asked.

Evvie shook her head. "It was his noble's ring. It was cut from his hand when he was assassinated, and it was never found."

The three looked at her in shock.

"How it ended up in my trunk is a mystery. I did not take everything out of it when I returned from Adrin. I left mostly little keepsakes and such that I hold dear, but do not pay much attention to. The ring was with those things when we were unpacking. I have no idea how it could have gotten there. Someone must have been playing a cruel trick on me," she said with no shortage of bitterness. "What a horrid thing to do. Such indignities I had to suffer in my marriage to him and to put the ring with my things…" Evvie paused and tried to recapture her poise. Dareth reached out and placed his hand on hers.

The aunties looked at one another and then at her, their brows furrowed beneath the ruffles of their caps. A servant entered carrying a tray piled with toasted bread and butter, boiled eggs, ham and sausage, and pots of jam and honey. The platters were placed on the oval table and the family served themselves from them. Evvie ate absentmindedly, her mind far away in the past.

"Never mind a dead man's ring, dear girl," Nerah finally said. "You are here now with us. That past is like that painting there." She pointed to a rendering of a horse standing in a meadow. "It is a moment of time captured long ago. It is no longer living, or breathing. You are away from everything that has connected you to that time. You have a new life and a new family. Do not let someone's cruel game intrude upon this."

Arah drank from her coffee. "Give us the ring so you do not have to look at it. We will find a way to return it to the family it belongs to."

Evvie sighed shakily. She glanced over at Dareth who was watching her with concern. She gave him a wan smile. He was the only one who truly understood what motivated Evvie's reaction. The ring was a cruel reminder indeed of a terrible time in her life. Its presence in her possession was a conundrum. It meant, to some degree, that the person who killed her husband wanted to be, or was, connected to her.

Dareth was obliged to see to some business upon his return. He was ordered to the warrior's guild to accept some sort of token for achieving his completion. He was not thrilled about having to leave Evvie once again. The aunties, however, were delighted to have Evvie to themselves. They outlined their plan for the day. They were going to take her to what was called the garden district, where they would meet Dareth's sister and a few other cousins and relatives for lunch at a the infamous glass house, where the Brii grew trees and flowers from the far south—some plants even from the Wyver islands that no longer existed in nature.

Evvie was given only a few moments to spend with her fiancé alone before being bustled upstairs after breakfast. She put on her half boots and was so excited to wear her new winter redingote with its fur trimmed cuffs and hood. She chose a low bonnet to put the hood over, and a frilly cap. Imbrah set three curls on each side of her head just like her new aunties, and they had a giggle about that.

Warm stockings, and the matching muff of crag-rabbit fur slid over her gloved hands, and she and the aunties paraded out of the little house into Ilmeeri square. The space was busy. The livery was being mucked out, the horses tied to rings on the stone exterior while a young fellow briskly saw to their grooming. A smith was trimming up hooves and re-shoeing. Several girls were sweeping the square clean of the dried up vine leaves that had fallen from the faces of the various buildings. One girl was gathering the burrs from the chestnut tree in a bucket.

An elderly lady, accompanied by an awkward teen boy, made her way towards them as the ladies headed for the gate. The aunts stopped and waited for the plump, silver-haired woman in the ridiculously large bonnet festooned with feathers, to approach them.

She was a wizened, ancient creature with a face full of lines and jowls most certainly gained from frowning a vast deal. She also had her own drest, now quite faded. Like Bask men, the women had more of them the higher the rank, but they all possessed the naming tattoo, which was applied at the first childhood rite, and they were usually on the top of the wearer's hand. Evvie recalled this from her father's books. And she had glimpsed faded marks on the aunts' left hands, along with a few on the wrists, but their long sleeves mostly covered them. They were subtle and less intrusive than the tattoos seen on the men.

The old woman wore black. Her wrists and neck were encased in dense pleats edged in delicate lace. Her bonnet was also black, with raven feathers and greenish black ones, and a few spriggy white accents. Her face was surrounded entirely by white ruffles, her cap tied with a bow under her chin. She drew up eyeglasses that hung from a chatelaine on her high waist, and put them in front of her yellow, watery eyes, taking in Evvie with a sweeping, appraising gaze.

"Well, this is the red witch the boy has brought home, eh?" Her silver brow arched as if she wasn't much impressed. "She's not even as tall as me!"

"Lady Dall, this is Evvie of Ravensroost," Arah introduced her. "She is a gem."

"A gem, eh?" the woman intoned dubiously. "What a sad day it is that one must go south to find a red witch. You look a little slight, girl. Northern girls are of stronger stock. Hopefully a little time in the village will get you up to muster. Can't do anything about your height though." She said the last with a sigh of resignation. "You will come and take tea with me tomorrow in the afternoon. Without these fussing creatures. I want to get a look at you without all that fluster." She waved her hand over Evvie's form, and then nudged the teenager forward to a house across the square.

"Never mind her. She's a harpy," Nerah blurted, looping arms with Evvie. It was true that Evvie was slight. Compared to the aunts she was small. Even her abigail was taller and stouter than she, but the aunties didn't seem to have a care in the world about it. They latched her between them, and exited the family compound, unapologetically consuming the width of the walk. But Evvie's shock of red side curls and her clear, crystalline eyes were enough to cause other people to step aside and let them pass.

It was a bright, but crisply cold day. Evvie's new garments were made well to guard against it.

"There will be snow by tomorrow, care to wager?" Nerah asked Arah, who merely scoffed.

"That there is the Brii conservatory. The glass house is annexed to it, and this is where we are going," Arah pointed to the side of the mountain consumed by the flying buttresses and nubby rooflines of the edifice. On the other side, in a distinctly different style and stone, was the palace, which took up most of the skyline with a bristle of towers and battlements. The road they climbed was steep, and it slowly wound upwards towards these crenelated confections of stone.

The city of Tirdonne was a marvel. Not just to Evvie, but a legend that was described throughout the land. The buildings were beautiful in their severe styles—artful stacks of rock and slate, with astonishingly detailed carvings in the dense indigenous rock.

The gardens were also a wonder on their own, made up of hardy plants that could survive and return after the many months covered in snow and ice. There were no flowers, but carefully chosen foliage and evergreens. Variegations and unusual colors that one would associate with autumn back in Carath: orange and red, golden yellows and orangey greens. Window boxes and planters spilled over with such vegetation, and the streets were lined with a variety of winter-hardy conifers and deciduous varieties, which were already bare of leaves. Vines and ivies enrobed building faces, mostly just webbings of thin, leafless stems as the cold had taken their vegetation, the dark recess of the windows glinting from them like eyes.

Smoke rose up in what looked like a forest of lines, which all swished east with the wind after reaching a certain height. The scent of wood smoke was everywhere.

The city was well designed in the width of the roads, and the walks. They passed walls and gates to homes and compounds, archways and small front gardens with trees overhanging the walk like a canopy. Then the homes turned to shops, and little plazas began to appear here and there—some made simply for walkers to stop and enjoy the prospect—overlooking the rooftops below, and down into the forest valley between Tirdonne and Avradelle. In the far distance, one could just barely see the ridge of peaks against the sky. It seemed farther to Evvie than it was, because it was so arduous a journey.

It felt wonderful to walk out in the daylight. The exercise put color in her cheeks, and the sights were more than enough for her to put the ring out of her mind and enjoy her time with the bickering aunts.

"Rell is an unfortunate looking thing, is he not?" Arah declared as they walked, speaking of the boy at the old woman's arm. Evvie had been informed upon exiting the compound, that Lady Dall was the Ilmeeri matriarch and was Dareth's grandmother. The boy was a lower cousin, with no visible drest. He was a ramshackle assemblage of awkward limbs inside clothing too baggy. He had gazed at Evvie with the fascination of a teen. He had not uttered a word nor even greeted any of them with a nod or a polite bow.

"He is a bit of a scarecrow. Natto asserted the child should go to the Brii enclave. He is not of *leadership* stock," Nerah agreed.

"An Ilmeer becoming Brii? Unheard of. That is a crime in and of itself," Arah sneered.

"And truly, how can young man so disadvantaged enter society and earn regard from his peers, when he's continuously latched onto Lady Dall's arm?" Nerah added.

"Disadvantaged?" Arah bristled. "What do you mean disadvantaged?"

"Have you looked at the boy? He's as homely as an old hound," the younger replied.

"Oh, but he is rich, and that will make him handsome enough for someone," Arah gloated loftily.

Evvie listened with an amused smirk. She imagined that even alone, these two women did nothing but natter on like this all day.

MIRANDA MAYER

Chapter 12

Their discourse for the whole of the walk was a never-ending litany of criticism and gossip about the clan's many members. They arrived at the glass house in due time, and Evvie had worked up an appetite from the long, steady climb. She threw back her hood as she entered the vast space, and gazed up at the soaring arcs of metal and stone where the glass was fitted. It was warm. Birds and insects sang and glided about the colossal space, landing on the forest of exotic trees and shrubberies filling the immense space.

"My goodness…" Evvie uttered. "This is astonishing!"

"Yes, yes. Come, the tea hall is this way." Arah said impatiently.

She was tugged through the densely foliated walkways of the hothouse. Evvie's eyes were cast continually skyward, watching the flowering vines and trees with awe as she was led by the aunties. They crossed a little bridge, and Evvie looked down to see a man-made brook winding about the floor of the massive hothouse.

They entered a small plaza where a cluster of tables and chairs made in the southern style were set about the space. Most were empty. There were two that were occupied—one beside the other— by a group of handsome Bask women, all gazing directly at Evvie.

"Welcome, my dearest sister! May I call you such? For we will be sisters, soon enough!" An elegant lady rose, tall and beautiful. She was dark eyed like Dareth, with a head full of raven curls wound around her head and framing her face. She wore a tasteful bonnet with a black gown, like her grandmother, embellished with white cotton and lace.

"Evvie, this is Dareth's eldest sister, Mrs. Reteen," Nerah muttered softly in her ear. Evvie curtsied. Mrs. Reteen reached out with her elegant white gloved hand, and embraced Evvie warmly.

"There is no need to introduce yourself to us, Miss Evvie. There's scarce a member of our extended family that doesn't know who you are already," she laughed merrily. "You are a shockingly pretty, tiny little thing, Miss Evvie," she declared boldly. "Even more so than we had imagined!" There were murmurs of agreement that rose up from the small cluster of women. Mrs. Reteen began to introduce the six other women sitting at the table. They were cousins and second cousins. Their names almost immediately slipped Evvie's mind, as there was so much chatter and excitement.

"How you will stand out at family gatherings," Mrs. Reteen declared proudly. "It makes me regret that I no longer live in Ilmeeri square. I would love to have you nearby, so that we can be as thick as thieves!" She sat down and Evvie and the aunts did as well. "None of us are residents of Ilmeeri square. We're all married off to men of other compounds, I'm afraid."

As they ate a lovely lunch, the ladies chatted with animation. It was an astonishing spread of cold meats and cheeses garnished with fruit and salads, and one very jiggly, creamy and delicious jelly. The Bask tea service was what fascinated Evvie the most. A tall, lanky gentleman in impeccable livery delivered the tea in a strange long pot with a thin, curved nozzle. He sent it into the cup from a great distance, with impossible flourish.

She was watching it with interest when she caught someone moving out of the corner of her eye. It was Mr. Ando Ryse-Mevvick; the man she'd met at Avradelle, and who'd accompanied them on the last leg of the journey to Tirdonne. He was walking over the bridge into the little plaza, his gaze fast on Evvie. He tipped his beaver topper at her, and strode past, his cane clicking on the pavement. She returned the nod politely and turned her attention to the company. She had forgotten about him by the time they'd finished eating and were rising to tour the rest of the hothouse together.

The group moved along the pathways, the younger ladies rather loud and full of laughter. The aunties had relinquished her and were leading the small horde of formerly-Ilmeeri women. Evvie walked next to her soon to be sister-in-law behind everyone. It was during a brief moment of awed silence as they gazed in rapture at the abundant flora that she heard the sound of a cane hitting the pavement. She twisted to find that Mr. Ryse-Mevvick was behind them. Mrs. Reteen followed Evvie's line of sight and her brow furrowed.

"Who is that?"

"A gentleman, of a brief acquaintance, Mrs. Reteen," Evvie answered.

"Call me Hella, Miss Evvie. We are to be sisters after all."

"Of course," Evvie replied. She glanced back again at the man who had trailed slightly behind some trees. "Dareth and I met him at Avradelle. He met us again at the inn at Midway. I'm surprised that I have encountered him again here. Do you not think it strange, Hella? To encounter him again?"

"He is Brii, and this is Brii territory, so to speak. It might not be that much of a coincidence," Mrs. Reteen replied. "However, seeing you are who you are, and knowing that you are so sweet and lovely, I would not be surprised if this man was so interested in you as to actively pursue you."

"That does make sense when you put it that way," Evvie conceded.

"It cannot do any harm to be cautious, Evvie," Hella added when she saw the confusion on her soon to be sister-in-law's face. "When I was about seventeen, there was a man whose fascination and desire was so strong for me that he threatened to kill any young man who dared to court me," Mrs. Reteen whispered. "My father had to *manage* the situation. The young fellow was from Rothro. I do not think he was quite prepared for what would happen when one threatens a Baskreth family. Poor thing couldn't walk for five months after my father got his hands on him. So never fear, dearest sister, for if any man approaches you out of turn and makes unwanted advances, you need only say the word, and the family will act as is deemed appropriate." She gave the man another glance and then they moved to rejoin the group.

"I do not think I'd be comfortable setting the family after anyone, in all honesty. It doesn't seem right. I suppose I could find a way to discourage him if that were the case. Without the necessity for repercussions that might end with him not being able to walk for months," Evvie rambled. Hella glanced down at her from her lofty height and her brow arched.

"You are unaccustomed to our ways, and it must be shocking to you."

"I am not sure it is shocking. Where I'm from, if you are a woman, men speak on your behalf. They act on your behalf, and they make decisions on your behalf. Seeing that Dareth would give me the chance to make my own decisions on the matter, I'd likely choose one that is not punitive. I would not wish to be responsible for anyone's pain." Evvie realized as she spoke that her admonishment of the act was in essence, a criticism of her sister-in-law, and she flushed, and stammered.

"Oh goodness," she shook her head. "I didn't mean…"

"Oh, Evvie, do not fluster yourself, please. I agree whole heartedly. No matter how possessive and threatening the fellow was, I do not condone the level of punishment he received. But you must remember, Baskreth are Baskreth. And northerners are northerners. And to back down from a fight is not in our blood. If the man had conceded the fight, he would have come out of it in better form. But he did not. And that was the result of it.

"I do not feel bad for him, for like me, he had a choice." Evvie smiled wanly, fearful she'd offended her new sister. But Hella looked quite content as they explored.

As the aunties and Evvie bade the cousins and Mrs. Reteen farewell, Evvie did not see Mr. Ryse-Mevvick. But she was almost certain she saw him again as they turned into the gate of Ilmeeri square, standing in lee of an alleyway, watching her. She did not say a word. She merely slipped inside, and took a deep breath as the young gate keeper locked the gate behind them.

Chapter 13

Evvie was awoken the next morning by Imbrah who brought her a full breakfast to eat at her little table in her sitting room. "Neither of the ladies feels well this morning," Imbrah murmured in a low voice. She crossed through the archway, placing the tray on the table, and then returned, pulling open the curtains. "Their lady's maids think it is all that walking yesterday. None of us could recall the last time the madams walked much anywhere."

"I feel terrible that they are going out of their way and endangering their health to entertain me," Evvie replied.

"Nonsense. The village has a fleet of coaches and carriages, barouches and curricles. There's no valid reason why they chose not to be driven, except they overestimated their abilities. They are both laid out in their beds, bemoaning the world. I've been instructed to take care of you, as your betrothed will not be able to see you until after you have tea with Lady Dall."

"Oh, gods, I forgot about that," Evvie mumbled. She crawled out of bed and yawned. She had to admit she, too, was feeling the effects of her long walk up the hill yesterday. The route home was much quicker and less taxing than the slog up hill, but they had strolled slowly and not pushed themselves too much.

What she was going to do for the whole morning and most of the early afternoon was beyond her. As appealing as sitting in her cozy little room, working on a project seemed, she simply did not want to start any new projects until she was moved to her permanent home. And she had nothing new to read, which was irksome as Evvie read a great deal.

Then it occurred to her exactly where she was, and her eyes brightened. "Imbrah, would you be willing to accompany me on a little excursion today? In particular, I would like to visit a bookshop and buy a few books, or find a lending library even. As we are near the Brii conservatory, I imagine there must be a number of such places close at hand."

"Oh, goodness, there are probably more bookshops in Tirdonne than there are readers," the girl laughed. "I will get you dressed, and then I will fetch my cloak and we shall embark on a search for books. I know of two fairly well-stocked stores only a short walk from here."

"Oh thank goodness!" Evvie sprang from her bed, and first attended to her toilette, freshening up her face and brushing out her hair from the long plait. Imbrah had tied in a few rags to set her side curls the night before, rather than use the hot iron. Evvie loosed the rags and curls of deep, rich red tumbled free. This time, they looked much less like those of the aunties, these a little looser and separated. She sat down in her night gown and let Imbrah set her hair into a simple up do which would be covered by a cap for most of the day. As Evvie would be dining with Dareth's father this evening, Imbrah would have to do something more intricate later. For now, the only things that needed attention were her side curls.

Imbrah set them beautifully. They were curled and buffed to perfection. She was then disrobed and dressed in her stockings and heavy cotton shift. Her favorite walking boots went on next. Her stays followed, and her bosom was neatly arranged in it before Imbrah tightened the laces snugly, but not too tight. A heavy winter petticoat skirt—with thin shoulder straps to hang the skirt to the high waistline—went over her head and was fastened closed underneath her bust. A solid cotton chemise with long sleeves went on over that and was also fastened below the bust. Finally, a woolen sleeveless day-gown in a vibrant burgundy red covered it all. Some tone on tone embroidery and cut-work decorated the hem and the bodice.

"You look scholarly in that jumper," the lady's maid noted.

Evvie turned to appraise herself in the long mirror. These new clothes would be thought plain by Carathian fashion standards, but she liked them a great deal.

"I can fetch my cloak and the like. You go and get yours. I willmeet you at the door."

Imbrah dashed away. Evvie found her purse with some coins in it, and she frowned. They were Carathian coins. She would require a bank to boot. Since she was going to go to the bank, she took another moment to root out a stack of notes she had brought with her. She might as well open an account at a Bask institution. She would transfer her inherited monies over another time. That would require a whole day of conference with a banker and the likely employment of a wyvern or two. She took the Certificate of Relict, which she kept in her writing slope, which was required for her to do any banking as a woman.

"You won't mind showing me to a reputable bank first? I only have Carathian currency," Evvie asked Imbrah as the girl rounded the corner, closing the buttons on a plain brown spencer with a sweet peplum. She also wore rust colored gloves and a soft-crowned bonnet of navy blue, with a narrow, rounded brim.

"That I can do. My uncle is a banker at the Bank of Tirdonne. I will take you directly to him. He will get you sorted, and he's only two east and one street up."

"Will that be warm enough?" Evvie eyed the thin spencer.

"I am born Bask. This is not so cold to me. In a year or two, you will be the same."

"And stop wearing this coat? Never!" Evvie laughed. Imbrah laughed, for she could only concur.

They set off to the bank. Evvie was determined to move quickly through the square for she did not wish to be stopped and judged by any more matriarchs or patriarchs or whatever other relative felt compelled to impede her. The gate keeper was quick to set the ladies free of the compound and they crossed the street at once. The two women strolled along the breadth of the hill, passing a few houses, entrances to a compound or two, and the occasional atelier. Only one more street and it was all businesses of one kind or another. Some with homes above floors, others with placards directing customers to offices up stairs.

The bank of Tirdonne was an imposing building that was, at present, covered in a corroded veneer of marble that had seen better days. The windows had black weep stains streaking down from the sills from the sooty rain, and some of the marble veneer had flaked off in spots. There was, however, a pair of tradesmen on the far edge of the building doing some repair work.

"Do not be despaired by the building's state. It is an old bank and deeply established. The oldest in Bask," Imbrah assured her.

Evvie pushed through the doors into the lobby of the bank. Inside, the ceiling soared up into a cavernous dome where statuary and friezes decorated the hemispherical space, interspersed by large windows to cast light into the halls. Long ceiling chains held task lighting in neat lines over extended counters where clerks worked with customers.

"My uncle is this way," she said. She led Evvie down a corridor to an office with the door left ajar. She poked her head in, Evvie close behind. A man sat behind a desk, scratching down some figures on a ledger. He looked up at the movement and broke a smile.

"Ah, Imbrah, sweet. What brings you here?"

"I've a customer for you, sir. She has Carathian currency to exchange."

"And possibly some notes to convert to Bask value and to deposit, sir," Evvie added.

Imbrah's uncle was all too pleased to assist. Evvie reached into her reticule and passed the certificate of Relict to him. He took it with a curious furrow of the brow, and then looked at it.

"Am I to secure this in a box for you Madame?" he asked.

She shook her head. "It is a certic..."

"Certificate of Relict, yes. I've seen it," he laughed gently. "What do you wish me to do with it?"

"Do I not need it to open an account?" she asked. He scoffed and handed it back to her.

"This is Bask Madame. We do not treat our womenfolk like children. They can open accounts without permission from anyone." He then gestured her to sit in a worn leather chair. She did, a little shocked. She tried to process the idea that any woman could walk into a bank and open an account. Just like that. It was a marvel. She was overcome with a sense of empowerment the more she thought about it. How freeing the notion was, to not be dependent on the permission of men for anything.

The banker summoned some clerks to carry out a variety of small tasks while he entertained his niece and her charge. Evvie's coins were brought to the currency office where their weight value would be measured, and compared to the most current posted conversion rates, and then exchanged for Bask coins. She signed her name on some papers to open an account, and was given a receipt for the deposit of the notes, a booklet to calculate her balance and interest, and a purse of weighty coins, which she tucked into her reticule. All this was completed in under an hour. With that, she had her own account in Bask. No waiting period, no process through the financial ministry with requests for proof of her father's and husband's deaths. She could scarce believe it.

She and Imbrah set off to the bookshops, Evvie still bemused by the experience.

The first stop turned out to be the only stop Evvie would need that day. It was a large, cavernous shop filled from floor to ceiling with shelves utterly heaving with books. The first floor had an open area up front with a desk for the bookseller, and then rows of shelves behind them. It nearly took her breath away, the sight of it. The tall space required a mezzanine for buyers to access the second story of shelves, and moreover, there was a rolling ladder to reach the topmost shelves pressing up against the crown molding.

Imbrah, who was not a particularly big reader, asked Evvie if she could leave her momentarily. "I willonly be a quarter of an hour."

Evvie waved her off, too enraptured by the scene before her. She curtsied to the bookseller, a dignified looking older gentleman with silver hair and Brii markings. He had white fluffy sideburns, and a pair of pince-nez spectacles affixed to his large, hooked nose.

"Is there anything you seek in particular, miss? I do not specialize in magical books, but I do have some historical type books on witchery over…"

"No, I like to pore over the choices, but thank you sir," she said quickly.

His gaze took her in, gesturing for her to explore. She clutched her reticule, contained her glee, and disappeared into the stacks.

She was lost somewhere in the fiction section when she suddenly felt a heavy presence she hadn't noticed before. She'd been peeking into the first paragraphs of a dramatic piece, and she turned to find herself face to face with Mr. Ando Ryse-Mevvick.

"Good gracious, sir. Are you following me? I seem to find you lurking about too often for comfort," Evvie snapped. She clutched the books she had gathered for purchase before her as if they could somehow shield her from him.

"I am deeply concerned. It has caused me to seek you out more than I probably should dare," he blurted.

Evvie's brow bunched up in puzzlement and she frowned darkly. "Concerned about what?"

"That man you have so unfortunately attached yourself to."

"You mean Mr. Ilmeer?" she asked.

"Indeed. A barbaric boor."

"I beg your pardon?" Evvie could not believe he would be so bold as to call her husband to be such a thing. "My betrothed is a gentleman through and through."

"I saw that he insulted you to tears at Avradelle."

"He did no such thing. I was confiding something deeply sorrowful to him. Those were *my* tears. And what business is it of yours?"

"Because you are wasted on that family! They are Baskreth. Limping dunderheads with a penchant for aggressive conduct. They fight for this, they fight for that. Everything is about brutality with those people. I cannot think how you can live in the midst of barbarians."

"I am utterly astonished and beside myself as to how you drew these conclusions about the Ilmeeri family. They are civilized, polite, kind people, and honestly, not nearly as different from my own family and people as I imagined. I expected it to be much more rustic here, but it is hardly different at all. Exactly how do you think yourself dissimilar or better than they are?" she snarled.

"The Brii are weaned on knowledge and enlightenment, Miss. We are the brains of the Bask people. We are the progress and the illumination that took our barbaric culture and brought it forward into the modern Age. We are the reason Tirdonne is known to the world as the center of education and learning. Your betrothed is a remnant of an archaic past that is fast fading away. You are wasted on him."

"I am wasted on him? I am not an object. I am a person. One who makes her own choices."

"You are more than just a person. You are a red witch!" he hissed. "You are the purest of the magical bearers, and the most powerful. Your existence and your presence here amongst the Bask whose ancient mythos centers on the magic wielded by the sacred witches—when so few of the true blood witches can be found—is a revelation. It is profound. And you plan to throw yourself into mediocrity, deny yourself the privilege and prestige of *hexxenmaeg*, and make yourself a common little wife rather than choose a path that will lead you to explore your powers and become an exalted, sacred and beloved daughter of Bask!"

Evvie stared at the man as he ranted on with an almost mad expression on his face. She had no idea what *hexxenmaeg* meant, or what the other nonsense he rambled on about. He reached out and clutched her arm.

"You are the first red witch to return to Tirdonne in many years. You are here for a purpose. Do not deny your destiny by throwing it away. By sullying yourself and your sacred powers by diluting yourself with Baskreth barbarian blood."

"Away, sir!" Evvie shouted, tearing her arm free. She wended her way around him and scurried to the bookseller's desk. The fellow looked up, startled. "May I stay with you sir, until I am certain I am safe? That gentleman is threatening me."

The old man's eyes darkened and his shaggy brow fell into a glower. "Have a seat my dear. I willsee to that man." He reached behind his desk and pulled out a musket. Carrying it, muzzle down, he stalked between the bookshelves. Mr. Ryse-Mevvick soon bustled out of the bookshop, and gave Evvie one last desperate look before vanishing from the window. The old man followed with his musket.

"That'll fix him. I willsee to it that a constable sees you home. Can't take any chances with a fellow like that."

Evvie waited for Imbrah to return. The bookseller—whose name was Ghert—sent a boy for the constable. He returned in time with a constable in tow. The constable was a Baskreth man who looked a much like Dareth. Not quite as handsome, but with the same frighteningly powerful proportions. He wore the uniform of some kind of militia. He escorted the girls back to Ilmeeri Square, and waited until the gate was fast behind them before he ambled away.

Evvie had bought the four books she had clutched through the ordeal, but there was no way she would have the ability to concentrate enough to read them now. She bustled into the house and back to her room, flopping down on the bed after stripping off her outer garments. She had no idea that things could be so difficult simply because she had red hair and pale eyes. She hadn't been here three days, and trouble had reared its head. She fought back tears, and closed her eyes. Tarren was not joking, this was utterly mad. Witch this, witch that. She couldn't wait for Tarren to arrive. She needed a friend who could understand just how utterly ridiculous the whole ordeal was.

Chapter 14

Evvie excused herself from tea with Mrs. Dall, claiming to be indisposed. She changed into a comfortable morning gown, and puttered about her room, reading one of her new books, leaving Imbrah to do her work unperturbed. It wasn't until close to lunchtime when Arah knocked and entered, still in a dressing gown, her hair in two silver plaits falling onto her shoulders.

"Evvie, are you unwell?"

"Not particularly. I'm... overwhelmed."

The older woman closed the door behind her and walked through to the sitting room. She sat down in the broad fan-back chair. Evvie, in a gray linen gown, sat with her stockinged feet drawn up on the sofa and a shawl wrapped around her. She'd taken her hair down and let it fall down her back in thick, crimson waves.

"What happened?"

"I went to buy some books, and the man we'd met on our way through Avradelle found me. He was at the gardens yesterday too, but Hella and I decided it was not so much a coincidence as it is a Brii institution. But he was at the bookshop today. He put his hands on me, and wailed about my being a witch, and that I was wasted on this family. It was a circus. The bookseller luckily kept a musket behind his desk and sent him packing. I feel like I will never be able to go anywhere without this witch-nonsense following me."

"You probably won't. But you should be treated with utmost respect, not as if you are an object of value to be hunted."

"It is just been a strange two days. The ring, now this… After all that travel. I think I am just too exhausted to bear it with grace. I have decided to take a day for myself, so I can rest and restore my spirit."

"I forgot about the ring…" Arah said. "Do you still have it?"

"Yes, it is on my chest of drawers in the bed chamber," Evvie replied.

Arah grunted and got to her feet. She shuffled off and fetched it, returning to place it on the work table. She gazed at it with a slight frown.

"At least this is one problem we can address. I will go and fetch Nerah." She bustled out.

Evvie was curious what she meant to do. She got up, shook out her wrinkled gown, and was just sitting at the table when the ladies returned. They pushed the saber chair and the fan back to the table. Nerah carried a square basket with a lid. She put it down on the table, plucked off the lid, and removed from the top a roll of silken cloth edged in embroidered figures. Arah removed the ring while Nerah shook out and laid the cloth over the table. Arah plunked the ring right in the middle of the table on the silken cloth.

Nerah then pulled out a crystal orb, two small animal skulls with holes drilled in them— both were coated in layers of colored wax drippings, indicating they were used as candlesticks. She jammed a black candle in each skull, and set them on either side of the orb. The ring sat before the orb.

Then she produced two little drawstring sacks, a thick deck of spirit cards, a small silver knife, and some strange wooden coins. Arah had brought in two robes of jet black, which the sisters donned. Nerah set to closing the curtains and blowing out the candles and lamps about the room until the only light was from the hearth and the newly lit candles on the table in their skull bases. The last thing that came out of the basket was a thick, leather bound book.

The women sat and Arah picked up the ring and waved it over the candles. She began to whisper words under her breath.

Nerah barked: "Show!" and she threw the book down on its spine. It opened, the pages parting and falling open before her. Her dark eyes studied the pages. "It tells us to cast an Origin," she informed her sister.

Arah waved the ring over the flames in turn again. The book was gently closed and set aside. The ring was returned to the strange shadow cast by the orb. Arah parted the deck of cards several times, and shuffled them. She then split the deck and handed one stack to her sister. She then picked up one of the little sacks and gave it to Nerah, too.

They pried the ties open, and shook out the contents. Bones, colorful pebbles and tiny skulls sprinkled out onto the silk. They put their card-stacks horizontally above them, face down. Evvie watched, both horrified and fascinated. The sisters then reached into a pocket of their robes and withdrew long sashes of black with strange symbols embroidered into them. They stretched them over their eyes, and tied them on the back of their heads.

They placed their hands on each side of the little heaps of bones and began to chant.

> "*All seeing eye, sees all but speaks none,*
> *All knowing power, speaks all with no tongue,*
> *Sees all that has happened, knows all that will come.*
> *See those that serve you, your gifts give us say,*
> *Hear those that serve you, grant us allay,*
> *Diffident, we serve you, never tempted astray.*
> *See us. Hear us. Humbly we pray*
> *See us. Hear us. Humbly we pray.*"

Evvie was hiding a smirk, when something odd happened. What felt like a concussion—almost like a blast of air—dropped heavily onto the table, and nearly blew out the candles. There was a deep rumble that shook the house, and the air seemed to suck out of the room. The fire in the hearth grew dim and blue. Evvie stiffened.

"Your presence is heard, our gratitude and humility is boundless," Arah murmured.

Nerah reached out blindly. Her hand fell upon the ring. She picked it up and held it over the heap of talismans before passing it to her sister, who did the same. The ring was then returned to its place in front of the crystal orb, between the candles, to the bizarre shadow. Nerah then picked up the silver knife and nicked her finger. She rubbed her fingers over the collection of talismans, smearing them in blood. Arah then grasped the knife, and she, too, shed blood onto the bones.

> *"An origin we seek, a path that was laid,*
> *Of places seen, of plans that are made,*
> *Where has this traveled, where has it stayed,*
> *For the answer of origin, the levy is paid."*

A strange, haunting whisper filled the room. The candles wavered against and invisible breath. Nerah dug into the pile of talismans, pulling out a small skull— a rat perhaps—with yellow teeth. She placed it with impossible precision before the ring. Arah pulled a card from the center of her deck, and laid it face-down beside it. Nerah then plucked a small, ruby- colored stone etched with some figures next to that. Arah produced a little pelvic bone from another unfortunate creature. Another card, and another, and then the whispering words whooshed across the table again, lifting some of Evvie's flyaways. She was utterly dumbfounded.

Nerah pulled away her blindfold, and her sister did the same. In the darkness of the room, and the flickering yellow light of the candle, the silver haired, black-eyed women looked fearsome.

"The Defiler," Arah whispered after turning the card in front of her pile to reveal a ghoulish, hideous creature writhing upon a bed of bodies.

"Death, cut with a blade," Nerah murmured, her fingers running a line below the little row of skulls and bones and talismans.

They turned the second card. On it was a woman with red hair and white eyes, standing behind her own shadow, her figure dimmed by its form. Arah and Nerah said in unison, "The Prósopo."

"The proxy."

"The avatar."

The sisters looked up at Evvie with haunted eyes then back at the remaining talismans.

"A trophy to the victor," Nerah mumbled. They both looked to Evvie in astonishment, and what was unmistakably a touch of pride.

"It was *you,* Evvie! *You* were responsible for this man's demise."

MIRANDA MAYER

Chapter 15

Evvie peered at her new aunts with a look of betrayal and shock. "You're both mad!" she blurted, instantly regretting the words the moment they came out of her mouth. She shook her head and sat down. "I'm sorry, that was unkind." She rubbed her temples. "But what you fail to understand is that I was nowhere near him when he died. He wasn't even in the castle. He was killed at Ethincourt, more than twenty miles from where I was."

The aunts had drawn the curtains back to bring in the daylight, and returned the items from the table to the basket box. They removed their black robes and fixed their wild hair, tucking it back, and into their white frilly caps. How different they looked now, with their oval, plump, ruddy faces surrounded by the snowy ruffles of their morning caps. Their wide, dark eyes focused on Evvie with guilelessness, silvery curls tucked against their temples.

"You do not know what Prósopo is, my dear. It is one of the many facets of red witchery," Nerah explained.

Imbrah was summoned to bring them tea. She looked stricken and afraid when she came in. It was likely the vibration of the house and the whispering noises that had permeated the residence during the spell that had done it. Evvie suspected it was because Imbrah was new to the home, and certainly unaccustomed to these things, just as she was. Imbrah served the tea in terse silence while this discussion flared.

"No, I do not know what prospo is," Evvie conceded.

"Pro-so-po, dear. The proxy. Red witches can cast… oh; perhaps the best word is an avatar?" Arah said.

"More a doppelganger," Nerah offered. "Of sorts. They do not look like the caster."

Evvie's brow furrowed and she shook her head in incredulity. "Again, I say that this is impossible. I cast nothing. I cannot cast anything. I'm not a witch!" She got to her feet and walked to the window, looking out onto the cold day with confusion. She remained there while the others settled in for tea.

"Oh, my dear, when one is a red witch, one casts magic. It is not like what we do. We black witches must recite words and call for the attention of the powers. We must sacrifice some of our flesh as consideration for *anything* we ask. For you, the powers are right there inside you, always. You are blessed because the spirits speak directly to you. No such luck for the other castes," Arah said before she slurped her tea.

"So you are saying I can cast without even knowing?" Evvie found this baffling.

"The powers have a will of their own. Red witches are sacred. That is why you are given these gifts. I very much doubt that the great powers would stand by and allow one of its prized daughters to continue to suffer at the hands of a defiler. You have the means to protect yourself, and the powers inside you will act if you do not. They are *part* of you. They *are* you." Nerah gazed at Evvie with a grave expression.

Evvie absorbed this with bewilderment. She returned to the table and sat down with a plunk into the chair, her skirts ballooning around her, hands slack on her lap. All this talk of defiling brought everything back with unwanted clarity, and she was overcome with shame and humiliation. She steepled her hands over her mouth and sobbed behind them. The aunts both rose, but Imbrah got to her first.

"Oh, Miss Evvie," she exclaimed. She sat down beside Evvie on the sofa and put her arm around her. "I shall fetch your gentleman. I think you need him. You've had a difficult day. Drink some tea, I will return soon." She stood and exited, leaving Evvie with her aunts, who had both returned to their seats, their brows furrowed in empathy.

Dareth arrived in turn. He had only just returned to the village from his various obligations, and was coming out of the Dowager Dall's home when Imbrah found him. When she informed him of Evvie's state, he crossed Ilmeeri Square in long, determined strides and impatiently paced the hearth in the parlor until Evvie made her way into his arms.

Evvie had borne the burden of her anger and her bitterness in silence since her return from Adrin. She had yet to confront the pall of humiliation and shame that hung over her head like a looming sword. The talk of the Duke of Ivran as the Defiler, his cruelty having been given a name, the actions of Mr. Ryse-Mevvick mirroring those of her late husband, her feelings having been given validation by her new family were all it took for her to succumb to the abject misery she felt about her brief but horrendous marriage.

Dareth did not even have to ask. He opened his arms and enfolded her in them. He let her weep against him until her sobs were hiccups, and her beautiful face was ruddy with emotion and wet with tears. He then guided her to sit with him, where she wept more. At length she began to speak. To give form to her humiliation, and to express her shame. Dareth, his arms boldly around her, only rocked her like a child, and listened, whispering kind words to her when she succumbed to a spate of tears. He knew many found him to be a large, fearsome looking man, and not without cause. But for Evvie, he had only gentleness and understanding.

"That man, Mr. Ryse-Mevvick, reminds me of my late husband. In the way he felt entitled to touch me without my leave, to look at me as but a thing to be possessed…" she said through her tears, her kerchief sodden.

"Well, I do not wish to impose my will on you, my dear, but I suggest that you do not leave this compound without an Ilmeer man in tow. At least for the next few weeks. If I am not here, then you take my cousin Jeckin. He is built like an ox and he would love nothing more than to pound in the face of a smug Brii who dares to assail one of ours," Dareth growled. "But I have no urgent obligations for the next few days. I have freed my days in anticipation of our wedding. We will have obligations we must attend to together, but if you wish to make excursions for books, or to explore the city, I am at your disposal. I would rather you not go alone or merely with your abigail or my aunts. I won't allow you to be further intimidated or threatened by a madman."

Evvie sighed shakily, hiccupping from her catharsis. She then told him about the magic, and the ring, and what the aunties had determined. He listened with an impassive expression. When she finished, he merely bent forward and kissed her forehead, then lifted her chin, and kissed her lips. He gave her an affectionate hug, and then framed her face with his large hands.

"You are where you are supposed to be; with the people you can now call your family. Whatever transpires, we are in it with you. We are to be married in but four days. When that happens, there is a whole village that is here to protect and to stand beside you, come what may."

Evvie took a moment to realize what he'd said. "Four days! I did not know that the wedding was so soon! I was told at least two weeks!"

"I was on my way to tell you about it when your girl found me. My father has asked to hold the wedding sooner. As the family patriarch, it is his privilege to decide. It is infuriating that he decided this last-minute, and it will necessitate enormous concessions on behalf of the temple and the hall, which my aunts engaged the moment they received my letter of betrothal from Carath. Weddings are grand affairs here, and his decision will create many problems with invitations and other details I do not know about. But he has assumed the costs of the inconvenience and put others to work to make the changes and put on a suitable affair for us.

"He wishes to leave for Metrev before the snows fall in earnest, and the cold has arrived early. I have agreed for his convenience, and truthfully, for mine. I wish to be with you freely without the supervision of my dear aunts."

Evvie laughed through her nose and touched his face lovingly.

"I saw to getting a seamstress here this evening, to make you a dress for the occasion, to your liking."

Evvie clutched his hand. "If I might be so bold, Dareth, I will tell you know how much I love and adore you."

"And I you," he replied, suddenly overwhelmed with emotion. "In fact, a testament to the depth of my affection is how I submitted myself to the agony of appeasing an angry mother Dall. When your girl found me, I was just leaving her house, after having defended you in your truancy."

"Her scrutiny would have been too much to bear after what happ…"

"There is no need for you to explain it, my dearest. I was jesting. She's an old harridan, and she requires some humoring. But all is well. We will take tea with her tomorrow, if you are well, of course."

Evvie laughed and caressed his jaw, her gaze cast adoringly to his. He returned the look of love and fondness with equal ardor, if not more.

"Now… is there anything you wish to do this afternoon? I am here for you."

"In all honesty, dearest Dareth, I wish to retire to my room for the rest of the day. It is nothing in reflection of you. I am simply beleaguered by today's events. My face is a mess, and my feelings are all out of control. I will need time to wrest them into line again," she said, clearing her throat.

"I understand. I am in the great house, if you require me. I am overseeing the preparation of our city residence. I have been also been making arrangements for improvements to the country house, for I suspect you, like me, would be happier away from the center of Tirdonne."

Evvie's eyes widened at this news and a smile spread across her face. "We are to live outside of the city?"

"Yes. If that is satisfactory to you. I perhaps was presumptuous to assume you wished it, too, but it is what I thought, seeing where you were from…"

"No, no, you were most precise in your assumption," she assured him. "I do wish to see this home. Is it far?"

"It is only an hour from here, in the western forest. I spent a bit of time there yesterday. We will go the day after tomorrow, if you wish. We will not be able to take residence for another month or so, as there are extensive repairs that must be made. It is an old house, and it lacks a great deal of modern amenities, which I am seeing to.

"My father has given this house to us, as a gift of my right. For I will battle for the Counthood soon. We will take possession of the house when I have assumed my father's title."

"Your father will pass title to you before death? Can that be done?"

"Oh, yes. In Bask it is common to pass the titles to younger men who can fight for them. My father will retire. It has been known, however, that some of these old men hold onto their titles and will fight those who seek it still. The house of Rettin, for instance. The father has maimed his own son to keep the title. At his death, his son will either have to fight others who are of sufficient rank, or submit it for others to fight for in the view of the King.

"My father will give the houses to me when I win the battle against Errek Teth, who has been vying for a Counthood for some time. He is a viscount now. His younger brother would stand for his title if he wins, but they will both be disappointed."

Evvie smiled wanly, clearly trying not to express her fear that he might be harmed in this match. At least now she fully understood how their lines of succession worked. All titles made available by retiring nobles or deceased ones, were open for qualified successors. Whether or not you were born to the house, you still had to fight for it if there were contenders.

He saw her trepidation and patted her hand thoughtfully. "My dear, I am a seasoned fighter. I joined the Carath Attash as an infantryman and fought foreign wars for amusement. I've seen more swordplay and musket fire than any of the pretenders who vie for titles. Most of them haven't even made their completions in earnest. I will soundly defeat Teth and anyone else who dares to think themselves worthy of the title. I will win it for us. For our children," he declared.

Evvie nodded reluctantly, and squeezed his hand. "Thank you for coming to me, Dareth. I have missed your company. I became accustomed to having you with me every evening."

"I will come and spend my evenings with you and the aunties from now on, then. We will dine with my father tomorrow; I hope that is acceptable to you."

"Of course," she agreed. "I will go and lie down for a while, my dearest."

"Go on. I will return for dinner." They both rose and he embraced her once more.

Evvie watched him leave, and then went to the window to observe him as she stalked across the way towards the main house in the square.

So many surprises and new things arose in this place, she thought. She had been in Tirdonne only a few days and there was so much to take in. She watched her husband-to-be, with his broad shoulders, and confident stride, move around the livery buildings, and vault up the steps of the great house.

In spite of all the tumult and madness, it was the life she wanted. It was with him. She lifted her chin and blinked away her tears. *Enough simpering*, she thought. Witch or no witch, murderer or not, she was in a new place, and had a new life. It was all behind her. And she was safe. Safe in Dareth's hands. And if it were indeed true, what the Aunties had discovered with their skulls and bones, she was safe in her own hands too, no matter how absurd is seemed.

Infused with a little bit of pride and resolve, she sailed back to her room to read until the milliner arrived to fit her for a wedding gown.

MIRANDA MAYER

Chapter 16

The seamstress, a sweet woman by the name of Ellea Hail, arrived with Evvie's gown the morning of her wedding. Evvie had pored over samples the woman had brought, looking at the intricate work, and shaking her head in incredulity that they could accomplish an entire gown with these elaborate embellishments in only three days. The woman had assured her, she could choose whatever she liked, so she did. The seamstress and her apprentices had obviously spent the prior days hunched over the garment, applying an impossible number of beads and embroidering and detailed pattern along the trained hem.

The gown was spread on her bed so it could be admired in its entirety. Evvie had chosen the finest muslin. One so sheer, it looked like it was made from spiders' silk. The fabric had been meticulously white worked all along the hem and down the center front of the skirts with clear glass beading and tiny pearls. The sleeves were long, and the cuffs were also beaded and edged in a lovely open lace which was also attached in a dense ruffle around the broad neckline. There was a bodiced silken petticoat the color of forget-me-nots to wear underneath. An enormous rectangular veil of the same sheer muslin had been edged in the same pattern. Slippers the same blue as the petticoat, with long ribbon ties, were placed beside the gown. The last piece was a light blue hooded cloak edged in white fur to wear for the journey to the temple.

"Oh, Mrs. Hail, it is absolutely beautiful. How in the world did you manage to make all this in so little time?"

The thin, older lady was placing a fresh strapped petticoat with a lace hem, a sleeveless chemise, and silk stockings as white as snow with pale blue clocking on the dresser. She turned, and grinned. "Lots and lots of work. But I have many hands. We are known for creating detailed pieces quickly. I have two speedy embroiderers, and there's a girl by the name of Hanna who beads like the wind."

Evvie's bright smile was stunning. She was overwhelmed by how beautiful it was.

"You will make such a handsome bride, ma'am," Imbrah declared, her eyes full of excitement.

Evvie was feeling much better since the horrendous day with the spell and Mr. Ryse-Mevvick. She had taken tea with the Dowager Dall, who was rendered impassive by the presence of her imposing grandson. He sat in his tall wingback chair, his legs crossed, a saucer in one hand, his tea in the other, looking as bored as one could possibly be. He occasionally made a comical face at Evvie while the old woman blathered on about the family's noble history, and how she was instrumental in forming the Baskreth Lady's Society which—she informed Evvie—she would be obliged to participate in. Evvie tried not to look at her betrothed whose mischief was enough to make her laugh out loud.

For the duration of the tea, the boy Rell was a quiet, strange presence. Seated slightly away from the three of them by the window, he looked on coolly, his dull eyes never leaving Evvie's face.

Dinner with Dareth's father was another experience all together. The patriarch of the Ilmeeri family was a huge man, with a terrifying presence. Evvie already felt small and powerless as it was. When she timidly entered the drawing room of the great house, the old man rose up from his chair to his lofty height. His hard, black eyes glared down at her, his black and silver curls wild and unkempt, the tattoos that festooned his neck crept up his jaw line and along his temples. Evvie shrank against Dareth and clutched his hand tighter.

Count Ilmeeri was severe, and a man of few words. The longest discourse they shared was when he greeted her. He bowed shallowly, his hard eyes taking in Evvie's slight form and her wide, hauntingly pale eyes.

"You *are* beautiful," he conceded. "If not a little waify. A few winters in Bask will stouten you up, no doubt. Come and sit. Tell me about your family." He lowered his frame down into a worn leather chair, and crossed his legs. He reached for a pipe like the one Mr. Ryse-Mevvick had smoked, with a stem as long as his massive foot, and a tiny wooden bowl on the end of it.

Evvie was struck dumb at the notion of being the focus of his attention as he stared at her expectantly. She obeyed and sat, but she was want for words. Dareth found a seat next to her and came to her rescue. "Father, are you truly going to put my wife-to-be through and interrogation after not even five minutes in her company?"

His father lit his pipe and sucked on it thoughtfully. "I s'pose it is a bit much," he admitted in his booming voice. "Well, girl. Speak as you desire, or do not." He picked up a glass of port and drank it down in a gulp.

"Father prefers to be addressed by his given name. The formalities taken from southern cultures do not agree with him. You may call him Magnus."

Evvie pondered for a moment, and then replied. "My father was the same. He disliked the Misters and Misses and Masters and Mistresses... he found it most tiresome. Perhaps it was his northern blood that made him so."

"Your father had northern blood?" Magnus demanded.

"Yes. The Ravensroost line originated in Bask, at least twenty generations or so ago. The great house was built about four hundred years ago by our Bask ancestors. My father was a student of the Bask culture. It was a lifelong fascination. I very much miss his nightly lecture on the subject, especially when he was talking about something new he'd read or discovered."

"He sounds like a good man," Dareth said softly.

"He was the best of men."

"And your mother?" Magnus grunted, puffing out a cloud of bluish smoke.

"She passed away in childbirth when I was nine. The baby, my sister, did not survive."

"That is unfortunate," Magnus murmured. He paused. "Dareth's mother has divorced me. She lives in Ghenta, now. By the sea, no less, with some Brii blaggard."

Evvie glanced at Dareth, who merely shrugged and gave her a half smile. Evvie knew of divorce only through her father's unending studies. Divorce was not an option for southern marriages. Once married that was it. The idea that a woman could divorce herself from her husband was something Evvie found almost empowering. Her father had explained how women were treated differently in the north. He had always treated her respectfully, and given her as much freedom he could muster, to choose her own fate. She had chosen to agree to the marriage to the duke, much to her regret, but had she not wanted it, her father would have respected that decision.

Evvie doubted she would ever want to leave Dareth. But knowing it was within her power to choose meant a great deal to her. And she would certainly enjoy other freedoms and privileges as a northern woman that her southern sisters would never know—like opening her own bank account without permission from a man or institution. She still lingered on this seemingly trite little accomplishment with a glow of empowerment. She felt emboldened suddenly, and she looked her soon-to-be father-in-law in the eye.

"Although it is unfortunate that your wife has chosen to take her life elsewhere," she said, "However, I cannot fault any woman with the freedom to choose for doing so. Where I come from, unhappiness in marriage was something one is expected to endure. And women get the worst of it. While the men are given no punishment for acquiring lovers, women can be tried for adultery if they seek out the same for themselves."

Magnus's brows rose up in surprise at the personal nature of her assertion, and how boldly she made it. He sucked on his pipe a few more times, letting out little puffs of fragrant smoke. He then quietly stuffed the bowl again. "Well, I cannot imagine a lady of your sharp mind and decisive opinion would thrive much in that kind of barbaric culture. I am glad you are come here. Now, I'm hungry. I think we should eat."

Dareth gave her a proud, approving look and rose to his feet. But it was Magnus who took her hand and led her to dinner.

Evvie sat before her vanity while Imbrah pinned one last meticulously curled lock into place. She picked up a diadem that none other than Lady Dall had brought. It was a crown of sapphires each surrounded by myriad diamonds that sparkled like dew.

The dowager sat in a chair nearby garbed from head to toe in sumptuous silk, again swathed in ruffles and lace around her pale face and hands, and dripping from her collar. She was also wearing a parure of the most exquisite rubies. She clutched her cane with one hand resting on the top, her fingers thrumming the air as if she was deep in thought. Her watery eyes were fixed on Evvie.

She had been astoundingly silent. She had only said: "You will wear this. I wore it when I was wed. All first ladies of the family wear it, and own it until the next."

Evvie did not make a fuss, although inside she was overwhelmed by the gesture. Her glistening eyes and humble nod of gratitude and assent was what the Lady would respect. Before their tea with the Lady, Dareth had told her that the old woman had no taste for fussing or quailing. Evvie was neither a fusser nor a quailer, so there was no danger of irritating her. She accepted the gift with grace.

Evvie met the older woman's gaze in the mirror, and she could see something in the wizened eyes that warmed her heart.

"That is good, girl. I think you have finished." The dowager rose laboriously to her feet, and shuffled to the vanity, shooing Imbrah away. "I have given you the obligatory token. But I have a personal gift to bestow upon you, and I will do it now. For I must go to the temple before you." She reached up and beaconed impatiently for her lady in waiting—a mousy thing of indeterminate age with a slight wisp of silver at the top of her head—approached. She was carrying a velvet reticule which she presented to the Lady Dall.

"You are a rich woman. I know this. I am sure you have no shortage of lovely pieces. But this one was mine when I was a girl. It was my first set. One my father had made for me upon my coming out. It matches the diadem in its colors, but these are truly yours now."

She displayed a magnificent necklace with bean sized sapphires cut into perfect oval cabochons. Nine in total across a pale, white gold setting with small diamonds surrounding each stone and a tiny, blue, star sapphires no bigger than a bead between each cartouche. She fastened on the necklace around Evvie's neck, and then reached for the bag and removed earrings, a bracelet, and a brooch that could also work as a pendant for the necklace.

"You decide how you want to wear the rest," she said. "The box is too shabby to give you. I hope you will have a new one made for them."

Evvie studied the intricate pieces. She liked the idea of adding a splash of color to her pale gown by adding the brooch at the center of her high waistline. She thanked the dowager soberly, and squeezed the woman's fingers when she dropped the earrings into her hand. The corners of the lady's mouth twitched before she regained her composure and turned away.

"I will see you when you are at the temple my dear. I am confident you will present yourself tastefully, when you take the name of Ilmeer."

"Of course, Ma'am," Evvie replied, bowing her head respectfully. Although the family seemed to eschew formalities, this woman seemed to demand it in her austerity. It felt as if this sat well with her, for she gave Evvie a perfunctory nod in return before she swished out in a rustle of silk, her mousy girl in tow. Imbrah sidled back into place and stared in awe at the gift.

The minute the door was securely latched, she blurted, "Good gracious, you have made an impression, haven't you? I've never heard of a single act of generosity or kindness from the Lady in all my days in this village. And my family has been in service here since before I was born!"

Evvie slid the heavy sapphire and diamond earrings onto her lobes. They sparkled beautifully below the perfect curls of crimson hair. She quietly applied a little rouge to the apples of her cheeks.

Her first wedding had not been replete with anticipation and happiness as this day was. She could scarce believe how pleased and excited she felt. She straightened and looked at Imbrah. "I think I'm ready for the gown now."

Imbrah emitted a little squeal of delight and skipped to the bed where the silken under gown rested next to the work of art that would go over it. Evvie stood in her undergarments, the cotton strapped petticoat that hung just above her ankles, and the pale blue slippers, ribbons twining around her calves.

"Take care over the hair. You've outdone yourself and we do not want to mar this creation," Evvie cautioned.

"Yet…" Imbrah said, picking up the gown and slipping her hands up the skirts to gather it bottom first on her arms. She wagged her brows suggestively.

"Oh, do not be vulgar," Evvie said, blushing deeply.

Imbrah carefully lowered the slip of a dress over Evvie's head and delicately worked the neckline into place, while Evvie slid her arms through the holes. Once past the hair, Imbrah tugged it down and adjusted it, before securing the drawstrings.

"Blue is a beautiful color for you. Especially with your hair. And your eyes look even lovelier set against it."

"That is very sweet, Imbrah," Evvie replied. She patted down the silk and smoothed it over the cotton petticoat beneath.

With a deep breath, she turned to Imbrah, who grinned and fetched the over gown. The beads and pearls rattled decadently together as she worked her arms into the fabric and lifted the garment over Evvie's head. Evvie raised her bare arms and slid them into the perfectly fitted, snug sleeves, while Imbrah gently drew the gown down over her hair and diadem. The beaded extravagance tumbled into place over the blue silk, the front hem brushing the top of her silk-stockinged foot.

"It looks so ethereal against this blue silk, ma'am," Imbrah proclaimed. "It is so beautiful. I am half dead with envy!" She circled around Evvie to adjust the gown, tugging it here and there before fastening the little buttons on the tiny diamond-shaped back of the gown. The sleeves were sewn into the back in little pleated points in the most delicate way. Evvie shook out her arms, and the beads, dainty lace and pearls tickled her knuckles. She peered down at the neckline, which Imbrah had so carefully aligned, and pinned the brooch at the center of her waistline, just below her bust. Imbrah made a few more fussy adjustments and then stepped back to admire her.

"You are so shockingly good-looking I want to vomit!" she said laughingly.

Evvie snorted and laughed too. "I feel like a young girl, fresh and innocent again," she admitted.

Imbrah tilted her head and looked upon her with kind eyes. "That girl is still in you. She never had the chance to make an appearance, what with all that is happened to you, you poor thing." Evvie smiled wanly. She had confided her past to Imbrah while she tied up her hair in rags the evening before. Imbrah related that she had endured something similar, and there was something deeply comforting to Evvie to know that someone truly understood. Imbrah seemed even kinder and more attentive today. "But now you can be her. So delight in all that is happening. This is a good family, Ma'am. Nobody cruel or unjust lives in Ilmeeri Square. There is only the grumpy dowager, and Aklin Ilmeer, Dareth's youngest cousin, who once dishonorably throttled a weaker boy. He was punished for it, and grew up to be a worthy man. Good people as a whole, they are. The servants know. This is the best family in Tirdonne as far as many are concerned."

Evvie took a deep breath and turned to look at herself in her mirror as best she could. What she saw was some new version of herself, for there was brightness in her eyes and anticipation in her gaze. There was none of the sorrow or the darkness she'd seen in her mirror before she left Carath. None of the anger or bitterness that she felt whenever she saw men look at her in a certain way. There was only Evvie as she should have been. Evvie before the scar on her wrist ever existed. Before she had betrayed her own desires to please a father she loved.

"You have a little time before the coach is here. I'm afraid we were a bit quicker in dressing you than anticipated."

"Never fear. I've been meaning to write a letter to my brother in the moment. This is the perfect time to do it. If you would be so kind as to fetch me some cold water to drink, I would be most grateful."

The water at Tirdonne came from a rock spring and was the clearest, sweetest water she'd ever tasted. She was thirsty for it.

She moved into the sitting room to the small table, and picked up the writing slope that was resting against the wall, folding it open and pulling out a sheet of paper. She opened the inkpot and took up her worn, almost nubby quill. The blackened tip was testament to its usefulness, and she had re-cut it so many times, there was scarce a decent shaft left and it was starting to look comically short.

She dipped it into the ink and composed a letter.

Dearest Effery,

By the time this letter finds its way to the relay, I will be Mrs. Evvienna of Ilmeer. I have written in confidence to you of my marriage and its tribulations. You know of the experience that I have borne upon my shoulders, and it crushed me into something unrecognizable. It was my greatest mistake. And I have blamed and hated myself for it since. But now I am here, about to marry the first man I have been able to truly trust aside from father, you and Farrick. Such mad things have happened in the few days I have been here. I can tell you without reserve that I am happy for this choice. I know Faye was deeply concerned for the seemingly impulsive decision I made to leave Ravensroost with a strange foreign man, but I knew in the very center of my being that it was what I was supposed to do. Call it intuition, call it fate, call it what you may, I am where I am supposed to be. Please assure Faye that I am indeed happy. I wrote her a letter and I am certain she will think I am being untruthful, for I had told her the enormous lie that I was happy when I wrote from Ivran as well, because I could not bear her to know the truth. At this very moment I am dressed for my wedding, and awaiting the coach to take me to the temple. Dareth has such a wonderful, large family, and they have welcomed me so kindly. I hope you will visit at your first convenience. Dareth assures me that there is a town house right in the family village that is available for your whole family. You will be astonished by the wonders you will see on your way. Do write me, and tell me of what is new. I want to know how your homecoming was, and to hear about Faye and Farrick and your family settling in. I miss you dearly. I will be filling a hamper of Bask treasures for your family for the Solstice celebrations. I hope you will send me some Akarat chocolate and some of Mrs. Ybrim's tea with nettle and elderberry. I have poured the last pot of my reserve yesterday, and am angry that I did not bring more! I will also include gifts for Faye and Farrick. I must ready myself, for I hear the sound of a coach below. I will be thinking of you today, wishing you were all here to see this happy moment. I am certain you are all here in spirit. Please give my best wishes to your wife and children. I shall write them a nice letter soon. I send my love to you, and hope you are happy at Ravensroost again.

Regards, your devoted and adoring sister,
Evvie

MIRANDA MAYER

Chapter 17

Evvie folded the letter carefully, wrote the directions on it, and tied a length of ribbon around it. With a little knife stored in the tiny drawer of her writing slope she chipped off some sealing wax from the bar. She sprinkled the shards into a little spoon which she hovered over the flame of the candle on the table. The wax pieces melted into droplets and merged into a pretty emerald pool which she poured over the intersection between the ribbon and the edge of the fold. She then pressed her seal firmly into the wax. When she pulled it away, there in the hardening wax was the perfect imprint of an E with a tiny raven perched on the middle arm of the letter.

Imbrah came into the room carrying Evvie's cloak and veil. "It is time to go, Miss."

Evvie stood. Her hands trembled a little, but excitement coursed through her. She proffered the letter to Imbrah. "Can you please take this to the relay at your earliest convenience?"

"Of course." Imbrah accepted the little paper square. She shook out the cloak and carefully placed it on Evvie's shoulders, lifting the hood up over her head and placing it delicately over her hair. She then followed Evvie down the stairs to the coach where she loaded Evvie in and then put the folded veil on her lap.

"The aunties will see to the rest of your preparations when you are at the temple. They are already there, eagerly awaiting you."

Evvie leaned back. She had not seen them at all since breakfast. They had come down in their dressing gowns all in a dudgeon, eager to get dressed and on their way. They had arrangements to see to at the temple and then at the assembly hall where the celebration was to occur after the ceremony. Imbrah closed the coach door and watched it draw away, circle the square and exit the west gate towards the castle.

Evvie spent the time in transit in contemplation. She thought of Dareth and her heart filled with warmth. She suspired as she gazed out of the coach into the city, her nerves getting the best of her.

The cool day had turned overcast and she noticed that there were tiny snowflakes falling intermittently. They lofted slowly, blown about by gusts of air. The coach slowed to turn onto the main throughway.

She peered out to see where they were going and, to her shock, she looked straight into the face of Ando Ryse-Mevvick. He stood on the corner as if waiting for the coach to pass, his hard eyes fast on hers. She leaned back to hide from him, but she could hear him shouting uncouthly.

"You should be mine!" he cried. "This is a mistake!"

She pressed herself to the back of her seat and willed the coach to move faster. She caught a final glimpse of him as the coach clattered up the street, away from his desperate face.

"Let this be the end of this nonsense," she muttered.

She arrived at the temple. As the coach drew near, the great bell was rung to celebrate her appearance. The aunts were both waiting for her at the bottom of the temple steps, and they helped Evvie descend from the coach. Arah took the veil from her and they bustled her into the colossal doorway to the Bask temple of Ebremott where the god would oversee the bonding of the couple and bless them with happiness and fruitfulness.

Evvie had only but a short time to read about this. She was never much of a devout believer in anything, so understanding these ideologies was a challenge for her. She knew Dareth didn't take it all too seriously himself, but he did respect tradition.

The vestibule had a bride's door through which she was ushered into a small dressing room. As her cloak was removed, Nerah gasped.

"Good gods above you are a sight, Evvie," Nerah said. "Dareth will be the envy of his peers. They've all come to see his bride."

"The temple is a crush, there are so many people squeezed into the pews," Arah declared.

"It is the most talked-about wedding in Tirdonne since Morrikay and Bettos, the Archduke and his duchess, I imagine," Nerah speculated. They fussed over her making little adjustments, tugging and primping her skirts, and letting out the small train that Imbrah had bustled for the ride.

"The veil," Nerah commanded her sister, who reached for it.

They each took a corner and let it unfurl between them, backing away from one another to stretch it out. Then one aunt moved behind Evvie and they lofted it up over her head and lowered it onto her hair and diadem. The veil was massive. It covered her down to her knees and fell long upon her train.

Arah then picked up one of the loveliest apples Evvie had ever seen. It was a perfect fruit—nary a blemish or bruise to be seen—mostly golden yellow with a bright blush of red on its cheeks. Nerah lifted the front of the veil and Arah put the apple into Evvie's hands.

"Hold it against your stomach, dear. Like so." Arah positioned Evvie's arms, and her hands. Once they were satisfied that she had the correct position, they let the veil fall down again and stepped back.

"I willgo and see if the temple is ready for you. If they are, I willcome and fetch you" Arah said.

Evvie nodded dumbly and waited while Arah exited the bride's room. Nerah continued to fidget with the gown and veil, making sure everything was exactly where it needed to be.

Arah returned and gestured for Evvie to follow her. She followed Arah to the great doors of the temple, and was positioned in front of the door.

"When the door opens, Dareth will be standing a few steps away from you in the aisle. When the choral begins, you are to walk to face him. He will bow to you, and then ask if you will marry him this day. You will respond by saying yes, and then he will take your left arm and walk beside you to the dais. It is in the center of the temple and it is raised by three steps, so mind how you walk. Do not stumble. That is a sign of bad luck. Walk to the center of the dais, and the orator will tell you what to do from there. Do you think you can remember that?" Arah whispered.

"Yes," Evvie croaked.

Auntie Nerah raised her fist and pummeled the door three times. Then both of them bolted through a small archway next to the great doors, leaving her alone. Evvie trembled. Standing by herself in the vestibule, she could hear the rustle and the murmurs of people behind the doors to the temple. She studied the carvings on it: the fruits and berries interwoven with vines and birds, snakes and little creatures. The predominant fruit was the apple. It was everywhere on the door, which was carved in relief from the floor to the towering top.

She jumped a little when the doors parted like curtains. They slid into wall pockets, revealing the temple. Two attendants moved to stand rigidly on each side of the door. The breathtaking temple hall was a circular space with a domed ceiling. The walls were encased in delicate plaster friezes—depicting all manner of scenes—and the dome had gilded scrollwork sun-bursting from the apex where daylight poured in and fell upon the dais in the center. The room was heaving with people. The air was actually too warm, the heat of so many bodies filling it. Who these people were, was a mystery to Evvie. She recognized only a scarce few.

But the sight that truly threw Evvie's concentration was Dareth. Her eyes almost immediately burned with tears at the sight of this magnificent man. Garbed in traditional Bask formal vestments, he was a beautiful sight.

He wore a loose, painstakingly pressed tunic of snow white that crossed in the front and was tucked into an intriguing pair of trousers. The grey leggings were extremely wide; however they were generously pleated in the front and back so that they hung like the skirts of a cassock around his legs all the way down to the top of his feet. The pleats were precise, everything flat and perfect. The waist of the leggings was wrapped around him with ties that wound down to his narrow hips making his shoulders appear even broader and more imposing. The sleeves of his tunic were long and wide. His drest were clear and visible along his neck, hands and part of his arms. The tunic was richly decorated with gold trim and embroidery. On his feet, he wore strange little black leather sandals with only a single loop of leather that crossed over his big toe to hold them on. His feet were covered in black stockings that had a little separation between his big toe and the rest of his foot so it could slide into the sandal without obstruction.

She had seen an illustration of something similar once in one of her father's books, but she was astonished by how graceful and masculine it was in person. He had his arms crossed as if he was barring her path. She took a deep breath, her eyes on this handsome monster as she approached him, stopping within arm's length.

He bowed to her, and then straightened himself, his eyes devouring her beauty, a barely contained grin crossing his lips as he gazed at this little woman who had so changed his life. "Evvienna, of the Raven's Roost, vessel of the powers, redcaste, and my promised one. I ask for your leave to wed you this day in the witness of all present in this temple of bonding and blessings. May I?"

"You may," Evvie replied clearly. She could feel the eyes of the people upon her. She had heard the gasps and whispers when she had stepped into the hall, but she had forgotten them the minute her eyes found Dareth. For that moment, there was only he and she in the temple.

Dareth stepped forward and took his place beside her, walking with her to the dais where a woman of astonishing height and size wearing a habit and cowl waited, only her face visible in the shroud of ivory and grey. Her arms drew up like wings of linen, and she began to speak, her voice like a horn, loud and shrill.

"Before me stands Dareth Hann Vell Ilmeer, Son of the Ilmeeri Clan, contender for the Counthood of Ilmeer, son of the Count of Ilmeer, achiever of full completion, holder of the Silver Wings, master of sword and blade. King's favored, and betrothed to a Crimson Witch, he beseeches the Ebremott to bless this union, and to sanctify it before the witness of his clan and his peers."

Evvie glanced down in order to hide the mirth that was bubbling up. She had been gazing at Dareth who, with the utterance of every title and accomplishment, was making subtle faces at her.

"Reveal the bride to the temple," the orator commanded.

Dareth picked up the front of the veil and folded it back over the top of her head. There was an audible, collective gasp from the pews when her face was fully revealed. Dareth put his hands under hers, which still clutched the plump apple. He was looking straight into her eyes. She returned his gaze, hoping he would not try to make her laugh again.

"Crimson Witch, your presence in the temple is a gift to the Ebremott. Such a marriage cannot be denied by these gods, for such pairings of Bask and Witch are fated by greater powers. *You* must give the Ebremott permission to bless your union, and you must give your betrothed permission to claim you. Do you give such permission?" the priestess intoned.

"I do," Evvie blurted. She was incredulous that the orator offered her such deference. That her presence was sanctioned by greater beings and that their little god could not intervene if it wanted. This boggled her mind.

"Then Ilmeeri, you may proceed," the priestess declared.

Dareth began to recite words Evvie did not understand. His narrative was long and meaningful. His feelings were clear, no matter what words he used. He then lifted her hands with his, and stepped closer.

"Take a bite," he whispered, as the apple now hung before her lips. She leaned forward and sank her teeth into the flesh of the apple, the sweetness filling her mouth, and a little of the juice running down her chin. Then Dareth took a bite. The crunch was loud and she wanted to laugh, but she instead made an effort to chew as delicately as she could and swallowed the piece of apple.

The Orator then took the apple and held it up towards the ceiling, calling out a litany of words to the Ebremott gods, whatever they were. The apple was then passed to an attendant who held a thick board and a knife. Another attendant cut the apple down the middle and began to remove the seeds. They were gathered into a tiny silver box and then given to the orator who presented it to Dareth.

"Blessed are the seeds of this union. We will plant them in our orchards where they will thrive, and your union will thrive. They will grow and bear fruit as your union will." Dareth took the box, kissed the top of it, and placed it in Evvie's hands so she could do the same. He then indicated with his eyes that she should return it to the Orator. She did.

"The seeds have been blessed. The union has been fixed. The marks must be made. When they are, this pair will be wed. This moment must be theirs alone. The witnesses must go." The people in the pews moved en masse, and exited the temple leaving only Evvie, Dareth, the Orator and some attendants.

Dareth looked at Evvie. "This might hurt a little. But you're Bask now. And you must have your first drest."

Evvie smirked crookedly and her stomach filled with butterflies. "Where?"

"Right here." He brushed the little spot just below her ear. "It will be small and it won't take long."

Evvie assented nervously. The Orator led them down the opposite aisle to the binding chamber. Inside the small space sat a pair of strange chairs with deeply slanted backs and thick pillows to secure the position of the head. Evvie was helped into one, and Dareth into the other. The pillows were so that the heads were angled to look at one another. He reached out and took her hand.

"Do not worry."

"I'm not worried, Dareth," she assured him.

His eyes smiled at her. An attendant arrived with implements and the ink. Evvie watched them prepare for the process.

"Who arranged all this?" she asked.

"The family, of course," Dareth replied as if surprised she did not know. "The effort was mostly led by the aunties, but everyone had some hand in it. The celebration especially. My grandmother paid a goodly sum towards it, as well. Our village has outdone itself, from what I understand. The worry that I would never find a wife was one everyone shared. They are also exceedingly pleased by my choice. The wedding is a point of pride with many families—and ours spared no expense. You will meet almost everyone who lives in Ilmeeri Square tonight."

The tattooists arrived soon after. Pulling up little stools, they rinsed their hands in basins proffered by the attendants, and dried them with pristine white cloths. Both silent, both in the ceremonial robes of the Bask mark-makers, they gravely set to work.

"After this, we will dance," Dareth told her.

She peered at her handsome ruffian of a husband. "You can dance?"

"Like an ox."

They both laughed. There was then a sharp sting. Evvie kept smiling, trying with all her might not to wince as the tiny needles pierced her skin.

MIRANDA MAYER

Chapter 18

Evvie felt like a different person. It was as if the warmth and slight throbbing of the fresh tattoo had reinvented her. Like she had become the Evvie that Dareth saw, and the Evvie that she'd been before she met him was gone. She stepped into the vast dining room of the assembly hall a new woman. Her veil removed, the small, stylized apple blossom on her neck, her hand resting on her husband's, she faced the whole of the clan with a newfound confidence. She was Bask now. She belonged.

There were at least two hundred people staring at them, applauding and cheering the announcement of their arrival. Four long banquet tables ran parallel to one another in the room, all set before a dais where the master table awaited them. Magnus, the aunties and a couple she had never met already sat there, filling up the ends of the table while the bride and groom seats—decorated with bunting made from evergreen branches, colorful autumn leaves and sprigs of berries—awaited them.

She and Dareth walked around the room, accepting congratulatory handshakes and greetings from smiling, unfamiliar faces, and then settled into their place at the center of the feast. The food was served and the hall filled with happy talk and laughter. Evvie was exhausted, and famished.

The evening was a blur. So many new names and faces to remember. She held new babies and made the acquaintance of a small horde of grandmothers and grandfathers. She danced with her husband who was not graceless—though he was stiff—but full of laughter as he forgot the dance's steps on various occasions and caused a trickle-down of disaster all the way to the bottom of the set several times, much to everyone's amusement.

How the Bask laughed! These were not the quiet, murmuring gatherings of the people Evvie knew from her hometown. Here they expressed themselves quite openly. There were no surreptitious glances, or covered snickers of gossips and rumor mongers. Couples kissed one another in company. People were red-cheeked and merry. Here there were smiles and chatter, jests and roasting, peals of laughter. There was a group of men by the fireplace who on several occasions broke into song between the many lively dances.

Evvie could not remember having a better time in her life. The family was so warm and easy. They did not lack formality, or couth, but their way was different from what she was used to. There was earnest fun here. It wasn't a game of social discourse, a quiet battle for a pecking order. It was a large crowd of people in actual celebration, gleefully amused and diverted. Not raucous, bawdy, drunken, or savage, as many southerners described the Bask.

After a particularly vivacious dance—partnered with Dareth's cousin Janus—Evvie was delivered, short of breath, to her husband. He was seated at the dining table which was covered now in dirty goblets and napkins, the centerpieces wilted, and the candles in the candelabras burnt down halfway. There were still some platters of grapes and a few sweet pastries piled here and about. The servants were methodically clearing the tables as the revelers danced in the larger hall through the archway. The room was very warm. The tall windows had been opened, and they looked down over the city and its sprinkle of lights.

"You look like you enjoyed that dance, dearest wife," Dareth bellowed as she approached him. He reached out and pulled her onto his lap. He was surrounded by men who all looked upon her with admiration.

"I did. I do not think I've ever danced so much at an assembly in my life," she replied breathlessly.

"It is time to go home, is what I think. Your girl and the servants have been moving your things to the great house today. I have sent your box cart to the country house, as I imagine you would want those belongings there."

"Yes, yes I would," she replied. She had to admit to herself that she was reluctant to leave, for the orchestra was preparing for more dances and there were still many people lingering. She didn't want the celebration to end. But she also wanted quiet and to be with her new husband.

He picked her up by her waist and stood her up, rising to his feet with a groan. "This was a day to remember," he declared. His friends looked on and murmured in agreement.

"The best wedding the city's seen yet, I dare say," another Bask man muttered. He was his brother-in-law, if Evvie recalled correctly. Husband to Hella. His wife was lost in a horde of women doing a circle dance Evvie was sad she missed.

Dareth sent a servant to fetch Evvie's cloak and his coat. As Dareth put his on, there was a strange ululating noise that rose up above the din of the assembly, and Evvie saw a man in a corner blowing what looked like a ram's horn. The music stopped, and the people ran towards the exit in a flock as a cluster of servants wound through them with big bowls in their arms. There was a tinkling sound too, metal ringing mutedly against metal as the party-goers frantically fumbled about.

"Get ready for the onslaught," Dareth warned her.

She let him help her with her cloak, and she looked up at him from underneath her hood. "Ready?"

He grasped her arm and they sallied forth into the multitude. Evvie was immediately assaulted by the overwhelming scent of lavender, and within moments of smelling it, the tiny blue dried buds began to rain down on her head, accompanied by the deafening chorus of bells being rung wildly by the celebrants. She and Dareth pushed their way through the wailing, bell-ringing, lavender throwing crowd, Evvie hiding her face under her hood to protect herself from the veritable downpour of lavender. They emerged from the mess and racket mostly unscathed, both grinning. Outside the hall, snow was tumbling down.

"Oh, Dareth look!" she said, pointing to the dusting that had already accumulated on the ground. It snowed so little in Carath.

"You'll hate it by the solstice," he laughed.

"I willnever hate it here," she retorted. "Even if it snows for a thousand years."

The warmth of the wine and port she'd imbibed filled her center, and she was loose and relaxed, as happy as she could have ever imagined on the day of her wedding. Dareth snorted with a soft smile, and helped her into the waiting coach. Meanwhile, at the doorway, they were serenaded a riotous, bawdy little song by the revelers:

Today they sowed the marriage seeds;
Tonight they now go home to breed!
You've sung, you've drunk and danced and fed;
Now do not come out until you've bred!

The coach rumbled towards the compound, and Evvie threw back her hood. No sooner had she done this, then Dareth leaned forward and covered her lips with his, prying her lips apart with his tongue, and sending her into a spin from shock and desire. She melted into him. Her brain was addled and her heart raced. She scarcely remembered the ride home. She laughed like a girl when he lifted her out of the coach and carried her through the tall doors of the main house, hoisting her up to their shared room. He kicked the door closed behind him, plopped her onto her feet, and kissed her again. She lost her senses to him, his firm, experienced, sensuous touch, and his manly scent.

Evvie experienced lovemaking as it should be for the first time in her life. Tangled in the limbs of her beastly husband, she felt only trust and passion, breathlessness and, ultimately, ecstasy. She awoke the next morning huddled against him, her head under his chin, her body notched into his. He was snoring softly, his heavy arm with its cover of beautiful tattoos draped possessively over her ribs. She was clutching his index finger with her hand, reveling in the sense of security and belonging. The freedom of just being with him.

She looked closely at his markings, which sheathed most of his upper body, every mark artfully blended into the next. The rows of ciphers and text crawled out from the stylized shapes like roots of a tree. She squirmed around so she could face him, and then studied the marks on his shoulders and chest, tracing them gently with her finger.

His marriage mark was not like hers. It was a cross section of an apple with two seeds done in an unusual style.

He was riddled with as many scars as he was tattoos. Her fingers tickled him awake, and he bent his chin down to touch his chest so he could look at her.

"What are you up to, my little white-eyed wolf?"

"Where did these scars come from?" She gazed up at him, and she saw the pupils of his eyes widen at the sight of her face.

"I'm Baskreth. We fight," he replied, his hand sweeping up the curve of her back all the way to her shoulder. Then he cupped her chin and his thumb brushed her lips. She accepted his simple answer. She sat up onto her knees, and peered down at him. He looked up at her, his eyes voracious. "Good gods, you are scrumptious…" He reached out and she squirmed out of his reach, giggling. He sat up and grappled at her, snatching her ankle and dragging her back towards him. She squealed and laughed merrily, and then relaxed, as he moved to hang over her in all of his beautiful mass.

"I've never felt so comfortable with anyone before," she told him, staring up at his dark eyes. "I have never felt playful with a man before."

He brushed her red locks from her face, picking out a little lavender blossom and tossing it onto the bed after crushing it between his fingers and taking a deep scent of it. "We were meant for one another," he replied matter-of-factly. "We can be who we are without reserve when we are together. As it should be."

She wrapped her arms around his neck, clutching herself to him. He dropped his chest down onto her and his arms slid beneath her, enfolding her entire being into his. She was pinned beneath his huge body, and it felt wonderful. There was a great, cleansing sigh of relief and knowing, and they held one another like that for a long, decadent moment. Dareth kept kissing her temple, her forehead, and then squeezing her again.

Their moment was marred by the sound of the bell. "Urgh, visitors," he groaned. "And father's at the hunting lodge today, so we could have the house to ourselves."

"Can we not turn them away?" Evvie asked with a lamenting sigh.

"Visits are good luck on the morning after. This is probably the first of several," he warned her. Evvie wondered if she would ever get used to all these little traditions that seemed so strange.

Evvie sighed irritably and extricated herself from the tangle of her husband's limbs.

"We can take up where we left off later," he grumbled with a half-smile.

She grasped his bristly cheeks and kissed him. "I love you, husband."

"And I you, wife," he retorted. He scooted out of bed and began to dress, not bothering to call his man. Instead, he tugged on a tunic and stockings, tucked the long shirt down into a pair of trousers, and then drew a banyan onto his arms, slipping his feet into some slippers.

"I willsee who it is, and get your girl to see to you in your dressing room." He pointed at a door across from the bed. "The private parlor is through there. The wash chamber through there," he pointed out two other doors—one large, the other a hidden one, built to look like the paneling. "Your dressing room opens from the wash chamber," he added. He pointed to another door on the same wall as the bed. "Those are my rooms," he said.

"So we are to live here with your father?"

"For the time being. He will move into Rand Hall at the west end of the square. He wants it done before he leaves for Metrev. After that, this house is ours, as is the country estate."

Evvie finally rolled to the edge of the bed and drew a dressing gown over her slight, naked body. Dareth seemed disappointed to see her covered up, but he pecked her on the lips, and stalked out of the room.

She looked soberly about the rooms; making herself familiar with this space that would now be hers. The broad bed dominated the center of the west wall, a modern bed with curved head and footboards, it had been nicely dressed in quilted down blankets and white sheets, but was now a jumble of pillows and rumpled linens. The bed faced the wide fireplace, which was smoldering still from the blaze that had awaited them the night before. The walls were paneled in dark stained wood, with a few lovely paintings distributed about the space. Two archways led to different rooms. One by the windows led to the parlor. She peered in to see a large space cozily appointed with sofas and chairs arranged near the fireplace, which was built onto the back of the one in the bedroom.

She did not see her work table or her writing desk in here, so she concluded they would remain at the country home. Instead, a brand new circular table had been set up in the bright embrace of a bay window, with two matching chairs set beside it. The tall windows were dressed in swaths of silvery grey sheers, hemmed with a gold brocade trim.

The floors were swathed in a single piled rug that was shaped to the room, even notched around the skirt of the hearth. The design was detailed and beautiful, with whorls of cream and wine, navy and bursts of green and gold. It was a room made for comfort and ease. She envisioned many a winter spent in this space, with Dareth nearby, the fire crackling. She was overwhelmed with a sense of comfort.

She moved to the washroom, in search of the dressing room. The space she crossed was a windowless box tiled in marble on the floor and paneled in white painted wood, with a massive ceramic bowl tub, a washbowl and decanter stand built into the wall, and a chamber pot chair. She pushed open the door to her dressing room and smiled at the sight of it.

The space was almost as large as her dressing room at Ravensroost. A brigade of built-in armoires dominated the back wall, along with several small slipper chairs, a sizeable sleigh bed she would likely never sleep in, against the wall enhanced with a draping of fabric arranged like a canopy above the bed.

Her vanity—the one her father had made for her when she turned fifteen, which deserved a place in a city home for all its refined design and delicate look was in this room. It was too dainty for a country home. There was also her favorite slipper chair from her bedroom at Ravensroost, upholstered and tufted in deep dark teal velvet. To see them here provoked a strangely humbling feeling of belonging.

The paneling was painted a robin's egg blue, and adorned with lovely paintings. A small door in the panels by the window led Evvie to Imbrah, who was just putting on her shoes in what turned out to be her dainty little adjoined room.

"Mrs. Evvie," Imbrah grinned. "You're awake!"

"I am indeed," Evvie replied. "Is there a chance you could scare up enough hot water for a quick bath?"

Imbrah rose and patted down her gown. "I willsee to it right away."

Naturally, the time it took her to join her husband was a bit of a spell. But freshly bathed with her hair braided and then wound onto the back of her head, she was ready to dress. She selected a demure gown with a high neckline, and a ruffed chemisette. A little lace tucked around the décolletage, and her wrists, and some comfortable slippers, and she was on her way to the drawing room, where she could hear the low rumble of voices.

She slid the door open and found her husband sitting with two men and a woman. The lady's presence immediately intrigued her. She focused on greeting everyone first.

"Ah, there you are my dear. As you can see, at least she has the consideration to make a composed appearance, unlike me," Dareth laughed. He stood, as did everyone else, and bows and curtseys were exchanged. "My dear, this is Prince Vedd, fourth son of the King of Bask. The Marquess of Alst, and his betrothed, Miss Ylenne Bravis," Dareth said with immense formality. "My wife, Evvienne of Ilmeer, soon to be Countess of Ilmeer."

Evvie curtsied again, and greeted them. "I do much prefer to be called Evvie," she said. Her eyes were on Ylenne Bravis who looked very much like Mrs. Zsall. Tall and willowy, she had the same long bones and narrow face as Evvie's friend. But it was the white hair and blazing pale greenish eyes that sealed it. Another supposed witch secured by Bask nobility, Evvie smirked inwardly.

What was most notable about Miss Bravis was the look of abject disdain that crossed her face like a shadow when she first saw Evvie. Evvie was shocked, but she did not reveal it. There was no valid reason why someone would look at her like that. She looked at the woman impassively, with a soft smile, which seemed to only infuriate the woman more. The Countess-to-be took a seat beside her under-dressed husband, and folded her hands on her knees, gazing with interest at her company. They too sat, and when everyone was settled in again, the young prince spoke.

"We've only just arrived from Wargate," the young Prince explained. "We heard we'd miss

ed the union. So we decided to be the first of the first morning visitors. We're very sorry for having missed your wedding, Dareth,

Ma'am. Your husband has been a good friend of mine since we schooled together. I insisted we stop and pay our respects to you both. We haven't even stopped at home yet." He laughed easily. Like most Baskreth men, he was dark and tall, but his shoulders were not as broad as the warriors, and he had a bookish air about him. His eyes were bright and intelligent.

"Well, that is extraordinarily kind of you. I'm afraid the impromptu visit has exposed you to a lack of preparation on our part," Evvie said.

"It is what is expected on the morning visits. The goal is to disturb the newlyweds as much as possible, which is an unfortunate and cruel tradition," Dareth added with a silly grin.

The Prince and the Marquess both reflected it. Evvie wanted to roll her eyes, but she maintained her poise.

"Well, I wanted to invite you and your husband to dine at the Annex tomorrow night. It won't be a big to-do. Just myself, my friend and his lady, and a few other people who might have attended your wedding, but who were not properly introduced," the Prince offered.

"We would be delighted," Evvie replied. She was a little irritated by the invitation because that meant that she and Dareth would not be able to go and look at the country house as planned that day. But she was courteous.

"Excellent. We shall see you at the sixth hour then. Now, if you do not mind, ma'am, I would like to poach your husband for a few moments to look at a horse I found at Wargate. As we will be out in the snow, I hope you will entertain the lady for but a short while until we are ready to leave," the Prince said. The white witch seemed to shudder at this request, but nobody was looking at her but Evvie.

"Of course, we can amuse ourselves while you talk horses," Evvie replied graciously, her eyes turning with an amused expression onto the hard face of the young woman. The men rose, and they bowed and exited. Evvie then turned her attention to her company and found only a glare of ire shooting at her. They sat there looking at one another—Evvie in perplexity, with a slightly mirthful twist to her lips—the guest in derision—for a good five minutes before Evvie said anything.

"By the way you are looking at me, I cannot help but think that perhaps we have met before, Miss Bravis?"

"Good gods, no," the girl spat, with disgust in her voice. "I have no desire to hang about with red filth."

"I beg your pardon?" Evvie's hackles rose up and she glared balefully at the guest.

"News of your arrival has been less than well received by the whitecaste guild," Miss Bravis said. She stood and moved to the window, presumably to see what the men were up to.

"And how is that relevant to me? Have I done anything to deserve this loathing?"

"You're a red witch, and that is all it has to be. We have history with your kind, and there is a reason red witches are no longer commonly found."

"I believe—if my recollection is correct—that red witches were never commonly found. Not as *common* as white witches, anyway," Evvie snapped. "I fail to understand your dislike of me. I have done nothing to deserve it."

"It is deserved. And you will know firsthand how unwelcome you are here in Tirdonne very soon," the woman fulminated.

Evvie stood aback, and stared at her in incredulity. "Are you threatening me?"

"Take it as you wish, *Countess.*" Miss Bravis moved quickly to the chair she had occupied, and sat. Just as she did, the door opened and the men returned. Miss Bravis's expression was immediately one of affability and kindness. As the visitors made their farewells and exited, Miss Bravis threw Evvie one last flaming glare before vanishing out into the snowy morning.

Chapter 19

"Where are you off to? I thought we'd go back upstairs," Dareth said jestingly as Evvie rose from the breakfast table. It was a late meal, because of the visitors. Mrs. and Mrs. Reteen had come by shortly after the first visit, followed by two of Dareth's school chums and fighting partners. She'd eaten hastily, and was eager for the clock to strike ten and for the visits to cease. Then she would be free to get across the square.

"I want to go see the aunties. To thank them for their hospitality and for arranging such a beautiful wedding." Evvie did not lie, but she did not disclose the whole truth. Until she knew more about this hatred fostered by white witches, she was not about to worry Dareth. "I won't be too long."

"Good. I was thinking perhaps we could take a visit to the country house today, since the dinner tomorrow has interfered with that. We can leave early this afternoon. No hurry."

"That is a wonderful plan, Dareth. I shall make a hasty visit to the aunts then."

He continued eating, reading from a paper that was spread out in front of his plate. She slipped out of the room and ran upstairs to put on her rabbit-fur-lined boots and her favorite coat for the quick jaunt across the square.

The aunties were lingering in their tatty morning gowns and frilly caps when she arrived. They both embraced her and congratulated her. Nerah examined the marriage mark closely and then they made her take her coat off and ushered her to a chair by the fire.

She offered a preamble of gratitude for their efforts and their kindness, and stated she would miss living under their roof. She then introduced the subject she really wished to discuss.

"My dearest aunts, I have been threatened by a white witch," she said. The ladies' eyes widened and they leaned forward to hear more. "Moreover, she deemed to threaten me on behalf of a guild of the whitecaste."

"Good gracious!" Arah exclaimed.

"Am I in any danger?"

"I highly doubt it. You're a red witch. They can pose little threat to you magically. Your own powers would prevent it, I would think," Arah assured her.

"Unless they have some means of doing so we do not know about," Nerah postulated. "We do not know what they get up to."

"Is there a Guild of Black Witchery?"

"Yes, the ravencaste guild, but we do not participate in it. It is mostly comprised of self-important, weak witches who do nothing but gossip," Arah replied.

"We will have to look into this," Nerah said. "Although there are some stories of rivalry, we are all sisters in magic. There's no reason that I know of that the white witches would hold such a grudge against you."

"It sounds like they hate all red witches by the way that woman spoke."

The aunties reflected on this, and shook their heads in bewilderment. "We may have to do some spell work to find more out, but mark my words, child, we will find whatever it is. We cannot have people going about threatening you," Nerah suggested.

Evvie frowned and leaned back into her chair. She suspired heavily. "I suppose I cannot just be happy in my new life. There has to be grudges and madmen, too."

"These things shall pass, darling. Now, you said you could not stay long. Do not dwell. Get up and get going if you are to go to the country house," Arah murmured.

Evvie rose reluctantly and embraced the ladies in turn. "I will return tomorrow. If you learn anything, please let me know. I have to dine with that woman tomorrow evening, and I want to at least be somewhat prepared." The ladies nodded in assent and sent Evvie along her way.

The coach ride to the country home was a rough, bouncy one. The road was neither paved nor much used. It was overgrown with weeds and grass, and the recent traffic of the tradesmen and builders made it rutted and muddy. Add the snow and slushy ice, and it was less than pleasant for everyone involved.

Ilmeer the estate was large and had four villages on it, tucked away in the folds of hills and trees. Evvie saw none of them on this trip, as the road they took to the hall and its small park led straight there. Although she did see branching roads leading away from it as they got closer to the manor.

Evvie was leaning against Dareth. His arm was around her, and she basked in the sense of security and oneness she shared with him. How she wished she could have met him sooner, but she knew that if she had not endured her first marriage, she would not have seen Dareth in the same light. Her misfortune served to prepare her for choosing what felt right for her.

He was astonishingly gentle and attentive to her. When he was with her, even when he seemed unfocused or preoccupied, he was still tuned into her presence, and aware of what she was doing or saying. And every once in a while he would quietly bend down and place a soft kiss on the top of her head. She watched the white-dusted greenery slide by with a distant, detached feeling, her hands gripping his arm.

"What is pressing on your mind, my dear? You seem troubled and anxious," he asked. "Is it that Ryse-Mevvick fellow again?"

"No," she sighed. She weighed the price of telling him, but it was so difficult to not be honest with him. "That woman, the white haired one that visited this morning…"

"What about her?"

"She threatened me." Dareth's arm withdrew and he twisted on the bench, turning Evvie to face him. "Explain, please."

Evvie recounted the brief conversation she'd had with Miss Bravis. Dareth's eyes darkened.

"I do not understand why she despises me so, or that this purported whitecast guild would dislike me so much as to conspire to harm me…"

He shook his head and threw himself back onto the seat. "You will stay here in the country starting immediately. The improvements can be waylaid until spring, if need be. I won't have you being threatened by common-blooded, inferior witches. And I willhave a word with the Marquess about his lady. Nobody speaks to you with such disrespect or nastiness and gets away with it!"

"Dareth, I do not wish to create rancor between friends because of the words of one unimportant person," she said. "I will manage this myself. Perhaps with the help of your aunts. But this is nothing that you should worry about. It has only disconcerted me. I am indeed eager to live in the peace of the country, but there is no need to curtail the work because of this."

Dareth looked at her with solemn trust. "Very well. But if it becomes a greater problem, I want you to promise me you will ask me to intervene."

Evvie silently conveyed her assent, surprised he didn't try to take over anyway. "May I ask you something about your aunts?"

"Of course," he said.

Evvie squashed herself against him, and he put his arm around her anew. "Witches are valued as wives in Bask country. Why are they not wed?"

"My aunts are *black* witches. There is sadly nothing greatly unusual about a Bask woman with a voice to the powers," he explained. "There are many, many ravencaste women amongst us. However, in the case of my aunts, their spinsterhood is because of a tragic romance which involved both sisters, and one gentleman. To this day, not a single person in the village can understand how they live together in harmony as they do. The situation was untenable from how my father tells it."

"You cannot be that vague and leave me hanging, Dareth," Evvie said grumpily. "And I would hardly call it living in harmony. They bicker and needle each other constantly. More precisely, Arah is continuously admonishing of her younger sister, and cutting her down at every turn. Nerah mostly ignores it, or responds with defiance. I cannot imagine it is pleasant to live like that all the time."

"That sounds about right. When she was but nineteen, Arah had her sights on a young Mr. Tayrus. He was a Brii man. A self-important sort of fellow with some standing amongst his people, though of what exactly I do not know. He was interested in Arah, by all appearances, but still had a roving eye. Because of her status and family connections, he lingered at Arah's side, giving her all the hope that he would ask her to marry him sooner or later. But it was clear he did not love her, and the proposal never occurred. Nerah came out that same year, and it turned out that it was she who had captured the elusive Mr. Tayrus's heart—and he had remained in the family's society merely to wait for Nerah to come out. Nerah—who had admired him as a girl, and was quite smitten and jealous of her elder sister—was delighted to learn that he loved her, and they were almost immediately engaged.

"Arah was beside herself, for she truly believed he remained in order to marry her. The heartbreak was world-ending for my poor aunt. Betrayed by her own little sister, her wretchedness was felt by all. My grandfather, naturally, was less than pleased by the tactics to which Mr. Tayrus had secured Nerah's promise, and his untoward intentions towards her older sister. So he paid Tayrus to go away. And to the disappointment of many, without resolve or determination, he simply took the gold and left."

"Oh goodness." Evvie was horrified. Her heart broke for young Arah.

"So you can imagine, there was great sadness in the home of the sisters. And enormous acrimony, one blaming the other, and both so vastly hurt and disappointed by Mr. Tayrus. They were never the same after that. Neither was interested in risking further heartbreak, and they became shut-ins. That is why they are not married."

"I see," she whispered, feeling only regret for the ladies who had so kindly doted upon her. "So their witchery is not the reason. What about white witches? They are common as well?"

"White witches are a little rarer—and from what I understand of witchly things, a sight more powerful than their darker counterparts, when practicing. But most witchery has fallen out of fashion. The ancient beliefs have faded a deal since the southern cultures have influenced ours so greatly. The Bask will not let go of ancient ways entirely, but the number of witches seems to be dwindling. There are commonly found ravencaste witches, but white, grey and greencaste, they are less widespread. I am not entirely certain how powerful any of them are, or how effective their supposed magic is, but they still hold some sway. But as you have experienced, the sight of a wolf-eyed red-head sends everyone into a lather."

"I wonder why the white witches hate red witches so much," Evvie ventured. "If that is truly the case. The aunts know nothing of this, nor did Mrs. Zsall speak anything of it. But she, like me, hails from outside of Bask. It is hard to know what is true and what is not."

Dareth shrugged. "Probably some ridiculous reason borne out of old superstitions which are utterly irrelevant today. But for some, it is enough to hold onto. I cannot imagine they would be of any threat to you magically, as I know that red witches are the darlings of the powers. You would be—if you were indeed a practicing witch—much more powerful than they by tenfold. To threaten you is an act of profound arrogance, looking at it through the eyes of a Bask traditionalist. If there is a risk of *physical* danger, I would rather you stay here at Ilmeer."

"I am safe at Ilmeeri Square, Dareth," she said. "As long as I'm in company, I cannot imagine they would try anything if that were the case. And the aunts are investigating the matter as we speak. It seems silly to be so alarmed by the words of a strange woman, but I cannot help but feel discomfited by the whole thing." Evvie groaned.

"I am here. The family is here. Anybody who dares to approach you with harm will regret it. All this blather of witchery seems ridiculous, as there is so little evidence of it being anything more than parlor tricks. It could be that the woman's threats are as empty as her head," he told her.

"Indeed," Evvie muttered, unconvinced. She nuzzled her head into the crook of his arm and gazed out at the brush closing in around the coach. She did not have a good feeling about the exchange at all.

The country house was far more than she had ever expected. Much grander than Ravensroost, it was an ancient stone construct sitting in a dense growth of old trees against a hillside where a towering, three-tiered waterfall cascaded down from a lofty, rocky cliff. It was breathtaking.

"That is Alouaine Falls," Dareth told her. "There's a pool at the base that is perfect in summer for swimming. There is not much park to wander. It is mostly dense forest. Though the land has been in my family for countless generations, we've not seen fit to clear much of the land for farming or gardens or whatnot. We have a small pasture over there, behind that outcropping, for the livery and saddle horses."

The coach rumbled over a bridge made of the same dark stone as the house, crossing the river which wound away from the waterfall. She spotted several large fish in the crystal clear waters along the bottom, which was lined in smoothened river stones.

Alouaine Hall was imposing and grave looking. Unlike Ravensroost, it was not much adorned with decoration. It was also larger than Ravensroost; less sprawling, but taller and with more rooms. It was flat-faced and dramatic with stepped gables and tall, arched, stone-carved windows with diamond-leaded panes that peered out into the lush greenery that surrounded it. There were several runs of lancet windows galleried on one side, and there was a conservatory hot house that clung to the far side of the house looking like a dusty, mossy gem. There were several bay windows resting on heavy timber corbels, and a patio— edged in pragmatic, rounded pilasters with a simple railing— leading out the back to the river. There were planters all about the exterior made of the same stone, overflowing with wild vines and moss. There were signs of the improvements being made: saw horses standing in pools of sawdust, patches of new masonry embedded in the old, and front doors that had been sanded down to the natural wood.

Inside, the hall was mostly empty of furniture and contents. Dareth explained that the furnishings had been stored in one of the better halls while they fixed the wooden floors and swathed the cold stone walls in wood paneling, plaster, paper and paint. The smell of wood lacquer permeated the open spaces. Workmen and women toiled. One lady was hanging new draperies in a vast empty hall, while a man was high on a ladder hanging up one of four candelabras from the thicket of trusses and beams that dominated the ceiling.

"It won't be long until they're finished," Dareth assured her.

Evvie was astonished that so much house would be for their use alone. But Dareth would be Count, provided he did win his battle.

They entered a smaller room at the back of the house where the walls were clad in natural timber. The mantle had been built out in milled wood, and workmen were replacing a set of windowed doors.

Evvie squeezed her husband's arm. "I love this room!"

"I knew you would. It is like your sitting room at home."

"Yes. Yes it is." She was brought back to that moment when Dareth had stood in the window with his bayonet dripping blood. She turned and hugged herself to him. His hand brushed her back.

"I will furnish it to your liking. You need only tell me what you need."

"No dark paneling in here. Have them paint it white. I will put some of my furnishings in here." Evvie clutched her husband's arm, utterly delighted by the house.

"I figured as much. Your work table, the one you brought, I already planned to have it put in here." He told her.

She peered up at him, her eyes wet with emotion. He bent down and kissed her, and then withdrew, peering into her eyes. "I want nothing more than to make this feel like home for you. Truly feel like home."

"As long as you're in it, it will," she said through a tight throat.

The workmen moved away and took the old door with them, leaving them a clear view of the back garden. The doors opened out onto a patio which overlooked the stony brook. The falls sang only a short ways off. "It is not as fashionable or fine as your home, Evvie, but it is yours nonetheless."

"It is perfection," she replied.

"Excellent. Then let us go home. In a few weeks, we will come here to stay."

Evvie hugged herself to him enthusiastically and then they made their way back to the coach.

Evvie gave herself one final look in the mirror before she went downstairs. She'd chosen one of her old gowns because she thought it suited her best. It was the gown she wore to the Mummer's Ball when she met her first husband, the Duke of Adrin. The gown was an unusual shade of raspberry. It was a slightly out of fashion by southern standards, but at the forefront of it in the north. She counted on the room being well heated, for the gown was but a thin, papery taffeta with thin, subtle tone on tone pin stripes. It had a train, which was acceptable as this was just a dinner and cards. The elegant, fitted, long sleeves were a bonus. She also had a pair of spare little silk slippers to match, with tiny cockades of paler raspberry and beads of pearl sewn to the tops of them.

Imbrah made her hair resplendent, and added in the mountain pearls the young girl from Avradelle had gifted her. Evvie added the matching necklace and earrings which Dareth had given her as a wedding present. She then bundled up in a woolen cloak of midnight black, edged in black fur, added a matching fur muff, and draped her shawl over her shoulder. She left her dressing room only to run into Dareth in the sleeping chamber. He was digging about in a dresser looking for something.

"Good gracious, woman. Do you make it your goal to devastate me with your beauty?"

"Thank you," she said.

"Have you seen my fob?"

She moved to the window sill, picking up the chain and ribbon made from braided ayle hair—a beast of the far north. Evvie had never heard of such a creature, but Dareth described it as part bear, part horse, with long white hair. The beast sounded horrifying to Evvie. Dareth had laughed. "No more so than a dragon, or a bear."

He now tucked the watch into the tiny pocket at his hip, and gave his waistcoat a tug. "I dislike these formal to-dos."

"You choose to be friends with a prince," she said with an arch of the brow.

"The good thing is that he likes Alouaine, so he is happy to spend time there in informal society as often as he can. So there are those wintry nights to look forward to. He is good company."

Evvie gazed at her husband, trussed up for parlor society. She smirked at him, and he took her arm. Seizing his wool garrick and a feathered bicorn on his way out, he loaded his wife into the coach and it cast itself uptown towards the palace.

The Annex was exactly that: an annex to the palace itself. It was a tall, narrow construct angling off of the main structure, which towered up to impossible heights. The annex was set on the lower portion of the palace, where parts of abutted the upper streets of the Sky district. Most of the annex was made from stone blocks, unlike the palace which had been carved from the hilltop.

The city was covered in several inches of snow. Everything looked clean and smelled crisp. It was mind-bogglingly cold. Almost as cold as Avradelle.

The coach drew into a tunnel before emerging in a small bailey where it came to a stop in front of a set of stairs. The steps led up to a broad door with windows that broadcast the warmth inside in bands of bright, yellow light.

Evvie and Dareth were ushered inside. Their outerwear was removed, and they were herded up three sets of stairs to a well-heated parlor where three familiar faces awaited them. There were several other guests, one of which was none other than Mr. Ando Ryse-Mevvick. Evvie emitted a burdensome sigh, and shook her head unobtrusively.

"I cannot escape this man," she murmured to Dareth.

Dareth looked over and frowned. "Well, you're married, so he has no reason to further pursue your attentions. If he gets out of hand with you, I will set him right."

Evvie peered at the guests, two of whom she could not stomach, and forced a smile onto her lips. She entered the fold with as much courage she could muster. Welcomed openly and heartily by the Prince, she melted into the cadre, and throughout the time before and during dinner she was unfettered by the presence of the two nemeses.

But after dinner, she was confronted by her unwanted suitor who came to apologize to her for his inexcusable behavior. She felt Dareth's eyes on her from the fireside, where he and the Prince and Marquess and two other fellows were enjoying some grog and sharing a lively debate. His watchful gaze remained fast on Evvie when the man invited himself to sit near her. She looked at him, and he looked at her tattoo.

"I am regretful of my actions. I truly am," Ryse-Mevvick said. "It is a strange madness that consumed me. It was fed by the knowledge that you are redcaste. I should explain, I am descended from redcaste lines, and am hexxenmaeg—only one of four that I know of now. My family valued that part of our heritage greatly, and hoped to have a daughter with wolf-eyes again. They put that hope on me. And the notion that you could have been the one to bring back the living line of witches, it was… intoxicating and it drove me to act rashly and stupidly."

Evvie listened quietly, unfamiliar with the term he used, and honestly indifferent to it. "I am not a mare to breed."

He winced at her sharp tone, and shook his head. "That was never the intention or idea."

Evvie nearly scoffed in laughter. But she kept her composure, and stared at her hands, listening.

He continued, unabashed by his delusion. "You are... you are beautiful, and your manners are so elegant. Your kindness and generosity to the inn's child, it charmed me so. It bespoke of a depth of character few possess. I have thought of little else since I first saw you. I let it consume me."

"I accept your apology, Mr. Ryse-Mevvick. However, I am now a married woman. A *happily* married woman in love with her husband. He will not tolerate advances from other men, and he already has a dislike for you because of what happened."

"And you shall have no more such advances," he said, his voice filled with defiance. He sat up straight and sighed. "I shall only say that the strength of your bloodline is weakened by your alliance with a Bask warrior clan. It is wasted. Red-witch lines are disappearing, and you have all but assured they will disappear altogether." His tone was bitter, but he caught himself and stood. "Ma'am." He bowed shallowly and stumbled off to join a group by at a carding table.

Evvie gave Dareth a bemused look, and engaged another woman in chat, before moving to join another card game.

Throughout the night the Brii man still gazed longingly upon her, while on the converse, the white witch Miss Bravis spent the entire evening glaring at her with open contempt.

MIRANDA MAYER

Chapter 20

Evvie slipped quickly out of the coach and into the courtyard of the Brii archive, her head covered with the hood of her favorite coat. She flitted through the broad, echoing space to the largest of the many doors surrounding it. She pushed it open, entering a cool—but not cold—space which smelled distinctly like old paper. She closed the door. Her boots clattered a staccato on the flagstone floor as she moved through a featureless vestibule towards an archway beyond which she could see a shelf of books behind what looked like a long desk.

There she found an old man carefully sorting books onto a cart. He was an odd, sweet-faced old fellow. His papery skin was covered in faded Brii symbols, and a shock of pure silver hair expertly coiffed and pomaded into a dashing do. His sparkling hazel eyes immediately locked on Evvie. He dropped his task the moment she threw back her hood, and he nearly floated to her with a look of intrigue on his face.

"Well, well, well, you must be the Red Witch rumored to have married a Baskreth Count, how enchanting," he whispered with obvious delight. "I am Edanbras. To what tremendous honor do I owe this visit, my most venerable Lady?"

Evvie twinkled at him with her pretty smile, and tugged off her gloves. Her cheeks were still ruddy from the cold.

He tilted his head as if in admiration of her loveliness. He, like southern scholars, dressed mostly in black, with pale stockings and an ivory linen shirt, of which she could only see the dismally pressed collar and the ink-stained cuffs over his knuckles. His waistcoat, breeches and shoes were also black. Over these he wore a black robe with a yoke in the back, to which yards of fabric were pleated. It was open in the front, and the shoulder panels were heavily pleated, which made quite a swish when he moved.

"I am here to learn more about witchery," she told him.

He grinned broadly. "Indeed you are. Any particular facet of witchery?"

Evvie wasn't quite sure where to begin. As much as she was curious about the white witch grudge against redcaste, she did not want to jump into the middle of the story without background, or she might miss something. "I do not know," she admitted, grasping her gloves and twisting them in thought. "Perhaps if I can start with something general, then it can lead me to something more specific."

"Something general about witchery. A history, perhaps. Of Bask origin, so that it is not biased with southern pragmatism. I think I can help you with this. If you would just excuse me a moment, I will look up the reference number." he held up a long, bony finger, and then scuttled away towards a towering cabinet built into the sidewall. It was studded with tiny drawers. He first referred to a large tome on a raised portion of the desk, flipping through a number of pages, stopping to run his finger down lines of text. Then, having found what he was looking for, he rolled a ladder in front of the cabinet and climbed it, pulling out one of the myriad drawers. His fingers marched through a file of standing cards, and, when he found the one he wanted, he plucked it out and waved it, twisting on the ladder with grin of success.

With the clank of his shoes descending the ladder, he was soon before her holding the little card. He put it down and slid a piece of scrap paper off of one of the many stacks peppering the long counter. He dipped the quill in a crystal vial of ink and copied the information onto the scrap before returning the card immediately to its tiny drawer.

He was a bit breathless when he returned. "Here is the stack number, which is the actual bookshelf cabinet. Stack twenty nine. They are all laid out in an intuitive manner. The numbers are on their ends—or the middle top if they are against a wall. Twenty nine is on the west wall. So you'll take a left when you enter the library, and then go towards the back. They are easy to find. Then this number here, eight; that is the shelf number. Shelves are numbered from floor to ceiling. You will need the ladder. There are plenty spaced about the edge of the room. And that number 11 means it is the eleventh book on that shelf. I've written the title just to be sure. That little 4 is the spacer size, that is for me."

Evvie grasped the paper and read the title. "A Heritage in Witchery by Tallin Bleeque."

"It is an excellent book. Not too heavy with the ideological drivel, and not mind-numbingly skeptical. It follows the history of witchery in Bask territories from the first written records of it all the way to present day…ish. It was published in Annum Seventy-One, so it is a two decades old. But it is quite relevant, and little has changed in respect to witchery since then."

Evvie nodded.

"There are reading booths all along the walls of the study room if you prefer privacy and are easily distracted. Or you are welcome to sit at any of the long tables in between. You will see the study room once you're in the stacks in earnest. I will see to it that you have refreshment, are supplied with paper and ink, and ample light," he added. "Oh!" He reached under the counter and withdrew a block of wood painted a bright red. "This is your spacer. Be sure to put it on the shelf in place of your book. It keeps the others from tipping and makes it easier to find the spot when returning the book to its place."

"Thank you, sir."

"Call me Edanbras, dear Lady. Should I call you Countess? No, not yet, from what I understand."

She let him ramble, and did not bother to reply. Instead, she reached into her reticule and took out one thick, plump little coin with the King of Bask stamped on its face, and a the serpent and rose stamped on the back. Edanbras, understanding the cue, reached for one of several boxes on the countertop, and slid it towards her. She deposited the coin into the slot, and he bowed kindly at her.

"Thank you for pre-paying. So many people do not. It makes it less of a task for me, as I do not have to chase anyone down demanding payment. Most considerate, dear Lady. Most considerate."

She had paid him amply, which would mean—if he was a responsible archivist—he would bring her a pot of tea. She offered him little squeeze of the hand and then took her slip of paper and went out in search of shelf stack twenty-nine.

The main body of the archive was vast. She had never seen anything like it. It took her breath away. The first shelf she passed on her right was numbered 124. It started at one when she took the left. And as she skirted the room, following the wall shelves, the inner portion of the room was chockablock with towering, double sided, long shelves with numbers on them as high as 192.

There was a stairwell now and again between the wall shelves indicating there was a second floor with shelves 200 to 400. The volume of books that would entail was beyond her capacity to imagine. She was glad she only had to find stack 29. *Some books might require one to assemble an expedition to find*, she giggled to herself. She knew she would spend time here. How could she not when there were at *least* four hundred heaving shelves of knowledge and imagination all in this one spot? The idea of all of the things she would learn made her shiver with delight.

Just at the turn of the wall there was an archway into the study room Edanbras had indicated, and next to that archway was stack twenty-eight where a ladder was leaning on its rail, waiting for her. She pushed it to the next bookshelf and climbed it to shelf eight. She counted eleven books in, and pulled out the unprinted spine of the book, opening it to ensure it was the one she wanted. She slid the wooden block into its berth, and then descended.

"Well, that was easy," she murmured. She then walked into the study room.

There were four other people in the room. Two were scholars, by the look of them, and one was a young boy. The other was the boy's governess who was laying out study materials on the table only a few seats away.

Evvie chose a table that was close to a wide-mouthed fireplace that had a moderate blaze burning in it. She threw her gloves down on the smooth surface, and then the book. She removed her coat and draped it over the tall chair.

The chair was upholstered in leather and the back and seat were tufted for comfort, as many patrons would likely spend hours in the library. When she had finally settled in and was reading along through the book's introduction, Edanbras arrived with a pot of tea, amongst other things. He looked as pleased as anyone could possibly be to be toting a tray for a lady. He put a little crocheted doily down and placed the pot on it. Beside that he set an empty cup and saucer, a sugar pot, a cream pot, and a little plate of biscuits.

"There." He refilled the lamp with oil, adjusted the reflection hood, replaced the ink pot, and tamped the slips of notepaper neat and put them within her reach. "I will check in on you in a spell to see if you require anything else." And off he tottered.

She opened the book and leafed through the pages. The first thing that drew her eye was the elucidation of the most basic aspects of witchery—beginning with the colorcaste wheel, and what aspect of spirituality they served; something that had puzzling her since she met Mrs. Zsall.

The Wheel of the Colorcaste Witches

Red Witch *– the first; the witch of the spirit and soul; the very source of the power within.*
She requires only will to cast magic.
Green Witch *– the second; the witch of the earth and of nature.*
Her tools of magic consist mostly of the use of natural herbs, wood and plants.
Grey Witch *– the third; the witch of the life waters.*
Her tools of magic consist mostly of potions and her keen senses; and prognostications in water.
White Witch *– the fourth; the witch of the air.*
Her tools of magic consist mostly of oils and insense. Her spells must be chanted and spoken.
Black Witch *–the fifth; the witch of the fire and death.*
Her tools are the talismans of bone and stone. She is the channel of the deathpowers.

Evvie was surprised and intrigued by this little chart. The book was more informative than she had expected, as it offered insight into the white witch rivalry. It was something that had begun early on in the written history. A jealousy of the power given to red witches by the old gods—which were oft-referred to as *the Powers*—and a sense of arrogance by white witches, as there were more of them than there were of their red rivals. The book mentioned various events where the two factions had clashed, and as she read on, the author implied that the decline of the red witch was due to the actions of the white witches. How, it did not specify.

Evvie had consumed a whole pot of tea, and had to refresh herself twice by the time she got to the part that detailed more about the distinctions between the types of witches. It was a mere summary, as the focus of the book was on the history of witchery, but what was notable was the mention of the Prósopo:

The manifestation of the Prósopo—also known to many as the red avatar—is one among many of the notable powers of red witches that no other magic bearers possess. The red witch can separate from herself a spiritual avatar which, once removed from her being, can become a palpable, viable entity. It can inflict harm on anyone and anything. There are scant reports of the witness of these beings. Some have purported to have seen great beasts acting in the witch's stead. But as red witches also possess the ability to thrall, these could have been mistaken for actual animals compelled by red witchcraft. Admus Veck, a notorious scholar of witchery, speculates that the avatars are likely to be unexceptional creatures, as they often do their damage without being noticed. He states in his thesis on the subject of red witches the following: 'The superiority of the red witch is beyond her greater abilities, but her capacity to exercise them with subtlety. She needs no talismans, no wild chanting or arm waving, nor does she need to spill blood. She needs to only will it and the powers will heed her. Her avatar would be, in all respects, a reflection of this understated preeminence which, anyone of logic would conclude, to be an ordinary, unremarkable person.'

In the context of superior order, red witches are to witchery as wolves are to the animal kingdom: creatures with no predators. They are the apex. The grey, green, white and ravencaste rank below the red witch in ability and relevance to the practice of the ancient religions. White witches are the only caste of the sisterhood to hold the redcaste in disregard. All other castes of witch have historically been cooperative and deferent to the pinnacle of witchery, as are the red witches.

Evvie reached for a quill and scratched down the name: *Admus Veck*. She then wrote *thesis on red witches* after his name. He would hopefully have greater detail about red witches and this Prósopo she was supposed to have. She then decided to read on in hopes of finding more details on the idea that white witches might have had some hand in the decline of red witches. Admus had called the redcaste the apex of witchery. That, like wolves, there were no creatures that hunted them. Then what would that make the white witches if that were the case? The book did not illuminate that subject any further than the brief mention.

When Evvie looked up, the governess was gone with her charge, the study was empty and, far in the back, an archivist was extinguishing the candles on one of the large candelabras. She stood, her back aching. She drew on her coat and closed it, stuffing the little slip of paper into her reticule. She returned the book to its shelf and carried the spacer back to the front desk where a new, younger archivist had replaced Edanbras. Evvie slid the spacer across the counter towards him.

"You returned it? How thoughtful of you. Thank you ma'am," he exclaimed.

"When will Edanbras return to attendance again?"

"Oh, he's on only a few times in the week as he also works in the records room. Next Highday, he will be here." That meant he would return at the beginning of the new week. She gave the man a nod.

"Excellent. I thank you. And my gratitude to Edanbras as well. Good day," Evvie said. She put on her gloves, and pulled up her hood. She hoped the coachman wouldn't be too put out that she had made him wait so long.

MIRANDA MAYER

Chapter 21

Evvie and the aunties set out to shop on Tower Street where the best shops of Tirdonne were located. It was a long, slow-rising street that climbed against the side of the hill. The street was named for the great drum tower of the Brii Abbey, its massive base and magnificent ridged talus butting into the row of buildings and part of the street itself.

They walked in tandem, each aunt on one of Evvie's arms. They were determined to stop at as many shops as possible, as well as take a rest for tea at Allendon's Tea House, which was famous throughout the land, including the southern cities. It was renowned for its unmatched standard of service, elegant tea room and its sticky buns.

After having browsed through a millinery, a shoe shop and a place where Evvie purchased a stunning high-boy for the country house, they ambled towards the tea room. "On a snowy day like this, it won't be crowded," Arah assured Evvie.

They passed a strange, narrow little shop with a sign that read: The Diviner's Rest. Nerah stopped, pulling everyone else to a stop. "We forgot about this place," she blurted.

Arah contemplated and then agreed with a decisive nod.

"She *could* have that book you want," Nerah turned to Evvie. "Let us have a look."

Evvie agreed, and they approached the small storefront. There was a window but it was covered in a lace curtain, so they could not see inside. They pushed open the door and a little bell rang cheerily. Inside, it was brightly lit by lamps and window light and there was an earthy, herbaceous aroma that permeated the place. Working at a single table in the center of the space was a remarkably beautiful woman of Evvie's age, but with hair as grey as the clouds. Her eyes were also like Evvie's. She wore a black gown with a crisp, white apron over it.

The shop, save for the window with the lacy light streaming through and a narrow door on the back wall, was solid shelves and drawers from floor to ceiling. The open shelves were stacked with beautiful glass jars filled to the brim with myriad compounds and substances. The top of the shelves and cupboards were laden with books. Every drawer and cupboard had a neat little label noting the contents. There were two chairs pushed up under the work table on the street side, and a stool on the other side. Everything in the shop was as neat as a pin.

The woman was crushing some dried leaves in a mortar when they entered, her bright eyes looked up and they fell upon Evvie. She picked up the bottom of her apron and wiped her hands. "My goodness! Welcome, Lady! Ladies." She curtsied to each of them in turn. "What, may I ask, are you looking for this morning?"

She carried the stool around to the other side of the table and gestured for them to sit. They did. Evvie fished in her reticule and pulled out the slip. "I'm looking for a book by an Admus Veck."

The grey witch pondered for a moment, and shook her head. "I am fairly certain I do not have that," she replied regretfully. "I have blank grimoires and spell books for the lower witches. Nothing of the historic nature. I am sorry."

"Well, that is inconvenient. But while I'm here, I willneed a few new talismans as two of my bones snapped and one of my little stones has gone missing," Nerah interjected.

"Yes. Your talismans are demanding change," the shop keeper asserted, and moved to one of the cupboards, removing two tall wooden boxes that stood side-by-side in the cupboard taking up the whole space. She plunked them on the table, and then fetched a velvet runner from a drawer, rolling it out the length of the table in front of the ladies. She opened the narrow lid of each box—which were also lined in velvet. She tipped them to reveal one filled to the brim with hundreds of bleached bones, and the other with as many tiny stones.

Nerah plunged her hands into each, whispering under her breath, and then withdrew a handful apiece from the boxes. She threw them onto the velvet and stared at them. She remained markedly silent, gazing at them with skepticism. The grey witch had righted the boxes and was looking at them, too.

Arah frowned. "That is odd," she muttered.

The grey witch circled the table to peer at the talismans in earnest. Evvie was puzzled by what was happening. "What's odd?" she asked, leaning aside so the grey witch could see better.

"A choosing is a simple process. Depending on how the talismans land, it is determined which ones you should keep. These are all oriented in a way that indicates that they should be kept. And moreover, they are in a prognostication pattern," the gray witch murmured.

The bones had landed in a particularly orderly fashion. Most of the skulls were upright, the little bones were either horizontal or vertical, everything neatly separated from the next, and all the stones were positioned so the figures etched on them were visible.

"We cannot simply ignore this," the grey witch murmured. "The talismans are telling us to seek further." She picked up the boxes and put them back into their cupboard, and then removed a deck of cards from a drawer.

Arah rose from the stool and put it back on the other side of the table. The shop keeper moved her implements aside to clear space in front of the bones. She cut the cards four times and then fanned them out on the table. "I think each of you ought to pull one."

Arah reached first and drew a card, placing it face up in front of her. Then Evvie, and then Nerah.

"That is intriguing," the gray witch whispered as Evvie drew a card depicting a lady who looked much like herself. Like the card that they had drawn the night of the spell.

The card Arah had drawn was a dragon being subdued by the sword of a knight. "The Defeated," the gray witch whispered. And then she looked to Nerah's card, which showed a golden knight standing on a heap of bodies. "And the Victor."

"This is madness," Arah blurted.

"Which talismans am I to keep?" Nerah asked.

"You are to keep them all," the shop keeper shrugged. "They have spoken."

"What am I to do with all these extra bits and bobs?"

"They will tell you what to do, have patience," Arah grumbled.

"I do not understand. What does all this mean?" Evvie interjected.

"The message is quite clear. The defeated will become the victor. And that would be her." The gray witch tapped her finger on the red witch card.

Evvie shook her head. "I'm sorry, this all too confusing."

"I imagine so. A southern-raised witch would indeed find everything about witchery confusing. But spend enough time up here, and that cloud will clear up soon enough. That'll be a copper Troy for the talismans," she told Nerah, who scowled and dug into her reticule for money.

Evvie stared at the cards until the gray witch picked them up and returned them to her deck. She tamped them and put them away. Nerah scooped up her plethora of new talismans and put them in her reticule. Arah rolled up the velvet runner and handed it to the shop keeper.

"I would say that the impromptu prognostication was good news," Nerah said cheerfully.

"Yes. But victor of what? And who was defeated?" Evvie murmured. Her thoughts returned to the missive about the white witches having something to do with the decline of red witches. The aunties were making as if they were going to leave, but Evvie lingered in her chair, her brow furrowed into a puzzled patch as she worked the knowledge through her brain. "How were the red witches defeated?" she asked out loud.

"The practice of magic has lost ground in the past two centuries. It is only natural that the rarest of the witches would be even rarer..." Arah replied loftily.

"That is not *entirely* correct," the grey witch interjected. "There was a period during the Eydoc era, at witchery's peak, when witches were divided against other witches. And red witches were under assault by the white witches. There was a spell that was created, a groundbreaking spell, which could protect the whitecaste against the proxies. Part of what made the spell unusual was that it required white witches to work in *unison* for it to succeed—which incidentally, was the beginning of the witch guilds. The whitecaste were empowered by this collective spell, and were able to inflict harm against redcaste witches now that their proxies were rendered powerless against white witches. This unification of the whitecaste made red-witchery almost impossible from then-on. That spelled the beginning of the decline of witchery in general, and saw the disappearance of red witches almost completely. Quite tragic, in truth. The whole thing. It brought each caste together, but undermined the very foundation of witchery all at once."

The aunts were aghast, standing with their eyes wide in shock, Arah's mouth hanging open.

Evvie was astonished by the flood of answers she got from a simple reply. She stood. "So the white witches drove not only the red witches away, but also drove witchery into the insignificance they've become today."

"It was they that turned this incredible gift into a mockery?" Arah barked, incredulous. Her brow furrowed in anger. "That is a crime!"

"And they still carry that prejudice with them, to this day. The way that woman spoke to Evvie!" Nerah grumbled.

The grey witch looked perplexed. "One should never disrespect a supreme witch," she muttered. "I apologize on behalf of our white sisters, my lady."

Evvie waved her hand dismissively. "Does that mean that they will try to harm me?"

"And that they can, because they have protection against her Prósopo?" Nerah added; her voice imbued with concern.

"I cannot say. It depends on the witches they are today. If they still possess that spell, or if there enough of them to put it into practice," the gray witch said.

They stood in silence. And then Evvie broke it with a smile. "You have been more helpful than I could have ever hoped for. I thank you ma'am."

The grey witch curtsied politely and they exited the shop.

"Well that was fascinating," Arah declared when they were back out in the cold.

"Well, shall we go to tea?" Nerah piped in. Her sister snorted and they all proceeded towards the famed tea shop. Evvie was beyond intrigued now. She would have to return to the archive. There was more she needed to know.

Evvie reached home while the sun was setting, as it did earlier in the evening every day. The snow had resumed, and was coming down in larger flakes. The sound—or rather lack of it—was mesmerizing. The city had been muffled into silence. Inside, Evvie was greeted by her husband, who was again wearing a banyan and box hat, in a state of comfort after spending the day at the counsel of lords. Evvie removed her coat and gloves, which were whisked away by a servant, and embraced him.

"You have a visitor," he told her.

Evvie's brows arched in curiosity as she followed him to the drawing room. There awaited the first white witch she had ever met, sitting patiently by the fire. The sight of her struck Evvie dumb, and she was overcome by a particularly strong rush of emotion.

"Mrs. Zsall!" she exclaimed. She rushed to greet Mrs. Zsall, so relieved to see the friendship mirrored by the young woman. She was a lovely sight, her pale skin flush and healthy, her beautiful white hair braided and wound about her head elegantly with a sheer cap placed upon it. She wore a woolen gown of blue that enhanced her beautiful eyes. "Oh I am so glad to see you!" Evvie exclaimed as they embraced with genuine affection. Evvie took the other woman's hands and squeezed them.

"And I, you!" Mrs. Zsall replied. "I have been looking forward to coming to Tirdonne since your visit. Before that, the idea of staying with my husband's family had only filled me with dread." Her laugh was infectious. "You look well, my Lady. And you are well married, your husband says."

"I am indeed. Blissfully so. You are here so much sooner than you had said."

"Yes, I managed to persuade my husband that the state of the roads would be too dangerous if I waited much longer. The winter has come, and when the snows come to Avradelle, the roads are impassable until Spring. And with the snows, comes less business through the tunnel, so my husband thought I was quite sensible to speak up, as he won't need me as much anyway."

"Well, good for you. And where are you staying?"

"At Kaynan Place. Although it is not as nice as the tunnel, they've given me a small apartment in the third house, as my husband does not have tremendous status in the family. There is only a girl to help me, but it will do."

"No it will not. Would your husband tolerate you coming to stay with me? I will see to it that your delicate state will be tended to with every convenience. And then you will not be alone. I will bring you your own nursemaid to assist you and then a midwife as needed."

"My husband cannot control anything from where he is," Mrs. Zsall laughed. "And if he knew how dismal the little room is, he would be very upset. But I have not written to him of it because I did not wish to distress him. I will tell him that the family has been kind and generous, but the offer of a Countess should not be turned down, do not you think?" Her eyes twinkled with mischief.

"I think that is a sensible way to present it," Evvie giggled.

"Your husband won't mind? You're only newly married."

"This is a big house, with many rooms and private apartments, my dearest Mrs. Zsall."

"Please, as I said before, you must call me Tarren," she insisted.

"Then you must call me Evvie. You can be my companion, and I yours. I will give you the west rooms as they are commodious and private, and they have an annexed set of rooms for a servant. Let us go to your family's square. I will speak to whomever I must to execute the invitation, and whisk you away with your trunks. I will tell my husband what has transpired. I'm so very excited that you are come, Tarren!"

Tarren smiled broadly and her cheeks flushed. Evvie rushed out to find her husband in his library. He was in no way averse to the plan. In fact, he was the opposite.

"It is good luck to have a woman with child about," he grinned. "Go on. Take one of my cards."

Evvie snatched one from the tray on the desk where he sat and gave him a kiss. It was intended to be but a peck, but it evolved into something infinitely more passionate, and Evvie had to pull away.

"You!" she accused him. He spanked her bottom as she drew away.

MIRANDA MAYER

Chapter 22

The Baronet of Kaynan was a stout little man with a big pot of a belly, and fluffy sideburns that stuck out from his face like goat whiskers. He was Brii, with few visible drest. He was, however, quite self-important, and the reception of the future Countess was a great to-do. When her coach arrived with its family herald upon it, both of the women could hear a terrible turmoil in the main house of the small, enclosed square called Kaynan Place. There was full panic as servants were shouted at, fires were stoked, and rooms tidied in a rush. A dog was frenetically barking to add to the chaos. Evvie and Tarren, with deliberate slowness, descended from the coach.

Kaynan Place was a quarter the size of Ilmeeri Square, and the houses were narrow and plain, a few nothing more than slim cottages. The north side of the clan village was dominated by the wall and taluses of the Brii conservatory. The shadow of it made the little square rather dark. The ladies, trying not to smirk at the sound of distress in the house, slowly climbed the stairs and rang the bell.

A harried looking housekeeper opened the door, and she bowed instead of curtsied. Evvie handed her Dareth's card. "If Sir Barrit is available for a call?"

The servant opened the door and ushered them into a small foyer where a chambermaid flitted through in a flurry of skirts carrying a yipping dog in one arm and dragging a protesting child with the other. Tarren emitted a little snort. Evvie elbowed her when the housekeeper bade them to follow her.

The housekeeper showed them into a room that had been hastily tidied. The servants had not managed to scoop up a large spill of beads under a chair and table by the window, and there was a child's shoe underneath Evvie's seat. The frantic looking woman invited them to wait a moment, that the Baronet would join them shortly.

"This will be your life, soon enough. Toys and shoes and beads, frantic tidying when unexpected visitors come," Evvie warned Tarren as the housekeeper scurried from the room.

"Do not think that this is not your lot, either, Mrs. Ilmeer. You are only newly married," Tarren replied smugly.

The door then opened with a thump as it hit the wall, and the Baronet and his Lady were there to greet them. Both ladies rose. Evvie offered him a polite curtsy, and Tarren did as well.

"Tarren, you did not say you were friends with the Ilmeeri Countess," the Baronet chided her. "Nor did you warn me of a visit!"

"I hadn't the chance to," she retorted. "It was spur-of-the-moment. My Uncle-in-law—the Baronet of Kaynan, Sir Barrit—and his wife, my Aunt-in-law, Lady Ayva. Uncle, Aunt, this is my friend Lady Evvienne of Ilmeer."

Evvie nodded graciously. "I am pleased to meet you, my Lord. My Lady."

He bowed again, and his Lady— a lovely, round-faced, rotund creature with sparkling hazel eyes—curtsied in respect. "I beg you sit, ma'am. I must apologize for the state of my home, as the children have been at play."

"Your home is perfectly pleasant, Sir," Evvie replied as she and Tarren took their seats. "I have come with a purpose."

"Oh? Do say," he asked. He plopped down in a chair. His wife remained on her feet. She merely moved behind him, clutching her hands.

"I am afraid I'm about to request permission to steal away your niece."

"Oh?"

"I met her at Diamond Rock, and we became instant friends. I am newly married and also a new arrival to Tirdonne. I have few acquaintances yet, and to see her familiar face brought me such comfort. So I have come in hopes of your allowing her to come and stay at Ilmeeri Square, and also at Alouaine Hall when we remove the household there. I would not keep her from your family of course, and she will visit and she may take visitors as frequently as she pleases."

"A woman that is with child requires special care, Madame. I feel obligated to guard you against this expense," he said.

Evvie found that the matter of money had come up much too quickly—and it was a clear way of saying that he would not provide her funding to live elsewhere. Evvie found that rather off-putting. Tarren turned beet red in embarrassment at his assertion.

"All of Mrs. Zsall's expenses for her stay would be my responsibility, sir. Including any special care she might require. Those things will be duly provided. If she receives an allowance from her husband or the family, I would hope she would not cease to receive it, as she should have the ability to purchase what she desires with it. However, anything additional that pertains to her lodging and her care, I have no objections to assuming the cost, as it is for my convenience she comes to live with me." Evvie was already aware of the small income Tarren's husband had provided for her to receive each month for her personal use. Tarren had told her of it. The family, Evvie assumed, would provide for her care, if she stayed. And they had not gone to great expense to make her comfortable for the duration of her pregnancy.

"I must apologize as this talk of funds must seem so crass," the Baron blurted, clearly aware just how cheap and ridiculous he had sounded. "We are not a rich clan. Of course Tarren will continue to receive her husband's allowances, and we are much grateful that you are willing to provide for her special care. As we were going to make use of qualified resources *within* the family to assist the young lady for her most special time—we would not have assumed any additional costs for her keep. But I would be remiss to deny her even better care when it is offered. Remiss indeed. Of course, she may go and stay at Ilmeeri Square. Of course!"

Tarren beamed.

"Excellent." Evvie declared. "Then we shall return to the square to help her settle in. I willsend a man for her trunks in a few hours. Oh, and I've brought you a snow turkey that arrived just this morning from Alouaine Hall as a gift to express my gratitude for your kindness in sharing Mrs. Zsall with me. He's twenty pounds! I will send the footman in with it."

There were oohs and ahhs at this declaration, and the girls took the opportunity to stand and exit, bidding kind farewells as they slipped out of the door. Tarren scurried to the third-house to quickly gather a few of her immediate belongings, and to see to the trunks being repacked. Evvie waited in the coach, huddled in her crag-rabbit coat, blowing out little clouds of steam to amuse herself. Tarren returned with a tapestry bag and plunked down on the seat across from Evvie.

"I cannot begin to express the vastness of my gratitude to you, Evvie."

"Do not worry about it. Come, let us go home." She knocked on the coach wall and it moved forward, exiting the archway into the lower city. "I think I ought to warn you, Tarren, there are other white witches like you in Tirdonne. I've only met one, but I've heard there is a guild of them."

"Oh?"

"Yes, and apparently, white witches have some sort of grudge against red witches."

"Truly?" Tarren's brows furrowed and she laughed merrily. "I suppose I ought to know this, but I'm not from Bask. Like you, the talk of witchery did not exist until I met my husband. Does that mean that I must bear such a dislike to you as well?"

"I imagine so, if the white witches had their way."

Tarren snorted. "Well that is just nonsense. Witchery is a silly superstition. It is mad that they still take such things seriously in these modern days."

"My feelings exactly," Evvie replied, putting the memories of the strange, inexplicable things she'd seen out of her mind.

"Lady Evvie, I will never bear a grudge against you for any reason. You have become my friend with no consideration of my place in society, the coarseness of my hands, my common accent, none of those things. You are kind and thoughtful, and you are welcoming me into your home like a member of your family. I would have borne this child with nobody I truly care about near me, living with a family that is cold to me, without half of the care I know I would have received if I'd stayed at Diamond Rock. My husband wouldn't hear of it, however. He does not trust the midwives of the tunnel with our child. He wants Bask midwives to see to me. Being here and knowing that I have a friend is of such comfort to me. It has made me much less apprehensive about what is to come. So, if any white witch dares to speak ill of you to me, I will condemn it."

"I'm so glad you're here, Tarren. I have felt… alone. I am used to my confidante, and I left her behind in Carath with her husband. My husband is my friend, but there is something that is missing that only a lady friend can fill. I feel so much better now that you are here."

Tarren reached out and squeezed Evvie's hand. "We are stronger together, are we not?"

Evvie nodded. They exchanged a meaningful look and leaned back.

"We should go shopping tomorrow," Evvie decided. "Let us find a milliner who specializes in gowns and stays for expectant ladies. Your little lump will grow fast! Faye's popped out from nothing in no time flat. Perhaps we should get a little gown or two for the baby once it comes."

Tarren's eyes were shining with delight. Evvie was so very pleased as well.

Evvie made sure Tarren was all settled in, and found a competent nursemaid to attend to her care during her confinement. She spent a comfortable night with the couple, keeping company with them in the parlor after devouring a healthy portion of dinner. The next morning, Evvie noted that Tarren looked a little peaked. Perhaps she might need some air.

"Would you like to accompany me to the archive this morning, Tarren?" It was a day that Edanbras would be there—she was eager to speak to him.

"If you do not mind, Miss Evvie, I would prefer to stay here in my room for a while. All the travel paired with the symptoms that accompany pregnancy, and I'm not feeling up to roaming about today. I think my body has found comfort this last evening and does not wish to relinquish it just yet.

"Should I fetch a doctor, Tarren?"

"No, that is not necessary. I have struggled with sickness each morning. I am quite accustomed to it. I will rest until the feeling passes."

"Very well. Do not hesitate to ring for assistance if you require it. I won't be gone too long, I hope." Tarren offered her a weak smile and Evvie bade her farewell. It was off to the archive for her.

Edanbras was as delighted to see her, as she expected he would be. She sailed in, the little slip of paper in her hand, and gave it to him. His brow arched in intrigue and he frowned with thought. "A thesis, eh? I will see what I can dredge up for you. In the meantime, I've taken the liberty of making a little list of books and shelf-sections that might interest you." He moved to a portion of the desk with drawers and drew one out. He returned with a sheet of paper with a variety of neatly written titles on it, along with the stack, shelf and book number written next to each one.

Evvie ran her finger down the list. "It is so thoughtful and kind of you to dedicate your time developing this reading list for me. Is there a chance I can borrow some of these? This list is almost daunting."

He leaned over the desk with a conspiratory air and whispered: "I will allow this for you and only you, but only one book at a time."

Evvie thanked him. "I might want to browse a shelf or two. This one seems interesting: Magic and Magical Heritage."

"That is stack 202. Second level." He grabbed two block spacers and gestured for her to follow as he moved quickly along the counter and came out from behind it. He led her to into the main library area and to a stairway up onto the next floor. He moved quickly and animatedly, like a squirrel. She had to almost jog to keep up with him. He led her to a large shelf, and then pointed in the direction of an arch with a corridor. "The second level study is through there. It is much smaller and most people prefer the one downstairs. Here are two blocks. If there is a book you'd like to take home, please bring it down to me before you leave."

"Of course, Mr. Edanbras," Evvie assured him.

He bowed to her and scurried off, leaving Evvie alone in a deserted portion of the library. Evvie saw a ladder about eight stacks down, and went to fetch it. The top five shelves were the ones he'd indicated on his list, so she rolled the ladder to where she needed it, and climbed up. She began pulling books out one by one, flipping open the covers to view titles. She drew one out that seemed vaguely interesting, so she placed it on the ladder rung and reached up to slide in the block when she spotted the edge of something familiar. It made her gasp loudly in shock. The book next to it was large, and it came out further on the shelf than the others. When she had removed the book of interest, she revealed the cover of the larger book. On it was the sigil of the Ravensroost family.

She could scarce believe what she was looking at. She put the block aside on the edge of the shelf, and reached up with both hands, pulling out the heavy tome. It was as long as her upper arm, from finger tip to elbow, and as wide as the same, ungainly to manage on the ladder. She replaced the book she'd drawn, and put both blocks into the spot she'd liberated.

Descending with care, she carried the book through the dark, narrow corridor to the second floor study. It was a small space indeed. Only six tables, three by two, and twelve booths along the wall. The hearth was large, and the room cozy. She plunked the book down and hastily removed her gloves and her coat.

Sliding into the chair, she lifted the cover. The title page read: Codexus Magia – Cynling ef Ravens Roost Deschetann Elevoth Burgsele – An 11; 14 Ct; 4th M. The book was more than six hundred years old! Two hundred years older than Ravensroost house itself. How was that possible? She could not accept as true what was before her eyes.

She carefully turned the page and was met with a beautifully illuminated illustration of a circle made of a serpent which was consuming the tail of a wyvern which was also swallowing the snake's tail. Inside was the symbol of the raven that was unquestionably the same as her family's crest. She leafed through the pages. There were many paragraphs describing what looked like spells, but not in the traditional form that Arah and Nerah applied. There were illustrations and drawings, and a few instances of familiar words, like the ever-mysterious Prósopo. The spells were signed by their authors, and the names changed as she turned the pages: one daughter of Ravensroost to the next. Each successor adding her insight for the next generation. The end of the book had a finger-width of thickness remaining of blank pages, and there was a delightful surprise for Evvie when she looked at the last author. Her name was Evvienne.

Evvie rose and put her coat and gloves back on, folding Edanbras' list and tucking it into her reticule before picking up the tome. She toted it down the stairs and to the counter, where Edanbras was standing at the desk, writing on a paper, with a thin little book next to him. He looked surprised to see her there. "What have you got? I found your thesis," he added.

"This book, it belongs to my family," she replied with a look of incredulity, her eyes misted with tears. "How could this be?" She let it fall onto his counter with a thump. His brows shot up in astonishment and he dropped the quill into its pot and rushed over to see for himself.

"This is a private grimoire, indeed," he murmured, opening it and studying the pages. "It is unusual for the library to have private texts. You found this on the heritage shelf?"

She nodded.

"And you're sure it is your family?"

Evvie nodded again. She opened her coat and displayed the chatelaine she wore at her waist which bore the family crest. "If you have a recent copy of the Peerage & Landed Gentry listings for Carath, you will find us there," she replied.

He indicated she wait a moment, and went to his reference book and then the card cabinet. He then climbed up, and opened two drawers, a card from each. He dashed down one of the stacks behind him, and returned only moments later carrying exactly the book she had mentioned. He leafed through it until he reached Ravensroost family's page. He studied it, starting when he recognized her name in it. He then put one card back, and—to her astonishment—he exited from behind the counter, and stood before the fireplace, where he tore up the paper and threw it into the flames. He approached her with a mischievous grin.

"That is an interesting book you've brought me, Mrs. Ilmeer. An interesting book indeed. Thank you for sharing it," he said aloud. There was nobody else about, but she imagined it was for her benefit more than anything. He then stopped before her and clasped his hands together. "A grimoire belongs with the bloodline that created it," he whispered gravely. He picked up the heavy book and put it in her arms. He also reached for the thin little book he'd found for her, and placed it on top. "That one you can return when you are finished with it."

Evvie bent forward and placed a kiss on his cheek. "That is one of the kindest things anyone's ever done for me," she told him. "Thank you Mr. Edanbras."

The man's face flushed like a young buck, and he grinned broadly, bowing deeply. She made her way out to her coach beaming with happiness. Moments like these made her negative experiences seem so banal. She climbed into the conveyance with her books, scarcely able to contain her exhilaration and eager to show it to the aunties.

MIRANDA MAYER

Chapter 23

"You found it here? In our archive?" Arah repeated for the fourth time.

"Yes," Evvie exclaimed impatiently. "The archivist let me take it. He said it belonged with its bloodline."

"Indeed it does!" Nerah exclaimed. "What a treasure to be found!"

The sisters struggled against each others' elbows to get a proper viewing of the book. Evvie looked them amicably and opened it for them. They both gasped at the beauty of the illuminated drawing.

"Oh look, the old language," Arah sighed as they lay the cover open and gingerly leafed through the book.

"The symbol for the thrall, look! We shall have to find a language scholar to decipher it," Nerah suggested.

Dareth was nowhere to be found, and poor Tarren was still feeling unwell, but the minute she arrive home, she'd sent a message across the square to the aunties. They had come bustling over immediately, dressed in their finery for an afternoon of visitation with families in the square. They had dropped everything the moment they'd received her note. They huddled together, Arah in her pale green and pink striped day gown, dripping with lace on her tucker, ruff, cap and ruffled cuffs. Nerah was a little less showy in an orangey-red gown with a white collared chemisette beneath it, and a plain cap with sheer lappets dangling onto the back of her shoulders. They both had enormous wool shawls draped across the high backs of their long-sleeved, heavy winter gowns.

"Ah, this is more legible," Nerah said, lifting a good portion of the pages and folding them over.

"Annum Eighteen, Sixteenth Century. That is when the entries stop. With a witch by the name of Evvienne!" Arah declared. There were more clucks and warbles, and the sisters leafed back a few pages to where Evvienne's few entries began, a good sixty years after the previous entries.

"The paper is so unusual," Arah mumbled.

"It is shex. Skin of a chimera's wing," Nerah murmured, touching it gently.

"The look and feel of the ink is fascinating," Evvie said, running her finger along the relief of the text. "I've never seen an ink so black."

"It is bellen ink. Made with wyvern's blood and soot from fire of willow and rowan—witchwood as it is sometimes called. Only true magical codices use this ink. You will need a pot of such ink for when you apply your own magic to these pages."

Evvie's eyes widened. "I am fairly sure I am not…"

"You cast a Prósopo. Whether you were aware of doing it or not is irrelevant. You are a red witch, one of a *true* line. This book came into your hands for a reason. It appeared where it did because it was needed. It sought you out because it was lost to your line." Nerah explained.

"Nonsense!" Evvie snapped.

"Oh, no such thing, my dear. And we're going to prove it to you! Nerah, you should go and fetch the basket."

"*You* fetch it, I'm not your servant," Nerah said querulously.

"Very well!" Arah huddled into her shawl and bustled out, grumbling under her breath.

Nerah gave Evvie an embattled eye roll and continued to pore over the book while they waited. Evvie wandered to the window to watch as Arah nimbly negotiated the slippery walkways of the snowy square. She disappeared inside the sisters' house. There was a good long moment where the only sound was the pages leafing. After a period of quiet, Nerah spoke. "Evvie, dear, come and look at this."

Evvie turned to find Nerah looking at her expectantly. "What is it?"

"This entry here." Nerah tapped the page. "By your ancestress Evvienne. She wrote something interesting."

Evvie slid to her new aunt, and peered at the page Nerah indicated. Nerah began to read aloud.

"The Prósopopei hast been defeat'd by wrested spell. Many did act as one, the white hexxen has't purloin'd its pow'r and did bid it in wrath upon the r'd hex. Arianne DeNoth and Enoille Vayne liveth nay m're, kill'd by handeth of spell—Vayne and DeNoth lines art anon gone f'rev'r.

"We w're compel'd to act to shield the lines, and did cast as one the ancient Masque. Talismans art enshielf, the lines art to beest concealed, and silence shall falleth upon the r'd hexxen—f'r at which hour the pow'rs deem t safe f'r the r'd hex to returneth.

"To the lady yond this codex of r'd charms and magic taketh, it cometh to thee f'r it wast wanting to beest found. Hark to it at which hour it speaks. Fare thine well. Evvienne of the raven's roost."

Nerah read it again, this time with modern words. "The Prósopo has been defeated by stolen spell. The white witches, acting as one, purloined its power and bade it to beset its wrath upon the red witch. Arianne DeNoth and Enoille Vayne live no more, killed by a spell. Now their lines are gone forever. We were compelled to act to protect the lines, and we cast in unison, the ancient Masque. Talismans are hidden, the lines are to be concealed and silence shall fall upon the red witches until the hour the powers deem it safe for the red witch to return. To the lady who receives this magical codex, it comes to you for it wanted to be found. Listen at the hour at which it speaks. Farewell, Evvienne of Ravensroost."

"I do not understand. The white witches acted against the red witches by using their Prósopos against them?" Evvie asked. "That is a bit different than what the grey witch described. She said it was a spell that protected the white witches from the proxies."

"Yes. That seems it was not what the grey lady thought. I am curious about this Masque spell that is mentioned. I've never heard of it."

It was then that Arah returned. In her arms was the sisters' box of magical paraphernalia. She looked exceedingly grumpy as she plopped them gracelessly down on the main table. "Could I trouble you, my dear, for some hot tea please?"

Evvie realized she was a terrible hostess. She apologized, and rang for tea. At that moment, there was a soft knock on the door, and Tarren came in.

"Oh, sweet dear, are you feeling unwell still?" Evvie asked.

Tarren smiled. The aunts stared at this girl with unveiled expressions of horror. "I am better. The queasiness has passed. What transpires in here, if I might ask?"

"Tarren, these are my aunts. Aunt Arah and Aunt Nerah. Aunts, this is Mrs. Zsall, but I'm sure she won't mind if you call her Tarren, won't you?"

Tarren shook her head good-naturedly.

"Evvie, what in the name of the powers is a white witch doing in this house?" Arah blurted impolitely, her face a mask of incredulous shock. The servant arrived at that moment, and Evvie had to quietly request a full tea before she could reply.

Tarren seemed unperturbed by the question, and replied. "I am no witch," she responded with a dismissive wave of the hand. "I grew up in the south. My husband and his family seem to think I am a witch as well. I'm sorry, but we southerners do not often give credit to the same superstitions as those in the north."

"Superstitions indeed!" Arah exclaimed, looking quite offended.

"Aunt Arah, you know that was my perception as well when I first arrived. I thought it all a joke. I still have a seed of doubt, I will not lie," Evvie admitted.

The aunts both nodded in concession to this and then mulled for a moment. "Well, what are we to do with a white witch in our midst now?" Arah sighed.

"Now you mention it, this young lady could be an unexpected advantage," Nerah suggested. "If she is open, of course, to exploring the white witch inside her."

Evvie looked at Tarren, who seemed quite amused and intrigued by this. She shrugged. "What are you planning?" She looked with curiosity at the wooden box on the table.

"Well, you will have to wait and see," Nerah replied teasingly.

Evvie laughed. Nerah opened the box, and dug through it for the grimoire, removing it from the container and putting it on the table. Just as she did, two chamber maids arrived carrying the tea for the ladies. They were furnished with cups and little plates for the two tiers of petite sandwiches, tiny cakes and other treats. The ladies partook of this, quietly seated in four chairs, two on each side of the work table.

"What do *you* suppose Mrs. Zsall will contribute to all this?" Arah asked Nerah, almost sneeringly.

Nerah licked her fingers of the icing from a little cake, and then dabbed her mouth with her napkin. "I am not surprised you do not remember the lesson, you spent so much time arguing with Lady Stone and stubbornly doing things your way to spite her. She did have useful things to teach." She sipped from her tea, gazing accusingly over her teacup at her sister.

"I know she did. I am a successful witch. I can cast spells with the best of them. I learned quite a bit in spite of having a middling mentor, at best," Arah retorted smugly, eating a cake in one bite.

"Nonsense," Nerah grumbled. "Lady Stone was a brilliant witch. And she had a depth of knowledge few witches possess today. Knowledge of old spells and witchly history that are now likely lost to time. You never appreciated the gift that mother offered us by arranging for our witchly education with Lady Stone."

"Oh, poppycock," Arah snapped.

"Well, if you had taken in the treasures she offered you would remember things like the Lifweard Arcana, or the Alliance of the Seasons." Nerah gave her sister and arch look.

"Oh…!" Arah exclaimed, her eyes widening. "Would we require a grey and a green too?"

"No. The incantation can work with as few as two kinds of witch. But the more there are, the stronger the magic," Nerah said.

"I'm sorry, but please, do explain all this. We're on the edges of our seats," Evvie told the older ladies, who were absorbed in their conversation.

Nerah poured a fresh round of tea, and then passed the sugar pot. "The Alliance of the Seasons is an old spell. It combines the magic of different kinds of witches in order to give more power to other spells. So, let us say, we wanted to conjure an illusion. We would perform the Alliance incantation with the presence of two or more kinds of witch, and whatever number will make the illusion more powerful and successful. The second spell—the illusion spell itself—is then cast and it is infused with the power cast from the Alliance spell."

"Doesn't one have to be a witch in order for it to work? Neither I, nor my kind friend, Evvie, have ever done anything of the like," Tarren said. "Neither of us ever even knew we would be thought to be witches at all, until we met our husbands."

"Oh, the first thing we're going to do is to cast an unbinding. This may or may not wake your latent abilities. I suspect Evvie's abilities are already there, she needs only to understand how to connect with them. But it will surely benefit you, Mrs. Zsall." Nerah said decisively.

"You mean one spell, and I could be a true witch?" Tarren's eyes shone with excitement.

"Yes. You will still have to study spells for your colorcaste, to learn more about it. But you will recognize your powers. But if we do this, you would have to promise never to become an enemy to Evvie," Nerah insisted.

"There is nothing in this world that would make Evvie my enemy, not even the idea of becoming part of a large sisterhood of magical women," Tarren insisted.

"So you already told her?" Arah asked.

"She is my friend. Of course I did," Evvie replied.

"Are you game, my dear ma'am?" Arah asked Tarren.

Tarren took a long, measured drink of her tea and put her saucer and cup down. She picked up a sandwich and nibbled on it. With a nod, she said, "I'm ready. It will do nothing to harm the child?" Her hand fell to the presently small swell of her belly.

"Oh, no. Little baby will be quite all right," Nerah assured her. Evvie took a last bite of food and washed it down with tea. "I think we should all refresh ourselves, and then the aunties will make whatever preparations are necessary."

Arah drew the curtains of the tall library windows while Nerah spread the silk across the table. "First we shall do the unbinding. Then, we will try the Alliance. We will guide you through it. Then, we will cast a Tell on the grimoire together, my sister and I will lead the spell, and we shall see what it has to say." Nerah said while she set up the candelabra and lit the candles.

Evvie and Tarren looked on in fascination, taking the two seats across from the sisters.

Nerah peered at Evvie and then Tarren. "Now. Let us scare up those dormant powers of yours, shall we?"

"I do not feel the slightest bit different," Tarren murmured, looking at Evvie who shrugged. Arah smiled and Nerah chuckled. The younger women watched with interest as the sisters fussed about their paraphernalia.

"Will I need these things too?" Tarren pointed to the spray of charms and the now extinguished fire in the tiny brazier they'd set before them.

"Every witch chooses her own tools. Red witches do not need them, but some were known to have their own kit, of sorts," Arah explained. "My sister and I have chosen very similar tools, or perhaps I should say; the tools that have chosen us are similar. I began with the cards, as they are the most common tool for black witches. I do not know what is common for white witches. You might want to go to the Diviner's Rest to see what speaks to you."

"The Diviner's Rest?" Tarren asked.

"One of only three remaining witchery shops in Tirdonne. The best one, really," Nerah added. "The other two are worth a visit. One is run by a black witch, and she serves mostly black witches, so her shop might lack what you need. It's where we go most often, as she has a great selection of items just suited to our needs as witches. The shop is called the Red Candle. The other one is in Highside, which is on the north face of Tirdonne, right on Annet road. It's a large shop, run by a pair of grey witches. It's called The Silver Coin. As it's on the main road in and out of Tirdonne, it is always busy, and the prices are higher than the other shops. People who shop there shop mostly for the experience of it, not because they are witches. Much of their wares are useless trinkets and souvenirs for travelers."

Nerah picked up the grimoire and stood. She barked, "Show!" and dropped it on its spine. It flopped onto its side and did not open. They gazed at it in puzzlement.

"Well that is something, is it not?" Arah murmured. She picked up the book again, repeated the word, and dropped it on its spine again. It merely hit the table, and then fell again onto its side.

Nerah looked bewildered. She frowned and got up, moving to the box, where she riffled down into the bottom, and withdrew a smaller book. Sitting down again, she opened the book and leafed through the pages frenetically, stopping a few times before finally finding what she was seeking. "An Alliance cannot be cast with a written spell," Nerah declared.

"Well... how then?" Arah looked at her book and her brow furrowed.

"I wrote in my notes: 'Light in the circle, hands all 'round. Let the highest witch expound.' *You* would have to tell us, Evvie," Nerah explained.

"I wouldn't even know where to begin."

"Well, let us just trust the powers, and give it a try. See what happens?" Arah suggested.

Evvie and Tarren exchanged another look between them and they shrugged in concession. The older women cleared the table of most of the items, leaving only the silk runner and the candelabra. She lifted Evvie's heavy grimoire and put it on the table between them.

"Well then. Give me your hand," Arah demanded of Tarren, who sat next to her. Tarren slid her left hand across the table, and grasped Arah's right. Arah took her sister's hand with her left, and Evvie reached out and clasped Nerah's plump, wrinkled fingers. And then Tarren reached for Evvie's hand.

The effect was immediate. Fists tightened on hands, and everyone stiffened as a powerful rush of energy surged through them. Evvie's body became rigid as a board and she threw her head back, her eyes going full white. A ripple of power exploded from her body and shivered the room and its contents. A swarm of whispers buzzed around them and filled the air with voices. Evvie knew, at once, that these were the voices of her predecessors. It was a knowledge from within herself, something deep and ingrained.

Her voice joined them, her mouth moving, whispers of long-forgotten words escaping her lips. "*Andetta bóc sylfum forgenga,*" she murmured. "*Andetta!*"

The Grimoire shuddered, and Tarren began to speak. "The Brii bred red, a thousand thousand years. They are the precious of the Powers; and whitecaste bore such covetousness. Such envy. Triumphing over the will of the Powers, offending the very energies that sustained them, they acted as one. The white witches found a terrible weakness. They sent the precious ones into hiding using their own defense against them.

The white witches aimed to destroy all redcaste but those that would not threaten them, for their powers would die with the last of the redcaste. They began by corrupting the Brii tradition. They intervened with the Red Brii lines, and they *became* the Brii bred. But some lines survived—the red witches chose anew by the guidance of their energies. They chose to begin the lines afresh. By a new path gifted to them by the Powers, blessed Baskreth hexxenmaeg. Warriors. To become warriors. They are no longer Brii. They are Baskreth lines now, Powers-blessed, witches and fighters, witchly warriors. Sent into hiding, into sleep. Moving south to where the whitecaste and the Brii rarely dwell. They sleep. They sleep. They await the awakening. When the bellen touches my page by will alone; no hand to write, the awakening will begin."

A burst of sharp growing warmth passed through their circle, and where their skin came into contact with that of their counterpart. A searing heat rented their connection apart. The four of them hissed through their teeth and reclaimed their hands, shaking them to cool them off. There was a moment of contemplative silence as they rubbed their hands cool and looked at one another in wonder.

It was then that Tarren smirked and laughed. "That was madness, and the most exhilarating experience of my life! I want to do it again!"

The four of them began to laugh at Tarren's gleeful grin and contagious giggling.

MIRANDA MAYER

Chapter 24

The little allied coven was all a' chortle. They packed up the box and moved to the upstairs parlor where the comfortable chairs were. A fresh pot of tea was ordered, and the topic of discussion was Evvie's history and Tarren's overt shame over the acts of her white witch sisters. But it was her enthusiasm that entertained the others the most. "I shall have to write to my husband to tell him that I am indeed a witch! He shall be so pleased!"

"Your husband is Baskreth, I understand?" Arah asked.

"Yes, he is. This child is Baskreth-born." Tarren placed her hand on her stomach. "I wonder what that means. If it is a girl, will she not be a witch? What I said when the book spoke, it sounded like the Baskreth lines are new and blessed."

"We cannot know. But I suppose we could convene again, and see what your little one has to say," Nerah said, leaning forward to put her hand on Tarren's little bulge of a tummy.

Tarren's eyes brightened. "I must go to the Diviner's Rest. We must *all* go."

"Oh, you can go on your own. Last time I went it cost me a lot of money," Nerah grumbled. Arah laughed.

Evvie was contemplative and quiet. She took in Tarren's happiness with hushed amusement, but her mind was on the words her Grimoire had spoken and how she had felt when she had grasped the hands of her fellow witches. There was a depth of emotion she was unaccustomed to. Something that had been buried inside her was emerging. A powerful sense of things falling into place—of understanding truly who she was. The only other occasion she felt something similar was when she met Dareth.

The aunties finished the pot of tea, collected their box and went home. Evvie and Tarren immediately noticed the heavy, sudden quiet after they departed. Tarren looked at Evvie. "What folly!"

"Indeed."

"Shall we go to the Diviner's Rest tomorrow? After I have overcome the morning illness, of course."

"Yes, we should. I think we both have questions that perhaps the grey witch can answer," Evvie agreed.

"Excellent! I think I should go and write my husband before the relay is suspended. It is snowing again." Tarren stood and gave Evvie a thoughtful look before sailing out of the room.

Evvie stood and moved to look out the window. Outside, the square looked as if it was curtained in layers of dotted muslin. Great big flakes of snow blowing in whorls slowly made their way down to the cobbles where the morning's tramplings and smudgings had been erased by a fresh layer of pure white snow.

Evvie loved snow. It happened so rarely in Carath. As she watched, she saw Dareth walking through the veils of snowfall, his greatcoat swishing in the wind, his boots forging a path through the white layer. The broad brim of his hat hid his face from her. As if he sensed her, he looked up. He smiled at her and waved.

How she loved him.

She waited for him to enter the upstairs parlor, and greeted him with a loving embrace when he arrived. Stripped of his outer garments, his face was ruddy from the cold. "My love," he said in his deep voice. "How are you faring this day?"

"Like a red witch!" she declared. "I made magic today."

"No!" he blurted with a large grin. He kissed her.

"Yes indeed. This is marked up as one of the strangest days of my life," she laughed.

"Well, I'm going to add to the oddity, because I've been slated to battle for the title today. It is scheduled for tomorrow evening."

"Oh dear," she murmured, her elation melting into trepidation.

"My sweet, you needn't fear. I will be overseen by a full red witch. That alone brings immense fortune to me."

She looked quite unconvinced. "Must I watch?"

"I'm afraid you must," he sighed.

Evvie pursed her lips and took his hand. "Then you must comfort me now, to prepare me for tomorrow."

He grinned, and let her lead him away to their apartments.

The snow was still falling when morning came, and Tarren and Evvie set out against the blowing wind and flying ice to the witchery shop. They bustled through the door, relieved by the warmth that embraced them. The bell rang cheerfully. The shopkeeper curtsied deeply to Evvie, and then looked surprised to see her present with a white-haired beauty.

"Good day, ladies!"

"Good day!" Tarren exclaimed excitedly, her eyes taking in the shop. "The Lady's aunts said I should come here to start my kit. We've been newly minted, so to speak."

The grey witch nodded knowingly. "White witches do not require as... as ample a kit as the black witch, nor do they use many of the same tools. I will present you with what white witches commonly use, and see if there are any that speak to you."

Tarren assented with a nod, her eyes sparkling with pleasure.

"I will need some bellen ink," Evvie added.

The grey witch indicated they should sit at her table. This day, there were six jars lined up along the center line of the table. A set of beautiful silver measuring spoons and an old scale and weights were set up on her work area, along with a turned wood funnel, and a tidy row of tiny glass jars awaiting filling. The scent of herbs emanated from them.

The shopkeeper moved to a drawer which was segmented into little boxes. In each box were ink bottles in a variety of colors. She pulled out one with midnight black ink inside, and closed the drawer. She placed it in front of Evvie. She then went to another drawer, and sifted through an organized heap of quills, drawing out a single plume as long as her forearm and as black as night, brushed with a luminescent blue. She put it before Evvie.

"If you use bellen ink, you should always use a great-raven's feather quill," the gray witch explained.

Evvie was astonished by the size of it. The maker had trimmed the vane to a neat point, and cut a sharp, artful nib. Evvie had no idea there were ravens that large. She took off her gloves and picked it up, examining it with awe.

While Evvie did this, the shopkeeper gathered items for Tarren. She pulled out a blindfold with embroidered figures upon it, and drew it over Tarren's eyes. Evvie watched with interest.

There were indeed different tools on offer for a white witch. First, the shopkeeper produced a flat box filled with rows of what looked like tuning forks of various metals. She put it before Tarren and said nothing. Tarren sat impassively for a moment, and then on what seemed like impulse, her hand rose up and snatched with uncanny precision, a silver fork from the box. Evvie's lips parted in surprise.

Then, the shopkeeper put a stack of small metal bowls on the table and laid them out in a line before Tarren, who chose a dark, silvery metal one. The gray witch then brought a stack of book-sized wooden boxes and put the tower before Tarren. Tarren, without seeing, put her finger on the fourth one from the bottom. The grey lady pulled it out and placed it before Tarren. She put each of the remaining items away, and finally brought Tarren a long box where rolls of fabric were lined up in a tidy row. Tarren blindly chose a silken one of slate grey with gold lettering embroidered into it. When she was finished, the blindfold was removed and Tarren gazed in wonder at her chosen acquisitions. She opened the box she'd chosen, and inside were little cubbies with three rows of five little jars, each filled and labeled with different elemental powders.

"You should also choose a blank book for your codex," The shopkeeper pointed to a shelf with a variety of empty books that were awaiting new owners. Tarren rose and moved to the shelf. She quietly browsed through them, pulling one out, rejecting it and running her finger along the others.

As the shopkeeper reached for Evvie's purchases to wrap them, her fingers brushed Evvie's. She drew back and a curious little smirk curled on her lips. Evvie's brows rose in curiosity.

"Is everything well?"

"Better than well, my Lady," the shopkeeper replied. She strode to a cabinet and pulled out a drawer. She picked up a small item, and carried it to Evvie, placing it in her hand and folding her fingers around it. "Blessings," she whispered.

Evvie opened her hand and saw a small charm of silver. A little fish tickled her palm. She peered down it in curiosity.

"The fish represents the life-giving waters," the gray witch said. "A little token of good fortune for you and your precious one," she whispered.

It took a moment for the words to sink in. Evvie went pale. "I... I d... I'm... I do not..."

"Oh! Goodness, I thought you knew!"

Tarren was just returning to the table carrying a deep blue leather tome, her eyes wide with curiosity. "Are you unwell, Lady Evvie?"

"Apparently better than well. I am with child, if this is what I understand from this fine lady."

"You are indeed with child. We grays are the wardens of fertility and birth waters. It is very early. But she is a strong little spirit in there. I could feel her beaming her existence at me as soon as our skin touched."

Tarren made a little squealing noise of delight and flopped into her chair, putting the book onto the stack of items she had chosen. She reached out and grasped Evvie's hand. "We shall be mothers together," she whispered with happiness.

Evvie's eyes swelled with tears. A blink, and the droplets fell onto her pale cheek. "I'm to be a mother!" *So soon,* she thought. There is life inside me! The idea was almost too great to bear. Would she be a good mother? Her mother was gone so early, she had not had the chance to learn how to be a good mother from her. Or from anyone. Her hand slid down to her belly, where the folds of her walking gown rumpled. She opened her palm again, where the little fish glinted at her. She could almost see mischief in its little silver eye.

Evvie arrived at home a bundle of nerves. She helped Tarren carry her new tools to her room.

"I shall need a basket like your aunties'," Tarren declared. "Being a red witch is certainly a less expensive endeavor than being a white one."

They set the things down on a sideboard in Tarren's room, and Evvie sighed. "I wonder when my confinement will begin," she speculated airily. "Or if I will be as ill as you are each morning."

"It doesn't last for too long, so do not fret dear Lady," Tarren assured her. She looked at her bowl and her tuning fork and all the other items she'd bought, and giggled. "I haven't the slightest idea how to use any of these things."

"If my aunties are correct, it will come to you as naturally as picking them did."

Tarren groaned. "My ankles are so swollen; they're tight in my boots."

Evvie helped her unlace them and remove them, shocked at the state of her ankles; which were puffy and squashy to the touch. "Poor thing," she muttered. "I willsee if the nursemaid can make some compresses for you. I'm sorry I made you go out today." She helped Tarren out of her walking dress, and into something more comfortable, finding her a pair of slippers. She then made Tarren sit by the fire, and called for the nursemaid to give her a healing tea and see to her swelling.

Evvie then went to prepare for the evening's events, unsure what would be appropriate to wear for such a thing. She thought perhaps it would be best to dress well, as if perhaps for a ball or a dinner, since there would likely be peers there. She sighed, unsure if she wanted to tell Dareth about this day's discovery yet. She did not wish to burden him when he was faced with a looming battle.

Chapter 25

Evvie wasn't sure what to expect when she, accompanied by her husband, arrived at a hall high up on the top of the Tirdonne peak, inside the heart of the palace. She was glad she'd chosen her finest gown of claret silk and her favorite elegant long gloves the color of mustard. She'd adorned herself in sparkling jewelry, and a diadem with gold foundations and ruby stones. Over that she wore her black wool cloak with black fur around her face on the stylish, draping hood, and a small muff to keep her hands warm on this wintry night. Dareth gazed at her with tremendous affection and admiration, and looked proud to have her at his side.

Dareth was in traditional Baskreth garb again. His skirted leggings were pressed to perfection and the white tunic had nary a crease on it. The wide belt of leather sitting low on his hips shone from polish, and hanging from a thinner, secondary belt over it was a hand-and-a-half sword in a matching scabbard. He wore a cloak rather than a greatcoat this time 'round.

They crossed from the high bailey into the hall. Their cloaks were quickly removed and whisked away. They joined a stream of people—glittering ladies and gentlemen in formal clothing, both traditional and modern— all flowing through the archway into the great hall. There, long banquet tables had been arranged around the perimeter with seats only on the back side so that the diners would be facing the center of the room. The tables were swathed in white linen and strewn with mounds of wintry juniper and holly with candlesticks bristling from them, all glowing with warm light. The tabletops also glittered in cut glass stemware, and shone with polished silverware and plates of the finest china.

What seemed like a brigade of footmen sorted people as they were announced and allowed to venture forth from the archway, ushering them to their assigned seats. At the top of the hall was a raised portion of the floor, and the tables sat higher than those along the side walls and the ones flanking the entryway. There, two tall chairs indicated that the King and Queen would be present, and their court would be seated on each side of them. As an aspiring Count, and a son of a Count, Dareth and Evvie were led to the middle of the King's side of the elevated tables. They were seated between a portly old Duke and the Prince who was Dareth's friend. Everyone rose and bowed courteously when they arrived. Dareth helped Evvie to sit, and left her in the care of the Prince, making his way out a small door off the side of the room.

"I understand the Marquess' lady has been unkind and disrespectful towards you," the Prince ventured, leaning over Dareth's seat to ask Evvie.

She blanched a little. Dareth had apparently confided this to his friend. "It is nothing I cannot tolerate and contend with on my own, your Grace," she said dismissively.

"I have no doubt of that, dearest Lady. I am, however, concerned that I might surround myself with people who do not respect the order of things. Such untoward behavior shall not be welcomed into my circle, and for that I will exclude them from further invitation."

"Only if you do it not for my sake, but for yours."

"Indeed. I would hope that you and Dareth would be forthcoming if such a thing occurred with any of our friends. I desire you both to feel welcome. As your husband becomes a Count, he—and in part, you—will be expected to take part in all the same obligations of the rank. That means spending a goodly time with the likes of me. I would wish to ensure that anyone in our circle is happy to be there, and not overcome by unnecessary unkindness and prejudice from lower people."

"Of course," Evvie said.

He looked at her, his dark eyes giving away nothing. "You look remarkably lovely this evening. You do your husband credit. I can only hope that someday I will find a wife as fine as you."

"I thank you." She flushed. As they spoke the crowd was distributed to their seats and was settling in. Stewards threaded behind the table, filling the wine glasses and furnishing the attendants with goblets of chilled water. As Evvie scanned the room, she saw Mr. Ryse-Mevvick seated down the left side of the room, almost midway. He was brazenly staring at her.

There was the sound of approaching drums, which drew her eyes away from this strange, obsessed man. Through the now cleared archway came two drummers. Behind them marched the King, and after him four ranks of fighters, two by two. To Evvie's surprise, one of them was a woman dressed—as they all were—in formal skirt-leggings and tunic, sword and belts. She had cropped hair and many drest, like her male counterparts. Evvie could not help but feel a tickle in her stomach for seeing it. There was something about the inspiration she felt witnessing this that was different and empowering. She could not stop staring at the woman. Dareth was before the woman, and he bowed his head to Evvie in assurance when she finally tore her eyes from the warrior lady and looked at him.

The drummers ended their parade with a final spate of rhythms, and then turned and marched back out. The King raised his arms and called out in welcome. "It is the honor of the King of Bask to host all titular battles for the noblemen of our nation. There are four contests tonight. For the Counthood, the born heir, Dareth of Ilmeer. For the Rise, Errek of Teth…" As he named off the remaining fighters from around the realm, Evvie studied the man.

The monarch was a towering, battle-scarred monster of a man. Taller than Dareth, his skin was riddled in tattooed drest which covered the back of his bald head and his neck. He was an overthrower, which meant he had defeated the previous king—who was from a line of kings—and taken the title for his family's name for the first time. He had been the youngest contender for the throne ever to fight and win in known history. He'd been King for thirty odd years and had taken down many a challenger, and still held his own. Evvie could see why.

He was a powerful man. Even edging into sixty. As he made his declarations, his gaze would fall onto Evvie. His expression was one of interest. And when his introduction was over, he threw up his arms again.

"Let the battles begin! Ilmeer and Teth to fight!"

The other fighters moved to the doorway to wait, standing in a neat line. The King threaded his way between the dais and the tables where he took the arm of the Queen and led her to their place at the center of the table.

He stood in front of the table and lifted his full glass, toasting Dareth and Errek Teth. "Fight honorably, gentlemen!" He then sat and the audience applauded. They fell into comfortable chatter as they sipped their drinks and awaited the fight. Evvie could not move. Her husband and his opponent were sizing the other up in the center of the room. They lifted their swords to their noses in salute and then bowed to one another formally.

The audience seemed quite unperturbed by all this, and to Evvie's astonishment, the servants appeared bringing the food. She was served, but she did not eat. She watched as her husband and Errek engaged in a sword battle. It was not the gentlemanly parrying of foils, as she was accustomed to. This was a forceful, violent act of savagery. Dareth's sword swung into a perfect arc and landed with a strange *tink* into the edge of his opponent's blade, which hung protectively over Erreck Teth's head. Evvie's balled her fists and watched in horror as Mr. Teth retaliated by flying at Dareth with a volley of swings which Dareth escaped with artful deflections.

Dareth moved, in Evvie's view, like a huge bear. Not with a lurching air, but one of practiced brutality. His expression would be terrifying if she did not know him to be a good, kind and gentle man. In the fight, he was anything but those things. His teeth clenched in a fearful grimace as he attacked Teth with ferocity and the unveiled intent to maim and kill. It occurred to Evvie that these battles might be to the death. Why would the audience be so easily engaged in casual discourse, drinking and eating if there was the possibility of someone dying before them? The thought alarmed her.

Apprehension turned her stomach as the men battled. Errek Teth was a smaller, bandier looking man than Dareth. He was at a disadvantage from the start. Dareth was a visibly practiced fighter. He seemed fully focused on his battle, almost fluid and assured in his movements. On the converse, Mr. Teth looked to be over-exerting himself, put off by unexpected attacks. Dareth deflected a volley from his opponent with easy grace, and then as if tired of the effort, went after him in earnest. Dareth swung his sword in wide arcs first, lunging forward with each strike, sending Teth into a retreat with corresponding blocks until he was against a table on the left side of the hall. Dareth nicked Teth's chin with the tip of his sword, and there was a gasp that rippled around the room.

"First blood, to Ilmeer. A toast!" the King bellowed, raising his glass.

Arms rose with glasses in the air. Everyone drank and then they clapped. Evvie thought it would be over, as first blood usually was in such duels in Carath. But to her surprise, the swords clashed again. This time the men flew across to the other side of the room, their blades shining, catching the light of the myriad candles all around them.

As if Teth realized he was now fighting for his survival, the battle became even more violent and desperate. He swung fiercely at Dareth, who sidestepped and danced around him, waiting for him to tire. They jabbed and sliced, kicked one another away, and—on several occasions—came to a position where each had their sword tips pressed into the other, forcing them to stop and pace into a circle before positioning themselves for another bout. It seemed like it would go on forever, or until they gave up in exhaustion.

Teth's mistake was allowing Dareth to get behind him. Dareth taunted him into a close parry, and then while Teth swung to avoid a blow, Dareth slid behind him, and grasped him by the neck with his arm. It was the first and only time they came into such contact. Dareth knocked the man's sword from his hand with a painful blow of his hilt, and it clattered loudly to the floor. The company fell silent, and there was an air of expectation. Teth struggled, causing Dareth to stagger back a bit, but he held fast, his sword edge rising up to rest against the man's chin. He turned to the King.

"Yield or die," Dareth growled menacingly. There was only stillness as the challenger pondered his choice. The King merely picked up his wine and drank.

"Yield or die!" Dareth barked, pushing the blade under the man's chin.

With grudging reluctance, the man replied in a derisive growl: "I yield."

Dareth threw him off, glowering at him. To Evvie's horror, and that of the many witnesses, Teth bent down and swept up his sword, whirling it around to Dareth, catching Dareth's chest with the edge of the sword, cutting his tunic and drawing blood. Evvie gasped audibly and her hand clapped onto her mouth to suppress the cry that escaped her lips. With no hesitation, Dareth seamlessly deflected the attack, sending Teth back a step, and then plunged the tip of his blade into the man's side. The audience roared in astonishment and some in victory.

Teth fell to his knees, looking incredulous as his hand came away from the wound covered in blood. It stained the pure linen of his tunic, blooming like a scarlet rose across his side. Dareth stood over him, his sword dripping dark dots onto the floor.

The King sighed with resignation. "The defensive battle makes for better entertainment, but that, my friends, is the truth of battle. Quick and decisive. Such dishonorable acts end in blood. Ilmeer is the Victor. Summon the healers for Teth."

Evvie watched in both fascination and disbelief as a small horde of white-robed figures came to fetch the wounded man. Dareth wiped his sword with a rag given to him by an attendant, gave both the rag and the sword to the young man, walked before the King and stepped up onto the dais in front of the narrow table. Another attendant brought the king a heavy livery collar made of large, smooth cabochons of beautiful green fire agate set in bezels of gold filigree which reflected the candlelight with almost a magical blaze. The pendant bore the bear, the horse and the raven. Dareth bowed his head forward over the table while the King placed the collar on his shoulders.

"The new Count of Ilmeer, Dareth Hann Vell Ilmeeri!"

The guests cheered and applauded, and Dareth reclaimed his sword once it had been sheathed, and put it back on the ring of his belt. An attendant quickly touched up Dareth's superficial wound, and put a little poultice on it before releasing him. The King then invited him to sit. Dareth circled the table, and came up next to Evvie, who watched him with a furrowed brow. He sat down, and her hand immediately fell onto his, which she gripped tightly. He gave her an assuring look, and she smiled wanly.

"You can eat now," he told her, looking at her untouched food.

Chapter 26

Evvie glanced down at her meal and exhaled in a laugh, squeezing his hand tightly. "I am sorry, this is not something I am accustomed to watching. It reminded me of the day we met."

"I suppose it would. But I did not mortally wound Teth as I did the other fellow. I could have, but I did not."

She gazed at him, thinking to herself, *because you are a good man.* She emitted a heavy sigh, and looked at him in earnest for a moment. "You know how much I love you, Dareth." His eyes grew warmer when she said that. "It doesn't matter how much confidence I have in your abilities, the threat of your being harmed is not one I can ignore. And looking at how little honor that man had, he might have killed you in some underhanded way."

"He tried."

"Yes. He did," she reiterated, her eyes falling on the bloodstained hole in his shirt, and the dark smudge of poultice underneath. "And that would have been a shame, for a child needs its father."

She let that sink in, and picked up her fork, releasing his hand to eat. He sat; slack jawed for a moment and then reached up and turned her chin to face him. In open company, he bent forward and kissed her, a grin of wonder on his face.

"That is truly the best thing to happen today," he said to her as he withdrew. His smile was soft and loving. "I love you, my precious wife."

"And I, you."

Dareth picked up his utensils, and dug in. The King ordered that the next bout begin. To Evvie's delight, it was the woman and her counterpart. This, she was excited to see.

Evvie's eyes lit up in pride as she watched the lady warrior fling herself into the fray without hesitation, and with great strength and skill. Although smaller, she was not at a large disadvantage. Her arms were sinewy muscle, and her body a powerful, finely hewn tool. She battled viciously.

"A hornet," Dareth called her succinctly, with no small measure of reverence.

"Is this unusual? A woman?"

"It is not common, but certainly not unheard of. There is the Queen Amarayne of the line that preceded our current monarch. She battled her brother and won. She was a formidable warrior. There have been a few notable ladies who have stood equal amongst the Baskreth."

"If our child is a daughter, she should learn to be like her," Evvie said with an excited sigh. "She's remarkable!"

Dareth took in her amazement as she watched the woman swing her sword and defeat her opponent soundly. Evvie's eyes misted up when the lady received her livery collar. She was now the Countess of Pryvett, ousting its heir with a decisive win. The heir was not an honorable man either, and he threw his sword at the table where the new Countess' family applauded loudly. The sword swept across their settings, sending the decorative foliage to the floor and shattering wine glasses, splashing wine all over the ladies and gentlemen. The sword slid over the narrow table, and shoved plates onto laps, and fell hilt-first with a clatter onto the floor between a couple, blade resting against the man's shoulder.

"Seems we have a spate of petulance today," the King laughed.

The company responded in turn with laughter, and that moment was forgotten. The next battle was to be fought, and the servants were coming out with tall, jiggly flummeries and creams. The mess was being seen to by other attendants and the event moved on. Evvie, still elated by the lady fighter, eagerly awaited the end of the battles, for there would be dancing and performances. She wanted to escape her place behind the table and meet the new Countess of Pryvett.

After two very quick battles—and the enjoyment of the final meal courses, and jellies—the tables were cleared and the floor quickly washed of the bloody evidence of the fights. Then there were musicians, and dancers, a singer, and finally, everyone rose to dance and to mingle. As if he could read her mind, Dareth took his wife's arm and led her to the little cluster of people where the Countess was engaged in conversation. She saw Dareth approaching and bowed to him. Evvie's grin widened. She was eager to get through the formalities so she could learn more about the lady.

"You've got double blessings, I see, Ilmeer," she blurted to Dareth, just after he introduced Evvie to her. "A new wife and a red witch no less. I am utterly humbled." The lady bowed again to Evvie.

"No. No, you mustn't be. I am humbled by *you*. For Dareth to see a woman do what you have just done is not unordinary. But to me, as a southern-born woman, this is unprecedented and wondrous. I have been overcome with pride and awe since I saw you walk in. Please let me shake your hand."

The lady tilted her head, and offered both of her hands to Evvie. "I do not spend much time in Tirdonne, as I prefer to be present for the inhabitants of my grant. This is the first time I've ever regretted it, because I am now fascinated and desirous of knowing you better, and possibly being your friend," the Countess said.

"Well, I will be at Ilmeer at Alouaine Hall for most of the year. We will spend winters in town."

"Then I shall make a rigorous effort to visit town in winter," the Countess replied. "I have always wished to know a *true* witch. My mother here is a black witch, or so she claims."

"Oh, Ilandra! How could you speak so ill of me to a red witch, my sweet?" An old lady in a gown of jet black with grey hair underneath a fine lace cap reached out to grasp Evvie's hand. "You are splendorous my dear," she whispered. "I am Lady Ahn Andros. I am most honored to make your acquaintance, Countess."

"Pleased to meet you Ma'am." Evvie curtsied and squeezed her hand.

"Witchery is such a lost art to so many. I am so thrilled that there is a redcaste in Tirdonne again. It will surely inspire the sisters, should it not girls?" the old woman asked to the batch of ladies around her.

Dareth was introduced at length, after Evvie had met the most important members of the Pryvett family. There were six in all—four women and two men: one warrior, one Brii. The Brii had been sitting on the Queen's side while Ilandra was fighting, and it was he Ilandra sat next to at the table. Evvie was astonished by the easy air about them, and how uninhibited the ladies were. These women were not merely parlor décor. They were all vibrant, thoughtful and clever, but more importantly, unreserved about it. She adored the whole lot of them at once.

Dareth remained fast at her side as she and the ladies learned more about one another. He then intervened with the conversation. "Ladies, I am fearful of rebuke for this request, but as I have *just* won my title, I was hoping to celebrate it with a dance with my lovely wife."

The women assented graciously and relinquished the witch into his custody. He walked with her to the top of the set below a Duke and Duchess, and they waited until the rest of the dancers fell into place after them.

"I thought the Bask were not dancers," Evvie said archly, but with a mischievous smile before the music began.

"We only dance when someone's been stabbed or married," he replied with equal mirth. "Have you practiced since the wedding?"

"No," she replied. "But I have the idea of the dances. They're like ours in many respects, just a little more complex."

"Wait until you try the quadrilles," he replied.

She had jumped into the dances at their wedding quite fearlessly, in spite of not really knowing any of them. But her knowledge of the basic movements—the hand-changes, casting, setting, half-eights, balances and single turns—she knew from childhood. She'd spent many an hour in the parlor with a dance-master, learning the music and movements to individual dances. So many now, she was well able to suss out the eight or so repeated figures for each dance as she followed without someone to call them for her.

The dance they were beginning was already familiar to her as she had danced this one at the wedding. The dance master had called it 'the Winter Waltz'. She followed the movements of the others until she knew the figures in sequence. After three or so repeats, she was comfortable enough with it to concentrate on her husband, who was not completely graceless on his feet, his skirted leggings sweeping stylishly as he moved, the pleats fanning out and spreading quite beautifully. He held one arm elegantly behind his back, and kept his shoulders square. She caught the love in his eyes as he gazed down upon her. She returned it. They did not speak. They merely basked in their affection while they wove intricate patterns through the sets of other dancers.

Evvie's bliss was interrupted coldly by being paired for a few movements with none other than Mr. Ryse-Mevvick, whom she had not seen down the sets when the dance was assembled.

"Countess, there is still time for you to leave this marriage, and for you to choose me. You should be with a Brii man by right. For the sake of your ancestors and the children you will have. The Red Witches exist only because of their rich Brii heritage. You will kill your family line if you remain with that man," he whispered hastily as they circled one another twice in a gypsy.

"Then how did I come to be then?" she asked him pointedly. "There are few Brii men in Carath, yet here I am. A redcaste." He frowned, but did not answer. "You promised me you would not persist, Mr. Ryse-Mevvick."

"I cannot help but lament the enormous crime that I am witnessing."

"I will not change my mind," she replied calmly. She was back with her husband for four more measures, and then once more she and Ryse-Mevvick turned together, his hand clasped tightly around hers.

"Please," he whispered.

She ignored him, and they moved down to the next set. When they reached the bottom of the set, and waited a turn to rejoin, Dareth gazed at her with concerned eyes.

"You look a little fatigued," he noted.

"I'm feeling a bit strange," she admitted. She was. Her head was a little woozy and her knees felt weak.

"Now is as good a time as any to step away from the dance, my dear. In your condition we cannot be too careful."

She nodded shakily, and they left the dance, Dareth supporting her by the elbow. It was good they did it then, for their exit would not disrupt the rest of the dancers. They were met by none other than the

King, who was quietly moving about the room, something no southern King would ever do. His wife was with him, her arm looped through his. The Prince was behind them.

"Has the dancing worn you out, dear Lady?" the King asked Evvie. She curtsied politely to the monarchs.

"My wife is in no condition to be dancing for more than a few repetitions," Dareth said with pride in his voice.

The Queen's brows arched and she said: "Oooh, I see." She reached out her hand. "Come then, and sit with me, for my ankles have been giving me pain." She led Evvie through the archway into a parlor where people were congregated for cards and discourse. A cluster of people vacated a grouping of chairs the moment they spotted the Queen and Evvie approaching with the King, Prince and Dareth in tow, along with a few other hangers-on. The Queen sat Evvie next to her.

She waited until the interlopers were fully cleared before she spoke. "When did you find out? It is very soon. You have not been married very long."

"Indeed, your Highness. I discovered it only recently. I was touched by a gray witch who informed me of what she felt," Evvie admitted.

"That must be Miss Ives, of the Diviner's Rest."

"Yes, your Highness. She is the only grey witch I know."

"There are a few in Tirdonne. They are almost as rare as red and greencaste. But not *quite* so. You should go to her again. Gray witches are the best resources for mothers. She will ensure that your child remains happy and healthy as it grows inside you."

"I will, your Highness," Evvie assured her.

The Queen acknowledged her with a subtle nod. She then turned her attention to another lady, who had seated herself across from them. The Queen's hand clutched Evvie's still.

As the evening wore on, Evvie—although thrilled by the personal attentions of the Queen—was growing increasingly fatigued, and Dareth was aware of it. In all politeness he excused himself from the King's attention, and stated he was obliged to see to his wife's health and wellbeing. The Queen, fatigued herself, was happy to relinquish Evvie, and to rise herself to take leave of the company. She walked with them out of the parlor to the main hall with her ladies-in-waiting behind her.

She bade Evvie goodnight, and asked that she come and visit her again soon. Evvie nodded in assent, and bade her Queen farewell. Dareth then reclaimed his wife and commanded that their coach be readied and their cloaks be returned to them. He moved towards the entranceway with his wife, momentarily deviated by a man by the name of Kavenah, who wished to make his acquaintance. Evvie was momentarily left to stand by herself by the doorway to the atrium, as she had just put on her cloak and was sliding her cold hands into the rabbit-fur muff in anticipation of the biting cold that awaited them outside.

Mr. Ryse-Mevvick appeared at her side as if from the shadows, and startled her. "Please, Miss Evvie, grant me a moment to make my case, to win your approval…"

"Mr. Ryse…"

"It is not too late. It is not," he begged her. "You are merely married. Divorce is but a signature away. Do not let your line be polluted by Baskreth blood."

"But it already is, Mr. Ryse-Mevvick. I am born of Baskreth blood." He froze and gazed at her in disbelief.

"I beg your pardon?"

"My line, just before it went into hiding from the white witches—oh, five or six hundred years ago—became Baskreth. The Ravensroost line is descended from a Baskreth marriage with a red witch. And now, I am with child by a Baskreth man again, as the new line requires for the powers to continue."

The man's eyes widened and his face grew red and he barked out loudly: "*What!? You're with child!?*" He screamed at her face. He was not able to say anything further, for Dareth's fist planted itself firmly on the man's jaw and sent him flying back into a drapery and then onto the floor. Dareth then bundled her up against him and they exited, leaving Mr. Ryse-Mevvick both writhing and openly weeping behind them.

MIRANDA MAYER

Chapter 27

Evvie awoke the next morning feeling ill in a way she never could have imagined. Imbrah was quick to fetch the nursemaid that served Tarren, and soon both Tarren and a young woman by the name of Ellie were at Evvie's side. Evvie retched into a bowl provided by the nursemaid, and tried to keep down the solution Ellie had made to calm her stomach. But it did nothing for her, and was vomited up as soon as it was inside her.

"Fetch the aunts at once," Tarren said gravely to Imbrah, who assented with a desperate nod, scurrying from the room.

Dareth barged in as soon as word spread around the house. The nursemaid looked fearful. "Can you not help her?" He gazed at Evvie, who was frighteningly pale, and who was heaving violently every few moments.

"I cannot. This is beyond what is normal, Sir. She needs a grey witch," Ellie told him.

He grimly acknowledged this request, and strode out of the room. The aunts came bustling in with only their morning gowns wrapped around them, and their hair hastily hidden underneath their heavy cotton caps, snow still clinging to their soaked hems.

Evvie groaned and turned onto her side again, her back to them. "It hurts," she whispered, clutching her belly.

The aunts immediately looked alarmed.

"Is she with child?" Arah asked Tarren, who nodded, her face white.

"Mrs. Zsall, if you would be so kind as to direct someone to have our girl bring our basket, and I think you need to get your things. Dareth went to fetch the grey lady. We have to prepare. You, nurse, help us move the table into the bed chamber..." the sisters began to bark orders.

When the grey witch, Miss Ives, arrived. Evvie had been given a soporific potion, which had calmed her slightly, and stopped the retching. But she was feverish and fitful, tears falling onto her cheekbones. Dareth was immediately ejected from the room, and while the family and Tarren prepared the table, the grey witch made a silent assessment of Evvie's state with gentle hands and her keen eye.

"It is a barrening beast," she declared. "But the powers are fighting it."

"Someone is trying to kill her baby?" Nerah hissed, her eyes wet.

The grey witch's grim frown spoke volumes. "It can be stopped. With an Alliance spell, it has no chance of succeeding, but we must act now. She is *very* ill. Come." The lady withdrew from her carpet bag a slender box of smooth oak. She unpacked a few items, and scanned what had already been put on the table. "We won't need those," she brushed the talismans and cards aside, and instead reached for a tightly bound wad of waxy leaves. She put it down in front of the lit candle, and moved the crystal ball there as well. She picked up Tarren's tuning fork, stuck the handle of it into a little stone base, and then produced several small bottles of herbs and liquids. She also took Tarren's little brazier dish.

"Sit," she instructed them. The witches sat, two across two, and the grey witch sprinkled some of her herbs into the dish, along with a dash of a strong-smelling fluid. She then picked up the roll of leaves and set an end of it ablaze, resting it over the dish where the leaves smoldered. She put her hands out, and the other witches reached out. As soon as the fourth connection was made, the roll of leaves flared up brightly, and a column of white smoke rose from the bright, white-orange flame. All of the witches had fallen silent, their eyes closed, their heads back.

Tarren reached for the tuning fork, and plucked it from the base. She struck it hard against the dish. Both rang out, and as she put it back into the base, the fork continued to peal and hum. The air around it hummed along with it, the smoke shivered as it rose up.

"Bryne beinnan glæm!" Nerah whispered.

The sheaf of leaves flared up again, and burned even hotter, consuming a portion of the roll, burning it shorter, and shorter, and brighter, and brighter. The embers soon crossed over the rim of the bowl, and as soon as they did, the sheaf slid down. When the smoldering leaves touched the liquid and the herbs, it exploded into flame. The smoke grew black and heavy, and it rose up in a sinuous column that danced to the sound of the tuning fork. Above them, it spread out, moving serpent like towards Evvie. The witches, hands clutched anew, hummed in a strange harmony along with the tuning fork, which still rang true.

The smoke began to fall over Evvie like a mist, filling space around her. However, there were some spots where the smoke did not fill, and those voids were taking shape, revealing a hideous malevolent-looking beast made of nothing but air. It moved sinisterly over Evvie, its body sliding like an ever-moving serpent. Its invisible claws dug deep into her belly. Its strange, terrifying face was shaped by the smoke around it, demonic and bristling with teeth. It looked up as the witches revealed it, and hissed at them, making the smoke whorl out with the force of its protest. The creature only began to dig more fervently into Evvie's being. The nursemaid, who had been standing near Evvie, gasped, and fell back in horror.

"Kill it," Arah snarled.

Their hands clutched tightly and the fire continued to burn in the dish. But now, it was the reflection of the flame in the crystal ball that was growing brighter. As the fire in the brazier weakened, the ball grew hotter and whiter. The candle flames leaned towards the glassy, glowing sphere as if it was beaconing them to it.

It grew so bright, Ellie had to hide behind her arm to protect her eyes. The light exploded outward, passing through the circle of witches—which only made it much, much stronger—and flooded the room. It cut through the air over the bed, shredding the invisible demon into nothingness with a horrifying screech, and consuming the smoke in a fiery flare.

Then everything was dark again. Evvie's tense body fell into a limp, unconscious state. Miss Ives let go of the witches' hands and moved to the window, drawing the curtain and letting in the morning light. She opened the window to air out the aroma of burnt herbs.

Ellie reached for Evvie's hand, and felt that the fever had abated and that she was still and calm. The grey lady gently pushed the nursemaid aside, and reached for Evvie, touching her belly and her throat, caressing her face.

"Both are safe," she concluded. She turned to the other witches. "There is someone who wants to harm her and the child. Best we prepare her to protect herself from further assailment. When she is awake and well, bring her to the shop. We will surround her with security."

The grey lady gathered up her things, and put them into her carpet bag. She then sailed out of the room without another word. Nerah and Arah moved to Evvie's side, and they looked down at her affectionately. Tarren stilled her tuning fork, which still sang just a little, and put it in its case along with the base. She poured the ashes from the brazier into the fireplace and gathered up her items.

"We are *strong* together," she observed.

"Hm..." Arah replied. "A whitecaste is no match for the red witch, if she knows what she's up against. We need to make sure she does. Yes, we are stronger together, but we won't always be here to intervene. She needs to start relying on her own magic to stop these attacks. And I assure you all, this won't be the last."

"Oh, Arah," Nerah exhaled in frustration. "Do you truly believe that *any* knowing woman would allow this to happen to their vulnerable child more than once? I think this is what it is going to take to turn Evvie into a beast of her own. I promise you, that once she is awake and sensible of what happened, there will be very little that will stop her from ending the threat once and for all."

Evvie slept well into the afternoon and awoke to a warm, darkened room, with the scent of lavender permeating the air. Dareth was reading a periodical in the chair by the fire, his feet crossed one over the other. She barely stirred, but it was enough to rouse him, and the paper fell to the table and he appeared at her side, his hands caressing her face.

"My dear," he murmured.

Evvie sat up. Her weakness of the prior morning when she fell ill, felt less oppressive, and her skin seemed a little less pale from what she saw in the mirror across from the bed. She still looked fragile and tired. "I'm hungry," she replied.

He stood, yanking the bell cord brusquely and then rejoining her immediately. He climbed up beside her on the bed, and let her curl up against him.

"What happened?" Evvie asked.

"As the aunties tell it, there was some sort of creature sent to attack you and the child. They said you were resisting unknowingly, but the thing was gaining purchase. I was tasked to fetch the lady from the witchery shop, and I succeeded in getting her here in haste. I do not know what transpired in here, but the sound of it was disturbing. They said that the creature was defeated."

"A creature cast by the white witches," Evvie ventured.

"I cannot imagine why they would endanger a tiny thing, not even grown," he murmured in bewilderment. "I do not even have an enemy to confront on the matter. I do not know who to threaten," he growled in frustration.

"These threats are to be my lot, I'm afraid," she sighed. "It will be my task to keep this child safe." Her hand slid down protectively to the place where the tiny thing that she already loved rested. Her confusion was being slowly replaced by anger. She sat up. The lingering effects of the spell-beast were already almost gone. Instead, Evvie was fueled by a growing sense of defiance. Dareth helped her to her feet, and then positioned her in front of him, as he still sat on the edge of the bed. He held her by the hips, and looked straight at her eyes.

"We can move to Alouaine if you wish."

"It won't change anything. They are a threat to us regardless of where I am. Now they know I'm here, and with a Baskreth child in my belly."

Dareth drew his hand down the side of her head, resting it on the back of her neck.

"I will destroy any person who dares to put this child in harm's way," she said hauntingly.

"You are likely the stronger of the two of us, Evvie. Witchery aside, you have persevered through terrible things, and here you are, still defiant. It makes me so proud to know that you have such strength. You lauded the Countess, but strength is not always in the swing of a sword."

She looked upon him with a gaze of trust and love, and she saw it reflected in his eyes, with what looked like a shred of pride. She leaned forward so her forehead rested on his. They stood in quiet for a moment.

"When I met you, Dareth, I felt that you would protect me from all that is bad in this world, because that is what I *thought* I needed. Being near you, it made me feel secure and shielded from my shame and humiliation. But you have shown me something completely unexpected. You've offered me a life where I am able to protect myself. You make me feel safe, not just for your strength and guardianship, but you make me feel safe for trusting that I can stand on my own two feet. And in this case, it is what I must do. For us and for this child."

"You are a red witch, Evvie. There is little you cannot do."

"It is more than that. I do not know my powers yet. But I know that I wake up in the mornings now without the sense of powerlessness I felt before. Not because of the idea that I am able to perform magic, but because you have shown me that I am not powerless. I can be alone and not be fearful or worse, angry. I was so filled with bitterness before you. Over all that had happened."

"Now you have an entirely new source of bitterness to feed from," he grumbled with a smirk.

She looked at him, and oddly, she smiled. "No. What I feel is not bitterness. I feel anger, and I feel a desire for retribution. But it is not fed by the shame I once felt. This is different. And I do not feel helpless. I feel... *empowered* by my anger. It is time I made myself familiar with what I can truly accomplish, Dareth. And I will set things right once and for all."

Chapter 28

The true illness that accompanied pregnancy arrived only a few days later. There was no alarm this time, for the symptoms were what they ought to have been, and poor Evvie spent part of her afternoons indisposed, as her sickness arrived with startling consistency about an hour after tea time. She barely ate as it was, for everything made her feel ill, and the scent of what were once her favorite things would send her running with her hand clasped over her mouth. Evvie could only eat a little toast with creamed cheese, boiled eggs, and a plain porridge with a dash of cream. She only drank plain herbal teas and iced water by what seemed like the gallon. Everything else made her green around the gills.

She had no specific plans to approach her problems at this juncture. She was too embroiled in the natural reactions of her body in its delicate state. But she did make a plan to visit the archive again early one morning in hopes of finishing up and being safely at home by tea time. Tarren, who was now moving past her time of illness, was full of energy and glowing with anticipation to be out and about.

So with a little less enthusiasm than her companion, Evvie climbed into the coach, bundled up against the cold. She'd had a little warm chocolate with her spare breakfast, and she was feeling a bit better than she had the evening before. Tarren was bright-eyed with excitement. The past few days had been quite uneventful after all that happened and even Evvie was getting a bit bored with being indoors for so long.

The snow, in any other location, would have been prohibitive to travel. But the Bask were well accustomed and prepared for the snow that never seemed to stop falling. The accumulation had already reached the height of the window sills of the ground floor, and there was no sign of it slowing down.

The various clan villages contributed to a common livery stable in each district. These stables existed solely for the management of the snow, and subsequently the water from the melt which—coupled with the shed leaves of the city's greenery—would often flood some areas of the city.

The horses that were used were the largest horses known to any man. Bred specifically for winter work, the Foth horses were mountainous, powerful beasts. Their color was either a blue or red roan, with black points, and heavy masses of raven mane and tail. Their withers stood higher than the tallest Baskreth soldier, and their hoofs were larger than dinner plates. They were tasked through the winter, to not only push the great snow ploughs through the streets, but to follow behind the ploughs with the scoops, which scraped up the piled snow and funneled it to the back of a large dray, which would in turn discard the snow into heaps at the edge of the city by the river, where they sometimes remained—barely shrinking—until the end of the brief summer.

The roads within and near the city were almost always navigable by horse, coach and foot because of these clever creatures. Although the snow was never quite completely removed, as the ploughs left at least an inch or two of compacted snow behind, those that traveled them knew to stud their horses' shoes, to switch wheels to sleighs, and to wear good boots with special tread on the soles. The snow of the past four days had been heavy and unrelenting, and the team of Ilmeeri horses taking the ladies in the enclosed sleigh to the conservatory were mired behind their district's plough horses and scoopers who were removing the days' worth of accumulation. Progress was slow.

Evvie was contemplative. Both of them were bundled up warmly in woolen blankets, enjoying the radiant heat of the fire-bricks that had been put into bins underneath their seats. The horsehair insulation inside the coach, coupled with the bricks, made for a cozy ride. Inside the coach, the dim, grey day was forgotten as there were lamps burning in the tiny sconces on the coach walls, casting their small oasis in a yellow, warm light. In contrast, the windows were scenes cast in blue and white and grey.

In all the chaos of the past days, Evvie had forgotten about the thesis by Admus Veck. She only remembered it now as the coachmen, growing impatient with the slow Foth horses, took a turn on a side street so they could find an alternate route. She wished now she'd taken the time to read it. She frowned.

"Are you unwell?" Tarren asked.

"No, merely angry at myself for neglecting to read something that might have provided me some answers."

"I would only say that you've had scarce the chance to sit and read anything, Ma'am," Tarren replied.

Evvie appreciated the support, and gave her friend a grin. "I must declare that I'm glad that there is one white witch that doesn't hate me, or want my child dead."

Tarren shook her head lamentingly. "Would that I could stop it. I do not even understand my own powers yet."

"That, we have in common, I'm afraid."

The coach slid into a road that had yet to be ploughed, and it jolted a bit as the sleds dragged through deeper snow. But the horses forged on.

Edanbras was there when the ladies arrived and he was elated. "Oh, I'm glad you've come. I almost broke the rules for you again," he said with a wry grin. "I was about to have these sent to you." He reached under the counter and withdrew a stack of four books. He slid them towards Evvie, and she turned them and read the titles as they were printed.

The first was a larger book with a rather old, worn binding. The title was impressed into the cover, and gilded, along with some decorative lines on the covers and spine. Though the gilding had mostly worn off, it was still legible. *Divinations of the Alambrean Circle of Five*. It was dated a little over a hundred years ago.

"I thought this one would be interesting to you. It is a collection of prognostications, many very old. The Alambrean Circle existed in earnest until the red witches began to disappear, but the circle continued on with only three: black, green and grey witches. From what I understand there are still witches serving on this circle in anticipation of the day that both a red and white witch would return to it." He gave Evvie and then Tarren a meaningful glance before moving that book aside, and revealing another. *The Five Ranks of True Witchery.*

"This is a book describing the different types of witches in detail, and what their powers entail. It might help you deduce what tools you will require and what sort of spells you can cast," he explained.

They already had Miss Ives for most of that, but Evvie took the book anyway. The next one was titled: *The Tenor of Red Witchery: a diary of the last.*

"This one purports to be a memoire of a red witch. It is categorized as fiction in our library, but there is a scribble of notations on its ledger entry as to the validity of that placement. Some say it is not fiction, but indeed a true parable of a redcaste's experience. Others claim it is but a ploy to sell more books by an unseemly publisher. I thought perhaps *you* ought to be the judge on whether it is a work of fiction or not."

He then reached for a final book. A shabby little thing bound in board and marbled paper with a cotton spine and a little label glued onto it. It had been in a lending library for some time, and it had been read a great deal. *Manifestations of Magic.* "And lastly," he murmured, "This is a little lark of a book. One with many illustrations describing the various outcomes of spells witnessed by the author. It is a silly little book, but I thought it might amuse you, and it is, in context to what you are researching, apropos."

Evvie liked Edanbras. He was so desirous of pleasing her. "Am I to believe that I am *not* to take any of these books home with me?"

"Again, this is not a lending library," he said firmly, his gaze scanning the desk and the stacks behind them for other souls. When he was sure they were still alone, he winked at her. Tarren gasped and giggled. "As long as you bring them back in a week or two. I think you already have one in possession that must be returned."

Evvie took his hand gratefully. "I had forgotten about it. So much has happened since I last was here." She tucked the books into the folds of her cape, under her arm. She then reached out with her free hand to squeeze Edanbras' hand after pressing a nice, freshly written bank note for a full twelve Troys sterling into his palm. With a smile, she and her giggling companion left, making their way to the Diviner's Rest.

The clock in the great tower had only just struck the tenth hour, and Evvie felt she had already accomplished so much! Miss Ives was just opening up the doors of her shop and appeared pleased to see Evvie in good health and spirit as she welcomed both ladies into the shop.

"I have no books for you, I'm afraid, Countess," she said, as if she knew that is what they sought that day. Evvie merely revealed the books she'd gotten from the archive and handed them to the witch, who looked at them in curiosity.

"Rubbish," Miss Ives mumbled, sliding the illustrated book aside. She pulled the Five Ranks book out as well. The other two she seemed intrigued by. "This one is particularly appealing," she said, leafing through the Divinations book. "There is a rumor that there is still an Alambrean Circle in Bask, but nobody I know can—or maybe will—substantiate it. What I would give…" she sighed. "Would you be opposed to letting me read it after you're done with it?"

"I am not even supposed to have it here. But you can have access to it at the archive if you wish," Evvie said.

"I have a better idea," Miss Ives offered. She moved with a rustle to one large cupboard, the top of which was laden in rows of books. She reached up on her tip-toes and drew down a plain, half-calf book with a blank text block and a shining ribbon marker. "Do you want copies of these too?" she asked Evvie, who grinned enthusiastically.

"Would I. I do not like having these in my possession. I would much rather return them if I could have a copy. How will you go about doing that?"

The grey lady merely laughed. "Some books won't copy—those written originally by the authors, in their own hand, if they were magic bearers. But these are all published and printed by a third party. It should be a simple spell. This is more something a green witch would do, but I am not a stranger to crossing into new territories, nor am I inept at this particular spell. I'm a bit of a book collector, so I've done it on more than one occasion. The ink that must be used is an unusual color but it will print the words regardless."

Miss Ives then fetched some of her paraphernalia and returned with a silver bowl and a little glass ink bottle full of a dark, rusty colored ink. She plunked down two more of these simply bound, blank books—one large like the first, and then one slightly smaller. She stacked the two large ones next to the divinations book, and put the dish below them. She lit a candelabra, and then cleansed the air with an herb bundle. Tarren and Evvie sat in fascination as she watched.

She waved the smoking herb bundle over the book and the blanks and whispered, "Ricay giemen mec." She then reached for her ink pot, unstopped it, and poured the ink into the silver dish. "Geanboc heleothwyde."

The air thickened and then a blast of wind from nowhere blew open the cover of the book Evvie had brought. The pages riffled and turned in the strange moving air until the book had blown from title page to the appendices. Then the ink began to seethe and roil inside the dish. As it did, it began to recede toward the center. The pool grew smaller and smaller until there was nary a drop of ink left in the dish.

"That is the big one. Here." She handed Evvie one of the two blank books.

Evvie opened it and, to her amazement, it was now filled with text. Miss Ives put hers aside and quickly cast out the same spell for the *Tenor of Red Witchery*, and handed Evvie the smaller copy. "The large books are two Troys. The smaller one is only one Troy. I ask no extra charge for the copying spell as you have both been excellent new customers."

Evvie reached for her reticule and drew out three silver coins, giving them to Miss Ives, who took them. She then took her new books and thanked Evvie.

"Let us return these to the conservatory before we go home," Evvie told Tarren. "Do you wish to purchase anything?"

"Yes. A book on white witchery, if you have one. I'm curious to know more about…"

"This book ought to give you some information right here." Miss Ives picked up the *Five Ranks of Witchery* book. "I can make you a copy. It will be cheaper than anything I have on my shelves, and will probably be better suited than the texts I have. Mine are for practicing witches who've apprenticed under their aunts and mothers. This will give you your first insights. The books that I stock will become useful to you later on."

Tarren soon clutched a copy of in her hands as she and Evvie climbed onto the carriage.

The day had darkened even more, and snow was falling again at an almost blinding rate. Evvie quickly ran into the archive to return the books to Mr. Edanbras in haste, and then they returned home through the snow storm arriving just in time for tea and sandwiches by the fire, where they both dug into their texts with alacrity. Both witches wished to know a good deal more about who they were and what exactly could be done with the powers they possessed.

MIRANDA MAYER

Chapter 29

My introduction to witchery

I came to be an apprentice to my great aunt Zella when I was not seventeen. From what I understood, I was starting much later than I ought to, but that was nothing of my doing. My family had chosen to live in Ketemheer long before I was born, or even before my mother was, leaving behind our Bask home. In Ketemheer, witchery is not just frowned upon, it is punishable by law. When my mother was killed, my father sent me to live with my aunt in Taromyen, east of Tirdonne. He said that it was important for my protection. I was surprised to see that my great-aunt had eyes like mine and my mother's. There, I learnt what I was, and she began to teach me exactly what being a red witch meant.

I, like most of the rest of my family, never put much stock into the occasional rambling of a Bask person, calling us witches upon sight of our red hair and pale eyes. But as my time with my aunt went on, I began to understand why my ancestresses chose to leave Bask, and why my father decided it was important that I learn more of what I was. Once this became clear to me, it became imperative that I share this with other latents—what I have dubbed dormant red witches—for I realized that innocent people like my mother would be in danger if they were not awakened to what they were.

My mother died of consumption, or so it was thought. But my father believed otherwise, and he said early deaths for the women of my mother's line was common. My great-aunt explained to me much later on that the deaths were not natural, and that latents were hunted down by some kind of magic, and killed. Why, I was never quite certain. My aunt was convinced it was because of other witches, but that was never proven. What I do know is that something is out there, prowling about the land, searching. And my father knew the only defense against it was to return to the roots my family had run away from. To learn the skills to defend myself should that prowling beast find me.

At seventeen, being told that I had the ability to create magic seemed ludicrous, and for weeks and weeks I believe my prejudice and doubt kept me from embracing what my mentor was trying to show me. That attitude prevented me from touching the powers that fed my ability. Understanding what the powers were, and how to connect with them, was the key. Once I opened myself up to that, I was able to learn very quickly how to let them pass through me and to mold them to my will.

As a latent, I struggled with it. Children are much more prone to open minds, and their thinking is flexible and imaginative. Starting a witch young surely must have made it easier than it had for me. For at seventeen, I thought I knew it all, and I scorned and laughed at my aunt for her silliness.

My aunt claimed that I used magic already in one way or another. That as a red witch, it came naturally to me. But I would not know, because the powers I connected to were intermingled with my unconscious, as they were not able to connect to my disbelief and doubt. But then, the longer I lived in her home, and the more confidences I shared, she began to point out little things that I had let pass by. Small tragedies that befell a childhood tormentor. The fire that took the house of one of my father's peers, who had been swindling my father over a parcel of land. Things that seemed incidental that I learned were likely not. My aunt showed me that coincidence was rarely so kind, and so frequent.

One evening, my aunt once again forced me to put down my novel and to meditate. Something she insisted upon, but I found so boring and dreary. She possessed a brass bowl with a mortar to match. She would sit with me and drag the mortar along the edge of this brass bowl, around and around until the bowl rang like a bell. The sound of it still rings in my ears sometimes when I am connecting with the powers to perform my magic. It is still ingrained in my memory for it is what helped me open up the door to the furthest reaches of my awareness and let in the legacy that my ancestresses had tried so very hard to make me forget, for the survival of my line.

My aunt also spoke to me. In a low, velvety, even voice she would recite this same story, of sorts. She would force me to listen. To lose myself in it. So often she

234

would do this—before I opened up to them—that I recall them word for word. As you are latents, I must stress the importance of these words. You must try to do the same with them. Before you read any of the chapters beyond this first one, you should do this until you understand why you must. Find someone who can read them to you as my aunt did while making a brass bowl ring long and evenly for as long as it takes.

I would lie on the chaise longue, and place my hands on my stomach. She directed me to breathe deeply, again and again, to pace my breath—four ticks to inhale, eight to exhale. She would tell me to let my body sink into comfort. To focus only upon her voice, and the peal of the bowl. And then she recited these words:

Let all your worries pass through and out of you and around you, like water flows around a stone.

Until they have seeped out of your limbs.

Let your body sink heavy, until it feels like you are too heavy to stand.

Breathe. Feel the rise and fall of your breath on your stomach.

Breathe.

Imagine you are in a cavern.

You hear water, drops like rain, falling into puddles.

You can see nothing. But the echoing drops tell you that in that darkness you are within that cave, and the weight of the earth is pressing in all around you.

The chill passes through your silks. The chill is heavy as is the darkness.

A drop of water falls nearby, and something catches your eye in front of your feet. You look down and see that there is a pool of water at the hem of your skirts, and it ripples. But you notice that there are pinpoints of light reflected on the surface, wavering with the motion set forth by the water. You look up, and there you see an aperture, and above it, the night sky.

You know, that this is where you must go. But there is no light to guide you out of this dark place.

So you must make your own light. You crouch down and, making a cup with your hands, you scoop up the water. You lift your hands to your mouth to drink from them. The water is so pure, so sweet, you feel its purity filling your body and slaking your thirst. As your hands fall away, droplets fall into the pool and the water ripples anew.

You see in the darkness a tiny light appear, soft and green, like a will-o'-the-wisp dancing. It reflects off the pools of water on the cavern floor, lighting a safe path for you to walk between the pools and pits of the ground.

Follow the light where it takes you. Cross the slick stone towards the dancing light.

As you approach it, it grows. It expands, the light growing brighter and brighter until it is white and almost too bright to look upon. You must stop walking for it is blinding you. It is then that you see it has grown as big as you—bigger— and it is melting into the form of a person, with the edges of its shape shimmering with light.

It reaches out its hands to yours, and you cannot help but receive them, and the moment your fingers touch this glowing form, your body is infused with its light. It fills you and you feel it radiating from your skin, and the chill is shed from the warmth of this light.

Your light casts out all around you, and it washes the walls of the cavern with its purity. You can now see the long, spiraling stairway circling this cavern, leading up the sloping walls to the aperture above.

The being steps closer, and it bends down to kiss you. You are not afraid. Its warmth, its purity and its light fill you only with love and trust. When its lips touch yours, your awareness is suddenly cast out into the darkness and you see not only with your eyes, but with your mind. Every crag of the cavern, every stone, every pool. The whole of the being that kissed you then steps into you, absorbing into your body, becoming you.

The cavern is dark again, but now you can see. You can see the cavern in all its detail, and it no longer feels like it is a pressing darkness around you. You forge forward, and make your ascent, circling slowly towards the piece of sky you can see, your path lit by your awareness alone.

You emerge into a field of swaying grass with air so sweet, fresh and warm caressing your skin, and blowing your crimson locks from your shoulders. You can see the sky, draped in its mantle of stars, the face of the moon rising up from over the water of a massive lake, and the crag of mountains behind you. You feel at one with it all. The radiance of your inner being glows within you. You feel your awareness shining out like the light that just stepped into you.

You lie down in the grass, and look up at the sky. You spread your arms and dig your fingers into the earth, and you know you are part of it in a way not everyone is. That it is part of you, and that your power comes from the fact that the very essence of the world rests inside you.

Your eyes close, because this knowledge fills you with warmth and comfort. The heaviness of your truth, and the purity of the air surround you. You are pure. You are powerful. You can sleep.

Evvie awoke from her nap to find Tarren slumped in her chair, her shawl draped across her legs, fast asleep. The book had fallen to the floor and rested at her feet. Her tuning fork lay on her lap under her hand. Evvie rose from the fainting couch and picked up the book, placing it on the table. She walked to the window.

Outside, a storm of epic proportions raged. The snow fell so thickly, she could not see the houses across the square. The stone house seemed little-affected by the storm. The wind was coming from the north side of the house, so the windows were snug in their frames, no whistling, and no trembling. It was impossible to know what time of day it was. Separated from the grey and white maelstrom by panes of leaded glass, Evvie stood barefoot in a simple cotton morning gown, her slippers on the floor by the chaise longue. The room was lit as if it were night. The candles had shortened a bit since they began the session. A fire crackled brightly in the hearth. Someone—likely Imbrah—had come and stoked it while they slept.

Evvie was aware of all this as she gazed out into the mad dance of snow and bleakness. She understood something else. She understood she was a witch. She felt it in the core of her being now. She felt the presence of that being of light that had stepped inside her. She had welcomed it, embraced it, and knew that what resided inside her now was a personification of the powers. The very life of this world and the universe now resided in her body. She was bred to carry them. She was their vessel. All red witches were the vessel. And she was not the only one. She could sense her sisters now; scattered and lost; their powers dormant.

She sensed they were different than they were before. They were not like their ancestresses. There was something new—a strain of warrior blood—that helped them rise from the ashes of their embattled predecessors.

Tarren woke with a start, and looked at Evvie. "Did it work?" she asked. "Or do we have to do it again and again, as this witch was forced to?"

"It worked," Evvie said quietly. She turned to look at Tarren. "The white witches have angered the powers. They use their magic against their own kind, and against the wishes of the Powers."

"It is incomprehensible, as to why," Tarren intoned. "I am ashamed of my sisters."

"The Powers have given us our advantage back."

"Us?"

Evvie nodded, and walked to the table, picking up the memoire they'd just used to wake her powers. "Yes. Like the witch who wrote this book said, there are latents. Witches with dormant powers. Descendants of the Bask lines scattered about the land. They do not know. Not yet. I have been given the ability to awaken them, but I will need a proper Alliance of the Seasons to do it."

Just then, the door opened and a servant came in. She was not able to announce the aunts, for they burst into the room without leave.

Nerah carried the book that Evvie had loaned them. The one with the Divinations. Arah shooed the maid out, and closed the latch.

"We found something enormously interesting, Evvie dear. Something tremendously fascinating," Arah declared.

They did not bother to ask Evvie about her endeavor. They were too tied up in what they wanted to share. They opened the copy of the book to a page marked with a bit of green yarn.

"Hear this," Arah declared with haste, putting her finger to the stanzas of beautifully written, graceful script:

"Rejuvenation cometh on the wake of a storm
Crimson wilt rise with power reborn
The slumbering awaken from seeds long sown
Their proxies wilt taketh a life of their own.
The snowy hex wilt payeth the powers their due,
Raven hexxen wilt stand in their lieu
One crimson sister sets 't all into place
At which she arises, by that lady's own grace
She wilt endue again, the lost circle of five,
And breathe hexxery back into life."

What the aunts read what Evvie now already knew. But the aunts were convinced this was exactly what was happening at this very moment. "We are living a prophesy as we speak!" they exclaimed in near unison.

"The red witches will be reborn in the wake of a storm! This storm! And look, it will be brought about by you, the one that arose by her own grace. Do you not see? You will restore the Circle of Five and witchery will become great again!" Arah tittered.

"*And*, we black witches will replace the whites in the castes. We shall be above them! Does that mean our powers will be greater?" Nerah blabbered.

Evvie turned elegantly and moved to the seating area, letting her body sink gracefully into a chair. It was only then that Nerah paused and tilted her head as she looked in earnest at her niece-in-law.

"Goodness me, Evvie. There's something changed, isn't there?" she intoned sweetly. She approached and scrutinized Evvie's face. Arah was too ecstatic to notice immediately, but her sister's sudden intrigue stilled her. She too circled the chair to look at Evvie.

"Goodness me indeed," she agreed. "We have a full fledged red witch amongst us now. Look at the aura about her. Is it not astonishing?"

"I never noticed it before," Tarren whispered in awe.

"I heard red witches were strong, and that they emanated powers from within, but I never knew how to picture that in my head. But it is, in its truest form. It is lovely," Arah murmured.

"We *must* find a green witch," Nerah suddenly exclaimed. "We have Mrs. Zsall here, and then there is the Grey witch from the Diviner's Rest…"

"Miss Ives, who was very much intrigued by the circle. She called it something… the Alambrean circle," Tarren said.

"Yes, I've heard that before, too. It must be a formal appellation for it," Nerah opined.

"Then there's us. For the circle to be complete we need a green witch. An alliance of the five is most certainly needed to awake the latents," Arah added. "Oh, good heavens, aunts. Can we not let the first thing sink in before we go out hunting for the other? Have you forgotten my condition? I've some things to consider before I even think about prophesies," Evvie said.

The aunts looked cowed at once, and they both fell into a rambling missive of apologies and excuses of excitement and zealousness. Evvie humored them. She was starting to feel the unease of nausea washing over her, and she stood to excuse herself. The way she felt, the last thing she wanted to worry about was a green witch.

Evvie was enjoying a boiled egg, chamomile tea, and toast and creamed cheese in the breakfast room with her husband and Mrs. Zsall the next morning. The storm still raged, but full daylight made it seem less fearsome. The quiet of the falling snow felt more peaceful than it was, the wind appearing tamer as its powerful gusts made the snow slow then slash into a violent dance. In spite of this, the door bell rang loudly, and the trio at breakfast looked at one another in surprise.

"I am astonished the old ladies are out and about this early in the day, and more so, venturing out into this snow," Dareth murmured, assuming that only the aunties would be silly enough to come visit on a morning like this one. He appeared tired, his eyes tinted in a little darkness, and his usual easy energy seemed tainted with a shred of lethargy to Evvie. He'd spent the previous day up at the chambers with some of his peers going over matters of the estate of Ilmeer, along with other titular responsibilities, alongside his father who was transitioning his seat to his son.

Dareth came home that night all a grumble. He complained that being in the infantry, at war, was simpler than the tedium of land squirage. He then fell into bed and Evvie, feeling a little faded after the interesting day and late-afternoon illness, cuddled up against his long, dense body, and wrapped her arms around him. She awoke that way, with one arm in pins and needles from the crush of his weight on it.

He was at present in his banyan, a deep blue waistcoat, some trousers and a pair of tapestry slippers he wore about the house. He had a little box hat on his shaved head. He ate a great deal more than his wife, whose appetite was sparing, and whose nose could barely tolerate the pile of bacon rashers on his plate, or the rank smell of the smoked fish he insisted on eating this morning. She had not complained about it, because she knew he would dispense with it immediately, and she felt it wouldn't be fair to always have him deprived for her sake. So she tolerated it as best she could, but she couldn't help wrinkling her nose a bit.

The butler entered and Evvie expected to see one or both of the aunts at his heels. Instead, he placed at her side the salver of silver which held a single card bearing the name of an unknown lady. Evvie snatched the card up, and read it.

"Lady Cethareen of Dalst. Do you know her, Dareth?"

He shrugged and grunted brusquely, shaking his head.

"Seems early to call, doesn't it?" Mrs. Zsall said over her tea.

"Indeed. Well, it must be urgent if it is this early. Go ahead and show her in. She will have to excuse our morning wear. We cannot have her waiting for us to finish breakfast and change."

The footman bowed curtly and exited. He returned with the lady in question, ushering her in and closing the door behind her.

Evvie and the others rose to their feet in politeness, and watched the woman enter the room. She was a willowy, lofty creature with a delicate face and rich mahogany hair that was curled to perfection on each side of her face. Over it, she wore a frilly cap, and then a startlingly lovely bonnet of granite grey with a riot of frilling and cockades and some pleated ribbon along with a dense flourish of feathers which were all dusted in snow. The hems of her heavy woolen cloak and walking gown were weighted down by little balls of snow that had accumulated there. She had fine leather gloves of rusty red, a voluminous muff of what looked like the fur of a wintered cat-wolf, along with a matching tippet over her shoulders. Her cheeks were bright and rosy, given freshness by the cool air. She was lovely. Evvie thought Lady Dalst had to be at least thirty five or forty, but she appeared youthful. Her eyes were lively, and she looked like she could scarce keep herself from grinning.

"Lady Dalst, please, take some tea with us, if you would. And please excuse our informal state…" Evvie began.

"Oh, please, let us not worry about formalities, dearest Countess." Lady Dalst sank down into a respectful curtsy in a rustle of wool, interrupting Evvie in the most easygoing way possible, her face aglow with happiness, unable to contain herself. "I came as soon as I could. There was a clear signal last night of the prophesy coming to pass. I set out first thing today without regard to the weather and the signs led me straight to you." She hesitated, and then stepped forward, reaching out her hand. Evvie took it, slightly befuddled. "I am Lady Dalst. I've come to help you awaken the red witches again, and to put those white witches right back in their place at last! I am the last inheritor of the Alambrean Circle of Five and the only green witch remaining in Tirdonne."

MIRANDA MAYER

Chapter 30

Lady Dalst was a vivacious, lovely woman, Evvie discovered. A rich widow, she enjoyed a particular independence, and possessed a spirit to match it. She had no airs, and she spoke plainly, but always smilingly.

She shed her gloves, cloak and other accoutrements, until she was wearing but her gown and her cap. She sat down with them, accepting her tea from the servant, politely refusing an offer of freshly baked scones, all the while exclaiming her delight and happiness to be the one to witness the rebirth of red witchery, which to her meant the rebirth of all witchery in earnest. "Red witches are the very source of the powers all witches possess. If there were no more latents, we would all lose our connections to the powers. I will be honest and say that for a spell, I and a few of my sisters of various castes of witch were worried that this prophesy would not come to pass. That we would all be lost in another generation.

"But that is not the case, is it? Oh, such relief. I cannot wait to inform my friends. I simply cannot," she exclaimed excitedly. She sipped her tea and then finally looked at Mrs. Zsall, her brows rising up in surprise. "I am sorry, I have not properly introduced myself." she told her.

Tarren merely waved her off, and remained fast in her seat, reaching across the table. "I am Mrs. Zsall, a friend to the Lady Ilmeer."

Lady Dalst took Tarren's hand. "Indeed. We were all quite in puzzlement as to how we would find a whitecaste willing to sit beside a red one and voluntarily choose to help enact what amounts to demotion of their kind... Of course I am perhaps being presumptuous, that this young mother-to-be here is open to the idea."

"Goodness, I'm new to witchery," Tarren said. "Almost as new as her Ladyship. I have not been raised here in Bask, therefore I have not been indoctrinated into whatever prejudices my witchcaste sisters hold against her kind. The Countess has only been good to me. As have her aunts, who also are witches. If I am to continue being what I am told I am, I would desire it only if I am in the same good company. I have no interest in old grudges or deceptions."

Lady Dalst's eyes twinkled with glee and she squeezed Tarren's hand. "I do believe we are all going to be excellent friends. And such wonderful things we will do for our nation and its people, as the Alambrean circle did long ago. Before the rebellion of the white witches."

Evvie quietly broke off a bit of scone, buttered it, daubed a little jam on it, and popped it into her mouth. The garnet-hued strawberry jam was the only food of any color and brightness she'd eaten that morning, except the yolk of her boiled egg. "I'm curious, Lady Dalst; perhaps you could explain to us exactly what it was that caused the whitecaste to rebel?"

"Many believe to this day that it was mere jealousy. That the redcaste were the vessels of the powers, and were not secondaries, as the other castes are. The witchcaste, before all this, perceived the distribution of power as a great wheel. The redcaste are the hub, and the secondaries the spokes. The tyre is the circle that binds us all. The hub is what holds us together. It was unheard of that any of the witchcaste would be discontent in their position. We all knew our roles. Our place in the world was paramount. We were the very foundation of the Bask spiritual doctrine. To create imbalance in that wheel, that would be disastrous for not only witch kind, but for all of the people of Bask," she asserted.

"And then came Della Aya," Lady Dalst continued. "Her name is the one that rings sour amongst all knowing witches, for she is the one that incited the rebellion. It began as a personal rancor with an adversary red witch. Her name was Guyell. That is the only name we know her by. The story goes that the two were bitter rivals. Some say it was over a man. As neither of you are from Tirdonne, there is a particular *kind* of man that witches are drawn to. They are almost always Brii. If the women who chose to marry did not choose a Brii mate, they were cast out of the sisterhoods and forbidden to practice magic, their children forever barred from apprenticeship."

"That is odd... Why?" Evvie asked. She could see that Tarren was also intrigued as they were both wed to Baskreth men.

"Because the children would be considered impure. Without the hexxenmaeg, their magic would likely be tainted and dangerous." Lady Dalst looked at the bewildered faces of her audience, Dareth's being the most mystified, and then shook her head. "Women do not have tenure over all magic. There are men who have magic, too. They have been bred amongst the Brii for centuries, but their magic is.. it is…" She frowned as she struggled to find a word for it. "Feeble. Their magic is feeble. They do not have colorcastes, nor does their magic specialize in any particular thing. They can only do things like cast passable glamors, or move an object. Mere parlor tricks, if anything at all. Sometimes the magic only manifests in the form of greater skills or talents. But as they are so very rare, they are the most desirable mate for a witch, as the daughters from such a union are born to double magic. And it is the same for the men. To have a witch—especially one of the higher witchcaste—oh, well, that is something of enormous prestige. To be born with the hexxenmaeg—even if you are the lowest of the poor—can lift any Brii man out of his poverty and make him important. The very essence of the Brii is erudition and culture, knowledge and wisdom. If a man is born with such powers, he rises to a caste of his own, and rises within it based on what kind of wife he chooses.

"Because the Mage Brii are rare, you would think that they have an easy choice. But that is not the case. Many witches do not choose to embrace a man. Or they do not wish to bear daughters. Many witches, especially amongst the black and green witchcaste, choose spinsterhood, or companionship in one another. Some choose to marry men who are not Brii, and choose love and children without the burden of continuing a line. That is why witches are not many. Because witches can only make witches if they marry mage Brii. But *all* Bask men covet the witch. All. But all that changed. Not just for the reds but for all of us. Because of all that happened, the powers gave us all a gift. Perhaps to compensate for the damage the witches would have to suffer for the actions of the one caste. The powers began to give Baskreth boys the hexxenmaeg." Lady Dalst looked at Dareth who merely grinned and leaned back in his chair. He crossed his leg over the other, and drank from his coffee cup. Behind him, the tall window showed the storm continuing to fall upon Tirdonne. Evvie looked at her husband, who just shrugged his brows from behind his cup. Lady Dalst recaptured her attention as she continued:

"I digress, the witches I spoke of, they likely sparred over the affections of a Mage Brii. And when the red witch won him, Della believed it was merely for her witchcaste and not for any other reason, and her resentment grew and grew.

"She began to influence her sisters, citing all the advantages and power that the redcaste witches had over them. And the resentment began to spread. And then, in some uncanny act of fate, the whitecaste discovered that if they acted as one, they could possess and even destroy the Prósopo of the Red Witch. For no witch could stand against the proxy before that day. But they discovered this weakness, and they used it. And many, many red witches died. It was a dark time for all witchery, for our powers were reduced so greatly by this wanton destruction.

"The white witches were shrewd, for they knew that the demise of all red witches would destroy their own powers, so they destroyed *almost* all of them. The ones that did not die were persecuted and harangued and maligned to where they could only flee Bask, retrench from their powers, and hide from the hatred of their snowy sisters.

"And that is when the Baskreth Mages began to appear. But the white witches would not sully themselves. They wanted the purest witch powers, and they believed that the Brii were the ones to possess that. So they slandered all witches that chose the new Baskreth magic bearers, assumed superiority over the rest of the witchcaste, and drove any dissenters out with their unified magic. They have ruled over Bask since. Almost five hundred years, I think. But here's the best part," Lady Dalst reported with a wry, gleeful smirk. "The Brii-born Hexxenmaeg have been slowly dwindling in number these past hundred years and the White Witches are in a panic. They still do not deign to marry outside the Brii. Most other witches who desire to continue the lines have long been marrying healthy Baskreth hexxenmaegs and bringing forth into the world more witchly daughters. But not the whitecaste. And they are most, most displeased."

"Well then… That explains one mystery," said Dareth, dropping his leg and leaning forward to put his forearms on the table. "Mr. Ryse-Mevvick."

Evvie peered at him, eyes wide. It made sense now. Ryse-Mevvick's almost insane pursuit.

"Oh! Indeed. You've met Mr. Ryse-Mevvick? He's rather notorious," Lady Dalst laughed. "A hexxenmaeg, indeed. A most celebrated one, for he is highborn to boot. There are many witches that vie for his attentions, but he is known to desire only the rarest of witches." She looked to Evvie with a knowing arch to her brow. "It is no wonder you've been acquainted. I imagine he must have come to you the second he saw your pale eyes and that stunning hair. How disappointed he must have been to learn you were taken." She laughed merrily, her eyes sparkling.

"Oh, he's more than disappointed. He's been pursuing my wife with fervor." Dareth's tone was dry.

"I believed he might have somehow been responsible for an attack on me recently. A magical creature was trying to harm my child," Evvie declared.

Lady Dalst went from amused to horrified in but a beat of a heart. "You have not cast your Prósopo? To protect yourself? You must! Here in Tirdonne you are in danger!"

"I only opened up to my magical abilities yesterday," Evvie explained.

"Nonsense. A Prósopo appears without spell. It appears when it is needed, when your instincts or your unconscious will demands it," said Lady Dalst.

"I had no idea anything would come for my child!" Evvie blurted.

Lady Dalst retreated, an apologetic look on her face. "Countess, you must—you simply must—meditate. And you must meet your proxy. You must give it power to do what it will."

"If the white witches can destroy it, what would it matter?" Evvie asked stubbornly.

"That is the thing, my Lady," Lady Dalst interjected. "I am fairly certain that the white witches can no longer do the damage they once could against the redcaste or any other witches. I think their ability to do so was finally vanquished about a hundred years ago or so, from some of the accounts I've read. You see, we are almost all descendents of a new kind of witch, with new blood in our paternal lines. The whitecaste are still products of the archaic lines. Our altered heritage has changed the nature of our magic. I have seen it in reading the grimoires of my ancestresses. My magic is different from the greencaste of old. And if the white witches could have destroyed your proxy, or manipulated it against you, they would have already. And trust me when I say that would be something you would have very much felt and noticed, because the Prósopo is an extension of you." Lady Dalst was very serious in her expression. Evvie looked straight on at her bright, pale green-blue eyes. "That does not mean that you are not in danger."

"The recent event makes that very clear," Evvie admitted.

Lady Dalst nodded gravely. "We must ensure your safety, and that of your child."

"Indeed," Dareth grunted. "What must be done to assure my wife and child's wellbeing?"

Evvie tilted her head. "We are left with only *one* thing to do."

"Reconvene the Circle of Five, of course," Tarren concluded.

Chapter 31

Evvie sat in the chair by the fire in the private parlor, a room she had yet to truly make herself at home in. Her husband read quietly nearby. The fire snapped and popped as a new log had been added. Other than that, the silence was palpable. Evvie's eyes were shut fast, closing out the warm orangey-yellow light that diffused about the room. She was inside herself. She was seeking something: The version of herself that was imbued with light. She was interrupted by a knock on the parlor door.

The housekeeper handed her a card. "Send him in, and, if you would, send someone to fetch Mrs. Zsall. Inform her that her husband is here. Please have a pot of tea made up for him. He must be frozen."

The housekeeper sank down into a curtsey and exited, ushering the owner of the inn at Diamond Rock into the parlor.

Mr. Zsall was a kindly faced, older version of Dareth, with a bit of fuzz growing in on his normally bald head. He clutched a sodden hat in his hands, and bowed deeply to both Evvie and Dareth, who had risen at his entrance. His woolen coat with its two capes was also covered in snow which was quickly becoming a shimmering layer of droplets in the warmth of the room. "I'm sorry to disturb you this evening, but I just rode in from Diamond Rock, and I wished very much to see my wife."

"Oh, Mr. Zsall, you have no need to apologize. Do sit by the fire, warm yourself up. I cannot believe you would ride all the way here through this storm." Evvie watched the servant take his coat and hat.

"I have a Foth. They will forge through anything," he said proudly. Once discharged of his outerwear, he moved hesitantly to the fire and sat down gingerly in one of the chairs.

"Have you not even stopped at your family village?" Evvie asked.

"No ma'am," he shook his head. "After I received word from my wife, I closed the inn and set out immediately. There are few travelers braving the northern roads right now anyhow."

"Ah yes," Evvie agreed. "She did indeed send you important news." He nodded vigorously and grinned proudly. "You will stay here, I hope, Mr. Zsall. As Mrs. Zsall is so comfortably settled here."

"Oh, I wouldn't dare to impose upon…"

"Nonsense," Dareth barked. "You will be our guest. We cannot have you residing where your wife is not. Unless you insist you must be with your family?"

"Thank you, Lord. My family is neither here nor there. I am not close to the clan, as I am settled in the tunnel. If you are so kind to have me, I would gladly stay," Mr. Zsall agreed.

"Then it is settled. If you have bags, we will see to it that they are brought in. And Kepp will see to your horse," Dareth declared.

Mr. Zsall beamed. It was then that Tarren entered. She was beside herself with surprise and happiness to see her husband. She threw herself into his arms and he embraced her affectionately.

"We will situate you in the apartments across the hall from your wife, and annex the robin's room for you as a common space, should you desire to receive guests and whatnot." Evvie rose to pull the bell cord. As she ambled across the floor, she shrieked out in pain, clutched her stomach, and crumpled to the floor wailing in agony. Tarren cried out and ran to Evvie, dropping to her knees beside her in a drift and puff of skirts.

"Evvie!" she shrieked.

Dareth and Mr. Zsall rose to their feet, but they stood rigid and unmoving. Tarren looked about her in fright, unsure what to do, and when she saw the state of the gentlemen, she froze in shock.

The eyes of the men rolled back until they were white, and both began to grimace fearsomely—baring their teeth and snarling like wild animals. Each gripped their hands into fists and shuddered violently. From their beings came shapes of beaming light that—once freed from their bodies—merged together into a greater entity that in turn resolved into a barbaric creature of enormous size. It was, in all essence, a Baskreth warrior, but one of the days before chivalry and gentlemanly airs. One of fierce and terrifying savagery: a bare-chested, tattoo-riddled monster of a man with bone necklaces around his thick neck, and skirt leggings of thick, roughly woven wool hanging from his narrow hips. In his hand, he clutched a terrible blade.

"Prósopo…" Tarren murmured with awe. The creature's white, glowing eyes turned to look at Tarren, and then a moment later it vanished. Its hosts collapsed to the floor with two indelicate thuds. Somewhere in the city—unbeknownst to the occupants of the parlor—four white witches were being hacked down in a violent spray of blood and gore. Their screams cut through the storm into the streets of Tirdonne and chilled the marrow of all who heard them.

Back at Ilmeeri Square, Evvie's keening had quieted, and she sat up suddenly with a confused look upon her brow. Tarren turned to peer at her.

"What happened?" Evvie asked. "I was in such pain…" she looked in shock at the men, who were lying inert on the floor.

"I think you were being attacked again. But the Prósopo appeared. It came from them. From our husbands."

"They are both Baskreth warriors," Evvie whispered.

The women looked at one another with astonishment, and finally got to their feet. They went to their men, who awoke as if they'd but fallen into an unexpected slumber. They all gazed at one another in wonder.

"Well…" Tarren marveled awkwardly, "it seems you've indeed found your powers, my Lady."

"Indeed, I have. When my proxy attacked my first husband, had it come from some unknowing Bask man too? I recall only seeing one Baskreth man during my time at Adrin. The stable master. I noticed him only because of my father's obsession with the Bask. Did *his* spirit, or awareness form into my proxy?"

"Who could truly know?" Tarren replied, gazing at Evvie. "Mrs. Dalst said that your proxy is an extension of you, but it was formed by the men."

"Yes. An extension of my will; taken form in the spirit of the Baskreth warrior." Evvie murmured. The four of them gazed at one another in confusion.

"I can only wonder at what you are talking about, dearest ladies," said Mr. Zsall. Tarren laughed uncomfortably and gave her husband a quick summation of the past few days. He appeared befuddled and intrigued.

Evvie on the other hand, had been quietly mulling, her lips pursed, and her eyes distant. She looked at Tarren and emitted a little sigh of resignation. "I cannot begin to know what my proxy has gotten up to, though. It seems to have a mind of its own," she conceded. She emitted a single laugh of shock and amazement. "I suppose we'll find out soon enough." She paused, her brow furrowing in confusion. She then shook her head briskly as if to catch her senses again. "Well then. I was seeing to your rooms being prepared." She straightened and brushed her skirts down, returning to the bell cord and giving it a decisive yank. Nobody but Tarren noticed that her hands were trembling.

The aunts arrived the next morning to join Evvie and Tarren for breakfast, and to talk a little before the green and gray witches arrived at the tenth hour. They'd heard rumor already of the event at the main house, and were eager to know more. Evvie and Tarren related the incident from the evening before and the aunties were unabashedly and unapologetically delighted.

"Oh la! I wish I could have seen it! It was a warrior? Oh my!" Nerah exclaimed, clapping her hands together and smiling broadly.

"Indeed! I am so very proud of you my dearest Evvie, so very proud!" Arah added. "An historic moment for witchdom! Mrs. Zsall, you must describe the thing from head to toe again!"

Tarren laughed at Arah's request. She had described it for the aunties twice already.

"I'm curious as to whether Mr. Ryse-Mevvick has something to do with these attacks on your child," Nerah pondered.

"Why would a white witch help him to do that? If his aim is to make Evvie his own and ridding her of the *impure* Baskreth child?" Arah snapped.

"I would think that the white witches would be happy to do *anything* that would harm Evvie," Tarren offered between sips of tea.

Evvie broke off some of her toast and buttered it with her trusty cream cheese. She listened intently while eating.

"We cannot know for sure. But Mr. Ryse-Mevvick would best leave Evvie be. It is in his best interest, for if left to do what she must, there will be a small horde of red witches for him to choose from," Nerah said airily, picking at what was left of a crumpet.

Arah rolled her eyes and shook her head, tugging at the lace of her cuffs. "You ought to have the gray lady look at your tummy, my dear, and see that little baby Evvie is safe and secure after last night's escapade."

"I will," Evvie agreed, "but I'm confident that the child is perfectly sound and will certainly remain so from now on, after last night."

"Mmm. Any news yet on that end?" Nerah asked.

"No. Not yet. But it will come. It is inevitable. The way the servants spread gossip, it is only a matter of time before we hear *something*," Evvie assured them.

Just then, there was a knock and a servant opened the door to Lady Dalst who bustled in as if she was a familiar to the household, shucking her outer wear into the servant's arms, and sitting down to breakfast. The four of them watched with surprise. Lady Dalst impassively reached for a clean tea cup, and filled it from the teapot.

"Well then, I am Lady Dalst, dear ladies, as you are not being introduced," she said to the aunts, who sat frozen in shock at the intrusion of the newcomer. "I am one of the city's only greencastes and keeper of the Circle of Five's legacy." She paused and reached for the sugar pot, plucking a couple of lumps out with the pincers and plopping them into her tea. She then strained across the table for a teaspoon. "I had some news early this morning, and I thought I'd come over early so we can discuss it. Seems there was a bit of bloodshed last night. Four witches dead." She stirred the sugar into her tea with the spoon, her pale green eyes on Evvie with expectation. She had everyone's undivided attention. They could have heard a pin drop in the room.

"I see," Evvie croaked. She blanched and frowned. "I was assailed. Likely by another such creature as attacked me before. I do not know what happened…"

"She fell down crying out, and then the Prósopo appeared," Tarren interjected.

Lady Dalst turned her face and her perfect bundles of side curls towards the white witch, with her brows arched, and her hand frozen with the cup of tea hovering before her mouth. "Indeed?"

"Oh yes."

"You saw it?"

"I did," Tarren insisted. "It was a great Baskreth warrior. Like the old barbarian bezerkers."

"Oh!" Lady Dalst exclaimed with an arch of her back and no shortage of titillation. Like the aunts, her eyes twinkled with excitement.

"It came right out of our husbands. Two glowing figures into one, and then it… it transformed into what it was. Drest covered its entire chest, arms and neck, some even on its face. A most formidable a figure if there were any," Tarren opined.

Both aunts and Lady Dalst listened on in fascination. "And then?" Lady Dalst prompted.

"He disappeared."

"That is it?" Lady Dalst appeared disappointed. Tarren picked up her tea, taking a sip. Lady Dalst put her teacup down, and stared at the table. "The Prósopo used to manifest as a ghostly creature that would possess whomever it needed to do its deeds. It did not come out of anyone. This is most unusual and unexpected."

"You yourself said our magic was different, that it changed because of the Baskreth blood," Evvie asserted.

"I suppose so," Lady Dalst conceded. "I never suspected it would be a enormous terrifying warrior that would cut a person to bits. Good gracious! Those poor whitecaste ladies do not know what's coming if they threaten you, or any of the new red ladies to come." Lady Dalst finally took a nice, deep draught of her tea, a strange little smirk on her face. Nerah drank too, but she did not bother to hide her chuckle of delight.

"I cannot say this sort of thing brings me pleasure," Evvie murmured. "I do not like that death is bestowed in my name."

"Only if invited," Lady Dalst rationalized. "The Prósopo is only invoked when you are threatened."

"A threat," Evvie murmured, her brow furrowing. "I have struggled with what happened to my late husband; at my hands. But I must confess, he invited it. As hard as it is to say; that someone deserved that fate. But he did."

The sisterhood agreed with decisive, supportive words. Tarren reached out and clutched Evvie's hand. "Your actions were just, Evvie. Of that I am certain," she assured her.

"From what you said, Evvie, he did indeed deserve his fate. For he drove you to such despair, there was the danger that you would perhaps try to end your misery yourself," Nerah said softly. Evvie looked at her, and they shared a long, meaningful gaze.

"I do not think I could have admitted that I'd reached that kind of desolation before," Evvie sighed. "But you are right. I had."

Nerah reached her hand out across the table and took Evvie's other one in it. "But no more. You are so very much loved and happy now. The Prósopo will protect you as it did then. It only knows how to do one thing: its job. And that is to shed blood in protection of you. It will be a brief lesson for those who seek to harm you or your child. Any act of enmity might well end in a death sentence. If you are lucky and your rivals have any brains, it won't have to happen too many times for them to get it.

"And let me add, what your Prósopo doesn't stop, your sisterhood will."

Evvie smiled at Nerah. She loved Arah too, but there was a kindness and gentility to the younger sibling that Evvie had to admit she preferred. Arah looked on impassively, and then spoke suddenly.

"Well… We have decided that Nerah shall be the one to sit on the Alambrean circle. I will not."

Evvie was astonished, as Arah had always been the dominant personality of the two. Evvie was quite sure that Arah would have bullied Nerah into being secondary. She wasn't sure what happened to change things, but Nerah looked quietly delighted as Arah pronounced this, and she reached for another fresh crumpet and slathered it liberally with butter and jam.

"There's no reason the two of you cannot alternate," Lady Dalst suggested. "That is not unheard of."

"No. We have decided," Arah insisted.

"Well, when we've all finished, we will need a round table and five chairs," said Lady Dalst.

"There is one in my private parlor," Evvie offered. "I hope it will be where the future gatherings of the Alambrean circle will take place."

Lady Dalst gave her an approving nod. "I have brought the ceremonial cloths and such belongings to the circle. Your servant has custody of them. Perhaps they can remain here as well?" Evvie agreed, and Lady Dalst continued. "That is most convenient. I've also brought the ancient grimoire of the circle. I looked to see if there was any precedent when it came to waking latent witches, but I did not find any."

"I am quite confident we will discover our own method. We have for all of our past alliances, have we not?" Arah asked.

Nerah nodded in agreement, the ruffles of her voluminous cap bouncing, and the lappets on her shoulders swinging with her movement. The ladies then remained mostly quiet as they finished their breakfasts, the sound of cutlery clinking on china and teacups ticking into their saucers the only thing to be heard as they waited for their fifth to arrive.

Chapter 32

Miss Ives arrived a little early, covered in snow. She, too, brought her paraphernalia which was carried by a tall, lanky Brii man who she quickly introduced as her affianced. He was clearly glad to melt away into Dareth's sporting hall down in the depths of the servant's realm. It was where Dareth went to practice his fighting skills, and sometimes where he and some of his friends would partake in boxing bouts as Dareth was an avid pugilist. The Brii man would probably find little to amuse him there, but for Dareth and Mr. Zsall, it was where they would spend a good deal of their time during his winter stay.

The women convened in Evvie's parlor, where she had found five delicate matching chairs taken from the attic, and distributed them about the hefty, round work table of dark-stained oak.

Lady Dalst declared this arrangement to be perfect. All the ladies settled into their chosen places at the table, except Lady Dalst who busied herself preparing the table with Imbrah's help. Imbrah was only too delighted to be part of it. Evvie was impressed by how attentive and unafraid she was. She was indeed an excellent abigail, and more.

Imbrah deposited the box of the Alambrean Circle's items on the window bench. The fire had been freshly fed by Imbrah, who also brought refreshments and laid them out on the small sideboard. She drew the curtains, and helped the ladies set about to prepare for the first true Alambrean circle in centuries.

Lady Dalst then called Imbrah over to the box and opened it, removing items in turn. She gave the girl a round cloth only slightly smaller than the circumference of the table and made of red silk. It was an old fragile looking, a simple hand-sewn circle, edged with patinated gold braiding in an interweaving pattern. Imbrah lofted it over the table and centered it perfectly. In the center of that, Lady Dalst placed a candelabra made from the antler of a wye-deer which in its beautiful natural symmetry was decorated in bands of silver. In the cups on each of the six antler tips, Lady Dalst placed six small, round candles the color of blood and lit each one. She then pulled out another container of wood from the Circle's box and opened the lid. Inside were five objects.

The first item that Lady Dalst extracted from the box was a skull, smoothened and yellowed with age. One of a great-raven, large for a bird, with hematite stones inserted into the eye sockets. She put that in front of Nerah. She then withdrew a strange, rounded little bell of meticulously polished silver, which she placed before Tarren. She placed a small chalice before Miss Ives, filling it with water from the carafe on the sideboard. She set an oaken wand in front of herself, and then drew out single, large, perfect natural crystal which she set in front of Evvie. She then put the box aside and returned to the larger container, where she produced a small cauldron that she put it in front of the candelabra.

All the while, Miss Ives scratched down notes into a small book, listing all the things that Lady Dalst was distributing about the table.

Evvie watched and then something came to her. "I must go to my room. I've forgotten something."

Arah's brow furrowed.

"The bellen ink, and the family Grimoire!" Evvie reminded her.

"I will fetch them," Imbrah offered, rushing from the room.

Lady Dalst pursed her lips and brewed with reflection. "For what purpose do we need these things?"

"The alliance spell we cast, to make my grimoire speak, it said that the latents would awaken only when I write anew upon its pages in bellen ink. Whatever we are required to do to make this work, this is the one thing we know," Evvie explained.

Lady Dalst's brows rose and she shrugged. "Well, we go with what we know, eh?" she replied.

The others chuckled, and only a moment later, Imbrah arrived toting the large tome and clutching the feather and bottle of ink in her hand. Evvie put the tome in front of her, and the ink and plume as well. She opened the little pot and put the cork aside in preparation for whatever would come. Imbrah moved to a chair nearby until she was needed again.

Lady Dalst then handed Tarren a raven's feather. To Nerah she gave a tiny bowl filled with little shavings of fragrant wood. To Miss Ives, a little robin's egg. To Evvie, a wooden coin with a five pointed star etched into it. The last object was a dried leaf of oak. Lady Dalst put another small, round candle inside the cauldron, and lit it.

She finally sat back and looked at each of them in turn. "These are objects that have been in the hands of generations of witches who have each served on the Circle of Five. These talismans are sacred, and they are believed to help strengthen the flow of power between the Alambrean five. These little tokens are required to initiate an immaculate Alliance of an Alambrean Circle of Five. We shall begin with it. From there, I do not know."

The ladies peered at their items.

"First we must perform the incantation of initiation. To beg the awareness of the powers. Place your hands first on the talismans. I will lead, and then you will follow," Lady Dalst said.

Arah, uncharacteristically, was silent. She had settled into one of the chairs nearby to watch the proceedings. Evvie wondered in passing what had truly transpired that the dominant sister stepped back and allowed Nerah to have her day. But she instead put her attention to the task at hand. She rested her fingers on the large, rough, beautiful crystal, and closed her eyes. Lady Dalst began to recite something.

"Steward of shadow, counsel of death,
Steward of words, and the power of breath
Steward of the earth, the agent of growth,
Steward of blood, life-waters doth flow,
Steward of the soul, of the vessel of mind,

The Circle of Five, our powers are twined."

Lady Dalst picked up her oak leaf and dropped it into the cauldron onto the flame of the candle, and then looked to Nerah, who added her feather. And so on around the table, each threw in their items. Evvie was last, placing the small wooden token into the growing, rather rank-smelling fire. The coin caught immediately and the fire swelled and crackled with the addition of the final item.

Lady Dalst reached out and took Evvie's hand in her right and Nerah's in her left. The rest of the ladies closed the link. The moment their hands were clasped, the fire in the cauldron burst into a white hot ball and sent out a column of acrid smoke that rose up to the ceiling. The whispering voices returned, and a wind from an unseen source picked up the curls and tendrils of the ladies' hair. Heads pivoted back and eyes stared up blindly, mouths working impossible words from a long-lost time. The house began to shudder and the air constricted around them. Arah's eyes grew wide, and she sank back into her chair. The fire in the fireplace turned a strange hue of purplish red, and the column of smoke from the cauldron began to undulate and writhe like a living thing, the tendrils curling along the ceiling, crawling along like fingers. The Grimoire shook and then it flapped open to a blank page, and the great black quill shivered and rose of its own volition.

Evvie felt something powerful take possession of her; something from deep within. The house shuddered again, *"Sweostor awacan, cunnan eow soth!"* The words spewed from Evvie's mouth in an otherworldly voice, which cut through the walls and shuddered the glass in their leaded panes.

The quill plunged its sharp tip into the ink and then retreated, hovering over the grimoire. It lowered and the nib scratched the very words Evvie spoke across the page in ancient script. Upon the utterance of the last syllable, and the last scratch of the quill, the fire in the cauldron again flared up and there was a great boom that shook the house, blowing the quill across the room. A wave of power drew away from the center of the circle of witches like a growing ripple.

Evvie's awareness felt as if it exploded from her body, filling the room and then passing through the walls. Her spirit traveled with the ripple; or perhaps, it *was* the ripple, she could not know. It was a growing sphere of visible light, that permeated the room and expanded through the walls, growing outside of the house—illuminating the snowfall in an ethereal, terrifying light that traveled ever outwards. It moved faster than anything Evvie could have imagined. She watched the land slide along at incredible speed around her, snowy towns and cities, villages and farms. Mountains and seas. Little flares of light burst along the expanding ripple wall now and again, bright and white-orange—as if the walls had caught on a little pebble or snag. Climates changed, countries changed, the sun rose and fell again; and when the walls of the ripple met themselves as they had circumvented the globe—there was darkness. Evvie returned to her body. The wall of light had extinguished every flame in the house, the village and the city, dousing every flame as it expanded outwards across the land.

With every burst of light along the ripple, every snag that exploded on its path, a redcaste witch was awoken.

The deed was done.

From the darkness in the stilled room, Nerah said, "Well that was rather swift and simple, wasn't it?"

Talk of the incident was all over Tirdonne and beyond, as it had extinguished all fires and lights on an evening of particular cold. So many servants in so many households were hastily ordered to restore light and warmth after the strange wall of undulating light had swept their fires out. Reports of various types began to come in as the morning progressed, and by tea-time Lady Dalst appeared with the aunties, followed by Miss Ives, who arrived alone this time. The six of them related the tales they'd heard over a genteel, full service tea, their conversation punctuated by the clink of china cups and the ring of stirring spoons. However the greatest surprise was the arrival of Miss Bravis, the only other whitecaste witch Evvie had met besides Mrs. Zsall.

She arrived alone, her hems caked in snow up to her knees, her expression dour and hateful. She had come in just as the repast was about to conclude and the ladies were finishing up their cups of tea and nibbling down the last of the lovely selection of items displayed on the tiered server. They were in good humor, feeling triumphant, curious to know if somewhere, in far off places, there were lovely, red-haired, wolf-eyed girls awakening to a morning in a whole new light.

The arrival of Miss Bravis put a quick damper on their pleasant tea. The six of them stood when she was ushered into the room, and she stood there staring in astonishment at the sight of so many witches all in one room. She seemed at a loss for a moment, but it was not a long moment. She glowered. "You are a murderess!" she hissed at Evvie.

"Are you indeed?" Lady Dalst asked with a believably shocked demeanor. Her eyes twinkled with mischief.

"She is. She murdered four of my sisters, and now... Now what have you done? It must be you, for nobody else could do what you have done!" Ms Bravis snarled.

"I have no idea to what you are referring, Miss Bravis," Evvie said quietly, clasping her hands over her belly with a deliberate action.

"We've been stunted!" Miss Bravis snapped. "I, and two other sisters I spoke to this morning. What have you done?"

"Oh, I've done no such thing," Evvie replied succinctly.

"Who are you people? And you? Why are *you* here?" Miss Bravis snarled at Tarren.

Tarren merely looked at Evvie and then back at Miss Bravis. "I am a guest of the Countess, and I am also honored to call her my friend."

"A white witch has no business being friends with red filth!"

"She's called me that before," Evvie informed Tarren, who frowned.

"I see." There was a dangerous edge to Tarren's voice.

"Miss Bravis, is it?" Arah asked. "May I ask why you have come?"

"I have come to warn the red witch that she's gone too far! There will be consequences!" Miss Bravis snapped.

"Consequences? Indeed..." Lady Dalst repeated. "What consequences do you threaten her with? And for what reason?"

"She has done something. Undermined the whitecaste. She has diminished the potency of our spells and our chants. Talk of it is already everywhere amongst the whitecaste. She cannot be allowed to do this!" Twin spots of angry red bloomed on Miss Bravis' cheeks. It was not an attractive look for her.

"From what I understand, whitecast drove the red witches to near extinction," Miss Ives said. "Did you really think there would be no consequences for that? It was a direct affront to the very powers that provide us our gifts."

Miss Bravis said nothing, she only glared at Evvie.

"Do you know what the Alambrean Circle of Five is, Miss Bravis?" Lady Dalst asked. Her pale eyes flashed onto the green witch.

"The Circle of Five no longer exists," the white witch replied shortly.

"But it does," Lady Dalst said calmly. "It always has. It hasn't always had all of its members present, but it does once more. You're looking at it."

Miss Bravis' eyes widened. She took a slight step back.

"Well, except for me," Arah cut in. "I'm only here for the scones."

"And fine scones they are, Ma'am," Lady Dalst remarked smilingly to Arah, before turning her gaze back to the visitor. "The Circle of Five was obligated to act long ago, to help preserve the balance of magic, Miss Bravis. It acted to protect itself, for its existence was important to restore what must be restored. The arrival of the Countess was what was required to fulfill the divination of the Circle. The redcaste acted with intelligence all those years ago, choosing ostensible impurity in order to survive. As many from the other castes did as well as the balance shifted. Their choices made the backbone of witchery much stronger, and changed the very nature of its magic. The whitecaste's refusal to embrace that change only weakened it. Your *stunting*, as you call it, is your own doing. The rest of the witchcaste have grown beyond your ken now that the Circle, and the flow of the redcaste's power, augmented by the Baskreth Hexxenmaeg, has returned.

"The Circle of Five awoke the latents last night, while you plotted and designed your assaults against the Countess. The deaths of your sisters were merely the consequence of attacking one of your own. Your magic, my dear Miss Bravis, will no longer sway the Prósopo. Know that any action taken against a red will very likely end with the same results. I think it would be wise that you warn your sisters of this, for we do not wish—not any of us—for any more blood to spill. I would think twice about vexing a redcaste again." Lady Dalst's easygoing, smiling air had hardened, her eyes frigid and piercing. Evvie felt the icy threat in the words of the last keeper of the Alambrean Circle's legacy, and what she knew had to be the strongest green witch in existence, for the legacy would not be entrusted to anything less. But as quickly as Lady Dalst had become intimidating, she melted into affability again. "Now, we were just discussing taking up a hand of Annuity, care to join?"

Miss Bravis only painted them all with a baleful glare before sweeping out of the room, leaving a trail of ice chips behind her.

Evvie reached out and took Lady Dalst's hand. "I find that I like you more and more, every day."

"I hope so. We're stuck together, the five... six of us. Now, let us sit and have a nice bracing game of cards, shall we? I shall wipe the floor with the lot of you."

"Fat chance," Miss Ives retorted, surprising them all. "It is my favorite game, and I'm *really* good at it."

Chapter 33

Winter relented, but it took almost a month and a half past what Evvie would have called spring to actually look like it. Although she was elated to see the light greens and yellows of new growth budding on the branches of the trees at Alouaine Hall, she lamented the end to the many warm evenings she'd spent with her friends, learning more about what it meant to be a red witch, and even more, one that sat on the Alambrean Circle. Her removal to Alouaine was bittersweet, for she would not see her aunts every day, though Mrs. Zsall was moved to a house near Alouaine Hall called Fir Lodge. Dareth had seen to it, as both Tarren and Evvie were utterly bereft at the idea of being separated. Dareth had to help Mr. Zsall find a way to expand his business to Tirdonne, and invested with him in a posh building which they were at present working to transform into a fine Inn. The Inn at Diamond Rock was passed down to Zsall's younger brother to run.

Mrs. Zsall's baby arrived in at the very end of the wintry weather, when spring had yet to show itself in earnest. Little Reeta was as wintry as her mother, and as precious as a little jewel. Evvie's swollen belly and her spiritual state was so that she could not look at the child without welling up with joy at the sight of her.

Tarren spent a good part of each day, when she could, at Alouaine, where she and Evvie would sit together, sometimes in silence for hours on end, reading books copied or borrowed from Mr. Edanbras at the archive. The ladies were becoming true scholars of witchery.

In the short period of renewal, and the warmer days ushering into summer, Evvie had her baby. It was a girl, too, and one with eyes as pale as hers, and—to everyone's delight—a shock of little red curls against her tiny head. Lady Dalst dubbed her Little Carrot, as it seemed to be the thing to call her, although her true name was Lily.

Evvie's belongings were now fully distributed about both houses, and Alouaine—fully refitted for this new generation of Ilmeers—was all that she hoped it would be. The elegant house seemed to welcome her and the new baby with open arms. Dareth fell into his routine of managing his land, and working on his business with his new partner Mr. Zsall.

One fine evening, Dareth and Evvie, accompanied by the Prince and his betrothed—a remarkably beautiful eastern woman by the name of Ayalla—attended a titular battle at the palace at Tirdonne. It was the first time Evvie had been out with Dareth in full evening regalia and, more markedly, without her child. She had a strange, empty feeling inside her body, leaving the baby in the care of the governess. But it was something she would have to become accustomed to eventually. She was very protective of Lily, although Lady Dalst assured her she should not worry. Prósopos existed even for babies.

It was the height of Bask's short summer and the trees were already looking a little wilted, the late summer blossoms fading. The people left the pleasant warmth of the summer evening to enter the palace, flowing into a crawl through the narrower entrance and spreading out again once inside the broad hall. There Evvie saw Countess Pryvett. Evvie picked up her hems and aimed towards her, eyes twinkling.

Just as Evvie wound through the crowd towards Countess Pryvett, she came face to face with Mr. Ryse-Mevvick, who immediately looked behind her to see if her husband was with her. He bowed curtly to Evvie, his eyes lingering on her glowing face, and her bright eyes.

"Good evening, Ma'am," he said.

"Mr. Ryse-Mevvick," she replied coldly.

He shifted uncomfortably and frowned. "I'm sorry," he managed to utter. "Truly sorry." He would not look into her eyes.

Just then, a pale hand slid out from between two people, the rest of the body following. A thin arm encased in a white glove wound around the trunk of Mr. Ryse-Mevvick's arm, and a pair of wolf-eyes swept Evvie up and down with a look of both shock and a touch of jealousy in them.

The newcomer's hair was magnificent—a sweep of crimson wound around her head and then finished on top in a cascade of perfectly set curls, interspersed with pearls that seemed to beam against the deep red backdrop. She was a waify thing, wearing a plain blue silk gown. There was a strength in her eyes, a determination in her thin, narrow face and freckled cheekbones. "Ando, dear, I thought you were going to wait for me over there," she said.

Evvie eyed her counterpart. "I'm sorry, I'm afraid I signaled him over. I had no idea I was causing him to leave you behind," Evvie fibbed. Although Evvie had an immediate desire to warn the girl of the man's instability, a part of her knew by instinct that this girl was no wilting violet—and more importantly, by the way Ando was nearly simpering under her gaze, it was clear that the red witch was the dominant force in this duo. Mr. Ryse-Mevvick almost appeared to melt under the power of her presence. There was also a strange, mad little look in her eye too.

Ando's expression went through a variety of emotions before he got himself together. "Theya, this is the Countess of Ilmeer. Countess, this is my betrothed, Miss Theya Danvell."

The girl's eyes widened, and her whole demeanor changed. She sank into a low, respectful curtsy and then rose up again, her expression contrite. "Ma'am, this is the greatest honor."

Evvie shook her head. "That is very kind, Miss Danvell. It is a great honor to meet the only other redcaste witch yet. May I shake your hand?"

The girl offered it and Evvie took it. Dareth finally appeared, his air menacing, but slightly softened at the sight of the woman at Ryse-Mevvick's side.

"Truly? I am the first?" Theya said in wonder.

"Yes," Evvie said.

"I heard the stories. That it was you that freed us. I am surprised more of us have not returned simply to meet you, and know you. To learn from you." Theya's eyes shone.

"I do not have much to teach, I'm afraid. I am only slightly less new at this than you are. However, I would very much like to meet with you again, if that would be acceptable, Mr. Ryse-Mevvick?" Evvie cast her gaze at the gentleman.

"You do not need my permission," he snorted. "Theya is her own woman."

"Then we shall see to it. Here, take my calling card." Evvie reached into her delicate reticule and pulled out one of the cards. "I am in the city all winter, so that would be the most convenient time to spend together. But you are welcome at Alouaine any time."

The girl palmed the card and curtsied gratefully again.

"How did you meet Mr. Ryse-Mevvick?" Evvie asked.

Mrs. Danvell looked at her betrothed with a satisfied expression. "I was coming to Tirdonne this spring to learn more about witchery. I came with my sister, and we took rooms at a guest house. I was unprepared for the deference I received. And invitations soon came in for events around the city. I met Ando at the opera," she declared. "He asked to be introduced by my friend Mrs. Renns, and was so attentive and kind to me from the moment he saw me. He is so respected by his people, and so full of knowledge. I've never met any man so polite and doting before," she exclaimed.

Evvie could scarce keep from laughing, and she avoided looking at Dareth because she could feel him biting back his laughter too. The most difficult thing to endure was to see Mr. Ryse-Mevvick's expression, for he most certainly recalled how utterly awful his behavior had been, and how out of turn Miss Danvell's account of him was to the truth.

"Indeed, I have no doubt Mr. Ryse-Mevvick must have been *most* keen on treating you with the utmost kindness and attentiveness, for there is *nothing* he reveres more than a lovely redcaste witch," Evvie replied with a forced smile. Miss Danvell merely offered a satisfied grin and she hugged Ando's arm tighter. He sported a stiff, uncomfortable expression. Dareth elbowed Evvie subtly as he too had seen the man's face.

"We should sit, my dear," Dareth said.

Evvie detached herself from the pair with a polite farewell, and Dareth led her to their place on the dais. They both chortled together quietly as they crossed the floor, both deeply amused by both Ando and his little red witch. They composed themselves as they sat down, watching the rest of the peerage file behind the tables to take their places. It was not long before the hall was settled and the drumming began as a new crop of contenders were led in by the King. Evvie's eyes swept the patrons of the room. There were no white witches to be seen. She had imagined she would at least see Miss Bravis here, but she did not. Miss Ives had remarked on the marked absence of the whitecaste from Tirdonne.

"They usually come to my shop with some regularity," she had informed Evvie. "I haven't seen any in at least five months. There were a few after that night, but that is it. There is a surge of new customers in black witches though, and I've even met two greencaste, which is unprecedented. No reds yet except for you, but I'm giving that a bit of time."

Evvie's gaze went back to Theya who was looking up at her at that moment with a hopeful smile. Evvie wanted so much to advise her against Mr. Ryse-Mevvick. He was not the ideal mate for a witch now. He was inferior against the Baskreth hexxenmaeg. That alone ought to be a reason to stay away, not to mention Mr. Ryse-Mevvick's questionable moral character. But they both seemed oddly content in mutual company. Miss Danvell definitely had a strong, willful character, and Mr. Ryse-Mevvick was happy to be at her whim, as long as he had his red witch. Perhaps Miss Danvell's nature was one that required a bit of manic madness in her mate. Who knew? Evvie could only wish them the best. She would guide Theya, but she would be sure not to let her get close enough that Evvie would have to spend any more time than necessary in the company of the man who might have tried to have her child killed in her belly.

She noticed that Mr. Ryse-Mevvick was sitting closer to the dais than he had the prior year. It seemed his alliance with Miss Danvell had indeed earned him a little social currency. A Brii man could only rise so far without fighting for his place. Evvie couldn't picture him in this hall with a sword. He would have to content himself with that table. She caught his eye by accident, and saw only shame and contrition in his gaze. What a strange man, she concluded.

The events of the evening were kicked off by the King's display and then Evvie focused on enjoying her meal. This time she didn't have to worry that her husband was going to be killed. He was right beside her, one forearm on the table, the other on his leg, his handsome brow crinkled in concentration as the first pairing bore their weapons. Dareth had helped train the younger fellow who was vying to unseat an heir to a Baronetcy. This time, it was Dareth who was not eating.

Evvie picked up her wineglass and leaned back into her chair. She thought about the arrival of her brother in the fall, as he and his family were committed to spending an entire winter at Tirdonne in the Kass house in the square. She had warned him it would be hard, but he insisted. She looked forward to seeing his family again.

At last, thought Evvie as she watched Dareth's acolyte cut into his opponents arm, and spray blood across the floor, I *am where I am supposed to be.*

Dareth, as if sensing her feeling of wellbeing, turned to peer at her. "You look happy, my dear," he said. Her eyes smiled at him, and she reached up to put her hand on his cheek.

"Never happier," she replied. He bent down, and gave her a loving kiss. She'd gotten used to this overt, public affection the Bask were so fond of. She kissed him back, her body responding to his touch as keenly as it had on their wedding night. For a moment, she was lost in him, and he in her. But they were pulled back to the present by a loud exclamation.

"First blood!" cried the King, and the guests applauded fervently. What savages her brother would think these people were, she laughed to herself.

Suddenly, the fight stopped, and the Baskreth men of the room all fell deathly still. They then shuddered and their eyes rolled back, terrifying contortions flashing across their faces. Then, from every man, a bright form emerged. The glowing forms flitted towards the center of the room where they formed two distinct figures of towering ancient Baskreth warriors wielding fearsome blades. The men slumped in their chairs and the fighters collapsed. The women gasped in shock and titillation as the creatures glared at them all with glowing eyes, and then vanished. Evvie looked at Miss Danvell and her eyes were wide with shock.

Evvie had felt no attack, no pain, but the Prósopos had been cast. Evvie stood and moved to the monarch, putting her hands on him. He stirred, and the other men about the room began to as well. "Are you unwell your Highness?"

"I feel fine, Countess," he replied quietly. His wife clutched is arm, as he straightened in his chair. "What happened?"

Evvie, curtsied deeply and begged his forgiveness. "Sire, I must apologize for the untimely intrusion on this event. I'm afraid there has been an attack on the redcaste witches, and the defense that occurs with or without our knowledge is the manifestation of a proxy in the form of a Baskreth berserker. There were two, as there are two redcaste here this evening. It was shocking and I would hope that you would please accept my most humble ap—"

"It is what it is, Countess. You needn't apologize for the mysteries of your sacred ways. Witchery and all it entails is part of the Bask legacy. It is part and parcel of our lives. No other culture fosters it as we have. None. The rebirth of the redcaste is all anyone can talk about, and this, as far as we are concerned is only a mark of good luck and fortune for those participating today." He then stood to his feet and turned to face the crowd. "These bouts have been blessed with the manifestation of Baskreth bezerkers! There comes no greater endorsement to the winner than that!" he shouted.

The stunned crowd hesitated for a moment and then burst into applause and laughter. Wine was poured, the swords were gathered and the battles resumed. Evvie looked at her husband, who was still disoriented from the moment of unconsciousness.

"Do they not care what happened that would cause the proxies to appear?" Evvie asked him.

"Nobody has ever questioned it, Evvie. It is the will of the old gods, is it not?" She frowned. She resolved to speak to the Circle at first chance. For now, she leaned into her husband's side, his arm wrapped around her waist. He kissed the top of her head, the way she adored, and he squeezed her, his eyes back on the fight.

MIRANDA MAYER

Epilogue

Miss Bravis descended from the coach to be greeted by Farla Hent, her mentor and the eldest, highest-ranked of the whitecaste in her guild. The old woman appeared impatient and relieved at once.

"You are the last. What took so long?" she murmured, reaching out her hands to Miss Bravis, who took them in greeting.

"You know very well what hindered me," Miss Bravis replied snidely. "A thank you would be nice."

The old woman harrumphed and relented. "Welcome," she said. "It is good you came dressed and prepared." Like the old woman, Miss Bravis wore a simple white long-sleeved round gown and white slippers.

"I anticipated you would want to begin as soon as I arrived," replied Miss Bravis.

"Indeed. Come, the others wait," Farla gestured to the younger witch to precede her inside the big house. It was Farla's family seat, aged and crumbling, much like its resident. The soft sandstone of the sprawling old house had been worn by climbing vines and algae over the years. It was one of the few places that had a traditional whitecaste coven bethel and ceremonial chamber for private use. It was the natural choice for this event. The house sat in an ill-kept park, six days west of Tirdonne in the Ebshire Mountains. Whitecast witches from all over Bask had traveled to this house, upon Farla's invitation, after a few months of heated correspondence with Miss Bravis. She and the five remaining whitecaste witches of Tirdonne of the original nine were determined to regain control of what the redcaste had taken from them; power over Tirdonne and in turn, Bask.

Miss Bravis moved through the echoing hall to the bethel, where the old pews and vaulted pulpit harkened back to the days of the old religion. The wheel of magic was depicted in the colorful window. The hub, which should have been a bright, blood red, was broken out and replaced with a snowy pane of white glass. The white spoke was now red.

In the chapel, a horde of women with pale hair milled. Forty-nine white-clad women of the guild, to be precise. Minus the four that had been so brutally killed during the winter. Miss Bravis' Tirdonne sisters had arrived before her, and were the first to greet her as she entered the bethel.

"Finally. You should have come with us." Miss Vanne chided her. She was the youngest of the witches, only eighteen. She was Farla's niece, and had been placed in Miss Bravis' care for training and mentoring. It was hoped that the young girl—a remarkably pretty white witch with a lion's mane of snowy curls wound up on her head in the most stylish fashion—would find a Brii Hexxenmaeg at Tirdonne. But she had not been successful yet. There were high hopes she would be the one to capture Mr. Ando Ryse-Mevvick. To everyone's disgust, he once more, found himself a red witch to pursue—spurning the whitecaste ladies for the second time.

Ryse-Mevvick's connection to Miss Bravis was abruptly severed when he revealed in jealousy to a mutual friend, that the redcaste had bred and was with child, and that all hope for him was lost. Miss Bravis took that information and gave it to the Zenta sisters, who were known for their skill at beast-summoning. The assault that resulted from his slip had sent Ryse-Mevvick into a rage and he vowed to never again even remotely consider something quite as common and undesirable as a whitecast again, even if that meant marrying a woman without magic at all. They had ruined any shred of hope that remained of his ever winning the redcaste witch's heart. The whitecaste of Tirdonne no longer had any use for him anyway. They would find proper hexxenmaeg elsewhere.

"I needed to collect some supplies for our endeavor," Miss Bravis muttered in irritation to the young girl. "I am not so late. I have arrived in time for the coven invocation."

She was then embraced by the coven, and pale, colorless women closed in around her to put hands on her as greeting. Many looked angry, and a few looked fearful. The whitecaste guild as a whole had been shaken by the unexpected retreat of the scope of their powers. To think that common black witches now possessed greater connection to the powers than they was an enormous insult, and many of the members of the guild had expressed this in the fluttering of letters that crossed the countryside after the eve of the redcaste awakening.

Farla called the witches to order, and Miss Bravis' small entourage took the front row of pews while the elder lady took to the tall pulpit and rang a large silver bell that hung on a hook by the lectern. The scent of essential oils wafted over them; tinctures of powerful blends, designed to concentrate the powers on the coven.

The ladies fell eerily silent. Miss Bravis twisted to peer back at the ashen faces and ghostly hair, the purity of the white gowns, the countless pale eyes hauntingly gazing forward. She reveled in it. *So many*, she thought. Even stunted, there was much power in this room. Enough to undo perhaps, the damage that was done by the redcaste and the renewed Alambrean Circle.

And undo it we will, she mused with a self-righteous smirk. Farla rattled off the welcoming sermon, and spoke the spell of application, which would help the coven focus as one on the spell they hoped to successfully cast this night.

It had taken four months to arrange it—the part of the spring and the whole of summer. It had come at great expense to bring the guild together. But in order to accumulate the power and the items they needed, the time was needed. Everything was assembled. The last of the supplies were offloaded from the coach, and being brought to the chamber of ceremony to be put into action as soon as the invocation and welcome was complete.

She had turned to face the front again, and patiently waited for the long sermon to end, breathing in deeply the scents of the essentials, feeling them infuse her with their power. Farla concluded her missive with another peal of the bell, and she gestured for the coven to stand. She then descended the steps of the pulpit and walked down the aisle. In order of front to back, each pair of pews, row by row, emptied and the occupants followed her in a neat line out of the bethel and through the great hall again, marching down the dark corridor to the round chamber of ceremonies.

The witches filed along the circumference of the room, while Farla moved to the stone table in the center, where the slight form of a thin, black-haired woman lay underneath a drapery of scarlet silk. She struggled, but Miss Bravis knew that there were rings embedded in the stone to which shackles were fastened, that kept her pinned quite tightly to the table. She had her mouth covered in a band of black silk, tied so tightly, the skin at its edges was white. Her terrified eyes were wide and searching the faces of the women that now surrounded her. She would find no empathy or compassion in the faces. Miss Bravis's face was a mirror of all the whitecaste present. There was only indifference to be found. And anticipation.

Whitecaste witches historically, were not the kind that made sacrifices for power. It was not a part of their tenets or practice. The ravencaste were the ones that let blood. Usually their own. The whitecaste had discovered after the rebellion, that shedding ravencaste blood was particularly powerful, especially when coupled with whitecaste magic. With their newly stunted state, Farla had declared it necessary to spill a vast deal of ravencaste blood to achieve their ends. It was the black witch that Miss Bravis had been obliged to collect before arriving. It had been what had waylaid her journey and what made her late. The terrified girl on the dais was the *supplies* Miss Bravis described.

The witches had found their places, evenly positioned along the wall of the circular hall, staring with avarice at the girl and the heap of items placed around the base of the dais. Herb bundles and incense cones, braziers and bottles of oils. Farla put a book on the girl's stomach. It lurched under her struggles, but it did not deter the elder witch from reading from it.

The guild had agreed to the spell Farla had written for this occasion. It was sent to all of the members of the coven for approval after Miss Bravis, and the Tirdonne witches had helped the elder refine it. All the elements for it were in place. The ravencaste's components that would boost their magic, as well as all the tinctures and oils they would require to fill the air with their magic; so they could breathe it all into their bodies and then cast as one to destroy the new red witches, leaving only the very youngest to live so their powers would not be destroyed.

Miss Bravis liked this idea the most, for the redcaste witch had only just given birth to a lovely little girl. And she imagined the child could be taken and raised properly by white witches.

The spell was the one that had turned their proxies against their red witches all those years ago. Farla had modified it, adding the black witch's blood to the mix, confident it would produce enough power to sway the new, Baskreth proxies to their will.

All that remained was to spill the black witch's blood. And they would use her element of fire to do it; to cast into the air her essence of magic, to imbue theirs with the very core of her power to be breathed in by the coven. So Miss Bravis trod forward after Farla finished speaking the spell's words, and she picked up the single candlestick that stood at the food of the dais. Farla picked up her book and withdrew. And Miss Bravis, with no small measure of personal pleasure, lowered the flame to the dish of oil beside it, setting it aflame. It, in part, set the other items and magical oils alight. Soon, there was a ring of bluish flames licking at the dais, and the girl struggled and screamed muffled cries behind her gag.

The silk soon caught fire, and her movements became more frantic. This was their first full sacrifice of a black witch. Miss Bravis had returned to her place, sharing the same look of dark fascination on her face as the black witch was set ablaze.

It was at that moment that the proxies arrived. So many they could not be counted. A horde of barbarians, armed with voulges and swords, maces and pole arms. Each one was as unique as the next, their tattoos covering their broad, muscular bodies, their shining skin as real as anyone's. Their bald heads, covered in figures and whorls, with eyes glowing a hot white. At first there was a prickly sense of jubilation and victory. The white witches had successfully summoned the proxies. One after another they arrived in wafts of smoke.

But then there was the sudden and horrifying understanding that they were not controlling these Prósopo.

Farla was the first to cry the alarm. But her cry was cut short as a massive blade hacked through her neck and nearly severed her head. Other weapons rose up and the chamber of ceremonies was suddenly filled with horrifying shrieks of white witches as their blood was splattered violently along the ancient friezes along the walls. Nobody was able to even reach the door.

One of the last things Miss Bravis saw was the artful rendering of the sacred Hevvea, the first white witch, being bathed in a spray of Miss Vanne's blood as her severed carotid artery spewed blood like a fountain. She fell against the image and slid down the wall, leaving a gruesome, dripping trail of blood.

Miss Bravis did not see what killed her. It came from behind. She did not feel the pain. She only felt the magic leaving her first—abandoning her. She felt her body crumpling, and could see the carnage around her as witch after witch was cut down by the horde of magical avatars. The black witch burned, and the proxies killed. And Miss Bravis took a long time to die. She was still gargling blood when the last of the proxies dissipated, and the whole of the scene was revealed in its horrifying carnage.

It was a chilling, grisly tableau of white and scarlet.

The irony of it was not lost on the dying witch. She even managed a wheezing laugh before she choked on it. And then, Miss Bravis died. Along with nearly every last white witch in Bask.

End.

About the Author

Miranda Mayer lives in the Mount Hood territory of Oregon. A polyglot, artist, avid historic costumer and lifelong equestrian; her interests are broad, and edge on geekery most of time. She is married with one child.

Miranda's stories range from Science Fiction to Urban Fantasy to Fantasy. She writes from her heart, imbues her writing with her quirky humour, and tries very hard to make her characters as real and three-dimensional as possible. Her unpredictable and rather Attention-Deficit-Disordered nature guarantees that her stories will take readers to unexpected places.

MIRANDA MAYER

Other titles by Miranda Mayer

The Trilogy of Tinna:
Tinna's Promise
Tinna's Might
Tinna's Reign

Red Slipper series:
The Wizard King
A Problem of Ghosts
The Beast with Silver Eyes

The Belletrist

Blackroot

With author Shéa MacLeod
Wolffe & Bane – Book 1: The Talisman Killer